P9-DVG-867

OURSELVES
TO KNOW

A NOVEL *by*

John O'Hara

RANDOM HOUSE · NEW YORK

And all our Knowledge is, ourselves to know.
ALEXANDER POPE : *An Essay on Man*

OURSELVES TO KNOW

As a boy and until I was sixteen I spent a large part of every summer at my grandfather's house in Lyons, Pennsylvania. We always sat on the porch on Sunday and my grandmother would hold court with the people on their way home from the Baptist, the Catholic and the Evangelical churches; and like all children I realized at an early age that older people did not treat each other as equals. A man and his wife were a little above you or a little below you. All the people who stopped to chat with my grandparents were a little below them, and they could not help showing it. In fact, I used to think it gave them pleasure to be respectful to my grandparents, even when my grandmother would sharply contradict them on matters of no importance. As a boy who was being brought up very strictly, I was often embarrassed by my grandmother's manner with older people. When they had said as much as she wanted to hear, she would turn away and chat with one of my aunts until the poor man and woman found the simple phrases to excuse themselves. "Guess we better be getting along," they would say, and my grandmother would say, "All right. Goodbye." I did not know then, of course, that quite a few of those people were in financial debt to my grandfather. I did not even know that some of them lived in houses that were owned by my grandfather. There were a lot of things I did not know.

On Sundays it would have been an act of lese majesty for an acquaintance of my grandparents' to use the opposite sidewalk to avoid the MacMahons' porch. The Baptist and the Catholic churches were two blocks away on the opposite side of the street, but all the Catholics and a good many of the Baptists always crossed over to our side before reaching Grandma's porch. On weekdays, however, my grandfather was at the store, or the brickyard or the lumber yard or the bank, and my grandmother was busy about the house and the yard. I was free to go off and play with my friends, but punctuality at mealtime was sternly enforced and I was almost always on the porch before the last bell of the noon Angelus had been tolled, waiting for my

3

grandfather to come home for dinner. Most of the men in the town carried lunch-pails to work, and the men who came home for dinner were the prosperous ones. I did not take special note of who they were; I had always known. They were the men who owned the stores, worked in the bank, had the higher jobs with the coal company, managed the small factories, or were engaged in the professions of law, medicine and dentistry. They all owned a pair of horses or an automobile. The only other men who went home for dinner were poolroom loafers.

There was one man who had his dinner at home, who had his dinner later than the others. He always went to the post office a few minutes after the Angelus was rung, and this habit of his meant that all the way to the post office he was going against the sidewalk traffic of men on their way home to dinner. The man's name was Robert Millhouser and he lived in a large house on the edge of town, a house in a four-acre lot that was enclosed by a white paling fence. I don't know when I first began to notice Mr. Millhouser, but it must have been when I was very small because I took him for granted. But I think I must have been seven or eight years old when I asked my first questions about Mr. Millhouser, and the answers were evasive and unsatisfactory.

Mr. Millhouser never walked on our side of the street and never appeared on Sunday, but if my mother or my grandmother or one of my aunts happened to be sitting on the porch with me, he would always take off his hat and make a little bow, without actually looking across the street at the person he was bowing to. But he knew who was there; if I happened to be alone on the porch he did not raise his hat or bow. And if I happened to be sitting with my grandfather or my Uncle George, he would touch the brim of his hat in a semi-military salute and smile in a way that you might have thought was only a man smiling to himself, but if you saw it often enough it was the very sweet smile of a man who took pleasure in being polite to the Mac-Mahon family. If there was someone on the porch when he was returning home from the post office, he would make the same polite gesture, and again in the evening when he made his evening trip to the post office.

My first question about Mr. Millhouser, which I asked one of my aunts, was: "What's the matter with Mr. Millhouser?"

"Why? I didn't know there was anything the matter with him."

I could not explain my question. I knew, as children do know, that there was something the matter, and so I said: "He acts funny."

"Not a bit," said my aunt. "He's very polite."

4

Then I suppose it was a year or two later that I said to my grandfather: "Grandpa, what does Mr. Millhouser do?"

"What does Mr. Millhouser do? He takes care of his *finances*," said my grandfather, and then, quite unlike him, he said: "Time to get the crank and roll up the awning, boy." I say it was unlike him because he and I loved to talk to each other and I knew I was being diverted from the subject of Mr. Millhouser. Also, it was not quite time to roll up the awning. It would not be accurate to say that I immediately became curious about Mr. Millhouser, since at that age I was not very curious about any grownup unless he was a policeman or a soldier or ran the miniature steam locomotive at the amusement park or was tattooed or played football at Lebanon Valley College. Mr. Millhouser was totally unlike my personal celebrities of that period. He was, in fact, a most uninteresting man except that my aunt and my grandfather had not wanted to talk about him *to me*. He *was* something or *had done* something that I was not supposed to know, and yet he always bowed to them and they bowed to him. After that, but not at all consciously, I began to notice things about Mr. Millhouser.

I noticed, for instance, that when my grandfather returned Mr. Millhouser's bow, he always said, "Morning, Robert." But when I went to the post office and Mr. Millhouser was there, only a very few men and women called him by his first name, and those who did were the people whom my grandmother treated almost as equals. The others would wait for Robert Millhouser to nod to them or speak to them, and they would nod or speak to him. But he ignored most of the men and women in the post office, just as he ignored some of the men who were homeward bound for the noon meal.

Summer after summer I went to my grandfather's and it was remarkable how few changes took place, but the summer I was fifteen and was wearing my first long pants, I was sitting alone on the porch one day and Mr. Millhouser came along and saluted me, but as soon as he did he realized that I was not my Uncle George, and he smiled and I could hear him distinctly say: "Oh, oh, it's Gerald. Good *morning*." He had never spoken to me before, and I of course was surprised that he knew my name. After that he always saluted me as he did my grandfather and my uncle, and it was such a satisfactory sign that people were aware that I was getting older that I could hardly wait to ask my grandfather about Mr. Millhouser. I waited until we were alone and would not be interrupted.

"Grandpa," I said. "What is there about Mr. Millhouser? What's all the mystery?"

5

My grandfather looked at his cigar and worried in silence for a few long seconds. At last he said: "It isn't a mystery, Gerald. It's people not wanting to talk about something. Your mother and father never told you anything about Mr. Millhouser?"

"I don't ever remember asking them. I only asked you and Aunt May."

"Well, you've got a man's pants on now and I guess you could be taken for a lot older than fifteen. There's some ugly things in this world, Gerald." He leaned forward and tapped the end of his cigar over the ash receiver. "Some years ago, I guess you were about two or three, Mr. Millhouser shot and killed his wife."

"You mean he murdered her?"

"No. You can't say that. Better not say it, either. Because he was put on trial for murder, and he was acquitted."

"But did he do it?"

"There's no doubt about it that he did it, but the law said it wasn't murder."

"Mr. Millhouser really shot his own wife and killed her?" I said. "But Grandpa, you and Grandma always speak to him."

"Yes we do, always did and always will."

"Then you thought he was innocent, or you wouldn't speak to him."

"He was an unfortunate man and we felt sorry for him."

"Did Grandma feel sorry for him?"

He smiled. "Oh, you Gerald, you. You're still afraid of your Grandma, long pants or no long pants."

"But did she?"

"Not at first."

"But you made her, didn't you?"

"I convinced her, but once she was convinced, she was convinced."

"Why were you sorry for him?"

"Don't ask me that, or any more questions about Mr. Millhouser. Your father can tell you the rest of it, or your mother, if they want you to know it. If they don't, they won't tell you. But it's not my business to tell you."

When I went home to my own family's I said to my mother: "Why did Mr. Millhouser kill his wife?"

"Who on earth told you about that?"

"Grandpa."

"Grandpa? Grandpa told you that? What else did he tell you?"

"Not much."

"How in the world did he happen to get on that subject? I've never heard him mention that for years, practically since it happened."

6

"I asked him why Mr. Millhouser was so mysterious."

"He isn't mysterious at all."

"Maybe he isn't, but you are and Grandpa was and Aunt May."

"I wonder how much Grandpa told you. Did he mention Mr. Vance at all?"

"Oh, it was on account of Mr. Vance?"

"I didn't say that."

"Oh, come on, Mother. I've heard of justifiable homicide."

"You know too much."

"The unwritten law."

"I'm going to have your father give you a talking-to."

"You can't stop what I know already. If I know it, I know it. So *can* that."

"Don't tell me to *can* that. I don't like that expression."

"You're not going to tell me about Mr. Millhouser?"

"I most certainly am not, and furthermore, you're not supposed to wear your long pants except on Sunday."

I went away to school the following September and the next summer, when I was sixteen, my grandfather had become an invalid, forbidden his cigars and whiskey, and too weak to come downstairs. He died that summer, and one of the things I remember about the funeral is the tearful face of Robert Millhouser, tearful but strangely handsome, as the casket was lifted into the hearse in front of St. Boniface Church. I had never really seen Mr. Millhouser's face until that day; he had always been raising his hat and looking away. But at my grandfather's funeral he stood still and erect, with his chin up and the slight August breeze blowing his white hair, his skin tanned, his mouth curving downward as in pain, and his tears ignored. By that time I had begun to notice some of the differences in the ages of adults, and I realized that Mr. Millhouser was definitely younger than my grandfather, rather than, as I had always thought, a contemporary. Standing there, a little apart from the others, he seemed to me a stronger man than the Mr. Millhouser whom I had seen so many times, taking his rapid short steps and making his shy, polite gestures on the way to the post office. He had the ascetic look that I later saw in the faces of a few priests, a few deaf people, a few West Point army officers, and a few men who had served long prison sentences.

They closed the doors of the hearse and we went down the stone steps to the undertaker's limousines, and I watched Mr. Millhouser, putting on his hat and starting to walk away in the direction of his house. Then he did what I knew he was going to do: he stopped and turned his head for one last look at the hearse. I don't know why I was so sure he was going to do that, but I believe it was because I felt that he loved my grandfather as much as I did, and would miss him even more.

I was riding with the other grandchildren in the second car, and we passed Mr. Millhouser on the way to the cemetery. "There's that crazy Mr. Millhouser," said one of my cousins.

"Shut your God damn stupid face," I said.

It was one of my Rochester cousins, a girl, whom I seldom saw and invariably quarreled with, but she had provoked me into a sort of defense of Mr. Millhouser and from that moment on I was actively on his side and as curious about him as my many other interests would permit.

My other interests were those of a boy my age: school, and my friends and enemies there; my friends and enemies at home; sports, particularly tennis; the movies; girls; clothes; travel; cars; reading; cartooning; dance orchestras; the constant effort to make people think I was older than I was; the daily conflict between wanting to be popular and wanting to be independent. My curiosity about Robert Millhouser was not in a class with those interests: when I thought of him I was curious about him, but I had so many other things to think about that he was not often in my mind. I might have forgotten about him if I had not gone to my grandmother's for a short visit during the summer I was seventeen.

I was sitting on the porch, waiting for lunch to be announced (dinner was an evening meal after my grandfather died), and Mr. Millhouser saluted me and I waved to him. But he suddenly stopped and crossed the street to the porch. I still had never spoken to him and had never been physically closer to him than I had been that day of my grandfather's funeral. As he came nearer I was flustered; I did not know whether to stand up or to pretend I did not expect him to speak to me. But he came right to the point, without shaking hands, without any preliminaries. "Gerald, are you at all interested in the Civil War?"

I stood up. "Yes sir, to some extent."

"I thought you would be. Your grandfather, and so forth. Well, I came across a book you might like to have, a book of pictures. They're not photographs, they're drawings, and they're not for children. Pretty gruesome, some of them. But I'm told they show what the war was really like. If you'd like to have it I'll send it down to you this afternoon."

"Thank you very much, Mr. Millhouser. I'd appreciate it."

He did not hear my thanks; he was looking, with a faint smile, at the high-backed rocking chair that my grandfather had always sat in.

He nodded. "Good day," he said, and left. The book was delivered later in the afternoon by Moses Hatfield, the Negro who was the only servant that lived in Mr. Millhouser's house. I thanked him and he said: "Take good care of this book, Gerald. You' Grandpa used to say this book showed war like war was, not like the Fourth of *Joo*-ly parade."

I cannot say that I took very good care of the book. At my mother's suggestion I wrote Mr. Millhouser a note of thanks, and then I put the book under my atlas, which it matched in size, and it remained there with the rest of the books that I had not taken away to school. For the next few years I stopped going to my grandmother's in the summer; we would motor to her house for one enormous meal between Christmas and New Year's, but after sophomore year in college I had my own car and I always left Grandma's as soon as I could break away. I did not, therefore, see Mr. Millhouser at all during my last year in prep school or in my first two years in college. I might never have seen him again if it had not been, once again, for that book.

My roommate was a history major and his history professor would occasionally drop in for a chat with Kevorkian, who was a straight-A student and eventually a junior-year Phi Beta Kappa. "I wish you could get hold of a book called Mittendorf's *Pictorial History of the Civil War*," said the professor. "It was published in Columbus, Ohio, around 1885, but I haven't seen a copy of it since I left Northwestern."

"I have a copy of it," I said.

"*You,* Higgins? *You* have a copy of Mittendorf's *Pictorial History of the Civil War?* Describe it," said the professor.

"It's about the size of an atlas, about an inch-and-a-half thick. The binding is green, and there's a picture of a drum and a cannon and flags on the front of the book." I did not like this history professor but I enjoyed this situation. "I could describe the contents for you, too."

"Where did you get hold of this treasure? Was your grandfather in the Civil War?"

"I had two grandfathers in the Civil War, but the book was given to me by a man who thought I'd appreciate it."

"And where is it now?" said the professor.

"In my room, at home, with the rest of my books."

"Higgins, I may have wronged you. Would you let Kevorkian and me have a look at it?"

"Well, it's never been out of my house—"

"Oh, you knew how valuable it was?"

"Oh, I always knew that."

9

"I'd be willing to make a trip to your home town, just to have a good long look at it. And take Kevorkian with me."

"You don't have to do that. I'll bring it back after Christmas."

"Higgins, you amaze me," said the professor.

I was well aware that the professor would repeat his astonishment to his chums at the Faculty Club and that a little story like that would do me no harm. Within the week I had a small reputation as a secret bibliophile, which I was not, and the college librarian wrote me a note suggesting that I might like to donate my Mittendorf to the library, which I had no intention of doing. At least not until I was in much worse scholastic standing than I was at that moment, and needed some favorable publicity at the Faculty Club. I am probably being unnecessarily harsh with myself; I finished college without using Mr. Millhouser's book for any sinister purpose, and when I knew I had passed all my courses I wrote to Mr. Millhouser and asked if he would approve my donating the book to the library. As a result of his reply I was able after many delays to obtain the material for the book which the reader now holds in his hand.

Mr. Millhouser was more than pleased that his gift to me would find a permanent place in the library at my college, and that the book was considered a useful one. He invited me to call on him, and I did so, and that first visit in 1926 led to many more. The story he told me follows, although naturally I have to tell it in my own way and not exactly as it was given me by Mr. Millhouser.

•

THE FIRST Millhouser to settle in North America was a friend and follower of Heinrich Melchior Muhlenberg. Franz Millhouser had gone to classical schools in Einbeck, Hanover, with Heinrich (or Henry) Muhlenberg, and Muhlenberg wrote to his young friend and urged him to join him in the work he was doing in the Evangelical Lutheran Ministerium of Pennsylvania. Accordingly Franz Millhouser arrived in Philadelphia late in 1745 and for the next ten years he helped to form new congregations in Pennsylvania, New Jersey, and Maryland. In emulation of the scholarly Muhlenberg he studied some law and some medicine at the University of Pennsylvania, and he died in Philadelphia in 1790. Except for his carefully kept church records and a few letters to his wife, he left no writings that told much of a personal nature. He married Anna Christina Weiler, daughter of a Lancaster clergyman, and they had three sons and two daughters. The sons attended the University of Pennsylvania, but only one of them studied for the ministry and that son died in Georgia where he had gone to assume charge of a new congregation. Another son remained in Philadelphia to engage in the practice of medicine; and the third, from whom the Robert Millhouser of this story was descended, was a lawyer and later a judge in Fort Penn. Judge Peter Millhouser was the first man of wealth in the family. He resigned from the bench a few years after he had been appointed, and almost immediately he amassed a considerable fortune in farming and timber lands to which title was obscure. He was murdered in his sleep by a person or persons who were never identified.

Peter Millhouser had four daughters and a son, Henry, the youngest child and the father of Robert Millhouser. Henry left the University of Pennsylvania in the middle of his sophomore year because of illness. He was thirty years old before he fully regained his health and was able to devote his time to the tangled affairs of his father's estate, which through neglect, mismanagement, and lawsuits had been reduced to a fraction of its value at the time of Peter Millhouser's murder. Through hard work on Henry's part and the natural increase in land values, the losses were wiped out so that at Henry's death the dollar value of the estate was greater than it had been at Peter's death. But the Millhouser fortune in 1870 was hardly comparable to the Millhouser fortune of 1810, and not to be counted among the first twenty fortunes of East-Central Pennsylvania.

Henry married late in life and built the house in the town of Lyons in which his only child, Robert, was born. He chose Lyons because it was on two railway lines and in the geographical center of the Millhouser holdings; the timber to the north and northeast, the farms to the south and west. Zilph Murray, whom he married, was an Ulster Irishwoman, a childless widow who had come to Philadelphia to visit her sister, but with no intention of returning to Ireland. When Henry met her at the home of one of his Philadelphia cousins he knew that he wanted to marry her, but her brogue seemed to warn him that she was a Roman Catholic, and her forthright manner and self-confidence further warned him that she was not one who would be likely to change her religion. Then upon learning that she was a Presbyterian, a Protestant, he proposed to her and was accepted with a speed that delighted him while it alarmed him. "I was wondering if I'd have to turn coquettish to make you speak," she told him. "Mind you, I was fully prepared to, and don't think I wasn't." The marriage from the start was a happy one, saddened only by two miscarriages before the birth of Robert.

Lyons was not a town for much social life in the middle of the century, and even if it had been, Zilph Millhouser would not have joined in. "Wouldn't you like to see some of the people in the town?" said Henry.

"I have, and if they'll keep their distance I'll be only too glad to keep mine. What would we do with them?"

"Feed them, I suppose," said Henry.

"And after that, what? A hand of cards? Not the Methodists, surely. Polite conversation? On what subject? No, Henry my dear, I'm content, so long as you are."

He was content. As a newcomer to the town he was liable to some hostility, but as a man of means he was carefully spared any display of it. His initial account at the bank made him immediately the largest depositor, and after it became apparent that he had no plan to dominate the town or to change the existing order, the hostility and suspicion disappeared and he was treated with the special deference due a man who has power but refrains from using it. The women disliked Zilph: the Protestant women could not believe anyone so Irish was not a Catholic; and the Catholic women, most of them Irish, hated her Protestantism. But their husbands quickly silenced all criticism of her, when it was made in their presence, and very few women in Lyons were safe from the beatings that were the usual punishment for opposing their husbands. They were often beaten for a great deal less than deliberate disobedience.

Robert Millhouser was fifteen and at Mercersburg when Henry died, and Zilph Millhouser, who was not yet forty-four, had a difficult decision to make. During her marriage she had formed no friendships with the people of Lyons and had been, as she said, content. It was a strange contentment; in the County Down she had never been far from friends or from the sea; in Lyons she was not half a mile from the great forest that came down to the clearing in the middle of which Henry had built their house. Westward the forest stood unbroken by a highway, up and over the mountain, into the next valley, up and over the Second Mountain and down into the Second Valley before a highway would be met. A mile from her house was already wilderness, and over the mountain, in the next valley, no Lyons man would go without a guide. Foolish men had been lost and died within the sound of the Lyons-Fort Penn train whistle. Only the men who wanted to kill moose and bear would take their guns into the next valley; those who wanted wildcat and deer had not so far to go. Sometimes during the late fall Henry would have guests for the night, men from Fort Penn and Philadelphia who would be up and gone before daylight and would not be back again for three or four days or a week, never with less than a buck, often with the head and hide of

12

the bigger game, to be mounted and tanned. Henry would not go gunning with his friends, but he took pleasure in being their host, in his pride in Zilph as their hostess; and when the men had gone back to their cities he would ask her again how much she missed the social life, since she was so good at it on these occasions. "Any woman enjoys entertaining men," she would say. "Your friends arrive here in high expectation and that makes them jolly, and then a week later they're back, pleased with themselves for being so courageous and so expert with their firearms. But they'd never be so jolly if their wives were along, and neither would I, Harry Boy, neither would I. I'm content."

The source of her contentment was in the closeness of their lives, their life; the satisfying nature of his dependence on her, the sure knowledge that there would be no such pleasure for him as there was for the men who visited them on their hunting trips, whose laughter as she heard it had never been heard by their wives. Now he was dead and the boy was away at school, and *he* had been part of that closeness, too; a grave and gentle lad, with more of his father than of her in him, who as he grew older seemed to look at her as his father had often done, fascinated by her vitality and her quick, humorous mind; standing, as it were, beside his father and watching her as his father often did, but denied the ultimate understanding of her that was the father's right as her husband. The boy did not share his grief with his mother. He was selfish with it and shared it with no one, and for a few days, a few weeks, the boy unconsciously made her feel like the foreigner that indeed she was, a stranger who had been his father's companion but had been so for not too long a time. In those dismal weeks the boy's kindness did not remove the fanciful notion that he was a creature who had lived as many years as his father had lived, and always with his father. And yet she understood the boy.

Henry had reached thirty before commencing his participation in the world of affairs, and he moved at a slower pace than most of his contemporaries; he was gentler in speech and, doubtless because of his own father's violent death, unaggressive in his business dealings, which constituted nearly the whole of his relations with the race of men. He had waited until the middle years before marrying, and she thereupon had become the sole and real and symbolic embodiment of her sex. As the boy grew older the father and son seemed to team up, and this, she knew, was all to the good. It did not make her love her son the less because the boy stood beside his father; she had Henry's love and he had hers, and it was easy to imagine that in watching the boy and his growth, she was seeing a repetition of the boyhood of her husband. She saw her husband in the boy, the father's boyhood years that she had not been there to see. And with Henry dead she could still have a true living memory of him as the boy who was so much like him grew into manhood.

There were other considerations, too. This had been Robert's home, his town, the home of his playmates. He knew the back streets and the back yards, the picnic grounds and the swimming dam. Here he went to Sunday School, here he had learned to read and write, here lived the doctor who had treated him for the illnesses of childhood, and to this place, she shrewdly guessed, he would always return. And so here she would remain. After the decision had been made it no longer seemed a difficult choice; but it had been a temptation, in the very first days without Henry, to sell the house, to move away forever. She had had no attachment for the town as such, she had made no intimate friends. With her inheritance she could live anywhere in the world, and there had been moments in which she had a strong impulse to return to Ireland, to live in London, her favorite city, or New York, her next favorite. But her greatest happiness had been with Henry and in this town, and if she could no longer have that happiness she could have a substitute for it; she could live where the happiness had been, rather than in some distant place where it never had been. She would live in this house until Robert married and brought another woman to it, and then she would go back to the County Down ostensibly for a visit, never to return to Lyons.

She wrote to Robert twice a week, a long letter on Sunday and a note on Wednesday, throughout the remainder of his time at Mercersburg and for the four years he was at the University in Philadelphia. She had her garden, her needle-work, her reading and her piano, and an additional interest. Once a fortnight Conrad Isaminger came up from Fort Penn to advise her on the conduct of Henry's estate. He would arrive on the noon train and would come to the house for the midday meal, give her the papers to sign, and have conversation with her until dusk, when Moses Hatfield would drive him back to the Central House for the night. She soon had learned more about Henry's estate than she had learned in all the years of her marriage, and in all but the legal technicalities Conrad Isaminger began to listen to her as much as she listened to him.

She had inherited fifteen farms and four large stands of timber, and in the second winter of her widowhood she had the farmers come to Lyons in groups of five so that she could meet the men and form her opinions of them. They all spent the night at the Central House at her expense, having been fed a large Pennsylvania Dutch noon meal

14

and given cigars before the business meeting that took up the afternoon. Conrad Isaminger acted as interpreter for those who did not speak English—two or three in each batch of five—and each man was encouraged to report on his farm's needs, from harness snaps to stump-pullers, without, however, any commitment on Zilph's part. As they walked back together to the Central House the farmers grumbled among themselves at the necessity of explaining anything to a woman, but Conrad Isaminger told Zilph that individually the men were not displeased. "That's very nice, considering," said Zilph.

"Considering what?"

"That if they didn't like it they could lump it. They know Henry treated them better than they'd ever be treated by anyone else, including yours truly . . . Let's get rid of the one called Hegelbrecht. He's a brazen liar."

"He's a pretty good farmer."

"He's a brazen liar, whatever he is. And I'll lay you odds his wife does most of the work."

"How did you know that?"

"Because I'm a woman and I know how he'd treat me if given the chance. I know the look."

"Yes, he makes her work like a horse, but they all do. The women expect it."

"I'm not against hard work for a woman, but not when she's doing it for a lout of his kind."

"All right, he must go. What did he lie about?"

"He wants us to buy him paint for the barn. The barn was painted three years ago."

"Yes, I think it was. Before Henry died."

"He thought I wouldn't know that, because it happened before Henry died. But I read up on all the farms, five at a time, every time we had the men come here. We'd get a bill for Hegelbrecht's paint and he'd divvy up with the hardware store. We'll keep a closer watch on bills from that store hereafter, Conrad. Do you happen to know how their prices compare with other stores?"

"Yes. Higher."

"We pay them cash in ten days to take advantage of the two percent discount, don't we? But most farmers can't do that, can they?"

"You bet they can't."

"Then let's stop paying cash to that store. Let's run up a big bill, and then when they ask us about it we'll put the fear of God into them. Or *you* will. Let their guilty conscience plague them."

"Yes, but what do you want me to say?"

15

"You think of something."

"There are several things," said Conrad Isaminger. "Pretty soon you're not going to need me, Zilph."

"Nonsense, Conrad."

"True."

"Unless what you're trying to say is you want to give up the work. What I've been doing is like playing games. I couldn't get along without you, if the truth be known."

A year later Conrad Isaminger proposed honorable marriage. He was sixty years of age, he said, and now that his children were married (his wife was ten years dead) he had nothing to come home to in the evening. He had a large house on the river road, full of rooms he never went into. He was lonely, and she would understand that. "All too well," she said. "But as a barrister you're not pleading your case very well. Conrad, the answer is no. Find a widow-woman in Fort Penn and persuade her. But it'll never be me. You're too young a man to give up your work, and I'm too old a woman to give up what I have here, to start all over again somewhere else."

"You could keep this house, and we'd come here for Christmas, whenever Robert has a school vacation."

"*We* could come here? You and I? Do you think Robert would come here after he once saw you sitting at the head of the table? No man will ever take the place of his father, and God pity the man that would try."

She received another proposal of marriage, and that was from the Reverend Emil Betz, pastor of the Lyons Lutheran church, and likewise a widower. He had called on her once after Henry's funeral; every previous year he had made the annual visit to the Millhouser house as he did to all the houses of his congregation. Zilph continued to attend his church after Henry's death, but aside from shaking hands with him after the Sunday morning services she had had no meeting with him until, on one of those Sundays, he asked if he might call on her the next day. She was prepared to increase her contribution to the church treasury, but in no way ready for the Reverend's intention.

"I'd rather stand up," he said, when she asked him to take a chair. "Sister Millhouser, we could do so much of the Lord's work together and please don't think this is sutten. I haff thought about it in my mind, ower and ower I turnt it, the pros and cons, backwarts and forwarts. A pastor neets a wife by his side chust as much as the woman neets someone to take care of her. There is so much of the Lord's work to be done—"

"Please sit down, Reverend."

16

"Will you wait till I finish yet?"

"Are you asking me to marry you?"

"Don't it sount like that?" he said.

"True, you did mention the word wife."

"I haff more to say, Sister."

"But please don't say it, Reverend. I can give you my answer now and it doesn't seem fair to have you go on."

"Fair? What has fair got to do with it?"

"Well, I know my answer—"

"But how do you know if you don't listen?"

"Because I'm not going to marry anybody, no matter how eloquent he is."

"But the Lord's work *has* to be done—"

"Well, not by me."

"What?"

"The truth is, I'm not a very religious woman, Reverend. One religion is much like another to me, so long as it isn't that of the Pope of Rome."

"You are a Lutheran."

"Well, *am* I? I became one when I married Henry, but if the truth be told, Reverend, I don't get much out of listening to so much German, Sunday after Sunday."

"I will teach you German."

"I'm afraid not. I don't want to learn it. Don't you think that if I'd wanted to learn German I'd have learned it from Henry?"

"It wondered me why he didn't make you learn it, a Millhouser yet," he said. "What are you going to do with all the money?"

"I beg your pardon?"

"A woman with so much money, what can you do with it?"

"I know what I'd like to do with some of it."

"What? You must tell me."

"I'd like to build a race track down at the other end of the town."

"A race track!"

"There are a lot of fast horses here, all around here."

"Ach, now. You make chokes."

"I have no intention of building a race track, but the thought did enter my head. That's because I'm the sort of woman I am, Reverend. No, I don't think you'd enjoy being my third husband."

"Third husband? Secont, you mean."

"No, I mean third. I was a widow at twenty-five."

"You had children?"

"No, but I was married for two years."

"What was your husband?"

"How did he make his living? Well, in much the same way Henry did. He owned land."

"A rich man."

"Oh, no. Always in debt."

"How did he die?"

"He broke his neck, poor man. He went over his horse's head and into a ditch," she said. "So you see, Reverend, I've had an odd sort of life. Marriage to Henry was as different to my first marriage as it would be if I were married to you. *Now* won't you sit down and have a cup of tea?"

"Thank you. I guess I go now."

"Carry on," she said, on an irresistible impulse. But he was on his way to the door and oblivious of her farewell.

Zilph created a short-lived scandal when the town learned that a party of three men from Philadelphia had spent several nights at her house. They were three of the same men who in the past had slept at the house before going into the woods for game. Zilph was not present during the men's visit; she was in Philadelphia on her annual Christmas shopping trip; but she had not bothered to inform anyone in the town that her trip coincided with the men's use of her house. When the two facts became known, the scandal died down, but in its place appeared an active resentment of her for her failure to explain the dual arrangement. There was no one in the town to whom she had ever explained or justified any act, but the feeling among the townspeople came from a vague notion that she should somehow have cleared herself of suspicion in advance, and her failure to do so, so unmistakably reflecting her indifference toward town opinion, was held against her. Now, at last, the citizens of the town had the beginnings of a righteous hostility toward her; she was a woman alone, still young enough to cause suspicion, and so contemptuous and wilful that she would not take steps to protect herself against proper reproach. All the years of her marriage to Henry, during which there had been no cause to criticize her, now were remembered as years during which the wives had been forbidden to criticize her. With Henry alive and beside her, and as devoted to her as she to him, she could be censured only for her foreignness and her aloofness; but as a rich and handsome widow living alone and with no disposition to communicate with her neighbors, she became in their minds a careless and then a defiant figure, and she would one day have to pay for it.

She was not unmindful of the near-scandal. Her maid was a young woman from County Waterford who got about among the Catholic Irish of Lyons, and who gleefully reported back to her mistress. "The

Protestants want your head again," she would say, ignoring the fact of Zilph's Protestantism, or, as Zilph suspected, hoping to undermine it. Margaret Dillon had come to Zilph through Mrs. Jeremiah MacMahon, wife of the young man who owned the smaller of the town grocery stores. The Millhousers patronized MacMahon's store because Henry Millhouser had wanted to give young MacMahon a little help when he returned from the War. "We can do that much for a young soldier," Henry had said. "And one head of lettuce is much like another." MacMahon's head of lettuce also turned out to be slightly cheaper than the one like it at Fred Langendorf's, and Mac-Mahon and his wife were so eager to please that Zilph rewarded them with all her green-grocery business and bought only dry goods at Langendorf's, a fact which did not weaken Mrs. Langendorf's suspicion that Zilph was of the Catholic Irish. One day Mrs. MacMahon said to Zilph: "I have a cousin of a friend of mine coming over from Ireland, Mrs. Millhouser. I don't know the girl, but she was a ladies' maid and well recommended in Dublin. If you hear of anyone'd have a place for her . . ." Margaret Dillon landed in Baltimore and was working for Zilph within a month of the conversation.

She was a black-haired woman with a large square face and a chin that seemed to be built to hold the strap of a policeman's helmet. But the masculinity of her appearance was misleading; she was daintily feminine in her care of Zilph's wardrobe, Henry's linen, the napery, the lace curtains, the piano throws, the tapestries. She was skilled with the needle, even with repairs to Henry's and Robert's suits. She could read and write English and she had picked up a smattering of French from the governess at her Dublin post. Her tolerance for Zilph's Protestantism was not a new thing; she had always worked for the one Dublin family, Protestant but patriotic, and her attitude toward them and toward Zilph was that they would be redeemed one day, if she gave good example and put a word in now and then. Zilph, an Ulster woman, was to be worked on politically as well as theologically, but Margaret Dillon had confidence in the power of her own subtlety. Although she was nearly twenty years younger than Zilph, the two women met about halfway between their ages: Margaret had the early maturity of the homely woman, and Zilph retained the youthfulness of the comely one.

Margaret had not come to the Millhousers' until the boy Robert was nearly ten. She had the Irish servant's gift for commanding obedience in the household's children without sacrificing her position as a source of sympathy, understanding, and an occasional copper. Winning Robert over in the beginning was easily accomplished by the small bribes of little cakes and root beer and by hiding things for him and telling small lies for him. Gaining his respect was as simple but for Margaret Dillon more difficult: she would slap him when he had it coming to him, and at other times she would refuse to speak to him. His complaints to his mother that Margaret had slapped him got him nowhere; Zilph would tell him he must surely have deserved it. He could not complain that Margaret was refusing to speak to him, and soon that became the more effective punishment, since it precluded the possibility of asking her for favors. In a year's time Robert and Margaret Dillon had had so many minor crises, matched fairly equally by her kindnesses, that it began to seem that she had always been part of the household.

The cook was an older woman, older even than Henry Millhouser, and as Margaret Dillon immediately commented, enjoying poor health. She was the only full-time cook in all Lyons; in all the other houses the wife did the cooking, regardless of the family's social and economic status or the size of the family. Mrs. Daub was a good cook and an excellent pastry chef, a fat woman who was often to be found sitting at her kitchen table with her eyes open and yet apparently sound asleep, with a half-eaten piece of cake and a cup of tea getting cold before her. Her breathing at such times was the breathing of a sleeping person, accompanied by a fluttering of the palate that was the next thing to a snore. After a while she would get to her feet and do some such kitchen chore as polishing the cookstove, as though all the time she had been sitting at the table she had been contemplating her next effort. She neither resented nor welcomed Margaret Dillon's arrival, and Margaret's backstairs ebullience and chatter went unnoticed by Mrs. Daub. "Conversation with Mrs. Daub is like tossing little balls of butter into a big tub of butter," she would say. Robert's longer experience with Mrs. Daub had taught him that if he went to the kitchen and asked her for something, he would have to watch her to see whether she nodded or shook her head. She seldom exercised the power of speech. She had no visitors, she got no mail, and her only trips away from the house were for Sunday evening prayer meeting at the Reverend Mr. Betz's church. She had been hired by Henry before he married Zilph. "If she isn't satisfactory, we can find someone else," Henry had told Zilph, and Mrs. Daub had been kept on because there had been no good reason to let her go. She gave the impression of laziness, and she was a lifeless person to have in the house, but the plain food was properly cooked, the desserts were always a treat, the kitchen was orderly and between meals smelled of strong soap, and the woman kept her person and her uniforms and her bedroom clean.

When Mrs. Daub did not come down one morning, Zilph was

summoned by Margaret Dillon, tending to go to pieces in the presence of death. "Go run for the doctor," said Zilph, to give Margaret something to do. Zilph did not know whom to notify; she had always put off asking Henry and Mrs. Daub herself, and in some desperation she sent off a telegram to Conrad Isaminger, who then took the next train to Lyons and learned from the chief burgess, the town constable, and the Lutheran pastor that Mrs. Daub had a husband who was living in Lyons, tended bar in the Central House, and had not seen her in nearly twenty years. They had had no children, there had been no divorce. William Daub expressed no desire to attend a funeral for his wife, until Conrad Isaminger pointed out that although Mrs. Daub had died intestate, her husband was probably entitled to his widower's share of her life savings, and that if he intended to accept any of her money, he owed her that final mark of respect. "I got no respect for her. Once, maybe, but not now no more," said William Daub. "Do I get the money even so, if I don't go to her funeral?"

"I'm afraid you do," said Conrad Isaminger.

"Then I chaintch my mind again. I don't go to no funeral."

The successor to Mrs. Daub was, inevitably, Irish and a distant relative of Margaret Dillon. She was older than Margaret and as cook expected to occupy a traditionally higher position in the household staff. Margaret did not see it that way, and the kitchen ceased to be the silent room it had been during Mrs. Daub's lifetime. "You'll do as I say," Theresa O'Malley would say.

"I'll not take orders from any greenhorn, least of all one that I got a position for."

"*You* got a position for *me?* Huh. I didn't come no three t'ousand miles to be spoken to contemptibly by a little snip that can't say for sure who's her own father. *I'm* giving *notice.*"

"If you don't, I will. I wouldn't be another night under the same roof wit' the likes of you. My father was Hugh Patrick Dillon and only too well you know it. It's no news to you that Hugh Patrick Dillon could father his own children and other men's as well. Two of your brats bear the greater resemblance to Hugh Patrick Dillon than to any Tim O'Malley. But your trouble, my fine woman, was that Hugh Patrick Dillon always come back to my mother after he'd had his way with you. And many like you. Give your notice, and I guarantee you it'll be accepted, with alacrity."

The kitchen was a lively place, even when the two women were not stating their respective views of the Dillon and O'Malley morals. Robert, home from Mercersburg, enjoyed sitting there and listening to them reminiscing about Ireland, making their comments on the citizens of Lyons, and sometimes singing hymns with a Latin pronunciation that was at variance with the one he was learning at school. Mrs. O'Malley had a small soprano that went well with Margaret's alto and they sang prettily, especially in the *Adeste Fidelis* at Christmas vacation, a hymn which gave Margaret the opportunity to wander all over the melody. His mother always made the women settle their own disputes. "What is it, Margaret—and I'll have no tattling," she would say, thereby putting an end to a complaint before it was uttered. Robert at eighteen was past the age when he could be slapped; he had become a handsome youth for whose approval the women constantly competed. Margaret would knit him skating caps, mittens, and mufflers, and embroider fancy waistcoats. Theresa, less gifted with needles, used her cash to buy him cuff buttons and cravats, mouth organs and penknives. The competition for his favor inevitably caused some of the bitterest quarrels between the two women, and some of Robert's earliest experiences in tactfulness occurred in the kitchen.

Outside the house yet very much on the property, his protective companion was Moses Hatfield, whose father was Abraham Hatfield, head of one of the ten or eleven Negro families in the town. Abraham worked for McDermott's Livery Stable and he had four sons, but jobs were few for male Negroes and only Moses remained in Lyons. The three Hatfield girls helped their mother, who took in washing, until they were old enough to find work in domestic service. Moses Hatfield was the youngest son and his father was delighted that Moses had no desire to go to Fort Penn and become a waiter as his brothers had done. Abraham Hatfield had started life as a Virginia slave, and was becoming a field nigger when he ran away, sleeping by day, traveling by night, until he came to Lyons and broke his leg in jumping from a hayloft where he had planned to spend the night. "Shoot me," he said, in fear and in pain. "Shoot me, master." But the farmer who discovered him bound his leg, fed him, and permitted him to sleep in the barn until he was able to walk again. The broken leg was now shorter than the other, and Abraham had a permanent limp, but he worked for the farmer through that spring and summer and early fall, receiving no wages but sharing the farmer's food and sleeping in the barn. After the small harvest, Langendorf, the farmer, told Abraham he would be unable to feed him through the coming winter, he needed everything for his pregnant wife and himself, but he would vouch for him in the town. Abraham reluctantly agreed to leave the farm and immediately found work at the Post House, taking care of the horses for a shilling a week, his meals, and the right to sleep in the stable. He lived in that fashion for three years, built a cabin, and took a young woman to be his wife. She was the chamber-maid at the Post House, a member of one of the two Negro families in the town. She worked until the day before her first child was born and returned to work the day after, taking the baby to the Post House and nursing it when she could. She could not give up her job; she needed the food she was given at the Post House; and the owner had already objected to Abraham's living in the cabin, arguing that part of his job was to sleep in the stable so that the horses would be ready to take the road at first light. Abraham and his wife were terrified. They knew that they were badly paid, but they also knew that there was no other work for them in Lyons and they had no friends any-where else, even if they could make their way to another town. But good fortune intervened. The second railway was completed, having Lyons for a terminal point, and a man named McDermott opened the town's first livery stable, board and hire, and after seeing Abra-ham Hatfield's care of the animals and the stalls at the Post House, he offered him ten dollars a month to be his hostler.

Moses Hatfield had no schooling, but he grew up in McDermott's Livery Stable, observing and imitating the speech and ways of a class of men who could afford to hire horses, live in hotels, smoke cigars, drink whiskey, and examine the large pieces of parchment that had no pictures on them but that told them where to look for the coal that was under the ground. McDermott in odd moments taught him to count to a hundred and to read the numbers. He learned to chant the letters of the alphabet in their proper order, and by the time he was eighteen he could identify the letters visually and by putting their sounds together, slowly read a name, a common noun, and a few verbs. But reading was hard work and it was not expected of him. The salesmen and the men with the spyglass mounted on the three sticks did not reward him for being able to read; they gave him coppers because he was strong and quick.

When Henry Millhouser was building his house Abraham Hatfield drove McDermott's wagon that was hired to transport the materials from the railway depot to the Millhouser clearing. Moses rode along with his father and helped with the loading and unloading of the lumber and brick and interior woodwork. He was about ten years old, but already able to harness or curry a horse. Moses would stand on an inverted bucket to make up for his lack of height, and in that way he was almost as tall as his father. He was witness to the building of the house from the breaking of ground to the final coat of paint, and when it was completed he was not forgotten by Henry Millhouser in the distribution of silver coins to the carpenter and the stonemason and their apprentices. But ten years elapsed before he saw the interior of the house with the carpet on the floor and the pictures on the wall and the furniture in place.

Moses was twenty years old and he heard one day that the Millhousers' coachman, Ryan, had dropped dead that morning. Moses finished his chores at McDermott's and then left without offering any explanation to his father. Abraham was now feeble and spent most of his time sitting on a feed bin and brushing away flies. McDermott went on paying Abraham but it was Moses who was doing the work, receiving tips but no regular pay.

Moses shrewdly guessed that the Millhouser horses would be neglected in the excitement of Ryan's sudden death, and he went to the stable, groomed the animals, watered and fed them, and hurried back to McDermott's without making his presence known to anyone at the Millhousers'. In the evening he again went to the Millhouser stable, watered and fed the horses, put down some hay and straw and bedded them for the night. This time he was seen by Henry Millhouser, who had suddenly remembered the horses and was on his way to take care of them.

"That was very good of you, Moses. Did you like Ryan so much?" said Henry Millhouser.

"No sir."

"Then why did you?"

Moses was silent.

"Are you fond of our horses that much?"

Moses remained silent.

"Oh! You like *us* that much."

"Yes sir."

"I see. You'd like to come and work for me."

"Yes sir."

"But if you came to work for me, wouldn't your father lose his job at Mr. McDermott's?"

"My pappy gonna die soon, yes sir. He mighty old, sir."

"Tell you what I'll do, Moses. I'll have to think it over, but I'll give you twenty-five cents a day to come out and look after the stock."

"Sir, how long it take you to think it over?"

"Oh, say a week. I'll let you know in a week."

Moses was silent again.

"You don't like that. Well, I must say you sized up the situation and lost no time in taking advantage of it."

"Sir?"

"You wait here a minute. I'll be right back."

24

Henry went to the house and explained the circumstances to Zilph. "Would you object to having a black boy for a coachman?"

"Oh, it might be rather stylish. Can he wear Ryan's livery?"

"Some of it, they're about of a height."

"Where would he live? The kitchen help might not like it."

"He wouldn't have to live here. But you wouldn't object?"

"No, I've seen them in London, Philadelphia. They do lend a bit of style to the turnout. More than poor Ryan did, with his big blue nose and the water running out of his eyes."

There was for Moses, after his years at McDermott's, so little work to be done at Henry Millhouser's that he was always available for trips into the woods with Robert. He showed the boy all he had learned from his own father, the slinging of a stone to stun a squirrel, the use of a forked stick to pin down a copperhead, the recognition of the woodland smells and of the calls of birds, the ability to move in silence, the selection of the edible berries and the good-tasting bark, the precautions against getting lost, the reading of the early signs of winter, the reliability of instinctive warnings when nothing appeared to be wrong. Robert was able to ride a horse, but he had not been taught any of the stable lore, the rubdowns with straw, the washing between a mare's teats, the plaiting of a mane and the dipping of a tail, the danger signs in the manure, the control of fractiousness. On schooldays Robert played with his friends; on Saturdays he would often go into the woods with Moses and spend the morning there. He admired Moses for the things he could do, and Moses enjoyed the boy's quiet but unstinted delight at accomplishments that Moses had always had. Moses could demolish a walnut with his teeth and break a carriage spoke across his knee. He had a repertory of imitations of all the barnyard noises. "Robert, you listen, what's this?" he would say.

"That's—do it again. Once again. That's putting on the brake going down a hill."

"No sir, it aint no such thing. It's sharpening a knife on the grindstone, boy. Listen to this."

"That's—that's—Bay Charley when supper's late."

"Why sure, boy. Anybody could tell that."

"Do the chicken-pen when there's a hawk in the air."

Robert was ten years old at the end of the War, which he remembered chiefly as a grownups' concern. "There's money in the town," he would hear his father say, and Robert knew that money in the town was related to the War, although he did not know why. He remembered that his father had been made angry by the Union Army. "We want to do all we can," his father said to his mother. "But we

25

can't run the farms without horses." This was a reference to the fact that the artillery came and took a horse away from every farm owned by Henry Millhouser. They paid cash, up to a fixed maximum, but the money would not buy a horse to replace the one that had been seized. One day when Robert was seven years old a lieutenant and nine other soldiers, cavalrymen, rode in and dismounted and examined the three Millhouser horses, the matched blacks and the gray. Robert was fascinated by the soldiers, who were unshaven and wore dusty uniforms, pistol belts and sabres and sabretaches. The lieutenant was using his sabre as a walking-stick and he was an arrogant man. "You," he said to Ryan. "What is your name? I suppose you're the coachman."

"Me name is Ryan, and I'm the coachman."

"Stand up when I speak to you."

"You're trespassing on private property."

"Oh, bother," said the lieutenant. "Sergeant, take the horses out of the stalls and lead them around . . . Saddle them up, take them for a gallop, and bring them back." He listened carefully to the breathing of each horse, ran his bare hand down their legs and under their bellies. "Good. We'll take the black gelding and the gray. Where is Mr. Millhouse?"

"There is no Mr. Millhouse," said Ryan.

"You're lying to me. Are you aware that I'm an officer of the United States Army?"

"I am that."

The sergeant whispered to the lieutenant.

"Then you go fetch Mr. Mill-hou-*ser*. And I want to remind you that you can go to prison for this kind of insolence."

"I'll speak to Mr. Millhouser. Fetching him is another matter entirely."

Henry came down from the house, and Robert felt a sudden pride in his father's dignity and superiority. "What are you doing here, Lieutenant?"

"I'm authorized to buy horses for the United States Cavalry," said the lieutenant. "I take it you're Mr. Millhouser."

"You're not authorized to march in here with your men and order my servants about or take liberties with my property. Put those horses back in their stalls. Order your men off my land, and then come up to my house and I'll be happy to show you a letter from General McDowd."

"You have a letter from General McDowd, sir?" said the lieutenant. "I didn't know that."

"No, of course you didn't, and you didn't make it your business to find out, either."

"May I ask what the contents of the letter are?"

"You may ask nothing at all until you've followed my instructions."

The horses were stabled, the cavalrymen rode off to the other side of the Millhouser fence, and Robert took his father's hand and they walked up to the house. They waited on the porch for the lieutenant, who dusted off his uniform with his gauntlet, straightened his hat and saluted Henry Millhouser. "Sir," he said.

Henry handed him a letter. "Be good enough to read it."

The lieutenant cleared his throat. " 'To all officers and men. The bearer of this letter, Mr. Henry Millhouser, of Lyons, Pennsylvania, is personally known to me and is to receive the utmost courtesy at all times. Any and all requests he may make shall have the effect of requests made by the undersigned. Signed. Benjamin R. McDowd, Brigadier General, United States Army.' Very good, sir."

"Yes, and I *have* a request. It is that in future you remember that you are in friendly territory and not in the state of South Carolina. You may go."

The lieutenant saluted, did an about-turn and marched off.

"Father, do we know a general?" said Robert.

"Indeed we do, son. We're related to this one. General McDowd is married to my first cousin, your Cousin Helen Millhouser in Philadelphia. Do you remember her?"

"I thought she was just Cousin Helen."

"Cousins can be very useful sometimes," said Henry.

A few months after the visit of the cavalrymen and a few weeks after the Fourth of July the noon train brought home two men who had been in the great battle at Gettysburg. Although they wore uniforms they did not seem to Robert to be soldiers; they were more like men he had seen riding home in a wagon after an accident at the colliery. Their beards were untrimmed, their jackets spotted and half buttoned, and one of them could not put on his cap because his head was wrapped in bandage. The other had lost a foot and his pant-leg was folded over and pinned. He could not manage his crutch coming down the steps of the coach and he threw it angrily to the station platform. He faced the crowd and called out: "Will some son of a bitch give me a hand?" But before anyone could reach him he lost his balance and fell forward, knocking down a man and woman who had gone to help him. The soldier with the bandaged head ignored the confusion at his feet and shouted: "Where's Mary? Mary, where the hell are you, God damn you to hell."

"Here I am, John. Here I am," cried a woman in the crowd.

"Well, come and get me, God damn you, woman."

The crowd then realized that although the man's eyes were not covered, he was blind. The remaining civilian members of the fife and drum corps were on hand to escort the wounded men to their homes, but no one now thought of a welcoming parade. The fifers put their instruments back in their boots and the drummers slung their drums over their shoulders and soon the station platform was deserted.

Robert did not recognize either of the first two men from the Gettysburg battle. Later on a few Lyons men, wounded or sick or not re-enlisting, came home from the War, and among them were men whose names he knew. The older brother of one of his friends was killed at Gettysburg but Robert's friend was not saddened except when his sister and his mother would weep, and Robert was not affected at all except by the mysterious experience of having known someone who would no longer be alive (Where did they go?). Robert's other outstanding memory of the War was a conversation he witnessed between his father and Ryan.

"Your honor," said Ryan, using a form he sometimes used in addressing Henry Millhouser. "I'd a man sleep in the stable last night."

"Why are you telling me, Ryan? You've done that before. It's all right as long as you and your friends don't smoke your pipes and start a fire."

"Ah, but this was no friend of mine. He didn't even know I knew he was there."

"Come to the point, man."

Ryan lowered his voice. "I t'ink he was a deserter, a deserter from the army."

"Did you see him? Did you talk to him?"

"See him? I didn't get a wink of sleep all night. Maybe a doze. I may've dropped off once or twice. But I didn't want to alarm the man, me not being armed and him very likely excitable and carrying a pistol. I *should* have a gun down there, you know. I didn't tell you I killed a rat with a stick, as big as a fox last week."

"Never mind about the gun now. Tell me about the deserter."

"The roosters woke him up and I could hear him, very stealthy, creeping, creeping down the ladder from the hayloft, then all of a sudden the black mare *ra-ha-ha-ha-ha!* And that started the gray pawing and then all three of the horses were causing a bedlam. The strange lad ran for the door and I up with the butt of an old whip, not much protection against an armed man—"

"And he got out and ran away. Was he in uniform?"

"Mr. Millhouser, why would I t'ink he was a deserter otherwise? I seen him running across the yard and through the little gate."

"Was he a Union soldier or a Confederate?"

28

"Blue. Blue. The same uniform them lads that come to steal our horses last year, they wore."

"Cavalry, eh? That's a probability. He knew the stable was there. He's been all through this section."

"Are you going to report it, sir?"

"I suppose I must. Yes, of course. And if I didn't, you would. Maybe not to the authorities, but to your cronies at the tavern."

"I'll do whatever you wish, sir, only I'd feel more comfortable down there if I'd a pistol, in case there's any more of these visitors."

"Oh, very well, Ryan. I'll supply you with a pistol. I can't have you fighting rats as big as foxes with nothing more than a stick, can I?"

"The bite of a rat can cause a man's death, and I'd feel safer with all these deserters going and coming."

Henry turned to Robert. "You're not frightened by all this talk, I hope, son."

"No, Father."

"Good. All the same, I wouldn't want you to repeat it to your mother or the women in the kitchen," said Henry. "And you, Ryan, don't you repeat the story either. By the way, I suppose you've got your weapon all picked out?"

"I've had a look at those in the hardware store. They've got a couple of little beauties there would serve the purpose."

"I'll try to remember."

"I've my witness here to remind you, sir," said Ryan, smiling at Robert.

"So you have, and you'll keep it where he can't get *his* hands on it."

"I'll be so careful hiding it the Old Boy himself'd never find it. The Old Boy is Satan, of course. The devil."

"Thank you for the explanation," said Henry.

They left Ryan and as they walked up the brick path to the house Robert said: "Are you going to buy Ryan a pistol?"

"Against my better judgment, yes."

"What is a deserter?"

"A deserter? A deserter. It's a soldier who runs away from the army."

"A coward."

"Generally considered so, but I wonder. 'Many are the hearts that are weary tonight, looking for the war to cease.' That song that Mama plays. A man must be very desperate to run away like that, knowing that if they catch him they'll shoot him."

"Who'll shoot him, Father?"

"The army, the other soldiers."

"But would Ryan shoot him?"

"No, I don't think Ryan would. If I thought he would I wouldn't buy him a pistol. I don't think *I* could ever shoot another man."

"But if you were a soldier wouldn't you?"

"But I'm not a soldier."

"But would you if you were a soldier?" the boy persisted. "You're not afraid of soldiers. I saw you that time. You weren't afraid."

"There wasn't much to be afraid of. They were on our side."

"But they wanted to take our horses."

"That always happens in a war."

"But they were on our side and you didn't want them to have our horses."

"Yes, if they'd asked me in the right way I'd have given them the horses."

"They didn't say please?"

"It amounts to that. It's more than that, but that's what it comes down to."

"You don't like soldiers, do you?"

"I don't like fighting."

"Mama says a good fight—I forget what she says."

"Clears the air. A good fight clears the air."

"How does it clear the air?"

"She means that sometimes people have a fight and when the fight's over they're friends again."

"I don't like fights either. I don't like to get hurt."

"Then stay out of fights, son. But fight when you have to."

"But I don't like to."

"No, but there will be times when you have to."

"No I won't, I'll run away."

"And be called a coward?"

"No."

"You see, it's worse to be called a coward, isn't it?"

"If I run away I won't hear them."

"There's a lot that you don't understand. Just don't get into the habit of running away from fights."

"I do if somebody's going to hit me."

"Well, I'd rather have you that way than to be the one that starts fights. You'll never be a bully. *That's* why I didn't like the lieutenant that wanted to take our horses. He was a bully. But do you remember when I showed him the letter, the general's letter?"

"I guess so."

"Yes you do. I showed him a letter, just a letter, but it was written by a general. You know a general is much higher than a lieutenant."

"Oh, I know that."

"Good. Well, remember this, the lieutenant was a bully but he was afraid of the general."

"He was afraid of you, too."

"In a way, in a way."

"And you didn't have a sword and he did. If you had a sword would you have stabbed him?"

"No."

"I would. I didn't like that man."

His father patted him on the head and smiled. "You're a good boy, Robert."

In April of '65 the station agent of the Pennsylvania Railroad, Ed Muller, took down a message that came in over the telegraph line. He let out a yell of exultation, but then caution prevailed, and he closed the station and borrowing a horse from McDermott's Livery Stable, galloped to the other end of town to the Gibbsville, Collieryville & Lyons depot. His friend Con Colby, the G.C. & L. stationmaster, held up a finger for silence and the two men together read the message that was coming in over the G.C. & L.'s line. General Lee had surrendered the Army of Northern Virginia at a placed called Appotox, according to the Pennsylvania telegraph, or Appomax, according to the G.C. & L. The war was over, the slaves were free, men would be brothers again, and General Grant had ordered that every Confederate soldier who owned a horse or a mule could take the animal home with him to start the spring plowing.

"Funny," said Henry to Zilph.

"What is, my dear?"

"General Grant is allowing the Confederates to keep their horses. I was thinking, wouldn't it be funny if one of the horses happened to be one the army took from us, and then was captured by the Confederates."

"Now who else would ever have thought of that?"

"Oh, you Irish aren't the only ones with a sense of humor. Sometimes we can see the funny side of things, too."

•

HERE I must explain to the reader that Robert Millhouser was perfectly willing to reminisce about his boyhood, to show me family documents such as letters and Bibles, account books and a journal in which his mother would ramble on for pages about her rose garden and then follow with an entry dated a month later in which she had written only: "Back from Philadelphia. A fortnight away from my own nest is much too long." Until his next-to-last year at Mercersburg Robert's letters were pasted in his mother's journal, then something must have happened that put an end to his letters, for no more of them appeared in the journal. "Did you stop writing home?" I asked him one day.

"Not entirely," he said.

"I did the same thing when I was in prep school," I said. "I guess I never wrote home unless I wanted an advance on my allowance."

"Is that so?" he said. He plainly had neither the desire nor the intention to discuss those interesting years as freely as he had his boyhood, no matter how hard I tried to draw him out.

"Did you join a fraternity at Penn?" I said.

"Yes, I did. St. Anthony—Delta Psi. But I think they were sorry they invited me. I was a third-generation Penn man—fourth, if you count my great-grandfather. And The Hall, as they called it, they set great store by such things. But I wasn't much of a fraternity man. There really isn't much to say about those years."

"What was Philadelphia like in the seventies?"

"I couldn't tell you."

"But you lived there for four years."

"I could just as easily have been living here. I went to my classes at the University, I attended the fraternity meetings that I had to attend. But I didn't go about socially."

"You had cousins there. Didn't you ever see them?"

"Never."

"Was there some sort of a family quarrel?"

"Oh, they were very polite to me. It was through one of my cousins that I was invited to join St. Anthony. But I really had nothing in common with them, if you except the common ancestors. My cousin didn't want to see a Millhouser in Phi Kappa Sigma or Delta Phi. They were our rivals. But I'm afraid he wished later on that this Millhouser had joined one of them."

"Who was your best friend while you were growing up, before you went to Mercersburg?"

"Leonard Vance."

"Leonard Vance." I tried not to emphasize the first name.

"The question you would like to ask, I'll answer. Leonard Vance was the older brother of Bartholomew Vance. There was still another brother, Chauncey, and two sisters. Bartholomew's the one you've heard of. Bart."

"Who were the Vances? What did they do?"

"Oh, your grandfather could have told you all about the Vance family. They were very stylish."

"Why did they come to Lyons?"

32

"They had interests here. Coal. The Vance Tract was named after them. And old Mr. Vance, the father, he had money in the G.C. & L., some of the original money."

"Then they must have lost it a long time ago, because I've never heard about them, with the exception of Bartholomew."

"Well, you know the Catholic convent, where the nuns live. That was originally the Vance residence, before the Catholics even built their church, the present church, that is. Leonard Vance was my nearest neighbor in those days, and my closest friend. We were in the same class in school. Then they built another house, in the North Ward."

"And yet with all the things you've told me about your boyhood, never a mention of Leonard Vance."

"I'll leave it to you to figure out why."

"I *know* why. At least I think I do. You didn't want to mention the Vance family. But I wondered why you never spoke of a particular friend, although you did like to talk about your boyhood."

"Leonard died the year I went away to school," said Robert Millhouser. "The other members of the Vance family belonged to a later period in my life."

"But Leonard didn't. He belonged to your boyhood, and he was your closest friend."

"I don't know, Gerald. I don't honestly know why I didn't tell you about Leonard."

"What other friends did you have?"

"Oh, they're all dead and gone. Leonard was the only one that mattered," he said, with a finality that I was reluctant to interfere with. "So now we have me graduated from the University and I spent the greater part of the next year abroad. Then I came home, back to Lyons, and lived with my mother till she died, in 1902."

"Oh, you lived abroad? Whereabouts?"

"I wondered if you'd let me get away with that big jump," he said.

"Mr. Millhouser, you can get away with anything you please. But we made a bargain, and if I live up to my part of it, I think you ought to live up to yours. Otherwise—well, I enjoy coming to see you—"

"But you don't want to waste your time. And you're quite right. But you must have patience with me. I'm not used to the confessional, although I suppose you are."

"I get there once a year."

"But you see I've never been. I'm a Lutheran, if I'm anything, and we don't confess."

"I thought some of them did, but never mind."

"Just be patient with me, Gerald, and it'll all come out, little by little, and you'll have all the material you'll ever need for your thesis."

"Okay. Now what about the time abroad? You mean Europe, of course."

"Four cities. Paris, Florence, Rome and London."

"You didn't go to Germany, or Ireland?"

"I was not there to look up my ancestors. I was there because I knew that once I came home to Lyons, I'd be here the rest of my life. I was right, too, wasn't I?"

"It appears that way."

"I had no curiosity about my mother's family. I really hadn't. I know I'm half Irish and I must have some Irish traits. But you'll have to decide what they are, Gerald. They should be easy for you to recognize."

"They should be."

"Half Irish or not, I've never thought of myself as Irish at all. I know my mother was married to a man named Murray and I know her maiden name was Hughes, but I always have to look up *her* mother's maiden name. When I went abroad that time I had the names of some uncles and aunts, but I told Mama I didn't expect to see them, and I didn't. And of course my German relations would have been as strange to me as I'd have been to them. I represented the third generation away from Germany, third generation born in this country. Is that right? Me, my father, and my grandfather. Yes. I've never even thought of myself as an American, let alone a German. I've really thought of myself as a Pennsylvanian. No, now that's not quite true. While I was abroad I was officially an American. Often mistaken for English and German because my French wasn't very good and my Italian was non-existent. The English thought I was German because of my Pennsylvania Dutch singsong, the rising and falling inflections, and the way I pronounced some words. But when I got home, and ever since, except during the late War, I've been a Pennsylvanian. In fact, a Nesquehela Countian. I haven't been away much, you know. I don't know that my life would have been very different if I'd gotten away more. I treasure those months abroad, but I'm an old man now, with plenty of time for an old man's regrets, and my failure to see more of the outside world isn't one of my old man's regrets."

"You said you treasure the time abroad. I wish you'd tell me why."

"My mother wouldn't approve of this, but I'll tell you. It wasn't Europe, Gerald. It was being in the company of Chester Calthorp, the finest man I've ever known."

"I haven't come across his name anywhere."

"Yes you have, but we've never talked about him. You've seen his name on my inkstand, and you could have seen it with a lot of other names in the fraternity picture upstairs in my room. Let me see where else? You've seen the initials on my walking stick, the one with the silver knob, in the hall. And signed to four paintings that you've passed many times without giving them a second look. Chester Sterling Calthorp."

•

SHORTLY AFTER the noon Angelus one day in July, 1877, Moses Hatfield was walking up the path from the stable to the house, fanning himself with the letters he had collected at the post office. "Moses, you got anything for me?"

"I hear you, Mr. Robert, but I don't see you."

"Under the grape arbor," said Robert.

Moses found him seated before an easel. "You painting another picture." He looked at the painting and at the scene beyond the easel and back at the picture. "That's good! That looks *like* it."

"I had to work fast. I wanted to get the midday light through the vines and the arbors."

"You got it darker than it is. It sure aint that dark in here."

"Yes it is, Moses. It's easily that dark, maybe darker, but you don't see it."

"You right I don't see it."

"Got anything for me?"

"Yes sir. Two letters." Moses took two letters off the top and handed them to Robert. "One and one makes two."

"Just a minute. Let me see the others." He went through the remaining letters until he found one addressed to his mother, in the same hand and of the same size envelope as one of his two. He handed them all back to Moses.

"Looks like the same person writing to Mrs. Millhouser and you."

"Moses, you could learn to read handwriting in no time. You can read names, and you even know these two were written by the same man. Why don't you let me teach you the rest?"

"Too hard. I don't mind print. I can read a lot of print, but people-writing is all different."

"But don't you want to read what your children write?"

"Cora, she can read it to me. My Henry writes on a slate, 'I see the cat.' Then he spit on the rag and wipe it off. I don't want to read something if Henry gonna spit on the rag and wipe it off. But I'll read print. D, a, n, g, e, r. I can read that."

"All right," said Robert in mock disgust.

It was always cooler in the diningroom. The windows were raised and the flies were kept out by cotton screens. Zilph and Robert, as a concession to the time of year, ate off doilies instead of a tablecloth and a typical meal was meat loaf and potato salad, but otherwise the atmosphere was no less formal in the summer than in the winter. Conversation was easy enough between them, but when they had disposed of a topic they would eat on in silence. Today they began in silence, broken by Zilph. "Did you catch the light you were after?"

"Very nearly. I'll try it again tomorrow. Moses said I got it too dark."

It was quiet again except for the sounds of fork on plate, ice striking the tall glasses of tea.

"Didn't you have a letter from Chester Calthorp?" said Robert.

"I intended to speak of it. Do you know what's in it?"

"I knew he was going to write you, and I know what for."

"Yes. He'd like me to finance a trip abroad for you. It opens up the whole question of money, doesn't it?"

"Money, and other matters."

"Particularly other matters. When you reached your majority you were still at the University, and I thought a thousand dollars was enough for an undergraduate."

"And it was."

"Besides your allowance. I've never asked you what you did with that money and I don't intend to now. It was a present. But we ought to have a talk about your future. I take it you want to go abroad for a year with Mr. Calthorp—"

"He's only three years older than I am, Mama. You don't have to make him sound like an aged uncle. Yes, I want to live there where I can visit the art galleries."

"And study painting?"

"No. I'll do some painting and at the end of a year I'll let someone good have a look at what I've done. If I have any talent, then I'll study painting. If I haven't any talent, I'll come home."

"Why do you want to go with Mr. Calthorp?"

"Why not? He's my friend, paints, speaks French and Italian. And we would share expenses."

"Does he paint all the time, or has he other work?"

"He does nothing but paint. He's musical, too, but that's a sideline with him. Everyone says he's very talented."

"Does he think you have talent?"

"Some. He says I have a feeling for it, but so far I'm only the rankest amateur."

"He says that, or you do?"

"He does. Oh, he's brutally frank in such matters."

"Is his standing so high that he's in a position to be brutally frank?"

"I respect his opinion. They admitted him to the Academy of the Fine Arts two years ago, and they're very strict. Anyway, he's the most interesting man I've ever known, even if he couldn't paint a lick. Mr. Eakins helped him get in the Academy, and there couldn't be two painters more unlike each other."

"That speaks well for Mr. Eakins, whoever he is."

"It speaks well for Chester, too. At least as a painter."

"Why does he take it upon himself to write me? You asked me not to think of him as an elderly uncle, but he writes like one. His letter could have been written by a man in his seventies."

"Oh, that's Chester's manner. Very stiff, very formal. In art matters he doesn't like to be considered young. And it's amazing how much he knows for someone his age."

"About painting?"

"About every subject under the sun. I'm sure he could be a doctor if he wanted to be. He studied anatomy at The Jeff and he goes there to watch operations, just like Mr. Eakins."

"Well, I understand why you'd like to go abroad with him. But have you any idea why *he'd* like *you* to go abroad with *him?*"

"No, but it's the greatest compliment I've ever received."

"He has money, this man?"

"Mama, the Calthorps all have money. I wouldn't be surprised if Chester was a millionaire, or close to it. He has his own valet and a good-sized house of his own. He could buy and sell us."

"How much do you think this trip would cost you?"

"Chester says I can do it on fifteen hundred dollars."

"That's a tidy sum, but not if you're taking a valet and living on that scale."

"We're not taking the valet. But we're not going to deny ourselves."

"Well, you have my consent."

"Thank you very much, Mama."

"But we are not millionaires, do remember that. Our income from the farms is so small that I'm only keeping them because your father always said to hold on to land. Our profit from the farms last year was under five thousand. The timber leases paid us about the same, but they won't go on forever, Robert. Conrad Isaminger would like me to get rid of the farms, and when you come back from your trip you'll have to discuss that with him."

"Maybe I won't be coming back."

"Perhaps not, but if you should, you'll have to begin to interest yourself in the management of the farms. A man can do more with the farmers than a woman can."

"I have no objection to your selling them now."

"Oh, it would be far more convenient to have all our money in shares, but I think you'll have to make that decision after I'm gone."

"We have ten thousand dollars a year? Just think of it."

"Do. Please do. Subtract twelve hundred for you, five hundred we pay Conrad Isaminger, the three servants, the cost of running this house, and the cash reserve I have to maintain for improvements and repairs on the farms—it isn't all there to be squandered. Yes, do give it a thought, Robert. If I don't watch everything, you may have nothing when I pass on."

"Who knows? I may make my living painting."

"That's it. Who knows? And who am I to stand in your way? It's your father's money, after all."

"It isn't, though, and you know it, Mama. It's yours, and rightly so."

She smiled. "Why, Robert!"

"He wanted you to have it, and you have it."

"Oh," she said, disappointed. "Well, I'll try to see that there's more of it rather than less of it when it comes your turn."

"I know you will."

"I'll get the letter off to Mr. Chester this afternoon."

"Mr. Calthorp."

For the remainder of the summer Robert was busy with plans for the trip abroad, busy to the extent that he had letters from Chester Calthorp almost daily, outlining, then changing, their itinerary.

We shall go directly to London [he wrote]. I have, as you know if you have been paying strict attention to my long-winded discourses, many dear friends in London, but they are only incidental to the principal purpose of our visit there, which is to introduce you to E. Tadburn, whom I consider to be the finest bespoke tailor in the world. He will study you, measure you, and politely but reluctantly agree to make you a suit. You will of course order several suits (and so shall I!). A year hence you will receive your first bill, which you will ignore. Six months later you will receive Bill No. II, at which time you will give him something on account, but under no circumstances more than half the amount owing to him. He is ridiculously inexpensive—eleven guineas for your first suit, ten thereafter until you reach the advanced age of thirty. I do not know how he will know the precise moment of your thirtieth birthday, but *he will know* and you will begin to pay more. Be that as it may, our first stop in London will be at the decrepid old establishment of E. Tadburn and your measurements will be taken and recorded. That pleasant task completed, we can enjoy ourselves with my English friends before proceeding to Paris. I am saving Florence and Rome for the winter months, then back to London for our last six weeks before returning to Penn's Wood.

Robert said goodbye to his mother in early September and was Chester Calthorp's house guest for two weeks before the sailing date. Chester had people in for tea every afternoon at the house in Spring Garden Street—"a foretaste of London," he said. They dined out every evening, always at the homes of men and women who had been or would be Chester's guests for tea. In the four years of his acquaintance and friendship with Chester he had met, through him, only a few artists, medical students and young musicians, and them only on the most casual terms. But in the weeks before their departure for overseas Robert and Chester were usually in the company of men and women whose tastes were musical and artistic, but who were readily identifiable as gifted amateurs—if they were gifted and not merely knowledgeable. They spoke familiarly of music and painting and of musicians and painters, but never of their own participation. Robert's first impression from them was of elegance, of high fashion among the women, of severe conservatism among the men; but nearly always among the men there would sooner or later appear some telltale clue to their love of beauty: a ring with a history, a scarf-pin of unusual design, a special scent on a handkerchief, a golden pocket-piece with an undiscernible motto. Or if it was not a tangible object it was often a speech habit or an eccentricity of manner that momentarily revealed what was hidden by the carefully restricted conventionality of their clothes and their social conduct. Most of the men had jobs, and when they stopped in at Chester Calthorp's for tea they still conducted themselves as men of business, until this congenial atmosphere and a whiskey-and-soda relaxed them. On meeting Robert for the first time they would study him in an effort to determine the exact status of his relationship with Chester, but after hearing that Robert was to accompany Chester on the European tour, they lost no more time in furtive investigation.

Two of the women were beautiful. One of them was overly feminine, but conscientious, dutiful, as to the care and favorable display of her beauty. She was in her late twenties, a Mrs. Hartung, whose husband never appeared at Chester Calthorp's house. She had little to offer conversationally but she was completely conscious of her contribution to gatherings such as these. Her mother's pride, and her own studies of her face and body had achieved for her some recognition as a work of art. She spent hours in preparation for parties, preferably the smaller ones like Chester Calthorp's, and every year or two she would sit for a new portrait, always by a different painter. The other woman, who was in her forties, was a beauty by legend and in spite of her neglect of herself. She sipped whiskey continually from the time of her arrival. She sat with her legs crossed, bent slightly forward, with her glass in her hand less than a foot away from her face, and with her elbow on her knee. She heard everything that was said to her, although she seemed not to be listening to the immediate conversation but waiting for the sound of an important bell, or perhaps an important voice. She, and not Mrs. Hartung, was a part of the secrets that were never hinted at but were in the air at Chester's parties. She was among the oldest of the women and of an age with most of the men at the parties, and Robert admired her and attempted to make her like him, but she snubbed him as no one had ever snubbed him. "Have you been abroad, Mrs. Sterling?"

"Yes, I have," she said.

"Chester and I are leaving on the twenty-fourth."

"So you are, aren't you?" She looked at him with such frank, personal scorn that her contempt for him was unmistakable. Then, and although he was sitting beside her, she held out her empty glass and said to a man whose back was turned to them, "Richard, will you fill my glass, please?"

"I'm sorry," said Robert. "Did I say something wrong? I couldn't have."

"Can't you sit some place else?" she said.

It was the only unpleasant incident in his two weeks as Chester's house guest, and he was so baffled by it that he did not mention it to Chester. To ask Chester for an explanation would have been, he suspected, an admission or a revelation of some inferiority that the woman had detected and that Chester had not noticed. When the guests were leaving she gave her cheek to Chester for a kiss, but to Robert she gave only a curt nod. No one among these friends of Chester's had exhibited any cordiality, but Alice Sterling was the only one who had been rude. And there was more to it than the calculated clumsiness of the Philadelphian to the stranger on trial.

They embarked in the *American Venture* and on the afternoon of the second day out they were the only passengers who were occupying their steamer chairs. "I'm pleased to see that you're a good sailor," said Chester.

"So far, so good."

"You're not feeling queasy?"

"Not so far."

"If people didn't know about *mal de mer* they wouldn't suffer from it."

40

"I don't know that I agree with you."

"Oh, I'm not talking about the human cattle in the steerage. They empty themselves at one end or the other because they are what they are. You've surely seen people like that at table?"

"Yes."

"You've seen them stuffing themselves like so many pigs at a trough. My point is that they care no more about how they take it in than they do how they let it out. To change the subject completely, or almost, you haven't told me how you liked my friends."

"You mean the past couple of weeks?"

"Of course, Robert. My *friends.*"

"Well, you've introduced me to other people I thought were your friends."

"Where?"

"In cafés."

"Yes, in cafés, but you've never seen them at Spring Garden Street. Oh, one or two."

"Or three or four, or five or six."

"You're begging the issue."

"Well, I don't know. I like all sorts of people. I like some sometimes, and others other times."

"That's a dreadful lie, you know."

"If you're not careful I'll challenge you to a duel."

"Don't ever. I'll choose épées and cut you to pieces. Haven't you ever seen my medals? My one form of athletic prowess?"

"I knew you were a fencer, yes."

"I could probably outshoot you, too, if it comes to that."

"Not so sure about that. I did learn to shoot."

"Oh, yes, I suppose you did, up in Daniel Boone's country. Did you wear a squirrel cap, Robert? I'm sure it was very becoming."

"I had one."

"Of *course* you had one. I never doubted that for a second. And leather stockings, like one of Mr. Fenimore Cooper's doughty heroes. But I've taken you out of all that, and now tell me, what *did* you think of my friends?"

"I'd be more interested in what they thought of me."

"Oh now, humility isn't becoming to you. A squirrel bonnet, yes. But humility, no. Reminds me, we must put Scott on our London list. Scott is the hatter I patronize, and you must too."

"My money isn't going to last very long in London, at the rate you're spending it for me. E. Tadburn, and Scott the hatter, and the Lord only knows who else."

"Peal. Bootmaker. But haven't I told you that it's against the rules to pay them under a year? Emily Hartung. Now what did you think of Emily? The train of thought there goes from debt to Emily, very logically. You didn't meet her husband, but poor old George Washington Hartung—would you call your son George Washington if you weren't related to him?—George W. has very little time for us. Emily keeps him on the verge of bankruptcy. Isn't she lovely?"

"To look at."

"Well surely you had no other thoughts. Or had you?"

"I don't see how anybody could have."

"George W. has, or did have. Not any more, I think. You must learn to understand women like Emily. There are experts, artists, in all lines of endeavor. Emily's an artist in her own field. And what is her own field? She occupies a chair, and she does it with such exquisite grace and so pleasingly to the eye, that she's unique. I'm as proud of her as I am of anything in Philadelphia. She could go anywhere in the world and be just what she is. Poor George doesn't understand that yet, probably incapable of understanding it and will have to die in debtors' prison without realizing that with all his grubby and slightly dishonest business deals, he was actually a patron of the arts. Uniquely one. Much more so than a rich man who supports a second-rate painter. Because Emily *is* unique, and second-rate painters grow on trees. I'd be very happy to paint Emily's portrait, but someone's told her I'm not good enough yet, so she won't sit for me. She's right. Five years from now, perhaps. Ah, but I'm content to wait. I think I've detected a tiny seed of evil in Emily, and in five years it will have begun to flourish and I'll be the one to put it on canvas. She may be the best thing I ever do. A lot of good men have done her portrait and I've studied them all, but not one has seen what I've seen. In fact, now that I recall all those portraits of Emily, they've all been characterized by a mysterious insipidity."

"Are you going to be a first-rate painter when you're thirty?"

"Before that. But I'm not going to tell anybody," said Chester. "You're very stimulating, Robert. If I say that too often you mustn't notice. You're one of the very few people that I trust with my thoughts. I wonder why."

"Yes, why?"

"Well, you're not jealous of me. So many of my friends are. And I know a little more than you do and I like to show off. But that doesn't explain why I trust you, does it?"

"No."

"Could it be because you trust me?"

"It might be. I do trust you."

"How do you trust me, Robert?"

"I don't know, I just do. You've always been honest with me."

"Oh, dear, we're becoming awfully platitudinous. And cold. Aren't you chilly? Let's go inside and have tea and rum?"

The voyage lasted twelve days; longer, it seemed to Robert, time-lessly longer because the shipboard life was all new to him. In the dining saloon they shared a table with an elderly Church of England clergyman whose wife had most of her meals in their stateroom; and with a middle-aged Jewish couple who spoke only when spoken to and who therefore spent a large part of their time frankly fasci-nated and almost equally frankly repelled by Chester's sophistication. I. Goldberg and wife were prevented by religious laws from eating much of the food that was set before them, but Canon Lovelace, who had some knowledge of the dietary rules, saw to it that little was wasted. "I say, Mr. Goldberg, won't you let me explain to the stew-ard? They must have something down there you can eat." Mr. Gold-berg was furiously embarrassed and said, "No, no, no, no, no," and his wife said, "No *thank* you, Father."

The canon had quickly given up on the young Americans. ("I'm sure he told his wife I was an insolent pup," said Chester.) They were American, they were young, they were rich, and the older of the two, if not actively disrespectful, was certainly lacking in respect for the cloth. He was of a type with which the canon was familiar at home and which was offensive enough there, but there was an added impertinence to young Calthorp's manner that came from his being an American. Americans, the canon believed, were not yet ready for such worldliness; those flippancies and cynicisms were legitimately, if regrettably, the product of an older civilization than he had ob-served in his month-long colonial tour. It did not make him feel more kindly toward young Calthorp when he, the canon, became so im-patient that he violated one of his minor rules of conduct: the canon made it a rule never to ask a man his religion, but in a moment of exasperation he said to Calthorp: "And what, may I ask, is your religious affiliation?" The canon thought he knew the answer: the insolent young pup looked like an Episcopalian.

"I'm a Quaker," said Calthorp.

The reply silenced Lovelace. As a C. of E. canon he enjoyed the divine privilege of rank among American Episcopalians, but he could not assume an attitude of righteous indignation toward a member of another faith. Table Six thereafter was not a jolly place to be.

"Oh, well," said Chester, toward the end of the voyage. "If the Goldbergs insist on starving themselves and the padre bolts and runs, that's not our fault. At least not yours, Robert. I'm the guilty party."

"You're not responsible for the Goldbergs."

"True, but they not only go away hungry. They detest me so that they think I'm partly to blame for their starvation. At least *he* does. Mrs. Goldberg secretly likes me. I've noticed that when I've got off one of my most offensive bons mots she has to suppress her laughter. Not that she appreciates the wit. But she knows I've said *something* that Poppa won't like and is bound to infuriate the established church. Steamer acquaintances. Just think, Robert, we'll never see them again, and yet who is there among one's friends that one has eaten thirty-odd consecutive meals with? Even with my closest friends, those you've been seeing lately, I try to arrange my engagements so that I don't have to see someone at dinner that I've seen that day at lunch. Tea doesn't count. I make a good meal of tea, but most people don't, and it isn't the same as sitting at table. I have an extraordinarily good appetite and I'm afraid it's beginning to show. E. Tadburn's going to be shocked when he draws his tape about my equator. Shocked, but not dismayed. It's all to the good for E. Tadburn. You, on the other hand, will never get fat."

"You ought to take more exercise."

"Bosh! My father rode every day of his life but toward the end of his life he had to be lowered into the saddle. Exercise has nothing to do with it."

"Lowered into the saddle? How?"

"From a derrick, I suppose. My father died when I was two years old and I don't remember a single thing about him, but I've studied portraits and photographs of him and nothing could disguise the fact that he was prone to embonpoint. I therefore assume that he was lowered into the saddle. With his belly it would have been almost impossible to swing his leg over."

"Maybe he had a mounting-block."

"Of course he had a mounting-block, Robert. You take things too literally. If you don't stop you're going to be hopelessly confused during the coming year. You must develop an instinct that tells you when to take me literally, and when not. If I say to you, 'Go to grass,' that doesn't mean you must scamper out to Regent's Park. It'll only mean that I've lost patience."

"Just as if I told you to go to hell."

Chester was silent. "I don't think I'd like that," he said after a moment. "I'm sure I wouldn't. If we quarrel, and we probably shall, you must be very careful what you say to me. I will turn on you like a cornered rat and say things and possibly do things that we'll both regret. I rely on you to be the steadying influence."

"Me?"

"Yes, you. Your stolid German nature."

44

"Well, I don't like to fight. I like things to be just so."

Chester smiled. "You sound so Dutchy. I'm relieved."

"But I'm like my father. He stood up to a whole troop of Union cavalry one time, because he knew he was in the right."

"Was he a Confederate, your father?"

"Of course not, you know better than that. Now you're the one that's taking things literally."

"Touché, Robert. A telling thrust. Let us go on with our packing. I must show you how to pack. It's a minor art, but an art, and I learned it from a real artist, my faithful Dan, who has probably been lying drunk in my cellar since the day we sailed." And he added: "And not out of grief over my absence."

England began for them that day, while they were packing. Chester adopted English pronunciations, at first, Robert thought, in a tentative, joking way, but before their ship had reached Bishop's Light his entire speech was imitative of an Englishman's, and since the nearest Englishman had been Canon Lovelace it was Lovelace he sounded like. The fact amused Robert, but he refrained from mention of the similarity. On the final morning of the voyage, while Robert was shaving, Chester said: "I cawn't face a hypocritical leave-taking with the dominie."

"Lovelace? All right."

"We cawn't cut him, but we shall take pains to avoid him. Let's hope he and his wife take their morning tea in their stateroom."

"Do you want to say goodbye to the Goldbergs?"

"No, but I shawn't avoid them."

The Goldbergs, carrying their outer coats, were finishing their tea when Chester and Robert sat down for breakfast. Mr. Goldberg said something in Yiddish to his wife and they rose, as did Chester and Robert. "It's been charming, Mrs. Goldberg," said Chester.

"Likewise," she said.

"Goodbye, Mr. Calthorp. We have to go now. Come, Momma." Mr. Goldberg was holding his bowler in one hand while the other was busy with his overcoat, and handshaking was therefore excusably avoided. He nodded briefly to Robert, and his wife followed him out of the dining saloon.

"Mr. Goldberg's coat, did you notice it?" said Chester. "Astrakhan lined and the finest broadcloth. Twenty guineas if it cost him a penny. And I'm sure you don't know about such things, but those were real pearls."

"Why are you surprised? They were traveling first class."

"I'm not surprised, Robert. I know he's on his way to Manchester to buy yards and yards of woolens. But we've been watching them starve. Now suddenly they know they're going to get a good meal and they *look* rich. That somehow offends me."

"Why?"

"Why? Because I don't like people to have money if they aren't people I'd like to know. Do you?"

"It doesn't bother me."

"You talk like a socialist."

They had booked rooms in Rumson's Private Hotel in Clarges Street, where Chester was known. He had also arranged for visitors' cards at two London clubs. "We'll use the clubs to write letters. If you haven't any letters to write, invent a reason. I always do. Just a note on a good London club's stationery will serve to remind some of my friends at the Philadelphia Club that they must at least hesitate before blackballing me. This year I'm going to write to old Mr. Wendell Banning. I don't like the way he looks away from me, as if he was rolling a lump of tar into the biggest blackest ball he could devise."

"What will you write to him?"

"Oh, 'Dear Mr. Banning.' I'll think of something. He was a friend of my father's. What I'll say will be, 'Look here, you dreadful old hypocrite, you wouldn't dare blackball me if my father were still alive.' In somewhat different language."

•

"I REMEMBER that conversation so well," said Robert Millhouser, "because it told me something about Chester."

"It did? What?" I asked.

"Not at the time, mind you. I had to think it over. I never was clever. But that conversation, we'd never have had that in Philadelphia. In Philadelphia, his native heath, as they say, Chester would not have admitted to me that he ever worried about being kept out of a club. But it was on his mind in London, and that told me a lot about him. Do you know what it was?"

"No, I don't think so."

"It showed me for the first time that Chester Calthorp had his worries just like the rest of us. He wasn't so sure of himself. To a young man like you that may not seem remarkable, but it was a big discovery to me. I'd known Chester for four years and I was fascinated by his charm and wit and, if I may use the word, fearlessness. He went against everything he was brought up to believe in, to respect. Pretty nearly everything he said and did was in opposition to

46

his family, and Philadelphia. Yes, I thought he was fearless. Then in London I saw that he did worry about things."

"I see."

"Conventional things, too. And that made me like him the more. I had always admired him for his independence, and fearlessness, and yet I admired him in London because the things he was going against, he wasn't against at all. Do I make myself clear?"

"Yes."

"Are you sure? I, for instance, I might have wanted to rebel against some of the conventions, but I never did. But Chester did. He did it so thoroughly that he was willing to become a figure of scorn. He didn't rebel quietly, on the sly. He did it openly and took the consequences, even if the consequences cost him things he wanted very much. Like membership in the Philadelphia Club."

"Did he ever make it, by the way?"

"Oh, never. Never. If it'd been anyone but Chester there'd have been an uproar, I'm sure. But in his case it was a very popular blackball. I'm told that a great many people in Philadelphia who had no love for that particular club, nevertheless were delighted when word got around."

"I imagine so," I said. "Mr. Millhouser, several weeks ago you referred to Chester Calthorp as the finest man you ever knew. Did you mean exactly that?"

"Why shouldn't I have meant it? He was."

"Well, this is your story and not mine, and I'd agree with you that he was an interesting man, probably a fascinating man. But the finest man you ever knew?"

"I don't expect anyone else in the world to share my opinion of Chester, but I'll stand on it. He was. When we read the biographies of famous men, men generally considered to be the finest, how much do we really know about them?"

"Isn't that judgment usually based on a lifetime of accomplishment? Good works, good deeds, and so forth?"

"I would say so. The great men, the Washingtons and Lincolns, yes. But I've never known any of the great men, the famous. I am an old man, past seventy years of age, and I've *been* old for nearly twenty years, Gerald. Most of my life I've lived here in this little town, and most of that here in this house. The noon mail, the evening mail, and the rest of that time in this house. Indeed, in this little room. What do I know of my fellow man, my fellow townsmen—and what do they know of me, Gerald? You may say it doesn't make any difference what they know of me, but it makes a great difference, because we're all limited in what we know of others by what they know of us."

"Do you believe that? I don't think I do."

"Yes, insofar as—what they know of us has a great effect on how they present themselves to us, and therefore, therefore, how much we can know of them. How often we are mistaken! We think we know one man very well, and something happens that shows we didn't know him at all. That's the sort of thing that happens in many close friendships. Think how often it happens in our relations with men and women who are *not* our close friends. That's when you realize how little we know of our fellow man. Who knows me? Who on earth knows me?"

It was not a question he expected me to answer, and I did not try.

His voice broke in the next speech, and it never had before. "Who knows an old man who destroyed his own happiness? Who wants to know him?"

"I do."

He quickly composed himself. "Yes, you do. You have curiosity, and perhaps you have compassion. I don't know. You'd come by it honestly, through your grandfather. And that brings us back to what we were talking about, the fine men, the famous great men. I would put your grandfather in among the fine men I've known."

"So would I."

"If good works, good deeds, as you said, if they're the standards. A lifetime of decent, honorable behavior. Jeremiah MacMahon lived that kind of life. But those are your standards, Gerald. Mine are not quite the same. Jeremiah MacMahon was a fine man by your standards, and I'll accept those standards. But I also have my own, and judged by my standards, Chester Calthorp is still to me the finest man I ever knew."

"Well, then I have to ask you what your standards are?"

"Yes, I knew that question was coming, and I'm still not prepared to answer it. Not in any way that will satisfy you. At your age you're still accustomed to finding the answers in the back of the book. Sixteen cords of wood. A earned $4, B earned $8, and C earned $16. But at my age—when I was a boy, fourth or fifth grade, we had an arithmetic book that had the answers in the back, like all arithmetic books. But in the *front* of the book they had printed a little notice that said, 'The answer to the problem on page 50 should be $12, and not $16.' Something like that. In other words, they'd made a mistake, in the printing, no doubt, but a mistake nevertheless. I remember that for me it cast doubt on all the answers."

"I see. And did that make you dubious about all answers?"

"Ever after?" Robert Millhouser smiled. "No. What a wonderful thing if it had! But I wasn't that perceptive. I was a very ordinary boy. Slow-thinking. Not very observant. And certainly not searching for truths. If I had tried to tell you that finding a mistake in an arithmetic book made me a skeptic the rest of my life—?"

"Yes sir, I'd have been skeptical," I said.

"All it did was, as I say, cast doubt on the answers in that particular book. True, I did remember the incident, and it's useful now, sixty years later, but I was much too young to build a philosophy on it." He paused, then went on. "I wonder if something like that could have happened to Chester. A quicker, alert mind like his, if *he'd* had that happen to him, *he* could have unconsciously developed a philosophy from it."

"If you believe that one incident can change a whole life. I don't happen to believe that."

"One incident changed mine."

"If you're referring to 1908, that wasn't an incident."

"I *was* referring to 1908," he said.

"If it was only an incident—" I stopped.

"Go on, 'If it was only an incident.' "

"Well, what are we doing? You and I, that is. I came to see you one day and happened to mention that I'd decided to try for my master's degree. You asked me what I thought the topic of my thesis would be and I said I wasn't sure. Then you suggested—"

"Not suggested, Gerald. I wondered. I wondered why a master's thesis had to be what most of them are. Scholarly and dull. And usually a secret between the candidate and those few men who pass on it. Couldn't a thesis be written in the form of a novel, or a biography? I thought it could."

"Yes. All right then, Mr. Millhouser, you didn't suggest, although you did use the power of suggestion. You volunteered to supply me with all the facts of your life."

"Well, at any rate those facts that I thought, and you thought, had some bearing on what happened in 1908."

"Exactly. But now you seem to be reconsidering. Now you refer to what happened in 1908 as an incident. I don't see it as an incident by itself, and I don't think you do either, Mr. Millhouser. However, if you've had a change of heart about going on with your confidences, your reminiscences, I can understand why."

"Can you, Gerald?"

"I think so. We're beginning to get in a little too deep."

"Yes, we are," said the old man.

"Then let's call it quits," I said.

49

"I'm sorry, Gerald."

"So am I, Mr. Millhouser. But frankly I was always afraid this might happen."

"You were?"

"Yes. There almost had to come a time when you'd have to tell me things that were so personal that it would be like opening up old wounds."

"Yes, but not only *my* old wounds," he said. "We've just about reached a point in my story—there are other people to consider. I have no right to tell you the things that we're beginning to get into. Nearly all those other people are dead, and soon I will be too. Let the whole unhappy story die with me."

I nodded several times. "I agree with you."

"You do, don't you? You have compassion."

"I hope I have," I said. I made an effort at humor; the old man was so uncomfortable. "I'll get my master's on—oh, something like The Religiosity of John Milton."

He looked up quickly. "How did you happen to mention Milton? He's a favorite of mine. Not of yours, I'm sure."

"No, not of mine."

He shook his head. "He's the poet of old men. You've no idea how close I've been to Milton. Do you know much about him?"

"Hardly anything."

"Then you were being frivolous about his religiosity. That's a disparaging term, religiosity, isn't it?"

"More so than not," I said.

"It may apply to Milton, it may apply. But how close he became to me in 1908 and since! 'All hope is lost/Of my reception into grace; what worse?/For where no hope is left, is left no fear.' You knew that he was married to a sixteen-year-old girl, of course?"

"I didn't know that, or if I did I forgot it," I said. "How old was he at the time?"

"In his middle thirties. He was more than twice as old as his wife. So you can see—? He was a comfort to me."

"Had you always admired Milton?"

He smiled, then shook his head. "No."

"Why does that amuse you?"

"It was the kind of question you often ask when you want to draw me out. No, I'd forgotten about Milton. I hadn't read him since I was at the University, and then not very understandingly. Then in 1908 the first two lines of the sonnet came back to me. 'When I consider how my light is spent,/E're half my days, in this dark world and wide.' I knew of course that Milton had been talking about his

50

sight, but *I* considered that my *life* was spent, and I had Moses Hatfield bring me a volume of Milton while I was in prison. I wanted to see if there was any parallel between that sonnet and my situation. There wasn't, but I began to read him, and I read him to this day."

"This isn't a question to draw you out, Mr. Millhouser. I'm in agreement with you about the life story. But for my own curiosity, do you read a lot?"

"I spend a lot of time reading, that's the more accurate answer. I don't cover very many books. I'm a slow reader and not—what is the word?—intensive. I'm not inattentive, mind you. But every evening after dinner I come in here, in the fall and the winter Moses builds me a fire, and I start reading. Sometimes I read right through until I hear ten o'clock strike, other times I let my thoughts wander away from my book. At ten o'clock I go around and lock up—Moses is getting forgetful. Then I sleep for a few hours, a very deep sleep. But then I'm often wide awake at three or four o'clock and I come downstairs again and read something either until I fall asleep in my chair, or straight through till daylight."

"What do you read, mostly?"

"Well, over on that bottom shelf will give you an idea. What do we see there? Those are books that you might call my active list, that I'm reading or that I've read and haven't put away. Milton, of course. Thackeray's *Pendennis*. Mr. Dickens, with the *Posthumous Papers of the Pickwick Club*. *Arrowsmith,* by Sinclair Lewis, which I'm afraid I'll never finish. It's so much like reading an article in a newspaper, although you probably won't agree with me."

"I don't."

"I didn't think so. *The Royal Road to Romance,* by Richard Halliburton. And *Pipefuls* by Morley. Nothing very heavy, but no out-and-out trash, either. I'd like to ask you a question, Gerald. Should I read Freud?"

"Why not?"

"Well, of course you've read D. H. Lawrence. I've only read *Sons and Lovers* by him, and almost every time his name comes up in a book review, they say something about Freud. I was very uncomfortable reading *Sons and Lovers*. After all, I've spent most of my life in a mining town. It isn't as bad as all that in Lyons. Or am I deceiving myself through ignorance? Be that as it may, I don't think I want to read Freud."

"You won't like him, but give him a try."

"I might do *that*," he said. "You know, I'm going to miss our meetings, our conversations."

"So am I."

"But you do understand why—"

"Of course, of course."

"Would you write to me once in a while? I'd like to hear from you, how you're coming along. And I'd like to write to you."

"I wish you would."

"I simply can't go any deeper into those other matters, and if I'd had any sense I'd have known that and never got you into it. I'm going to send you a present. I don't know what it'll be, but some memento of these meetings. I'd offer you money, but I feel sure you wouldn't accept it, and anyway there's no way to put a price on the time you've wasted on me."

"I've enjoyed every minute of it. I might even send *you* a present, too."

"Splendid. I get one present every year, from Moses at Christmas-time. Your grandfather used to send me a basket of fruit and guava jelly and things like that, but since he died, Moses is my only present-giver."

He walked to the door with me and smiled as we shook hands. I started to walk off the porch and then I remembered that I had left my pipe in his little room. I turned around and I saw his face, and I saw him, too, as he did not mean to be seen; the dead sadness in his eyes, the defeated sag of his lower lip. I thought of his line from Milton: *where no hope is left, is left no fear.*

It took him a shattering effort to say, "Did you forget something?"

"My pipe. I think I left it in the little room."

"I'll fetch it," he said, quickly turning away.

I waited on the porch and he brought me the pipe, handed it to me with a purely muscular smile. "Goodbye," he said, and closed the door.

In another week I was at Princeton, where I was to work for my master's. I could not know it at the time, but I was a spectator in one of Princeton's final years as "the pleasantest country club." At my college, Lafayette, there had been three or four fraternities that more or less corresponded to the best clubs at Princeton in that they were predominantly made up of prep school rather than high school grad-uates; they were wealthy; and they took in a large number of legacies. In fact it was quite remarkable how many boys at Lafayette had brothers at Princeton. I had gone to Georgetown Prep, my family were well fixed financially, and my father, although not a Zeta Psi as I was, had played football at Lafayette and was a busy alumnus. I was therefore not quite so dazzled by Princeton as some of my new acquaintances in the Graduate College, who had meritorious records at remote Presbyterian institutions; but there was still no likelihood of my confusing Princeton with Lafayette, nor undergraduate life at the one place with graduate study at the other.

I learned immediately that I would not have to write a thesis, which was just as well since I had been marshaling arguments in favor of my now discontinued novel-biography of Robert Millhouser. They would not have been very convincing to the men at the Graduate College; for the next year I would be studying Old English, Medieval Narrative, and either Spenser or Milton. One result of my final conversation with Robert Millhouser was that I chose Milton over Spenser.

In 1926, although it was possible to obtain a master's degree at Princeton with one year's work and without writing a thesis, there were several papers to be written and it amused me enormously to take for the subject of my long paper The Religiosity of John Milton. It also annoyed me to have to contemplate the prospect of spending the next year in the dust that accumulated between the eighth and the seventeenth centuries. I wanted to teach American Literature, starting at a large prep school like Andover or a small college like Hamilton. I had missed out on Phi Beta Kappa because I could not (or would not) devote enough time and effort to pull up my marks in math and the sciences, and I entered the Graduate College, I admit, with "the wrong attitude." But I wanted the Princeton M.A., and so I did it their way.

I relate these facts about my first days at Princeton because all of them created a mood which in turn made me want to express my thoughts—my impressions, misgivings, plans—to someone other than a girl or my family. Inevitably this second appearance of John Milton in my life, and the autumn melancholy of nights under the Princeton trees reminded me of Robert Millhouser, and I wrote him a long letter, which he answered.

October 14, 1926

Dear Gerald:

I was so pleased to receive your letter amongst the impersonal but all too personal communications that I usually receive on the 1st of the month. Perhaps I ought not to complain about bills; were it not for bills on the 1st of the month I would sometimes find it difficult to maintain the illusion that I am still in "the land of the living!" Fortunately, however, I may rely upon the butcher, the baker, the candlestick maker (electric light company) to remind me that I was alive last month and that I had better "look alive" before the 15th if I did not wish to starve in darkness.

Your first impressions of Princeton are very interesting, especially to one who has never been there. I had several friends who went there from Mercersburg but as you know, my own family, beginning with the first Millhouser to set foot on this continent, have always chosen "dear old Penn," and the only other campus that I have ever seen is that of Fort Penn University. One of the regrets I had on my trip abroad in '77 and '78 was that I never seemed to find the time to visit Oxford. Chester Calthorp had several English friends in residence there, but they preferred to come down to London. I had also thought of paying a visit to Harvard and Yale, as well as Princeton, but when I returned to Lyons in '78 I found Mama recuperating from an attack of la grippe and I immediately plunged into the work of managing the affairs of my Father's estate (mismanage would probably be the more accurate word) and I seldom strayed away from Lyons thereafter. If you will permit me to offer a word of advice, may I urge you not to postpone doing the things you would like to do? It is so easy when one is young to fall into the habit of thinking that one has a whole lifetime ahead in which to see and do everything, but then lo and behold, one is forty, then fifty, and many opportunities have passed, some of them forever. Seize the opportunity now, whilst you are young. I hope that you will find time occasionally to keep me up-to-date on your doings at Princeton. Needless to say, I wish you every success.

Very sincerely yours,
Robert Millhouser

I read his letter once and put it in my desk drawer, where it lay forgotten for a month or more. Somewhat to my surprise, and very much to my delight, I had begun to take a real interest in Old English, for reasons that would require explanations too long for this chronicle. But when next I came upon Mr. Millhouser's letter I was in a different frame of mind from that in which I wrote my first letter. I reread his letter more carefully, especially the latter part of it, "seize the opportunity now, whilst you are young." I was sure then as I am sure now that he had no such intention, but his words acted as a new stimulus to my curiosity about him and his life. It was now frankly curiosity, without the excuse of writing a biography-novel for a scholastic degree. If the truth be told, it had always been curiosity, going back to the time when I had been given those evasive answers to my childhood questions about Mr. Millhouser. I decided that I would follow his advice, to create, if not to seize, the opportunity, while he was still alive. Accordingly I wrote him a second letter. I made several drafts, and this is the semi-final one, in its essentials the same as the one I sent off:

54

Dear Mr. Millhouser:

I was very much interested in what you had to say regarding the temptation to procrastinate. The immediate effect of your advice was to inspire me to write a letter to a girl in Washington, D.C., whom I had met in Easton last year. Her reply was so friendly that it is now no longer necessary for me to admit that I have never visited our nation's capital. Seriously, though, the advice came at a good time for me. I continue to enjoy my work here and I am overcoming a tendency to put off those extra visits to the library when I have settled down in my room after supper.

In that connection, I am also prompted to invite myself to call on you during the Christmas holidays. I shall be at my grandmother's for the customary family reunion and will telephone you to see if it is convenient for you.

Sincerely yours,
Gerald Higgins

I got no answer. I had deliberately withheld the date of my visit to my grandmother's so that he could not say he would be busy that day. When he failed to answer my letter my suspicions were more or less confirmed; he was reluctant to resume our conversations, and he may even have seen through the casualness of my letter.

But during the holidays my grandmother gave me some news that made me want to apologize to Robert Millhouser. "Your friend Mr. Millhouser's been very poorly," she said. "Very poorly. He was taken with a severe cold and couldn't shake it off, and finally Moses had the doctor in and lucky he did. Young Dr. Willetts said one more day and it would have been good-bye, Mr. Millhouser. They had to give him oxygen. You ought to at least take him a jar of that guava jelly Grandpa used to send him this time of year. Poor man, I know he doesn't have many visitors."

There was no doubt about the seriousness of Robert Millhouser's illness. He received me in the little room, held out his hand and apologized for not rising. He had a shawl about his shoulders and a wool blanket across his knees. He was fully dressed, but it was obvious that his clothes no longer fitted him, which was unusual for Mr. Millhouser. In all the years I knew him he had always been carefully well dressed; although he seldom traveled away from Lyons, and his wardrobe was certainly not extensive, he managed to keep up with the less drastic changes in styles. He was the first man in Lyons to wear low shoes the year round, the first to wear a soft shirt with a gold pin in the collar. He had an instinctive sense of correctness in

55

clothes that was different, for instance, from my grandfather's good taste. My grandfather paid a lot of money for his suits and shoes and hats, and they were excellent and quiet. But Robert Millhouser indulged in the slight touches that added style without overdecorating himself. (I happened to know, because I had seen it, that he had a "Delta Psi Tea Company" gold charm on the end of his watch-chain, but his reason for not displaying it was that of delicacy; in 1908 they had not accepted his resignation, but he kept the insigne hidden in his pocket.)

At his full height he was not a tall man, but now he seemed lost in his clothes and the other coverings. His shirt collar hardly touched his neck and the knot of his tie made me guess that it had been tied by Moses. "You were very kind to come," he said. "Dr. Willetts isn't entirely in favor of my being downstairs, but if you can walk five squares the least I can do is slide down the banister to greet you."

"You must have had quite a siege," I said.

"Yes," he said. "If Moses hadn't taken matters into his own hands —that man is eighty-one years of age, and he wanted to carry me down here today. I think he could have done it, too, but I wouldn't let him."

"He's a dear man, Moses."

"You sounded like your grandfather then."

"The Irish sound. You know he picked that up from my grandmother. Grandpa didn't have a real brogue. He wasn't even born in Ireland, but I suppose you couldn't be married to Grandma without catching some of it. She's a talker, bless me if she isn't."

"Now you're putting it on, Gerald."

"Yes. I'm glad I've been so close to it, though. It helps me to imagine the sound of conversations in Old English."

"You're liking Princeton now. That's good."

"Yes, I'll be sorry when I have to leave."

"Then why leave?"

"Because I want to start teaching."

"Why do you want to teach?"

"I have no good answer to that. I have a *lot* of answers, but I don't want to waste your time with them. I suppose the best one is that in college and prep school I thought I'd be much better than most of the teachers, and the good ones I had, I wanted to be like them. I don't really know."

"I'm surprised that your mother didn't want you to become a priest."

56

"Is that a question?" I said. "She did, six or seven years ago, but she's given up."

"Have you given up your religion?"

"The practice of it, yes. Long since. I'm a heretic on so many counts that if my grandmother knew about them I wouldn't be allowed in her house."

"But what about your own mother? And your father?"

"My mother prays for me, I'm sure."

"And your father?"

"I think my mother must pray for him, too. He goes to Mass with her every Sunday, but that's all he does. That, and give money. He's anti-clerical, and so am I."

He nodded slowly. "Your priest came in to see me last week. Father Schultz. I'm sure he had the best of intentions. Neighborly. But I was glad to see him go. I don't want to be converted. He didn't say a word about religion, but we've never exchanged more than polite greetings before, and he made me very uncomfortable." He spoke very quietly, unemotionally, but gave me the feeling that he was on the verge of saying a great deal more. Suddenly he said: "I've had a purpose in this talk about religion."

I said nothing.

"I'm not an atheist, Gerald. I believe in God, and I've been wondering why my life was spared when it wouldn't have made any difference to anyone if I'd just quietly gone to sleep. Why *was* I spared? I'm not afraid to die, and I didn't pray to hold on to a few extra years on earth."

I thought of "where no hope is left, is left no fear," but I remained silent.

"Why? Why? Why? I asked myself so many times that I practically forced an answer. Or I forced a question that was practically its own answer. What had I been doing that I had not completed? Well, God was certainly not interested in the still life that I'd been painting when I caught cold. I don't think He cared whether we finished the work on the driveway before the weather got too cold. And I'm sure the dear Lord isn't guiding me in my correspondence with Drexel & Company. There was only one thing I hadn't finished." He looked at me and waited for me to speak, but I wanted him to say it. "Our story," he said.

I still did not speak, I wanted it all to come from him.

"The swallow in his flight," he said. "That's what I believe. The God of us all. I had no fear of dying, and I have none, but I do have some fear of leaving that story unfinished. I so strongly believe that

I was kept alive to finish something, and that's really the only thing I can think of."

Now it was my turn to feel reluctance. My old disillusionment and distrust of priests and their claim to infallibility was back with me. I did not want to participate in a project with a man who had convinced himself that he too had divine guidance. I wanted to hurry away. But I stayed.

"You're not saying anything," he said.

"Well, no. I think you have a lot more to say."

"Oh. I was afraid that you—well, never mind. I *have* more to say. I don't know any young people, Gerald, and I don't expect them to be as polite as you are."

"Thank you," I said.

"I wasn't completely truthful with you when I told you why I didn't want to go on. Back in September, I mean. You and I have never been completely truthful, have we?"

"I suppose not."

"Well, we all try to protect ourselves. I said that I wanted to protect some people long dead, but I was protecting myself, too. And where you were not truthful was in not coming right out and saying that I was a dull old man except that I had murdered my wife."

I was shocked, but I managed to say: "How could I say that to you, Mr. Millhouser?"

"Not to me, Gerald. To yourself. Did you ever really say it to yourself?"

"No."

"And yet that was the truth, wasn't it?" he said. "A dull old man who walked past your grandfather's house four times a day to get the mail. Then when you got a little older you were told that I had shot my wife and killed her."

"That is true, yes," I said.

"I'm sure that if you'd got the story from anyone but your grandfather it would have been much worse. How much did he tell you?"

"Almost nothing. To this day I could tell you all I know in a couple of sentences."

"What are they?"

"That you shot your wife and that Mr. Vance was mixed up in it, and that you were tried and acquitted."

"Good Lord, is that all they told you?"

"That's all, except that my grandfather said you were very unfortunate, something to that effect. Something sympathetic."

"How well I know that he was sympathetic! The only one that was, for a while. What did he tell you about Bart Vance?"

"He didn't tell me anything about Vance. My mother let that slip one time, his name, but then she didn't say any more. I don't even know what happened to Vance."

He sighed. "Now I'm beginning to think that I have to *tell* you the whole story to protect the people involved, not to keep it from you. But not today. Can you come back tomorrow?"

"Yes, of course."

"Are you sure you're not giving up anything?"

"I'm going to a dance in Gibbsville tomorrow night, but I can be there in an hour," I said. "Just so I'm there in time to change."

"Come in the morning and stay for lunch. I'll start where we left off, in London. And possibly by the time you're ready to leave, you'll know the whole story. I'm grateful to you already. I know that this is the right thing to do. Some good always comes of the truth, and I'll sleep better tonight knowing that I've passed the truth on to you, or will have this time tomorrow."

I could see that he felt better. He was tired, but he was more alive than he had been earlier in our conversation. And as for me, my momentary misgivings as to his religious fanaticism had vanished— lost, quite possibly, in my own new conviction that it was my duty to learn the truth about Robert Millhouser so that the truth would not die when he died. (In my middle years I always catalog this under The Religiosity of Gerald Higgins.)

The next morning at ten-thirty he greeted me in the glassed-in porch that some people would have called the conservatory, some the sunroom. It was warm and cheerful. "I saw you drive up," he said. "What make car is that?"

"It's a Jordan. A graduation present."

"Ah, *that's* a Jordan. I've seen their advertisements, but I don't think anyone in Lyons has one."

"At home they're known as the bootleggers' car. All the boot- leggers have them. The agency is owned by a bootlegger."

"But that didn't keep you from buying one?"

"No. Two of the bootleggers have raccoon coats, too, but that didn't keep me from buying one."

"You certainly need it if you drive with the top down in this weather. The thermometer outside my window said eleven above at half past seven," he said. He looked at me with frank approval. "I see you're all ready to leave for Gibbsville. Chester Calthorp had a tweed suit with knickerbockers. His jacket was in the Norfolk style."

"I had one a few years ago."

"Have you been enjoying yourself in Lyons? I mean, has Lyons anything to offer a young man these days?"

"Yes, I went to a dance last night at the Odd Fellows Hall. They had an orchestra from Fort Penn. The Winter Ball."

"The Winter Ball. I guess that must have taken the place of the old Assembly."

"It did. My mother told me it did. But now it's all school and college people."

"Are there enough of them here to have a ball?"

"Oh my, yes. They must have had at least a hundred couples and fifty stags."

"Two hundred and fifty. In my day I doubt if there were more than a hundred, all told. No stags, of course. The grand march began sharply at nine, always led by some member of the Langendorf family. I attended several of them."

"Oh? Who was your partner when you were in college?"

"Let me see. Never the same young lady twice, you can be sure. That was partly because of caution on my part. The Assembly was a very serious matter, very serious implications to ask a young lady to the Assembly, so I never did. I waited until some despairing mother or even her despairing daughter would write and say that if I hadn't already invited someone, why, Mary Jane's out-of-town beau had had to change his plans."

"Is that what they did then, too?"

"Yes. Or one of the girls I knew would all but order me to invite one of her friends."

"And you could be ordered?"

"Oh, I didn't mind, just so long as we all understood one another. I'd put on my full dress and Moses and I would go forth in Mama's landau and I'd make myself agreeable until the witching hour. Some young lady thereby had got to her Assembly, and I'd come home feeling that I'd done a good deed, and Moses and I would sit in the kitchen and get slightly intoxicated, then he'd usually carry me up to my room and put me to bed, and that would be that. You don't really want to know the names of the young ladies, do you?"

"I guess not."

"Two of them have passed on, one is married and living in Lancaster, and the other's here in town, a grandmother, hasn't spoken to me since 1908. No, that's wrong. She hasn't spoken to me since *1906*. She didn't approve of my marriage. There were two categories. Those who didn't approve of my marriage to a girl thirty-three years younger than I. And those who stopped speaking to me when I was tried for murder. I've never been upset by the latter category. I've come to realize that at least some of them stopped speaking to me because they simply didn't know how to act. A few of those, mostly men, do speak to me today. But women are an unforgiving lot. They're worse than that. Did you know—no, you didn't know—that after I killed my wife there was talk of lynching me?"

"No, I didn't know. I've never heard that."

"Shall I tell you about that now, or shall we go back to London?"

"Whatever you wish," I said.

"Unfortunately, if I try to tell you everything in the order that it happened, I'm afraid I'd overlook some things. We'll try it again later, but first, while it's on my mind, about the lynching. I wish your grandfather could have told you that part, but then I guess he never would have and it should be told. It shows what kind of man Jeremiah MacMahon was. Do you see now, Gerald, why I've changed my mind? Why it's right for me to tell you this story? You'd never have known this about your grandfather."

He settled back in his chair, with his head resting on a small pillow and his hands lying loosely from the arms of the chair. He moistened his lips, looked at the ceiling, and began: "They didn't arrest me right away, you know. Tommy Fenstermacher was the constable and I'd known him all my life, he'd known me. Same grade in school and so forth. Played together, and his father had often done work around the place. One of those handy men that could do odd jobs of carpentry and bricklaying, gardening. He could never hold a steady job because he was the kind that would go off on three-day sprees and the contractors couldn't depend on him. And I suppose he was a dangerous man to have around on a building. But my father used to find things for him to do and the Fenstermachers were always grateful to my father. Consequently, when young Dr. Willetts reported that my wife was dead, and that I'd shot her and was waiting to be arrested, Tommy came out and he was terribly embarrassed when I opened the door. I said, 'Tommy, I'd have gone down and given myself up but I didn't want anyone to think I was trying to run away.'

" 'That's all right, Robert,' he said. 'I didn't come to arrest you.'

"And I realized that he *hadn't* come to arrest me. He'd come because I was in trouble. I began to cry. It had only been an hour, or two hours, I guess, since the thing had happened. 'I did it, though,' I said.

" 'You get a lawyer, don't say nothing to me,' he said. 'Or if you want me to I'll tell George Holliday to come out, myself. You go have some rest, Robert.' Then he got Moses to take him upstairs where my wife was and in a few minutes Tommy came down and put his arm around my shoulder, didn't say anything except that he was going to have to notify Dr. Dixon, the deputy coroner, and Dixon would probably be out to remove the body, along with the undertaker. Then he left.

"That was done. Dixon came and my wife's body was removed to the undertaker's and I was here in the house still not under arrest, and when Dixon told Tommy Fenstermacher he'd better go out and arrest me, Tommy said they'd have to get someone else to do it, he wouldn't. The only other man who could arrest me was Leon Bensinger, the chief burgess, and he was in Johnsville on business. There was talk in the town that the railway and coal company police could arrest me and I believe they not only could have but should have. But they didn't want to and they all refused to take out a warrant. They didn't want to risk losing their jobs and I don't blame them. They weren't really peace officers. Their job was to protect company property and guard payrolls.

"George Holliday, my lawyer, came out and he and I waited for someone to arrive and take me off to prison, but we waited all afternoon and evening and nobody else came. And yet I could feel something ominous. Ominous? Yes, ominous. I was ready to die for what I had done. I'd been ready for a long time, but that's another part of the story. I expected to be arrested and put on the train and taken to the county jail in Fort Penn, tried in court, found guilty, and executed. I had known all those things would happen. But nothing was happening. George Holliday would look at his watch, stare at it and stare at it, snap it shut, put it back in his pocket and walk around. We talked, George and I, but most of the time we just waited and when it began to get dark I suggested to George that he go home and have his supper. He looked at me as though I'd lost my mind, not unreasonable in the circumstances, but I don't mean it that way. 'I couldn't possibly leave you,' he said. Then Moses came in and said supper was ready, and after supper Moses said he was going to get the mail before the post office closed and I didn't stop him. But I wish I had.

"What happened was that Moses did go to the post office and got the mail out of the box and when he was leaving he heard a woman say, 'There's his nigger.' Moses wasn't used to that. When I was a boy I'd often called him a nigger when he'd do something that made me angry, but I always did it from a safe distance, because if I was anywhere near him he'd slap my face. And in Lyons the colored were treated pretty well. They had their own church but they went to the white school and played with white children. There was even one colored man who was a member of the G.A.R. and he always paraded with them. I'd never heard of any trouble. But when Moses heard that woman he didn't like it a bit, and he turned around to say something to her and she said to him, 'Yes, you. You and that murderer you work for.' She began shouting, 'What kind of a country is this, where a man can commit a murder and send his nigger for the mail as if nothing happened?' Then some other women joined in with her and before he knew it Moses was trapped in the post office and some men started yelling, too. You know, only one door, and post office windows are all barred. Then a white man in the crowd said, 'Get out of my way and let this man alone,' and he pushed his way through the crowd and took Moses by the arm and got him out. The man was your grandfather, Jeremiah MacMahon. He knew them all by name and you may be sure they all knew him. He was one of the richest men in town by that time. But even so he was well in his sixties and it took courage to do what he did. More than courage. You can call on courage to do certain things. But there are other things that require principle. Do you see what I mean? You could stop a runaway horse and that would take courage. But here a principle was involved. A black man outnumbered, a crowd of bullies. And there was something else that I didn't think of for a long time and I never knew whether your grandfather'd had time to think of it, but Moses was a powerful man, prodigiously strong, and if they'd come at him, someone would have been killed. Moses is only two generations removed from the jungle, remember. His father was a slave, his grandfather was brought to this country like an animal. There surely would have been two more killings in Lyons that day if your grandfather hadn't stepped in. At least two. That crowd of bullies in the post office would have marched down to Darktown and God knows what would have happened there.

"But your grandfather did what he did. He took Moses by the arm and held on to him and walked all the way out here with him and told him not to leave the place. He saw that George Holliday's rig was still in the yard, so he didn't stop in to see me. Instead he went to Fred Langendorf's house and told him what had happened in the post office. Langendorf said yes, he'd heard about it already and more besides.

"The Langendorfs were *the* richest people in town and not Catholic, so Fred Langendorf was the most important man in Lyons. He told your grandfather that he had heard talk that the Blue Ribboners were going to lynch me. Have you ever heard of the Blue Ribboners? They were the predecessors of the Klan. A lot of the men in the Klan today are sons of the old Blue Ribboners. Everybody knew who they were then, just as we know now who belongs to the Klan. They hated the people who had money, but they hated Mitchell and all the union people too. And of course Catholics and colored people and Jews. They were poor themselves, most of them belonged to the poorer churches. Quite a few farmers were Blue Ribboners, and the town Blue Ribboners were usually uneducated; very seldom would you find a good carpenter or mechanic among them, although they did have some members among store clerks and men like timekeepers on the railroad and politicians in the South Ward and the East Ward, where the poor people lived and still live. Most of the time they didn't really do any actual harm. They had their meetings in the woods in the summer and somebody's barn in the winter and they distributed pamphlets that came all the way from Missouri. Most of the pamphlets I saw were written about the Pope, your Catholic Pope. They made very juicy reading, some of them. But they didn't do much. The younger ones, rowdies, sometimes gathered in front of the Catholic convent and called out naughty suggestions to the nuns and once they did throw some stones and broke a stained-glass window in the church. But they usually kept to their own part of town.

"But now they were dangerous. Fred Langendorf told your grandfather that they were having a meeting at nine o'clock that night back of the Reading depot, the old G. C. & L., and there was no telling what they might do. Fred blamed it all on Tommy Fenstermacher for not arresting me, and that *was* wrong. Everybody that Tommy'd ever arrested had it in for him, and most of them were from the East Ward and the South Ward, and when a rich man committed a murder and wasn't arrested—you can imagine what they said. One law for the rich and one for the poor. And then your grandfather, a Catholic, standing up to them to save a colored man. And there was one other thing. They didn't like *me*.

"It's not hard to see why. If anybody was typical of the idle rich, I was. I didn't have an office in town, I did all my work here, kept all my papers here, my filing cabinets. And I had almost nothing to do with anybody in the two poorer wards. When they saw me I was usually on my way to the bank or the post office. When I'd get a haircut they'd all stop talking as soon as I entered the barbershop and hardly say a word till I left. I didn't belong to any of the lodges and neither had my father. Then when I married an eighteen-year-old girl, me fifty-one, the *women* had something to talk about too. And those women had always hated my mother. Mama died four years before I got married, but in a place like Lyons four years is nothing. And if they don't know everything about you, what they invent is not likely to be in your favor. Some of the women never got over the time Mama let the hunting party use this house. On second thought they'd decided Mama hadn't gone to Philadelphia after all. Oh, I've often been here on a Sunday afternoon when they'd go for a walk and I'd see them staring at this house. A man and his wife would walk all the way around, looking the place over, staring at the upstairs windows. Heavens only knows what they expected to see. The men would try to keep moving but the women would lag behind, staring, staring. Even if their suspicions had been correct, whatever they were, they couldn't have seen anything. It's a good two hundred feet from the fence to the porch, and all the windows were curtained and shaded, not to speak of the walnuts and spruces and horse-chestnuts obstructing their view. My wife had once said that they were expecting Satan himself to appear. She had a wry sense of humor.

"To get back to your grandfather and Fred Langendorf. We had a company of the National Guard in town then and Fred thought of telegraphing the governor, but your grandfather said that wouldn't be very sensible. A good proportion of them were Blue Ribboners, and anyway, the governor wasn't likely to call out the Guard on the strength of a rumor. But something had to be done, and the question was, what? Get together the respectable element and put a guard around this house? No. Your grandfather said that would mean shooting. And there just wasn't any organization in town big enough numerically to stand up to the Blue Ribboners. At least none that didn't have some Blue Ribboners among the members.

"By this time it was around seven o'clock, and Fred had sent for three or four other men who had influence. Dr. Sam Merritt was one, and Bert Shoemaker, the printer. Ivor Brown, the druggist. Albert Connor, had the wagon works then. All still alive, by the way, except Ivor Brown, and I guess you know them all. A couple of others dropped in, too, but those I know for certain. Decent, good men and a lot younger then than they are now. I mention that fact because twenty years ago some of them were actually young men, and it wasn't just the older men that were worried. They were all ages, and they were all worried about what could happen if there was a lynching in their town.

"I don't know, but I would imagine that in a meeting like that and with the time growing short, all sorts of suggestions were brought up, and I still don't know who originated the one they decided on, but I'll wager they weren't unanimous on the first vote. Whoever originated the idea, he was a brilliant man.

"This is what they did. Four of them agreed to go down to the Reading depot and be there when the first of the Blue Ribboners arrived, around half past eight. They agreed they wouldn't say anything unless they were spoken to first. They just stood there on the freight platform and watched the early birds arriving. They spoke to them by name. All four spoke to every man by name, and that was all. And it confused those early birds. The Ribboners were very uncomfortable standing there and as some more arrived *they* didn't feel very comfortable either. But by nine o'clock there was quite a crowd, men *and* women, and the first thing every new arrival noticed, or was told, was that those four prominent men were there. Finally one of the Ribboners said to Fred Langendorf, 'What are you doing here?'

"And Fred said, 'We heard you were having a meeting.'

"The other man said, yes, they were having a meeting but they didn't invite Fred. 'I came without being invited, we all did,' said Fred.

" 'Well, you can go away,' the man said.

" 'Not till we find out what the meeting is for,' said Fred.

"And then a woman called out, 'We're going to hang Millhouser.'

"Fred looked at the man. 'Is that what you're having this meeting for?'

" 'What if we are? What business of yours is it?' the man said.

" 'It's everybody's business,' said Fred, and that's all he said. Then he turned to the three others and said something to them that the crowd couldn't hear. All he said was, 'Let's go,' but the crowd didn't know that. Then the four men walked off together without a word. They hadn't done a thing to inflame the crowd, no arguments. But every man there knew that he had been seen and recognized by four of the most influential men in town, and of course the crowd didn't know what those four were going to do next. What they actually did was to go to Fred's house and wait."

Robert Millhouser stopped speaking and looked at me and smiled. "How long do you think they waited?"

"I don't even know what they were waiting for," I said.

"Of course not," said the old man. "They were waiting for the sound of three quick, short pulls on a locomotive whistle. And they only had to wait about ten minutes.

"You see, Gerald, the reason I can't tell you whose idea this was is because I don't think it *could* have been any one man's. It must have been thought up by at least two men. Fred Langendorf and his three went down to the Reading depot and did what I told you. But in the meantime the other men, five others, I think there were, split up. Two of them came out here to my house, one of them your grandfather. The others went and got Billy Williams, the superintendent of the colliery, and drove up to the colliery and Williams ordered a train made up, consisting of a locomotive and caboose. They got up steam and then without even any lights they brought the train down to the Pennsy yards and I was put on it, accompanied by George Holliday and your grandfather in the caboose."

"Who drove the engine?" I said.

"The night watchman, he was an engineer. A yard engineer, I guess you'd call him. Anyway, accustomed to running a locomotive. As far as that goes, there was no danger of running into another train. There were no trains running between here and Soyersville at that hour, and at Soyersville, Billy Williams got a regular crew. The firemen, though. Ask me who the firemen were."

"Who were they?"

"Bert Shoemaker and Albert Connor. Can you believe that they ever shoveled coal in a locomotive? They did, though, as far as Soyersville."

"And what happened to you?"

"I was taken to the county jail in Fort Penn. One of the oddest things about it was that I was in prison without being arrested. George Holliday had to wake up a judge he knew so that I could be put under arrest and committed without bail. I can remember that judge, how upset he was. The whole thing was most irregular. The arresting officer was actually a prison guard and I was already in a cell! The warden wouldn't sign me in without the commitment papers, although I was in and behind bars. And I stayed there until I went on trial."

"What happened in Lyons? What did the crowd do when they found out?" I asked.

Robert Millhouser did not immediately reply. He was momentarily lost in the memories of that night. "Excuse me, Gerald. You asked me a question?"

"I was wondering what happened to the Blue Ribboners. Were they angry when they found out they'd been tricked?"

"That I can't say for sure. But I would conjecture that individually they were glad enough to do nothing, to find an excuse to go home. The Blue Ribboners were very small potatoes and they didn't have a strong leader. I've heard that only two or three of the younger ones came armed. They had shotguns. I doubt if many of them even *owned* pistols. The household weapon in a section like this is the shotgun, useful for going after rabbit and pheasant and for killing rats, but an awkward thing to carry around when you're going to break a law. I've often thought about that crowd, that were going to lynch me. Their hearts weren't in it, and I'll tell you why I've come to that conclusion. I think the women egged them on to it, as much as they did do. The men must have decided that they'd go to the meeting and do whatever the crowd did. But they didn't go armed. If they'd been determined to hang me, you can be sure they'd have brought their guns. I just wish I knew what went on in two or three households before that meeting. The whole thing to me smacked of angry women. Witness Moses Hatfield's experience in the post office. If there'd been a right time to do anything, that was the time, with Moses there. But your grandfather stepped in. Then in the next couple of hours the women tried to stir up their husbands and the husbands resented that. There aren't very many homes here where the husband will take orders from the wife, even today, and twenty years ago, less so. Then when the first arrivals at the depot saw that the respectable element had their eyes on them, that took the wind out of their sails."

"Did most of them just go home?" I asked.

"So I gather. The only saloon open was Stiney Burkitis's, and the Ribboners never went near that place. Stiney was a Lithuanian and an enemy of the Ribboners, and the Ribboners weren't drinkers in any case. At least not the kind that frequented saloons. As they say nowadays, they drank Wet and voted Dry. Church people. Anti-Saloon League. So they really had no place to go, and apparently they just went home.

"Naturally I've read a great many newspaper accounts of lynching mobs since then, and compared them with my experience. I've come to the conclusion that the Ribboners weren't really incensed that I had killed my wife. They might have been if I'd killed one of their women, but my wife didn't qualify in that respect. I've also noticed that you can't stir up a mob to lynch a man for a principle. To be specific, these people were angry because they told each other that there was one law for the rich and one for the poor, and that *is* a principle, but it isn't a principle that they could get violently angry about. It really had no application to the lives of these men individually. They had always known that there *is* one law for the rich and one for the poor, so there was nothing new about that. They could resent it all their lives, but there wasn't much they could do about it except to get rich themselves and come under the jurisdiction of rich man's laws. Then they would cease to be Blue Ribboners because organizations like the Blue Ribboners thrive on hating the rich and hating whatever else the Ribboners are *not*.

"Remember this, Gerald. If you had emptied the pockets of all those men at the Reading depot, I doubt if you'd have collected a hundred dollars. They were people who were always pinched for cash, had never had any money, but for three generations they'd seen the Irish and the Hunkies and Polacks come and work in the mines and make twice as much cash. Do you know, it's awful to think of the life of one of those men, one of the Ribboners, I mean. They have *never* had any pleasure. Sexual pleasure? I can't believe it. Sexual activity aplenty, but mean, secret, guilty activity, full of cruelty and totally lacking in love. Oh, their faces when I see them at the post office. Sometimes when the mail is late and we have to wait a little while. A woman like Dorothy Stiegel, do you know her? The woman that owns the beauty parlor? She'll come in and these men will stop talking and stare at her figure, all stop talking at the same time, all stare at her the same way. Not full of lust. Full of cruelty. They'll have their thoughts, and then they'll all start talking again, as abruptly as they stopped. One life, and to live it like that!"

At this moment I knew that Robert Millhouser, whether *he* knew it or not, was fully ready to tell his story. I felt sure he did *not* know it, and it was important to keep him from becoming alarmed. "Do you think they know what they're missing in life?" I said.

"What they're missing? No. But that they are missing *something*, yes. Their sadness is due to their inability to—to—to recognize, or define, what they're envious of. They think it's money. They think they'd be happy if they weren't poor. Happy, of course, is not a word they would ever use. Happy, or joyful. They think they'd be better off. Yes, that's it. Better off. If they had money they'd be better off. They could have one of your Jordan cars, they could have Dorothy Stiegel. But I'm afraid that the good Lord didn't create Dorothy Stiegel for them, any more than Mr. Jordan built his automobile with them in mind. Now don't ask me what the good Lord is doing for those people. A good and just Lord would seem to have been very unjust to those people, not quite fair. They're not doing anything to *deserve* heaven, are they? Assuming you believe in heaven. But neither has He, the Lord, equipped them with the intellect to behave so that they might deserve heaven. The conclusion, I suppose, if you believe in God, and heaven, is that those people are put on earth to irritate us, and when they die they'll all go to a certain corner of heaven that is reserved for people like them. If that's the case, then I suppose those dreadful people are really the Lord's angels, as I understand angels. Every son of a bitch—excuse me, Gerald—in the world is an angel, not quite human, not given a complete soul like you and me, but put on earth to try our patience and make us deserve heaven, or hell. An interesting conceit, don't you think? The notion that every s. o. b. is one of God's angels? Does it shock you at all?"

"Well, yes," I said.

"I suspect you're teasing me. Why does it shock you?"

"Because from now on I'll be inclined to treat every son of a bitch as though he *were* one of God's angels, and that's going to be very tough for me to do. Also, theologically, if I treat every son of a bitch as an angel, won't I be opposing God's will?"

"Oh, you have a very devious mind, Gerald. Are you sure you've abandoned the idea of becoming a Jesuit?"

"Be careful, Mr. Millhouser. You're liable to rush me into a hasty marriage."

"So that you can't become a Jesuit?"

"So that I can't become a Jesuit, right."

"I've only ever known one Jesuit," said Robert Millhouser, seriously.

"I'm a little surprised that you knew even one. Where would you have known a Jesuit?"

"In Italy," he said.

I waited, but he did not go on. I was very young, and I had not yet learned that conversational rests do not embarrass older people. I had also failed to realize that the effort of conversing was tiring to him. Presently he spoke: "We're having our lunch out here, Gerald. Do you want to wash?"

"Yes, I will, thanks."

"Good. You'll find my room at the top of the stairs, turn left, then second door on your right, and my bathroom is through the bedroom. Unfortunately Moses has to bring me a pot. The doctor was in to see me this morning and if I go upstairs now I have to stay there. One trip down and one trip up is all I'm permitted."

I took my time on the second floor, partly out of politeness, partly because I wanted to look at the rooms. Robert Millhouser's room contained a large four-poster, a black tufted leather chair now covered with a blanket, a spinet desk and some ladderbacks and Windsor chairs. Beside the bed was a marble-topped *cabinet* on one side, and on the other a wooden bench that might have been a luggage rest. Bracketed to one of the bedposts was a reading lamp, office-type, with a flexible arm. The floor was carpeted in a brightly colored flower pattern and on both sides of the bed were small Persian rugs, both about evenly worn, which I took to indicate that their positions were changed at the signs of wear, since obviously Robert Millhouser used the luggage rest when he was putting on his shoes, to judge by the shoehorn and by the Romeo slippers on and beside the luggage rest. But I looked in vain for portraits, photographs and all other objects that would have made this room uniquely Robert Millhouser's. Whatever the furniture pieces may have meant to him, he kept no other reminder of family or friends in this room. I was so astonished by this lack that I made a check to determine if I had the right room; inside the room there was a large clothes closet, with his suits and shoes hanging and treed, and with drawers for his shirts and underwear, and in the bathroom adjoining I noticed a washrag still slightly damp, an old leather case with seven straight razors, and on the window-sill a shaving brush left to dry. It was his bedroom, undoubtedly. And then of course I realized that the very absence of personal souvenirs made it even the more his room than any number of photographs and mementoes could have done. It was wholly and entirely his room, beautifully furnished and completely bare, in its fashion as bare as a Trappist monk's cell. Even his hair brushes were the kind that could be bought in any drug store, and not the silver-backed pair that I would have expected to find.

Outside the window, fixed to the ledge, was a flag-holder that had not been used to hold a flag since its last painting. Through the leaf-less branches of the trees I could look down on the town from this small height, and in the distance I saw the snow-covered culm banks and beyond on the far mountainside the streaks of snow where the stand of timber was thinned out. I had not been aware that there was this view from Robert Millhouser's house; most of my time in Lyons had been during the summer, when the Millhouser trees had all but hidden the house, even from the vantage point of my grandfather's attic. But now I was seeing the town as Robert Millhouser could see it every day from late fall to early spring, and my heart suddenly jumped as I thought of him looking out this window all winter long, day after day, every morning, seeing his world to the limits he had created for it. For just that startling moment, following so soon as to be part of my discovery of the bareness of his room, I *was* Robert Millhouser. And I did not want to be.

Precisely at this stage of our relationship I had an impulse to put an end to it. In our earlier meetings, before I went off to Princeton, Robert Millhouser had interested and entertained me with his stock of facts about his family and the people of Lyons. A gracious and intelligent gentleman had complimented me by taking pleasure in my company. No older person except my grandfather had ever taken so much trouble to honor my intelligence, and my relationship with my grandfather was so unlike that between Robert Millhouser and me that only the youth-age factor was common to both. (I did not even bother to consider my relationships with my teachers in school and college; they marked my papers and therefore possessed a power that I could not ignore, and I was perfectly well aware that I was not so stimulating, so unusual a student that a teacher would want to make me his protégé.) Robert Millhouser had admitted me into his present life and had reopened to me many of the facts of his past—up to that point beyond which he did not at first feel free to go; then had done his recent *volte-face*. In the very beginning of our summer meetings I had been actively conscious of being in the presence of a man who

71

had committed a murder (I continued to think of it in that term), but as time passed I seldom thought of him as an uxoricide. I had *never* thought of him as a man "with blood on his hands." You simply did not think of him that way, this neat, neatly handsome, quiet man whose face showed suffering and loneliness. I had not yet succeeded in re-creating for myself a scene in which Robert Millhouser would commit murder; I would, in my imagination, get as far as the moment in which he fired a revolver and as a consequence of which his wife lay dead. But I did not in my imagination see his wife, nor could I finish the scene.

I turned away from the window and by that simple act I was back in the intense solitude of the bedroom, mindful of the fact that Robert Millhouser downstairs was making water in a pot; but more embarrassed, I was, to be intruding on the intimacy expressed by the cold austerity of the bedroom than if I had been standing on the sun porch during the functioning of his bladder. Circumstances had combined to bring me now to a third phase of the relationship; the factual phase had been the first, the second was the withdrawal followed by the *volte-face* and the start of the deeper confidences, and the third phase—it had begun. The signs of it were the several references to his wife, the exposure of some of his sub-surface thoughts, the introduction of sex, the incident of the chamber-pot, and the over-all relaxing of the restrictions he had once placed on his conversations with me, signified by his use of the epithet son-of-a-bitch. And within myself, for evidence of the third phase, there was the shocking experience of discovering that unconsciously I had proceeded to a state in which I could see and feel as he saw and felt. I was in the midst of inventing an excuse to cut short my visit when Moses called. "It's all right now, Mr. Gerald. You can come down now."

Robert Millhouser looked refreshed. He was rubbing his hands as though he were washing them. "You were very tactful about my infirmities," he said. "Waiting up there till I'd finished. That's the most disagreeable thing about my present state of health. The doctor wants me to have a trained nurse, but I haven't reached that extremity, not yet. Can you smell this soap?" He made a tent over his nose with his fingers.

"Yes, it smells good."

"It's Roger and Gallet's. I have a weakness for it. That, and eau de Cologne. It goes back to the time I was in prison. Before that I suppose I was as clean as most men, took a bath nearly every day and shaved every day without fail. In prison they didn't allow me to have my own razor, but I was permitted to have a barber come in and shave me and trim my hair. Then after I was—released—I couldn't get rid of the smell of prison. It seemed to be lodged in my nostrils and I bought this scented soap and I believe I must have washed my hands with it twenty times a day, scrubbed my teeth, gargled, smoked a perfumed French cigarette. But the word prison, just the word, brings back that heavy smell. It's some sort of disinfectant that they also use in the toilets in railroad stations. But imagine breathing it for four months, every breath you took? But on to pleasanter subjects. I hope you like what you're getting for lunch. I told Moses that there was one thing not to serve. Turkey. Am I right?"

"Yes, I've had turkey four times in four days and we'll probably get it again tonight."

"You're not getting it here. Ah, there we are," he said, as Moses and the maid brought in the trays. "Oh, forgive me. Something to drink? We have some pre-Prohibition Mount Vernon. How would you like that?"

"I'd like it fine. Straight."

"Moses, let her do the serving. You bring us a bottle of that Mount Vernon, will you please, and get a move on?"

The maid placed the dishes and food on the card table that was set up in front of Robert Millhouser. My place was across the same table. Moses returned with the bottle and one shot glass.

"Where is my glass?" said Robert Millhouser.

"You don't get one, not till evening," said Moses.

"My un-trained nurse," said the old man. He was served a large plate of beef broth in which toast was soaking, and a glass of milk. I was given fried ham with a white gravy, a baked sweet potato, succotash, hot biscuits and strawberry preserve. I was hungry and so was he and our conversation was casual through the meal. Then, in spite of myself, I yawned.

"How would you like to take a nap? You're going to need it and this would be a good time to. You have a busy evening ahead of you. You could stretch out on the sofa, or for that matter, go upstairs and get into bed. My pajamas might be a little tight, but if you don't button them. Wouldn't you like to do that?"

"Frankly, it makes a lot of sense," I said. "Will you have Moses wake me at two o'clock?"

"That would give us plenty of time to talk," said the old man.

He rang the silver bell and Moses appeared. "Mr. Gerald is going to take a nap," said Robert Millhouser. "Get out a pair of my pajamas for him, please."

"He take a nap in your room?"

"There, or the room on the other side of the hall."

"I don't know do we have sheets for the other room."

"Well, then put him in my room."

I got undressed and put on the old man's pajamas while Moses lowered the shades, turned down the bed and waited to be dismissed. I thanked him and he left and I lay down, but I did not go to sleep. In spite of my tiredness I was being kept awake by something that I could not forget or remember. It bore some relation to my feeling of the bareness of this room that I had experienced an hour earlier, but I could not determine what it was. There was something missing from this room that was not like the silver-backed hairbrushes that I had imagined Robert Millhouser would own; it was something I had been *told* was in this room. But what was in *any* room that I had been told would be there? Then I remembered one of our summer conversations: Robert Millhouser had once said to me that there was a fraternity picture in his room that included a likeness of Chester Calthorp. It was certainly not in this room, and on an impulse that was irresistible I got up and went to the room across the hall.

There were all the souvenirs, pictures, trinkets that I had expected to see in Robert Millhouser's bedroom and that had been so strangely missing. The second room was crowded with such articles as cigar humidors and cigarette boxes, walking sticks and riding crops, a rattlesnake's tanned skin with buttons, churchwarden pipes and ale tankards, diplomas and albums, chunks of marble and polished anthracite. And everywhere, books and framed photographs. Most of the likenesses were indistinct, but it was not difficult to see a repetition of facial and figure features that showed the aging of Robert Millhouser's mother, and I recognized Moses Hatfield in three pictures that probably covered a period of about thirty years. But the Delta Psi picture that had impelled me to come to this room was useless; the light had not been good in the first place, the young men wore heavy moustaches and sideburns, and some of them wore their hair brushed down at an angle over their foreheads. Moreover, they did not sit in regular rows, and as a consequence it was not possible to tell from the lettering on the mat which man was C. Calthorp or even R. Millhouser. I was angry in my disappointment and ready to return to bed, but as I looked at the collection once again I noticed that something was missing in this room, too. Nowhere was there any likeness of Robert Millhouser's wife, but that was easy to understand.

I now went back to the first room and got into bed and fell into deep sleep. When I awoke I reached out for my watch, which rested on the marble of the *cabinet;* it was five minutes before two. I lay there in extreme comfort and as my consciousness returned it became clear to me that this room, this bed, were the room and the bed in which Robert Millhouser's wife had died. I needed some confirmation

74

before I could call my notion an established fact, but confirmation was all that it would be; in my mind there was no doubt. Robert Millhouser kept his personal mementoes in the other room, but in this room he slept.

At two o'clock Moses knocked on the door and came in bearing a tray with a small pot of coffee. "Ah, thank you, Moses," I said.

"You get a good little nap?"

"Fine." I poured the coffee while he raised the window shades. "This was Mrs. Millhouser's room, wasn't it?"

He had his back turned, so I could not see his face, but he stopped moving. "You say something to me?"

"Yes, I asked you if this was Mrs. Millhouser's room. It was, wasn't it?"

"I'm sure I can't say, if it was or if it wasn't."

"Well, no matter," I said. "I'm sure it was, but I'll ask Mr. Millhouser."

He faced me. "Don't ask him. I tell you. Yes, this was her room." He looked at me with a sort of tentative hostility. "Mr. Gerald, *why* you come here?"

"Why, Mr. Millhouser and I like to talk."

"What you got to talk to Mr. Millhouser?"

"You don't think we ought to talk?"

"You a boy, Mr. Gerald, he an old man. What an old man say to you?"

"We talk about the old times, before I was born."

"Why he talk about old times?"

"He likes to," I said.

"He don' talk to *me* about old times."

"Well, you were with him then, Moses."

"He don' say do I remember that time, or that time, or that time."

"Because he knows you do remember."

"No sir. Because he don' *like* to remember those old times, that's why. Folks like to remember old times, they talk about old times. Folks don' like to remember old times, they don' talk about them. I talk about old times, but I don' talk about old times to Mr. Robert."

"Well, I'm going away this afternoon."

"You come back soon?"

"I doubt it."

"Mr. Gerald, where you go?"

"Princeton, I go there to study."

"How you spell that Princeton?"

"P, r, i, n, c, e, t, o, n, Princeton."

"Too fast. You write that down for me?"

"All right."

He handed me a pencil and a piece of Robert's notepaper. "Print letters, not writing letters," he said. I printed the name without wondering much why he wanted it.

"Thank you, sir. Wish all you' folks a Happy New Year. Mrs. MacMahon, you' mother, you' daddy."

"Thank you, Moses, and the same to all your folks, but I'll see you before I go."

"Well, I think you best go now, Mr. Gerald. Mr. Robert he sound asleep and I best not wake him. I tell him goodbye for you."

I was angered and he knew it and was prepared for it and prepared to take the consequences, if any, of his interference, but what consequences could there be? I gave in. "I'll write Mr. Millhouser a note, *and you see that he gets it,* do you hear?"

I had been dressing while we talked. I sat at the spinet desk and wrote as follows:

Dear Mr. Millhouser:

Moses does not wish to disturb you and is quite adamant. Therefore I am off for G'ville but I would appreciate a note from you confirming your receipt of this hasty leavetaking. It has been a great pleasure to talk with you and I trust we can resume our correspondence. With all good wishes for a Happy New Year,

Sincerely,
Gerald

"You give him this, Moses, as soon as he wakes up. And if you don't give it to him, I'll know it." There was a stick of sealing wax and a tiny candle on the desk. I melted the wax and impressed it with my class ring, which was on the end of my watch-chain. I held up the ring for him to have a good look at it, then quite maliciously put it back in my pocket. Downstairs he helped me on with my fur coat, but neither of us spoke again, and I eased the Jordan off the property without warming up the motor. I was halfway to Gibbsville before I was able to laugh.

•

January 8, 1927

Dear Gerald:

I must apologize for my delay and for Moses' conduct, which was well intentioned but altogether unnecessary. It is one thing for him to treat me in cavalier fashion but to treat my guest so is another matter entirely. You may rest assured that he has been punished in the only manner that I have found effective. I permit him to bring me various necessities but I do not allow him to linger for a chat. It is a severe punishment, for Moses is a talkative man and an imperious one. Many years ago, when Moses first came to this family, the difference in our ages was greater than it is now, when we are two old men and the dark angel hovers over both of us. (Apropos our last conversation, the dark angel is an s. o. b.) In those days I had to obey Moses and he formed a habit then that he has never quite broken, namely, that of giving me orders and expecting them to be obeyed. Once or twice a year I am compelled to remind him of the difference in our stations, otherwise I should lose all authority in my own house and be forced to submit to even greater tyrannies than I do as it is.

But I do not wish to deceive you with the humorous tone of my remarks in the preceding paragraph. I have been greatly disturbed by Moses' action, which was, in effect, to send you away as though with my consent and approval. It is possible that I might not have been able to continue our conversation on that afternoon, but it is not my intention to abandon our collaborative effort. I say this to you now more freely than I might do if you were in the room with me: more than ever I believe that the truth and the truths of my life should not be buried with me. The form in which you choose to set them down is a matter for your own judgment and inclinations; whether as a disguised work of fiction, or as a factual case history. I leave that entirely up to you so long as I have some assurance from you that if any blame is to be fixed upon anyone it shall be me. I have no fear of any judgment in the life to come; I believe that the Lord is mercifully aware of my frailties as He is of the frailties of us all. But so strongly do I feel that there are lessons to be learned from the facts of my life that I want nothing to interfere with our collaboration. Therefore, if it is agreeable to you, I wish to resume our correspondence, starting with this letter. I shall write something every day, as much as my strength will permit, and mail it to you once a week.

Unfortunately this method of supplying you with the necessary information has one great handicap. You will not be able to ask me a question as it occurs to you, as would be the case if we were conversing, but you may feel free to put your questions on any and all matters in the letters you write to me. I may say that I am looking forward to the task I have set myself. I have never done any writing, but I have an enthusiasm for this task that I trust will make up for the total lack of a literary style.

The enclosed sheets represent four days' effort. It should go more rapidly as I begin to get the swing of it. I can think of only one more thing to say at this juncture: I know you have a great deal of interesting work to do in preparation for your degree and I cannot and do not expect you to take time off from your own work. However, I shall not put off writing to you for that reason. "No man knows the day or the hour," and I shall send you material weekly, covering the salient facts of my life up to about the year 1910. Nothing has happened to me since then that is worth recording.

With my thanks to you for your patience and very mature understanding and with my very best wishes to you in your own work, I am

Sincerely,
Robert Millhouser

The first batch of "material" consisted of nearly forty pages of completely legible handwritten autobiography, written in rich black ink on yellow legal tablet paper. He did not need the vertical guide lines on the left side of the sheets; his handwriting was so precise that it could almost have been typescript from a Hammond typewriter. I wrote Robert Millhouser a note of acknowledgment, and explained that I would not read what he sent until I had finished my first long paper at the Graduate College. A month passed before I read his manuscript, which he had paginated so that it could be read continuously, and by that time more than three hundred pages had accumulated. I took the manuscript with me on a short visit to Pinehurst and when I finished reading it I knew that he, or *we* were on the right track.

He had a remarkable memory, as good as any I have ever known. He remembered everything that had happened to him, everything he had seen, and he remembered all he had told me in our conversations. But the reason his manuscript made me feel that we were on the right track was the sense he imparted that he was not holding anything back, a subtly but notably different effect from the one I got during our early conversations. True, I was not ready to receive the deeper confidences then, any more than he was ready to give them. In those summer conversations I would sit and listen and always know that the incompleteness of his story was not only due to the fact that much of what he was telling me was hearsay; obviously much of what he told me had been told to him, since some of the events had occurred

78

before he was born. But the *style* of his narratives was inhibited, and only when he began to get into the Chester Calthorp phase of his life had he seemed to relax, to *confide*. Then, as the reader may have suspected, Robert Millhouser must have become self-protectively alarmed at the direction his reminiscences were taking; and then, and right then, he gave himself a choice of two courses: to be utterly candid, or to terminate the reminiscences. As I have already stated, he stopped the conversations and then did the quick *volte-face* which brought us into the present phase, when he was actually eager to make what I, with my Catholic background, now called a full confession.

It amused me to think of myself on the other side of the grille, listening to the secrets of a man three times my age. In prep school we had often talked about sneaking into the box and listening to the girls from F Street while they told the priest their most secret thoughts, words, and deeds. But now I was older, more sophisticated, and a serious candidate for a master's degree. In many ways I have never been so aged as I was at this time, my year at the Graduate College; no longer to be called a college boy, and militantly mature. I stayed amused only for a few minutes, or until my new maturity reasserted itself. This was deadly serious, literally so.

I had not read many pages of the manuscript before I realized that I had my work cut out for me. He had given me carte-blanche as to the use I would make of his material, and it was just as well that that was so. Consciously or not he was an admirer, I suspected, of the late Henry James. His prose style was similar to, if not imitative of, James's travel essays, which had been written at almost the same time that Robert Millhouser and Chester Calthorp were visiting some of the same cities—Paris, Rome, Florence. I even caught him in a plagiarism that I believe was unintentional: he wrote of "the swarming democracy of your fellow tourists," which he did not put in quotation marks and which I remembered from my limited reading of James. Robert Millhouser scarcely wrote a sentence without at least once using a double modifier, but he was no Henry James, and after a while I learned to read the manuscript for information and not for its elaborate statements of his impressions abroad. From time to time I sent him notes, usually containing queries, but there were surprisingly few questions that I needed to ask. In June I got my master's degree and promptly went to Europe, visiting the same cities that had been visited by Robert Millhouser, Chester Calthorp—and Henry James. I returned in the middle of August and went to stay with my grandmother so that I could have a few days with Robert Millhouser.

In eight months he had completely recovered his health. The always tightly drawn skin of his face was as remarkably unlined as ever. His neck was, I would say, a full size smaller in his collar and the neck cords were more numerous and defined; otherwise there were no immediately apparent signs that less than a year ago an oxygen tank had stood between him and death. On our first day together we compared travel notes and said nothing much about the manuscript. I did not feel, however, that the time was wasted. I told him that I had applied for teaching jobs at several prep schools and colleges and had been accepted at two places, and that I had bowed out because I wanted to devote as much time as possible to our project. He was pleased (as well he might have been), and he brought up a subject I never had discussed with him, never even thought of: his plans for the disposal of his money at his death. "I've waited all this time to make a will," he said. "Very unbusinesslike, you may think. Not really, though. It's a fair sum. It would be a nice amount to inherit all at once. But I have no one that close. Only cousins, most of whom I've never seen, none of whom I know at all well. So rather than have to decide who got what, I was going to die intestate and let the courts make the decisions for me. But last spring it occurred to me that for financial reasons you might have to stop working on our project, and I didn't want that to happen. So I had a talk with Milton Holliday, my lawyer, George's son. You must know Milton? I told Milton, in confidence, that I wanted to put aside $5,000 so that you wouldn't have to give up the project for financial reasons. Milton advised me that as long as I was going to do that, I might as well make a will, and I did. It was rather fun, once I got started. Ten thousand to Moses. A thousand apiece to the Lyons churches. A thousand to the Delta chapter of Delta Psi. They refused to accept my resignation in 1908, you know. I've never gone back, but this may remind some of them that I've always remembered their kindness. And it was a kindness, at a time when kindnesses were few and far between. I must confess it was a bit devilish of me to leave the same amount to my fraternity that I'm leaving to the churches. It's an ironic touch that only you and I know about. My fraternity, that had every reason to accept my resignation, stood by me. But the holy people of Lyons didn't. Not one of them came to see me, here or in prison. If my will is published, maybe some people can draw their own conclusions, but I doubt if they will. Let me see what other bequests. Five hundred apiece to my cook and my maid, if they're still in my employ at the time of my death. The rest in equal shares to my cousins or their heirs. That rhymes, doesn't it? The rest in equal shares—to my cousins or their heirs. I'm feeling very well, Gerald. It's nice to see you again." He patted my knee.

"It's nice to see you in such good spirits," I said. "But I don't want you to give me any money, or leave me any. I have some from my Grandfather MacMahon *and* from my Grandfather Higgins. More than enough to go on and take my Ph.D., if I wanted to. Not that I want to, at the moment, but the money is there."

He nodded. "Nevertheless, I have put in trust the sum of $5,000. You can draw on it now, it's in the Lyons bank, or you can leave it there. Or you can draw half of it now and leave the rest there. It isn't part of my estate and it isn't referred to in my will. It's not actually a trust fund. It's really a $5,000 savings account, drawing interest right now, and in your name." He tapped the tips of his fingers and thumbs together. "I've given this a lot of thought. You solved some of my problem by turning down the jobs teaching. I want this project finished, if possible in my lifetime. I promise you not to interfere, and when you've finished, if you care to show it to me, I'd naturally be most anxious to see it. However, I won't insist. If you let me see it, I may correct your facts, if I see any errors. But otherwise I won't interfere. I depend on you to comply with our agreement last Christmas. If there is any blame to be fixed, it must be on me."

"I may not see it that way. I've thought of that."

"Believe me, that's the way it was, and whatever kindly feelings you may have toward me, that's the way it was. I haven't come to that part in my manuscript. In any case, to get back to the money. I want you to have it because by the time you've finished you will have spent at least the better part of two years on our collaboration."

"I suppose so, maybe a little less."

He shook his head and held up his hand as a signal not to interrupt him. He looked straight ahead and away from me. "This is what I've been leading up to, and I want to be careful how I express it. If I'm clumsy, you may want to give up the whole project."

"I don't think you'll be clumsy."

"Well, then, I'll say it, and I promise you this is the last condition I'll impose, but it's a big one. When you have digested all the material I've been sending you and will send you, and you begin to do the actual writing—I want you to write the truth, not necessarily as I saw it, but as you see it. Then, when you've finished the writing, I want you to put the whole thing away in a safe place. I don't want you to show it to anyone for at least twenty years. Now wait a second. I know what you're going to say, but let me go on. I don't want you to show it to anyone else, for at *least* twenty years, because twenty years from now, I want you to get it out of the vault, or wherever you plan to keep it, and read what you have written. You'll be in your forties then, middle-aged, and you'll have lived a great deal.

81

I want you to *write* it as a young man, but I want you to pass judgment on it as an older man. You may object to that because you feel that your judgment is as good now as it will ever be. It isn't, Gerald. Believe me, it isn't. You have compassion now, as I've often said, but no man your age has as much as he will have when he's forty-two or -three. Hold still, I haven't quite finished. Then, twenty years from now, if you think my story has any value, I hope you will publish it, privately or otherwise. And that's all."

"Well, I suppose you *have* anticipated my principal objection," I said. "It isn't whether my judgment is going to be any better twenty years from now. But if the story has value, why withhold it for twenty years? Why not publish it privately when it's finished, and get some good out of it now?"

"Because twenty years is a minute in time. Oh, you'll see. Also, and I haven't considered this before. But twenty years from now you may regret having put your name to the project. You may wish you had waited. You'll understand that, too, but I don't expect you to understand it now."

"Twenty years," I said. "That's almost as long as I've lived. That's a lifetime."

"No it isn't. It's a very incomplete lifetime," he said. "Gerald, waiting for twenty years is a kind of self-protection for you. Also, if you write it now, knowing it's not going to be published for twenty years, you're not going to have to hold back as you might if it were going to be published a year or two from now. In twenty years, all the principal people in my story will be dead."

"I thought they were already dead."

"No, they're not. I lied to you."

"Who is still alive, for instance?"

He looked at me as though he were prepared to have me strike him. "Chester Calthorp is still alive."

"You told me he was dead."

"I lied to you. He's still living. I don't think it's likely that you'll ever see him, but you're bound to find out that he's alive."

"Where does he live?"

"I won't tell you, Gerald, and I must ask you not to try to find out. You must respect my wishes in this. In fact, I must ask you to give me your word of honor that you'll never try to get in touch with Chester Calthorp."

"I'm sorry, Mr. Millhouser. I can't do that."

"Then I'm going to *put* you on your honor. As an honorable man, as your grandfather's grandson, as a man that has been receiving my

82

most intimate confidences for eight months, you're honor-bound to respect my confidences. And I consider that what I've just told you is part of those confidences."

"I don't. You just said I was sure to find out that Calthorp is still alive."

"He means nothing to you except as a principal in my story. You never would have heard about him otherwise, his name wouldn't have meant a thing to you."

"That's certainly true."

"Therefore he *is* part of those confidences that you must respect. There is no other way to look at it. Not for a man of honor. You know, Gerald, I would not be obliged to accept your word of honor if I thought it was worthless. I could refuse to accept the word of a dishonorable man. And what is the difference? The difference is simply that you trust some men without their giving their word, and others you can't trust under any oath known to God or man. I trust you, and this is one time when it's literally true that I *impose* my trust in you."

I rejected the compliment. "You haven't been completely candid with me, Mr. Millhouser."

"I agree. I haven't. But you haven't changed. You're still a man of honor, and if you want to give up our project, you're entirely free to. But I don't release you from your duty to respect all that I've told you. I haven't even any fear that you won't respect it."

"Not even a little fear?"

"That's unworthy of you. You can be angry if you like, but don't have recourse to cheap cynicism," he said. "I think you'd better go now, Gerald. Don't you? You see where we're headed? And we've had a good friendship." He reached out his hand and I shook it and left him. I drove to my grandmother's and left word with the maid that I would not be home for dinner, and then went to Paul Burkitis's speakeasy and joined some friends of my Lyons boyhood. Paul's whiskey was raw but pure. I remember very little of that evening except that at about two in the morning we all went out to the Glen for a swim and the shock of the cold water sobered me up.

I was having an eleven o'clock breakfast and my grandmother came in and enthroned herself at the table. "You had one too many last night," she said.

"Did I, Grandma?"

"There'll be none of that while you're in this house. What you do at home is for your father and mother to deal with, but I tolerate no roistering in this house."

"Did I roister?"

"You scraped the fender on my car, and I'm sending the bill to your father."

"I'll pay it."

"Then pay it. It'll be three dollars. But I've a notion to make your father pay it and tell him the circumstances and the condition you were in."

"Ah, it's a severe woman you are, Grandma. A severe woman and that's the truth."

"Burkitis's, wasn't it? I've a good mind to have that schwakie run out of town."

"You sound like a Kluxer. All I did was scrape your fender, and I'll pay for that."

"Call me a Kluxer and I'll break this cane over your head. I take no impertinence from your mother and I'll have none from you, remember that. Robert Millhouser phoned. That's where you got started on the drink, I suppose."

"No, come to think of it, he didn't offer me a thing."

"He left word you're to call him. What's this odd friendship with you and Robert Millhouser? What are you doing, gab-gab-gabbing with an old man three times your age? You *and* your father, going to Protestant colleges."

"One Protestant college. The same one. Is it a kiss you'll be afther giving me, Granny-of-mine."

"Don't come near me. A whiff of your breath'd knock a horse over dead. If you're contemplating another such performance, go up now and pack your valise. Sober, you're always welcome. With drink in you I don't want you on the premises. Mind now, I'm in earnest."

"Was it talkin' to Robert Millhouser you were, Grandma, or did he be the greatest misfortune converse with the hired woman?"

She blinked her eyes very slowly and turned her lips inward. "The name of Higgins is one I never thought Irish, so no more of your sarcastic imitations of a brogue. *I* spoke to him. He asked were you home. Yes, but sleeping off a drunk I should have told him, but for the shame and disgrace. Then please ask him to telephone me. Good day, Mrs. MacMahon. Good day to you, Robert Millhouser . . . If you wish privacy, pull the door to, and I'm sure no one in this house is the least bit interested in your conversation."

The telephones—there were competing lines—were in a niche under the front stairs. I called Robert Millhouser on the Bell system because I knew that on that line he had extensions upstairs and down, and on the Nesquehela Valley line he had only one connection. "I was

84

hoping to catch you before you left town," he said. "Just to say good-bye and wish you good fortune."

"I'd like to talk to you," I said.

"Come right out," he said.

It was true that I wanted to talk to him and true, too, that he was the only man in Lyons I did want to talk to. He gave me some iced tea, which was good for my thirst, and as we talked I felt better. I have held back from the reader all the details that were contained in his manuscript; they will be revealed later, in toto. But here I can say that they were of such an intimate nature that they inevitably affected our relationship. I think it is accurate to attribute Robert Millhouser's cheerful mood on the previous day to the fact that he had been for eight months unburdening himself. Conversely, I knew, or I know now, that regardless of my genuine enthusiasm for the project, I was a somewhat uncomfortable confidant. Here, too, I will call the reader's attention, perhaps unnecessarily, to the numerous occasions when the project was nearly abandoned; in almost every case it was Robert Millhouser who was changing his mind or practically inviting me to change mine. I make this comment now because as of this July day in 1927 I had already learned that Robert Millhouser was a somewhat capricious man, not at all the steady person that his quiet life and regular habits had led me to believe him to be. In less than a year I had had to reject my lifelong impressions of Robert Millhouser, and while doing so I had been the not unwilling object of confidences that would have been remarkable in their candor if they had come from someone my own age. From a man aged seventy-two they provided a test of my own maturity, and it was a test that secretly I was often unequal to. I think now that if the early events he described had not occurred when he was about my own age, I would not have continued the collaboration. But he had managed to transport me back to the 1870's, to make that time and all of his time come alive to me, and he had done it through his own personality and not by his imitations of Henry James. I understood vaguely the reasons for this power: he was a man who had killed someone close to him; he had the quality of refinement that contradicted his most scandalous act; he was punctiliously polite to me; and he was that rare man, the completely self-sufficient man, dependent on no one else and thereby giving off an impression of quiet strength and dignity, and this strength and charm were available to me. I had no good answer to my grandmother's curiosity, any more than Robert Millhouser had been able to answer his mother when she asked him why Chester Calthorp sought his company.

When I arrived that day at Robert Millhouser's house he did not press me to tell him why I wanted to talk to him. He permitted me to describe what I could remember of the night before, which I did in fragmentary fashion while gulping his iced tea and smoking many cigarettes. "I've been wondering," he said, when I finished. "Are you flaming youth? Are you what I read about?"

"I guess I qualify. Yes, I guess someone that didn't know me would put me in that category. I have one of the right cars and a coonskin coat, and I even have a silver flask."

"Then you're not, really, are you?"

"Who is? Whenever I read about my generation I think they must be writing about the University of Michigan. I don't know anybody there, that's why I pick that particular place. But I don't know any at Princeton, I didn't know any at Lafayette."

"Any what?"

"Flaming youth. I know plenty of wild ones, male and female, but by the time they reach print I don't believe in them."

"Yes, but Gerald, if someone saw you at two o'clock this morning, driving your sporty runabout and carrying on at the Glen . . . ?"

"I guess so. Yes, I qualify."

"Superficially. But you don't want to be classified with the younger generation."

"I don't mind being the younger generation, because I am. But I do mind being flaming youth."

"But you do everything they do. You didn't mention any young women at last night's goings-on. Were there any?"

"Not last night."

"If there had been, what would have happened?"

"Depends entirely on the girl."

"Sexual intercourse?"

"It's been known to happen."

"To you?"

"Why not? It depends on the girl."

"Does that happen all the time? I mean, do the girls always give in? Is that part of flaming youth?"

"Not by a long shot. Most of the girls don't, but not *all* of them don't."

"Well, the better class."

"Generally, no. Some, yes."

"Then most of them are virgins when they marry."

"Oh, I didn't say that."

"Then they're *not* virgins when they marry?"

"Maybe fifty percent of them are, the kind of girl you're talking

86

about. It's only a guess, but if you live in a fraternity house and you stop to think of the girls you know that have gone the limit, I don't see how there can be more than fifty percent stay virgins right down to the altar. That's allowing for some bragging by the Don Juans. You allow for that, but the girls don't tell the truth by any means. I know a girl that was supposed to be a virgin, but I can tell you myself that she isn't."

"Of your own personal knowledge."

"My own personal knowledge."

"Tell me about her."

I laughed. "I'll tell you. I wouldn't tell anyone else. She's a girl that lives in Allentown, her brother is a classmate of mine."

"Fraternity brother of yours?"

"All right, yes. I've known her for four years and every time her name came up the good brethren would say thumbs-down, nothing there, not even necking. But I've been laying her for four years."

"Laying her?"

"That's what we say. A girl is a lay, or she's not a lay."

"So you lay a lay?"

"I've never heard that before, but it's logical."

"Where does this take place?"

"At her house, mostly. I've gone there for the night and she'll come to my room or I'll go to hers. Once in a while when she's going to be alone, in the afternoon."

"And no one suspects?"

"No. That's over, though. She's engaged to be married."

"But weren't you ever in love with each other?"

"Neither of us."

"But she must have loved you at first."

"She didn't, though. She had this reputation—she was brought up so strictly. I guess I was the first one that ever made the effort, and there it was. It was so easy that I was scared."

"Was she your first?"

"Well, my third, but the first nice girl. My first was right here in Lyons, when I was fifteen."

"South Ward, no doubt."

"No doubt."

"But your friend's sister—"

"I never had a real date with her. That is, I never took her to a football game, or a dance or anything like that. She had some guy at Lehigh that was stuck on her, then she broke that off and this year she announced her engagement to a fellow from Wilkes-Barre."

"Have you seen her since she announced her engagement?"

"Once. She wanted to make sure I'd never told anyone about her. I convinced her that I hadn't and so we had one last lay—the last lay of the minstrel, I thought later—and we parted very good friends. She said she was going to be faithful to her husband, but if it didn't pan out she'd let me know."

"She must have been in love with you."

"No, I'll tell you. I don't think you'll understand this, but I was the only Catholic that was ever allowed in her house. You probably don't know Allentown. There's one ward there that's solid Irish, but the town is old-fashioned Pennsylvania Dutch. In 1927 they still believe that the Pope has designs on this country. This girl's family, they're nice, quite well-off, decent people. The father went to Muhlenberg, the mother went to Bishopthorp. They have a very comfortable house out near the Traylor. This girl had her own car, a Ford coupe, and the father had a Cadillac with a big Shrine emblem on the radiator. The first time I was invited to the house my friend, the girl's brother, told me not to say anything about being a Catholic. Well, why would I? I don't go around asking people what they are, and I certainly don't tell people when I meet them, 'I'm Gerald Higgins and if you say anything against the Pope I'll punch you in the nose.' If there's anything going to be said against the Pope, I'll say it."

"So I've noticed."

"Well, the girl felt the same way about Catholics as her father and mother. And I finally got it out of her, what she felt about me. She could never marry me, she didn't want to marry me. Not that I ever asked her to. But she *liked* me, she liked me more than anyone she'd ever known. And *I* figured out—she didn't tell me this—that she could be as female as she wanted to be with me, and yet never have to think of me as a potential husband. Of course her family did find out that I was a Catholic, eventually, and they made an exception in my case. By that time they were used to me. And they were very pleased that I didn't seem to take any interest in their daughter."

"Forbidden fruit," said Robert Millhouser.

"Exactly. And I was a Zeta Psi. That carried a lot of weight. As one of the boys used to say, 'If you're a Zete, you rate.' "

"Your being a Zeta Psi doesn't explain her amatory interest in you, Gerald. I imagine that you're a very—forthright man where women are concerned. Have you ever been in love?"

"I'm in love now, with a girl in Washington, D. C."

"Oh, yes."

"Why do you say, 'Oh, yes'? I've never mentioned her before."

"Yes you have. Not by name. But in one of your letters you spoke of going to our nation's capital to see a girl."

"So I did, by God."

"Is all going smoothly?"

"It never did run smooth, according to W. Shakespeare. Oh, it's—it's good."

"I'm glad to hear it. I'm not going to ask you about her."

"And I know why," I said.

"I rather imagine you do."

"Because I've been talking about the other girl."

He nodded. "We understand a lot of things, you and I."

It was my turn to nod. "Specifically, we both know that I want to go back to work on the manuscript, on your terms."

He smiled. "I've known that for at least fifteen minutes, Gerald. You've been matching my confidences with some of your own. That's the first time that's ever happened."

"It probably won't be the last," I said.

And so, once again, I take up the story of Robert Millhouser, begging the reader's indulgence for the interruptions, and offering the explanatory assurance that the story behind the story is relevant. I have often wondered, as I watched newsreels of structural workers on skyscrapers and mountain climbers on precipices, what the anonymous cameraman was thinking and doing.

●

LONDON BROUGHT OUT a different Chester Calthorp, and the differences were more fundamental than the affectation of an English gentleman's speech that Robert had noticed in the ship. To Robert's complete surprise, Chester gave himself up to the enjoyment of simply being in the city that he admitted he loved best, and in so doing, in so frankly enjoying himself, he became a young man again. Robert had expected to see an even more austere Chester and one who would be at great pains to make himself out to be older than his twenty-six years. Publicly, on their walks and in the shops and clubs and the town houses they visited, Chester comported himself with careful dignity. It was in their rooms at the hotel in Clarges Street that Robert saw the other Chester, so unlike the blasé man of Spring Garden Street.

"You like this town," said Robert one evening.

"Like it? Like London? You imply that it would be possible to *dis*like it."

"We haven't *seen* much of it."

"I can tell by your heavy emphasis on *seen,* and the merry twinkle in your German eye, that you're referring to the fog. My dear Robert, have you ever been on Delaware Bay? Do you forget the number of times that you walked past the Delta Psi door because it was invisible to the eye?"

"What else would it be invisible to?"

"Well, to answer your question as it should be answered—to the imagination. I can bear with Philadelphia for such long periods of time because now and then something will remind me of London. When it isn't a house, an object, or the sound of a hansom cab, it's a man or a woman. The men and women I choose as my friends. Four, five, six generations of residence in Philadelphia has made them Philadelphians, it's true. But if you shut out their atrocious speech and study only their faces and figgers, they could be English. And of course they are, racially. They still belong to the English race. As purely English as most Englishmen, when you stop to think of it. My favorite Philadelphians know their ancestry and so do I, and it's been English marrying English all through those five or six generations, with an occasional infusion of Welsh and Scottish. But no more, I should say, than half the English families. Your gray German eyes—"

"That I got from my Irish mother."

He hesitated. "Is that true? If it is, you know, it almost *proves,* not *dis*proves the point I was about to make. I was about to say that you're sometimes taken for English because you are a throwback to the Saxons. Till you open your mouth. But of course if your mother had the same eyes, the point is too obvious to dwell on."

"Is that what you were about to say?"

"No, but that was quick thinking, wasn't it? Don't think you can trick me or trap me, Robert. I'm having much too good a time, and when I'm enjoying myself I'm especially alert. Are *you* having a good time? I hope you are. It would be a great disappointment to me if you weren't."

"It'd be a disappointment to me, too. But I am having a good time."

"For the moment I wasn't thinking about the disappointment to you. I was thinking of myself and no one else, as I usually prefer to do. As we all do. As you just did. You weren't interested in my disappointment. You were interested in your own, although we weren't talking about yours, we were talking about mine. *Ja? Nein?"*

"Das ist richtig."

"Is that German?"

"I think so."

"I could never learn the beastly language. Not to imply that it would have baffled me. I can *learn* anything, if I'm of a mind to. Things that one *learns* come easy to me, and there'll always be some-

90

thing I'm learning. But the fascinating experiences of the intellect don't occur as a result of study. Oh, heavens, no. They are the result of following, or not following, one's instincts. *Then* they *become* subjects for study and, possibly, one has learned something. But the learning is secondary to the experience of following the instinct. By the way, I want you to find yourself something to do Monday week. I've accepted an invitation that didn't include you, and I don't think you'd enjoy yourself. There I am, thinking of your happiness, your well-being. I must guard against that."

"Where are you going Monday week? Or is that none of my business?"

"If I were to say that it's none of your business, would you be grievously hurt? Yes, you might. I am dining with Lord Repperton."

"Who is he? Have I met him?"

"You were introduced to him, but obviously you made no impression on each other. He was one of the guests at Sara Paulsby's. Does that help you?"

"Not a bit."

"Well, I don't propose to help you much more. A tall, very slender, youngish man."

"Dissipated?"

"Yes. Although I shouldn't put it in such a grandmotherly way. Dedicated to his excesses."

"I'll bet he'd rather be called dissipated."

"And you'd lose. It was Repperton himself that told me he was dedicated to his excesses. We got on famously. Can you find something to occupy yourself that night?"

"Yes. I'll go to bed early. We've been on the go ever since we got here."

"Ending all too soon."

"We don't have to leave when we said we would. There's nothing in Paris that we *have* to do."

"But there is. More to the point, when you come to London you let your friends know how long you intend to stay. If you stay longer —no. It just isn't done. I don't like strangers hanging around Philadelphia, either. I want them to go when they said they would."

"That suits me. I may like Paris better."

"Chacun à son goût."

They had lunch at a club every day but Saturday and Sunday, alternating the two clubs at which they had guest cards, an arrangement that sometimes had them eating turbot on successive days and mutton on successive days. But Chester was as loyal to English cooking as to most other customs of the country, and as a recent product of a university and before that of a prep school, Robert had not had time to become fastidious about food. Chester had prepared thoroughly for their visit to London, and their evenings in town and their two weekends were all spoken for, except for the two Mondays that Chester had left open. On the evening of Chester's engagement with Lord Repperton they had a glass of sherry in Chester's room. "No full dress?" said Robert.

"No," said Chester. "As a matter of fact, Robert, I may be very late and I might not even get home at all. So don't you wait up for me."

"Not a chance of that," said Robert. "I'm looking forward to twelve hours' sleep. But why don't you pack a small handbag?"

"I can do for myself," said Chester, peevishly. "If you want me to throw a sop to your curiosity, I wasn't invited for the night. It just may turn out that way."

"Don't bark at me. If you want to get drunk with his Lordship, great!" Robert got up to go.

"Please, Robert, don't *you* be petulant. That's my prerogative."

"No it isn't. I'm not your guest on this trip. I'm your traveling companion and that's all. I pay my own way, and if you're going to bark at me I'm sure I could find my way around Europe by myself."

"Oh, dear, now what have I done? Shall I be abject? I'll hold it against you, but to restore peace I'll *be* abject. Temporarily."

"Oh, rubbish."

"Robert, I must tell you. Douglass Repperton is the man I most wanted to meet in London. The one man in London that Alice Sterling wanted me to meet. You remember my cousin Alice Sterling, she was so haughty?"

"Yes, I remember her, not with any pleasure."

"She doesn't know you. She doesn't like to be baffled, and you baffled her. Most people do baffle Alice because she makes it difficult for people to get to know her. But she's a dear old whore and I'm fond of her."

"You took the words right out of my mouth," said Robert.

"A painless extraction, I'm sure of that. Now Robert, I've been looking forward to this evening. It'll be such a triumph to tell Alice I dined with Repperton, at *his* invitation and without any assistance from her. So don't you make me leave here with *you* on my mind. Don't be selfish, Robert."

Robert Millhouser laughed. "How could I be, to someone as unselfish as you are."

Chester bowed his head in mock humility. "I daresay you're entitled to your *mot juste,*" he said. "Now we're even, so wish me a pleasant evening and go have your cambric tea and sweet dreams."

It had been their custom to have breakfast together in Chester's room. At ten o'clock, when there had been no knock on his door, Robert rang for the waiter. "Has Mr. Calthorp had his breakfast?"

"No sir, he has not. Does Mr. Millhouser wish to order, sir?"

"Yes. Has Mr. Calthorp's room been occupied?"

"No sir."

Robert gave his order and was eating his egg when Chester tapped on the door and entered. "Good," he said, looking at the food. "You didn't wait." He walked to the window. "Do you want to see a handsome turnout? Quickly."

"Let me finish my breakfast. I don't care that much about horses. Did you drink quantities of port?"

"Why won't you look at Lord Repperton's horses? One of the sights of London, not to be found in your guidebooks. Matched in every respect, and so are the coachman and footman. The men are twins. Come look, don't be stubborn."

"Have them wait till I've finished."

"Too late now, they've gone."

"Ah, me. Too bad," said Robert. "What is it they say? 'The port is with you.' Was that how it was? 'The port is with you, Douglass.' 'The port is with *you,* Chester.' Did you uphold the honor of Philadelphia, show him you could drink any Englishman under the table?"

"What we drank was much too good for any such contest. And it wasn't port. It was French brandy, which we'll be having in its native habitat in forty-eight hours' time."

"But I gather you did have a good time."

"A delightful evening. And you?"

"I wrote some letters and I borrowed a book from you. *Hiawatha,* by Henry Wadsworth Longfellow."

"Then you had no trouble getting to sleep. At least *I* carry it with me wherever I go, and I can open it almost anywhere and as if by magic—I've told my acquaintances at The Jeff. If I'm to undergo surgery, no chloroform, please. Send for my *Hiawatha,* hold it at arm's length, and there's my anaesthesia. They could take out my gizzard and I'd awake refreshed. Curious, of course, about the embroidery they had done on my round pink tummy, but otherwise none the worse for my experience."

"Well, I'd never read it before."

"Oh, then I must buy you a copy. In one small limp-leather volume you have an entire apothecary's shopful of soporific. When you get old, and *Hiawatha* has lost its anaesthetic potency, I'll prescribe a much stronger draft. Plato's *Republic.*"

"You chatter away without bothering to find out whether *Hiawatha* put me to sleep."

"But I know that it did. I can see that it did."

"Well, you're right."

"To be sure. I must say that your Irish mother has shown great good sense in not trying to force *Hiawatha* on you. It isn't a book for children. The names are much too hard."

"She read me *Evangeline*."

"Oh, then let's clear out of here quickly. How can you bear to be in this England, with its naughty, cruel King George? I reread *Evangeline* at the University. It was uproariously funny, Robert. Or didn't you think so?"

"I thought it was very sad."

"But that's what you were supposed to think, and *that's* not *thinking*." He yawned. "Heigh-ho. I did rather well, didn't I?"

"How?"

"Oh, surely you didn't think you could embarrass me by finding such trash in my book-bag. You did think so, didn't you? 'I can scarcely wait to twit dear old Chester. Chester with *Hiawatha*.' You were going to have a bit of sport with me, weren't you? Well, I knew that the moment you spoke. I know you very well, Robert Millhouser. Sometimes I—"

"Sometimes you what?"

He shook his head. "Never mind, never mind. Now let me see. Today must be White's because yesterday was Boodle's and tomorrow is Boodle's so today must be White's. I was very good at algebra. Wasn't it fun to remove a vinculum?"

"I think you're still a bit tipsy."

"Tipsy? I'm roaring drunk."

"Then go sleep it off. Here, do you want your *Hiawatha?*"

He turned toward the door. "I'll sleep. Not the sleep of the just, but I'll sleep."

"Hold on, what about lunch?"

Chester paused with his hand on the door-handle. "Don't count on me. For mullet or mutton. Don't count on me. I can go longer without food than without sleep. Wake me for tea, please."

Until now Robert never had seen Chester Calthorp show any effects of alcohol. He had, therefore, no recollection for comparative purposes. If this was "the morning after the night before" it told nothing of the night before, the amount consumed, the pleasure experienced, the remorse induced. Robert himself, brought up through childhood on sips of beer and wine and heavily fortified mince pies and plum puddings, possessed a high tolerance for alcohol and had

94

been drunk four times in his life—after his own and three other fraternity initiations. He was known as a man with a cast-iron stomach and a hollow leg, the conventional tributes to his drinking capacity. But too much liquor made him neither destructive, belligerent, lubricious, extravagant, witty, sick, or sad. At the fraternity initiations he had joined his brethren in song, and in due course had quietly gone to sleep. Chester had been present at two of the four initiation parties, and Fish House punch, a pleasantly aromatic, pleasant-tasting concoction, filled the bowl. Robert did not keep count of Chester's glasses, but if Chester had been made drunk, Robert would have remembered it. More notably, Chester had *not* been drunk. In the years of their friendship they never had discussed drunkenness, and Chester's abrupt announcement of his present condition was doubly significant: for its mention of drunkenness, *per se,* and for the remarkable admission. It was, Robert thought, part of that side of Chester that had only appeared in London, but on second thought it was *not* part of that side. It was part of Chester, undoubtedly, but to be drunk and to say so did not belong in the rigmarole of gentlemanliness that Chester so gladly obeyed in Philadelphia and in London revered. On this trip, Robert now knew, he would get to see, and possibly to understand, a Chester Calthorp that in Philadelphia was so concealed as to be nonexistent. But it would be the real Chester.

In Paris it was a still different Chester Calthorp, different, that is, from the Philadelphia presentation. Two weeks and a few days in London had been sufficient for Chester to be processed to the degree that would produce the polish and attitude he chose to display to the French. "They'll be getting ready for their Exposition," said Chester. "But since I chose to ignore ours entirely, I'll ignore their preparations. We can be comfortably elsewhere while the Paris Exposition is actually in progress, but if I know the French, and I do, we are liable to get a foretaste of what next year's tourists are in for. Now the best way to prevent that is to encourage them to think we're English. That shouldn't be very difficult. Indeed, it should make some things easier for you. Your command of the French language, for instance. It's woefully inadequate, isn't it?"

"Most likely."

"Good. And don't try to make it any better than it is, at least when you're dealing with hotel people, servants, shopkeepers, cabmen. Be as English as you know how. Assume the attitude that the French people should bloody well learn the English language, and that their failure to do so is due to laziness and chicanery. I repeat, that is the proper attitude for dealing with people who want to separate you from your ready cash. It is *not* the correct attitude when we begin to move in artistic circles or high society. There you can make an effort, of a different kind. You can put your best foot forward, and if it turns out to be a *faux pas,* let them know that you're an American. The French intellectuals still don't know many Americans, but they feel kindly toward us. I don't know why, but they do. But I warn you, never let a shopkeeper know you're an American. They have only seen rich Americans, and too many of them, heaven knows. Oh, yes. I've told you to be as ignorant as you please of the French language. But not of the French monetary system. Aha, no. If you want to create the illusion that you're English, you must begin immediately to master exchange. As an Englishman, a convincing one, you will know the value of the centime as well as the franc."

"I've just begun to master the shilling."

"Have you mastered it?"

"I guess so."

"You know what three-and-six is, quickly."

"About fifty-six cents."

"Hmm."

"I mean eighty-one cents."

"I had a scheme, but it won't work. It works with me, but I'm more familiar with English money. Whenever I want to be really English with a French shopkeeper I make him explain to himself, not to me, but to himself, the differences between the franc and the shilling. I'm afraid that a man who thinks three-and-six is fifty-six cents would get hopelessly confused, not to say impoverished. For the first month or two, you'd better let me make the purchases, over, say, ten francs. You'll catch on. Watch me. I'm rather proud of my ability to outwit the little bastards. The Calthorps have always had an acute sense of smell, where money was concerned, and if I'd gone into Calthorp & Company I'd have shown those Drexels. It humiliates me to have our letters of credit on Drexel, Morgan instead of Calthorp, Morgan, or Calthorp, Harjes. But I will say for the Drexels, they've made it easier for me to take up painting than it might have been if the Drexels hadn't been artistic, too. Philadelphia history, dear boy. Pay no attention. It can never be of the slightest value to a resident of Lyons, Pennsylvania."

"Well, to tell you the truth—"

"And you always do."

"Always. To tell you the truth, Philadelphia history isn't going to be much help to me now, and another thing, I may not go back to Lyons, Pennsylvania. Lyons, Nesquehela County, Pennsylvania."

"If you can paint. But we won't get a professional verdict on that for another year, so let's make ourselves as comfortable as we can."

96

Robert was not sure he liked the sound of that; it conveyed to him the first hint of what actually was to come. At home he had been convinced of Chester's sincere desire to devote himself to his own painting as well as to be an encouraging and strict mentor to Robert. His only misgivings in Philadelphia had been based on his doubt of Chester's ability to renounce the social life he thoroughly enjoyed. As against that doubt, however, there had been the fact that Chester did accomplish a considerable amount of work in Philadelphia and therefore (but not really therefore) would be more likely to work harder in Paris. Robert's doubts and misgivings soon became, in Paris, fears and convictions.

They took a flat in the 18th arrondissement, half the top floor of a four-story house. Chester, during the negotiations, wore his most somber clothes; all black, he explained to Robert, in the manner of many painters, so that the agent would believe that he was a painter; but black of good quality so that there would be assurance of his ability to pay. Chester spoke knowingly and critically of the north light and slightingly of the furniture so that he could argue with the agent that there should be a deduction for storing the chests and chairs he objected to. He was fully aware of the uselessness of the argument; the agent would neither remove the furniture nor reduce the rent. But having gained his victory the agent felt more kindly toward the American and when the papers had been signed, agreed with Chester that the pieces lacked beauty. "You see, of course, what I've done?" said Chester to Robert. "Monsieur Langlois knows that I never expected to win. He knows that I know what he knows. But we have conducted ourselves in proper fashion. I have given him the opportunity to score a victory and to feel proud of having done so. He can report his victory to the owners, thereby raising himself in their esteem, having earned his commission, and having earned it in a business duel with a worthy opponent, me. When we want a favor that won't cost any money, Monsieur will be on our side. You, on the other hand, can't call me money-grubbing, because if I were, I'd charge you a small commission for negotiating this happy affair."

"To be sure. When do we start work?"

Chester waved his arm in a 180-degree arc that was supposed to indicate all France. "There it is. Paint it."

Until now Robert's only audience while sitting at an easel had been Moses Hatfield, and when he took his equipment outdoors he could not banish the self-consciousness that afflicted him while trying to paint. The silent but always present onlookers of all ages and stations would watch him for a few minutes and then pass on. But silent or not they were French, Parisians, and he could not finish so much as a charcoal sketch under their expert scrutiny. At Chester's insistence he next joined a life class, which strictly speaking was not a class but only a group of painters and sculptors who paid a small fee for studio space and the services of the model. Robert never had seen a mature female body in the nude, and his hand shook. In French his nearest neighbor made a small joke about overindulgence in alcohol, and Robert was grateful for the ready-made excuse and replied that he did not think he could paint that day. He did not return to the class, and explained to Chester that the air in the studio had been so bad that he got a headache. Chester promptly hired a model to come to the apartment.

The woman disrobed and went to the platform and asked Robert how she was to pose. But before he could give her an answer she became suspicious and asked him if he was really a painter, or a degenerate. "You do not look at me as a painter would look at me," she said. "To the contrary. If that is the kind of model you require, I do not co-operate." She quickly dressed and held out her hand for her money, but then seeing his extreme embarrassment she said: "I think you are not a bad man but lacking in experience. Paint me from memory and I will come again. If I like what you have done, I will stay." She was not more than twenty-five years old, but she patted his cheek as though he were a small boy.

When she had gone he made a quick sketch from vivid memory, not so much to qualify for her approval as to have something to show Chester. "It's not bad. It has humor," said Chester, later. "According to your discerning eye, the subject is in her fourth month and has a malignancy in the left breast, poor thing. But I thought you were going to paint her. Don't waste money on first-class models if you're only going to sketch them."

"Do you think she'd like it?"

"Who? The model? Don't give that a thought. And certainly don't give this one a thought. She has gonorrhea. Have I told you in time, or am I just a few hours too late?"

"I wouldn't touch her."

"No, I don't think you would. But you owe them nothing but common politeness. Their opinions are worthless, and so is their approval." Chester studied the sketch again, then turned to Robert. "You're quite sure that I'm not too late with my warning?"

"Of course I'm sure. Why do you ask?"

"The sketch has more than humor. What I took to be humor may be, on second thought, voluptuousness. It isn't humor, Robert! It's carnality. Let's not have her back again."

"I don't care. She's nothing to me. But I don't like your thinking that I had anything to do with her."

"Nor do I like to think it. I really don't want to nurse you through a dose of clap. You've never had one, have you?"

"Of course not."

"Don't say of course not. It wouldn't be the first time a young man's shyness and reserved manner could be traced to that."

"Damn you, I've never even fucked!"

"Oh," said Chester. "Then please forgive me. I mean that from the bottom of my heart, my black suspicious heart. I want you to forgive me, do you hear, Robert? Unless you do, I'll leave this room and never come back. I swear it. I'll leave, and never see you again."

"Oh, I forgive you. Nobody can ever tell what you're thinking anyway."

"But I meant that. If you hadn't forgiven me, I'd have left. I couldn't bear your unforgiveness."

"Well, don't make so much of it."

Chester's repentance lasted several days and was difficult to live with. It manifested itself in small favors and conversational courtesies and finally in the gift of a set of matching shirt studs, waistcoat buttons and sleeve links. The design was an intricate filigree in gold, containing in each unit a small star sapphire.

"Chester, I can't take a present like this from you."

"Why not?"

"Because presents should be exchanged, and I could never buy you anything as beautiful as this."

"Did you mean as beautiful, or as expensive?"

"In this case, both," said Robert. "The design is beautiful. Look at that workmanship. But it doesn't take an expert to know that it's expensive."

"I consider the exchange completed. Your answer to my question was artful, and beyond price. We'll say no more about it, shall we?"

"Yes, we'll say more about it. I can't accept it."

"Then give it to the *charbonnier!* When I buy a friend a gift it's because that gift is exactly suitable to that one person. If he doesn't agree with me, I've been wrong, and I don't want to see it again to remind me of my error. *Don't* give it to the *charbonnier.* He has dark brown eyes and black hair. It wouldn't suit him."

"You're making it difficult for me."

"As difficult as I know how. I'd like to make it impossible."

Robert laughed. "All right. You have. I'll accept it."

99

"Well I should think you would. Hereafter don't be so upstate-stodgy. So Dutchy."

"I wanted it all the time, to tell you the truth."

"Oh, I know that. That's not Dutchy. That's Dutch. German. You know a good thing when you see it. Now stop thinking about it. Just adopt it into your wardrobe. If you want to give me something in return, I'll take an early Millhouser, Paris period. It may turn out to have value thirty years from now."

"At the rate we're going, it'll be thirty years before I have an early Millhouser to show you."

"Why all the haste? We've been here scarcely a month."

"Closer to two."

"Is it that long?"

"You know it is."

"I could if I stopped to count, but don't chastise me for your indolence. And it hasn't been two months, not in Paris. It's been two months since we sailed for Europe. In that brief time you've made your first ocean voyage, you've had a whirl in the grandest city on earth, and you've had your first taste of Paris. What would you have been doing in Lyons, Pennsylvania? Cutting out pumpkins for Hallowe'en."

"Or painting."

"Don't dare speak of painting in Lyons, Pennsylvania, when you've only just arrived in Paris. In a hundred years there's never been a picture painted in Lyons, Pennsylvania."

"I could resent that."

"Not successfully. This is Paris, the home of painters. Not of painting, but of painters. Painters may not do their best work in Paris, but they must come here. You won't know till you leave how much Paris means to a painter."

"You accuse me of indolence, but in the same breath you manufacture excuses for not painting yourself."

"But I can paint. I'm already an excellent second-rate painter. So far you are only a dauber. It remains to be seen whether you'll ever be a first-rate dauber, but if you should ever turn out to be a, uh, fourth-rate painter, you'll owe some of it to the time you spend in Paris."

"Why?"

"Haven't I explained it to you?"

"No. You've only said that painters may not do their best work here, but they have to come here. You didn't say why."

"That should be a sufficient answer, but for you I'll try to explain further, with very little hope that you'll understand. In the first place, the wine is cheaper. Now I dare you to make some stodgy upstate comment on that. I dare you to."

"How can I? The wine *is* cheaper."

"You're a coward. You know that I've set a trap for you, and you smell my cleverness."

"Sure."

"Oh, all right. The wine is cheaper, and you're dying to say what has that got to do with painting, but you're a coward. I'll tell you what it has to do with painting. Painters are not only poor, they're stingy. Great bursts of generosity and extravagance don't hide the fact that they are stingy. *They have to be.* Every time a painter starts a new masterpiece—and he must every time he starts—he knows inside himself that he is limited to the size of his canvas. He would be limited even if he had the Great Wall of China to work on. Therefore, because he is limited by the size of his canvas, he is working under restrictions. The restrictions are three in number. They are the dimensions of his canvas—let's say twelve inches wide by eighteen inches long. In that twelve-by-eighteen area there are only a certain number of square inches in which he has to put everything he wants to say. Consequently, every fractional, minute stroke must count for something, every bead of paint in every stroke must count. He must have absolute, perfect and uninterrupted control. Infinite control. Infinite because it gets down to amounts of paint that are too tiny to be measured, and that is achieved only through a combination of muscular and nerval co-ordination that originates in the brain and the soul, and instantaneously passes down the arm to the tips of the fingers. Knowing this, even though he may never have thought of it, the mind of the painter becomes habituated to the exercise of his control in small things that are outside his art. And since we live in a practical world, a world in which the necessities and most of the pleasures are bought and sold, the painter's control is exercised most frequently in money transactions. Not, I hasten to add, in transactions that involve the sale of his work, but in dealings with the butcher, the baker, and above all, the purveyor of wine. Exhausting." He sighed.

"I'm inclined to agree with you," said Robert.

"Sum up for me."

"Well, the painter is so accustomed to thinking in small, restricted areas of canvas that the same thinking affects his spending of money. Painters usually like wine, wine is cheap in Paris, and Paris—but why Paris? Why not any place where the wine is cheap?"

"Are you suggesting that they would all go to Chicago if the wine were cheaper there?"

"I'm not suggesting anything. I'm just asking you a question. You say Chicago, but I say, why not Bordeaux?"

"What is there in Bordeaux? If you want me to explain why not Bordeaux, I can. I've been there. It's a way-station. Things are always going or coming there, the things they make. Ships and sealing-wax, as Mr. Lewis Carroll would say. And that's literally true in Bordeaux. They build ships, and they manufacture resin, which is in sealing wax, unless I'm mistaken. Bordeaux is too close to Spain, and obviously there are more Spanish painters in Paris than in Madrid. Bordeaux is laid out to facilitate the comings and goings I spoke of, and obviously Paris is not. Paris is built for meandering, and for getting lost, as you've already found out. Bordeaux came to your mind because we were talking about wine. Forget wine. In fact, let's not ask ourselves an unanswerable question. I don't even remember what it was."

"I do, but I'll forget it if you like. However, you said something I would like to go back to. You said an artist—"

"A painter."

"A painter is restricted by three things, and you went on to mention the width and length of his canvas. But you never mentioned the third thing that restricted him."

"I didn't, did I?"

"Well, what is it?"

"The cruel, secret knowledge of the limitations of his talent."

"Do you believe that a painter has that knowledge?"

"If he's any good he has. That's how I know I'll never be first-rate. I am good, I'll be better, but never great. I am a cripple, Robert. But if you ask me to explain that, you will be wasting your time, your extremely valuable, precious time, that you feel you're wasting already."

"Then I won't pursue the subject, but you believe that a painter is restricted by three dimensions? Those of his canvas, and the third one, imaginary, his fear of his mediocrity?"

"I didn't *say* mediocrity! A man can be first-rate and still have that fear. Oh, indeed! The great ones have it earlier and later than the fourth-raters, they always have it. Their greatness is in going on and on until they know they've gone as far as they can, then they still go on doing their best work, sometimes for a year, sometimes for ten years. Then, if they're lucky, they die. If they're easily frightened, they kill themselves while they're still able to do their best work, with some left undone."

"Would you ever commit suicide?"

"How could I? I don't care that much about anything. And I've protected myself by engaging in a large assortment of activities, so that if one thing ceases to interest me, I have others that will."

"I don't believe you. I think you care very deeply about some things."

"Then that's the most intelligent observation you've ever made about me," said Chester Calthorp. "I care greatly about a great many things. Have you always known that?"

"I guess so."

"Yes, you always have, without knowing why or what. One of the few, you are. Why should it be you instead of some other, *complex* man that can understand that much about me? You, simple and direct, rather than one of my mischievously complex friends. I shall have to give that a great deal of thought, and meanwhile make myself more complex so that you will have more trouble solving the great riddle of me."

"Oh, you're not so complex."

"Glad to hear you say that! Proves to me that your understanding of me is far, far from complete. For just a few seconds I was afraid of you."

"Because I may have understood you?"

"Naturally. And I was afraid *for* you. Because I'm convinced that only a complex man can understand me with any completeness, and I don't want you to become that. I owe your admiration for me the courtesy of, ah, some stimulation. I want to bring you out, to shake you out of your lethargy. But I don't want any harm to come to you in the process."

"You're not the first one that's tried that."

"Aha? Who else? Tell me all about him."

"At Mercersburg I had a Latin teacher."

"Yes."

"Well, he was the only one that went out of his way to treat me like a human being. I wasn't very good at Latin, and he used to be patient with me, explain things after class."

"How old was this man?"

"Oh, I guess about thirty-five or forty."

"And did he shake you out of your lethargy?"

"I don't want to joke about him, Chester. He hanged himself to a tree. That wasn't very long after my father died, and I didn't get over it for a long time. He didn't exactly take the place of my father, but he was the only one of the masters that—well, treated me like a human being."

"How did he do that?"

"Oh, for instance, when I'd recite, he'd correct me without making

103

me feel like an idiot. And he did one thing he shouldn't have done, I know, but he did it."

"What was that?"

"Before an exam. He said to me, 'Millhouser, if I were you I'd pay particular attention to—' and then told me the pages that we were going to have to translate in Caesar. Mind you, I had to study the stuff, but at least I knew what to study."

"Did you share the information with your classmates?"

"I told some, and I guess they told the others. I know we all passed."

"Did you have him in mind when you asked me if I'd ever commit suicide?"

"No. But after I said it I thought of him. Oh, he wasn't anything like you."

"How was he different?"

"From you? Well, he was poor, dressed shabbily, his beard was always in need of a trim. In the summer he always worked on a farm near Hagerstown, so that he wouldn't have to spend any of his school pay. There was a story that he was married once and his wife ran away with a medicine show. I don't know how true that was. His ambition was to save enough money to go to Rome and visit the catacombs."

"Did they ever find out why he hanged himself?"

"They said he was drunk. They found a jug near the tree."

"Is that *all* they said? Didn't they offer any other reason?"

"If you mean Mercersburg Academy, they didn't offer that much. They said he died suddenly, and that was all. But the fellows had all sorts of stories. Somebody stole his savings. He was caught with a wench. I never found out for sure."

"What did you *guess* was the reason?"

"The money was my first guess. But when I got a little older I wondered if perhaps he wasn't just tired of life."

"Ah. How old were you when you evolved that theory?"

"Twenty, I guess. He used to say to me, 'High ideals and lofty aspirations, Millhouser. High ideals and lofty aspirations.' "

"Odd. I had a tutor that used the same words exactly."

"I'll bet I know where your tutor went to college."

"I'm not sure that I do. Where?"

"Franklin & Marshall, in Lancaster."

"Franklin. I don't remember the Marshall. But now I remember the Franklin, because I assumed that it was one of our minor halls of learning in Philadelphia."

"It's a damned good little college in Lancaster. It's called Frank-

104

lin & Marshall now. The Marshall part used to be in Mercersburg, but not since I went there."

"You can't expect me to keep up with all these little upstate, upstart seminaries. You were saying?"

"I was saying that I could guess where your tutor came from, because he used the phrase 'high ideals and lofty aspirations.' It's a Franklin & Marshall saying."

"Is it? I'm sure you'd find it some place else, too."

They remained in Paris until after Christmas, Robert's first Christmas away from home. It was not, however, a time for homesickness. They spent several days in Switzerland and were back in Paris for a New Year's Eve party which for some of their friends lasted beyond the Feast of the Epiphany. Chester was now making no pretense of applying himself to his painting. He had been taken up by a group of Englishmen and Americans who were at, or trying to get in, the École des Beaux Arts. He excused himself lamely. "I may try for a diploma," he said. "Philadelphia could stand some new architects."

"Then why don't you? It would be better than just loafing," said Robert.

"On the other hand, loafing, as you call it—"

"Is an art in itself."

"Is it? Do you say that?"

"No, but you were going to."

"Was I? I was *really* going to say that loafing is something I've never learned to do. I've always been so busy."

"You kept busy at home, but I haven't noticed you overworking yourself here."

"You'll never see me overworking myself. The very word carries its own warning. Overworking—it conjures up a picture of an emaciated dray-horse lying on the cobblestones, usually being flogged by a heartless Irishman. Or half-Irishman."

"That's me, I suppose. Chester, I wouldn't mind if I thought you were having a good time. But you're not."

"I'm not?"

"It doesn't seem so to me. Even your architect friends get some sleep. They have to because they're working. Where do you go when you don't come home all night?"

"I visit other friends."

"That I don't know?"

"That sometimes *I* don't know. I observe that you are not wearing your watch and fob."

"Yes I am," said Robert. Then looked at his waistcoat. "Well, I'm not, but don't change the subject."

"We are on the subject, very much so. You ask me where I go? I am learning to be a *filou,* a pickpocket. Here is your watch and your Delta Psi charm."

"Oh, for God's sake, Chester. One of these nights you'll be found lying in an alley with a knife in your back."

"They've been having more success with neckerchiefs. It's almost impossible to stifle the scream of a stiletto victim. Garroting doesn't summon every flic in the neighborhood."

"Is any of this true, that you're hanging out with crooks?"

"I relieved you of your watch, and I couldn't have done that six months ago. I did it quite well, too. As a rule it takes a team of three. The man who bumps you, the man—or woman—who lifts your watch, or your notecase. And the third party, who runs away with it after the second party has tossed it to him. You should be very proud to learn that the best bump-man is an American. Everyone is perfectly willing to believe that an American is clumsy."

"I am proud, and proud of you, especially. The next thing will be when you join one of those teams, just for the excitement. Or have you already?"

"I can't answer yes or no to that question. It may provide you with guilty knowledge. But I *can* say that I am looking forward to the racing season."

"If half of what you say is true, you're liable to get in trouble with the police."

"Naturally."

"And so am I."

"Oh, well, now I never thought of that aspect of it. I truly didn't."

"Not that I suppose it'll make any difference to you."

"Now that's not fair, Robert."

"Fair? What do you care what's fair or unfair? I have a certain amount of money that I got from my mother to come over here and do some painting. At the end of a year I was going to show the work to a competent judge. Depending on whether or not he told me to go ahead, I was going to go home, or stay. But good God, I haven't done nearly as much work as I hoped to do, and the winter's half over. I'm afraid the time has come for me to clear out."

Chester studied him. "Where would you go?"

"Rome, I guess. Rome, and Florence."

"You don't know Italian."

"I can pick it up, enough of it. And I can fall back on the French I know."

"You know so much kitchen French. How does that happen? In a salon, you're lost. But household, kitchen French, you're quite fluent."

"We had an Irish maid that spoke French. But the hell with that. Chester, I've got to get out of Paris."

"Will you take me with you?"

A more or less satisfactory arrangement was made with M. Langlois, the renting agent, and in the middle of February they arrived in Rome.

For more than a month Chester was at his easel every day while the light held. He was dissatisfied with every painting he finished, but he worked with an intensity that Robert never had seen and that was at times frenetic, especially in the final half hour of good light. But for the most part he was happily preoccupied, humming unrecognizable tunes, smoking long thin cigars, and taking occasional sips of cold, thick, black coffee. At the end of the day's painting they would eat their salad, bread, and cheese, drink a light wine, and talk, smoke, read, or sleep until the hour for dinner.

In London, the city Chester loved and in which he said he was happiest, he had been nervously brilliant, sardonically witty at the expense of anything and anyone, beginning with himself. In Rome, during the first weeks of their stay, and so long as he was painting every day, the nervousness was not present. In the interval between their stopping work for lunch and going out for dinner they would catch each other's mood, and often they would sit and smoke in silence. At other times they would talk for hours, the conversation dominated by the mind of Chester Calthorp even while Robert was speaking, but missing were the sardonic interruptions and the urge to coruscate that was an entertaining but frequently annoying characteristic of Chester's conversation. It was apparent to Robert that the nervousness, or the nervous energy, had been expended in the highly intellectual and physically tiring effort of concentration that went into Chester's painting. For the first few minutes after they finished a day's work the extent of Chester's physical effort was very noticeable. His right hand would shake in the sudden relaxation of the severe control of the preceding hours, and he would spend extra minutes cleaning his brushes until the shaking stopped. Simultaneously he was, as it were, washing his mind of its concentrated control. He would move about the room, shaking the damp brushes, putting them in their tall porcelain bowl, but unable to stop gazing at the painting; now shaking his head, now raising his eyebrows in an expression of semi-approval. Then, "Well!" he would exclaim, and purposefully drape the dust-cover over the canvas. "Shut up shop for the day."

All their conversations began with some discussion of painting, but it was only a point of departure, and they would proceed to painters, to travel, to history, to philosophy, to politics, and finally, to painting again. Chester now painted nothing but flowers. "I am not a botanist, I am not a horticulturist," he said. "Any gardener would be appalled by my ignorance of flowers, and that's the way it's going to stay, too. I love flowers, for interior decoration and for what they do to a rather drab world. But I am not interested in them, and they are not interested in me."

"Then why don't you hire a model?"

"Because I am playing a trick on myself. A trick of discipline. Flowers don't stay fresh much more than a day, so I must work fast."

"Very clever of you."

"Isn't it? It would be much too easy for me to start work on a nude figure. I could do one in my sleep, and often have. But those eleven snapdragons, or whatever the Italians call them—I can't do *them* in my sleep. No doubt I'll try, tonight, but it will be a tantalizing dream, I can tell you that. Why don't *you* hire a model? It won't distract me. Nothing does when I'm working."

"Well, maybe I will."

"Have you ever seen a surgical operation? You haven't, have you? Or a cadaver dissection?"

"Never."

"I could get you in to see one. Either. And I've been wondering. You're going to have to study anatomy. I could buy you a skeleton and teach you the bones. You could learn that in two days. But that's only the beginning. The mere bones of it, truly. No, I think we'll postpone anatomy. You keep on with your apples and lemons, and next month on good days you can go out of doors. The worst of the bad weather will soon be over. Spring, and then we'll have the *unhealthy* weather, malaria weather, but we'll be elsewhere for that. Lyons, Pennsylvania, isn't malaria country, is it?"

"Probably not as much so as Philadelphia."

"Decidedly not. Well, we'll stay here till then and you can go on with your experiments—"

"Experiments?"

"Isn't that what you're doing? Aren't you experimenting?"

"Well, yes. But how did you know?"

"At this stage, all painters experiment, Robert. Later on, when you think you've found yourself, artistically speaking, you will stop experimenting for a year or two, putting into practice all that you've

108

learned. Then you'll enter into the most discouraging, most satis-factory period. You won't think of what you've learned, it'll be there, but you won't think of it. You'll have your technique of hand and brush. You'll know what you can accomplish with a forty-five-degree turn of your wrist. Those things will be automatic. But the dis-couragement and satisfaction, they will interchange from day to day, sometimes from hour to hour. You will be *painting*, then, and not be-fore. Composing. Not in the sense that composition is used in an art school. But in a musical sense. Strange, isn't it, that when we want to illustrate a musical point, we use painting terms—heavily shaded, adumbrated, and such. And now I have to use musical terms. Well, what if I do? The period I am speaking of, that will follow your mas-tery of scales, the bass clef, finger exercises, and so on, that you will do automatically without thinking of them and without being a musi-cian! You will have that equipment, and your earliest experiment-ing, and you will know what you want to do. But it will elude you, then you'll catch hold of it, then it will slip away again. I think I am about to enter that period of my career as a painter. I hope so. In fact, I know so. My flowers, I do them to get ready. Somewhat like an athlete, somewhat like a pianist, who dips his hands in warm water.

"When I look so anxiously at my flowers, I'm not judging a pic-ture. I am passing judgment on my progress, my own progress, my return to painting. Me. Not the picture. I made some mistakes today, I will not make them again tomorrow. I am hurrying here, too slow there, too strong here, too weak there. And it isn't technique. It's in-spiration. Now, do you know what inspiration literally means? It means taking air into the lungs, and I mean it literally. Art has its own oxygen that only artists can breathe, and they don't breathe it all the time. But they're not artists if they don't breathe it. It's too bad that inspiration has come to mean what it does. A bolt from the blue, that puts a man to work. A bit of luck that solves all of an artist's problems. A short cut for the lazy dauber, or the lazy musician, the lazy scribbler. Inspiration is nothing of the kind. If you are not an artist who works and has worked, inspiration does not occur. The artist creates his own special oxygen, and he has his special gills, or lungs. By the process of inspiration he extracts his own special oxygen with his own special gills, and if he has also mastered his technique, he will do some first-rate work. He may not do a single, fully first-rate painting, but there will be a first-rate quality to everything he does. Within a stated period of time, of course. Not while he's too young, or too old.

"I should like to amend something I told you in Paris. I feel now

109

that I can be first-rate. I am encouraged by my love of painting. Greatness? Perhaps not. Greatness is the judgment of other men, and usually men who don't know greatness when they overlook it. But first-rate, I can be that. I may reject the Signora Hartung when someone tells her I am good enough to paint her. Can you at all imagine the Signora Hartung? She hangs the ribbon about my neck. 'You have been found worthy, you may paint me,' she says. And I rise from my genuflection and say to her, 'Dear madam, life is cruel, and cruelest of all to beauty.' I think I must hate that woman. She used her beauty to keep me in my place, consciously and deliberately, and knowing all the while that she's my inferior in all other respects. Her father, you know, is the mayor of one of your upstate communities. She is nobody at all, and when poor Hartung goes to prison, as he must, I'm far from sure that I'll help her."

"Cold, but beautiful," said Robert.

"And beautiful, but cold. Not haughty. Just cold." He was silent and frowning. "Ah, yes! I was wondering why she came into my mind. Yesterday I saw almost exactly her face in a carriage. An Italian aristocrat. Coat of arms on the door. Crest on the coachman's buttons."

"Did you know the woman?"

"It wasn't a woman. It was a young officer. But it was the face of Emily Hartung."

Not many days after the preceding conversation Chester and Robert were at breakfast, reading their mail and newspapers. "My word!" said Chester. "We can't work today. Do you know what today is? It's Washington's birthday."

"Is today the twenty-second? So it is."

"We must take a holiday. What shall it be? Florence, or Naples? Naples. It's closer, and there won't be the temptation to linger that there would be in Firr-rrenze. We'll save Firr-rrenze for a long visit."

"Today is really the twenty-third, now that I think of it. Wednesday, the twenty-third. This is Friday's newspaper, and Friday was the eighteenth."

"Oh, then we have no time to waste."

"No time to waste, did you say?"

Chester ignored the implication. He looked up the railway schedules in a Bradshaw. "There will be a train for Napoli in two hours. Put on your things and pack a small valise. We'll only stay a day or two."

On their way to the station and while waiting for their train Chester kept up a chatter that Robert knew was intended to prevent any protest against the impulsive trip. The chatter ended only when they were in the railway carriage and the train was moving south-ward. For a few minutes they were alone, and then they were joined by two men, one young, one in middle age. The older man, a serv-ant, saw to the comfort of the younger, and departed. The younger man looked at Robert, at Chester, and said, in German: "May I smoke?"

"It's your language, Robert," said Chester.

"I think he's asking if he may smoke," said Robert. "Try him with your French. He probably speaks it."

"Ah. English," said the young man. "I beg your pardon, I thought you were German."

"We are not English, we are Americans," said Chester, in Italian.

"You speak Italian," said the Italian, in Italian.

"A little, but my friend doesn't. And your English is I'm sure as good as my Italian," said Chester, in Italian.

"Then we speak English. May I offer you a cigar?"

They accepted cigars from a gold-crested alligator case.

"It is quite a clear day but there is quite a chill in the air," said the Italian.

"Yes, spring isn't here yet, is it?" said Chester.

"Spring is not here, not yet. Your first visit to Italy?"

"My third, but my friend's first."

"Your first visit to Italy? It is quite dissimilar to America, isn't it?"

"In many ways," said Robert. "Have you been to America?"

"Unhappily, no. My uncle has spent much time in Washington."

"In the Italian embassy?" said Chester.

"Yes. How clever. I am so sorry, have we met?"

"We haven't met, but I have seen you before, and you may have seen me. A few days ago in Rome, you were in uniform, riding in a black coach with yellow wheels."

"I remember well! My carriage was detained, and because of that you were detained. Very annoying to both of us, I am quite sure. Did we not smile at this detention, you and I?"

"Yes, we did."

"Hopeless, the progress of a carriage. Quite hopeless at certain hours of the day. Ah, then we have met, so to speak. I am Alfredo di Cattaneo."

"I am Chester Calthorp."

"Robert Millhouser."

"You are Millhouser, and you are Calthorp? And yet Calthorp seems more German than Millhouser. Was your mother German, Mr. Calthorp?"

"No, I have no German blood that I know of."

Alfredo di Cattaneo shook his head. "I am quite uneffective in such matters. My uncle will tell you that much. If we were traveling in Sweden, Mr. Millhouser, I should believe you were Swedish. In Germany, German. But you, Mr. Calthorp—Swiss! German Swiss. I shall never be a diplomat."

"On the contrary, I think you're doing very well at this very moment."

"Thank you, thank you," said the Italian.

"I take it you're in the army?"

"No. I have a commission, but—ah, *the uniform.* I am a count. That was my ceremonial uniform. Very beautiful, don't you think? I wear it to weddings. I was on my way to a wedding when I saw you, Mr. Calthorp. I enjoy to dress up for a wedding. I wear my funny sword. Beautiful. The Pope gave it to my father, to me, in fact, when I was born. You are in the army of your country—United States of America?"

"No," said Chester. Robert shook his head.

"And you cannot be a count, in America. Then you have no uniform to wear at a wedding. Too bad."

"I seldom go to weddings."

"Seldom? Seldom. *Infrequently?*"

"Infrequently."

"Forgive my English, please. Seldom. Infrequently. Is that an Anglo-Saxon word, seldom?"

"You have me there."

"I think it must be an Anglo-Saxon word. I speak five languages, all very badly. If I fail to recognize an English word, I declare it to be Anglo-Saxon." He grinned. *"You* say, 'It is Greek to me.' I say, 'It is Anglo-Saxon to me.' The same joke."

"Charming," said Chester.

"You will be staying in Napoli, long?"

"Back to Rome tomorrow."

"Oh, good. Then you must come to lunch, Sunday week? You will be in Rome, Sunday week? You can come, yes?"

"We'd be delighted to come," said Chester.

Alfredo di Cattaneo took out a thin Florentine leather card case and a slender silver pencil and wrote on a card. "I shall expect you at two o'clock. Frock coat, if you don't mind. My father is very old and very conventional. And a small deception? You will say that we met at the American embassy? If the question should be asked."

"Of course, and thank you very much," said Chester.

"Yes. Very much," said Robert.

"You will forgive me? I have to read documents. I am meeting a foreigner who arrives by steamer tomorrow, and I must know what to say to him. The answers to all the questions he may ask, the questions I am to ask him." He smiled. "I hope that he too is studying *his* questions and answers."

"Diplomacy," said Chester.

"Ah, yes. Kindergarten diplomacy."

"Isn't it all?"

Di Cattaneo pretended to be shocked. "Then I must give you the diplomatic answer. Yes, and no. Excuse me, please?"

They invited him to join them for lunch.

"I am desolated," he said. "My man will serve me. The basket, the hamper. But I cannot invite you to join me. There is only enough for me. Had I but known . . ."

"You will have a chance to study your questions and answers," said Chester.

"And when you return we can have conversation again?"

They lingered over their lunch, and not much time was left for conversation when they returned. They shook hands on the train, with expressions of the highest mutual regard and pleasant anticipation of Sunday-week. Chester and Robert observed that di Cattaneo was met on the platform by handsomely uniformed officers of the army and navy and frock-coated civilians, all older than di Cattaneo, but all saluting, bowing, and jostling each other to get near him.

"He must be very important in their Foreign Office," said Robert.

"That, or important regardless of the Foreign Office. I must look him up."

"For a while I thought you had."

"Do you seriously think I arranged this coincidence?"

"I don't now, but I did."

"If I'd wanted to meet Count di Cattaneo I could have arranged it a little better than that, my lad."

"Don't call me your lad. I apologize for my suspicions, but—"

"If I hadn't been working so hard, we'd have met di Cattaneo and many others like him. I am very well connected in Rome."

The Naples trip was not a success, and when they returned to Rome it was apparent that Chester's zeal for work had subsided. Robert resumed his work, but he was on his own. Their quarters in Rome were somewhat less commodious than the Paris apartment. One room, two stories in height (and almost impossible to heat), served as studio, diningroom, and livingroom. From this large room there was an open stairway leading to the bedrooms and bathroom, with a balustrade of unfinished cedar running along the stairs and balcony. The kitchen off the large room was well equipped but not well stocked, since they dined in restaurants most evenings. Their beds were made, the apartment kept clean, their mail and parcels delivered by Nicolena, who functioned as concierge. She spoke only Italian and stubbornly refused to admit a single word of any other language to her vocabulary. She was resentful of their refusal to take her on as cook, which to her would have meant her meals, her arrangements with the food merchants, and the 100 lira a month that the previous occupants had paid her. She had a husband in a foreign country, and on Sundays she was absent on visits to her numerous children, grandchildren, and great-grandchildren. She did not steal, but if a purse was left on a bureau, she would move it while cleaning, and forget where she had moved it to.

After the Naples trip Chester rearranged his days so that he would go for long walks during the hours in which he had recently been painting, and Robert was left alone until evening. As he came to realize that Chester was determined to sulk indefinitely, he likewise withdrew. He also took to going on walks in the city and eating the midday meal wherever and whenever it pleased him. Then a couple of days before the di Cattaneo luncheon Chester said: "I have an announcement to make, if you care to listen."

"Yes, I'll listen. I'm immensely relieved to learn that you haven't lost the power of speech."

"I have been a surly, ill-mannered lout. I magnified a small grievance until it became a large one. And I can only say that if I've made you uncomfortable, I've been just as much so. That, for me, is an apology, first-class, and I award it to you for patience beyond the call of duty."

"All right, Chester. As usual, you've come out of it with your self-respect intact."

"Would you have it any other way?"

"Yes, this time I think I would. This time I think you owe me an apology without any bullshit."

"Don't ask too much of me, Robert."

"You forget. I didn't ask anything."

"I know you didn't. My apology was freely given."

"Yes, but why? You're going to think I have a very suspicious nature again, but I think your apology now is only because we're going to that lunch on Sunday, and you don't want it to be awkward."

"Your suspicion does you credit, sir. That is precisely my reason for apologizing."

"Then we understand each other."

"Much better. I keep underestimating you. You're very perceptive."

"And you're damned patronizing."

"From habit, though. Not conviction. I respect you more and more. You're quite a fellow, and by the end of our two years I think you'll have shaken off that lethargy entirely."

"Two years? Do you think we'll last that long?"

"That's entirely up to you. I'm staying two years, with you or without you. There was never any contract signed, nor do I see why we should sign a treaty of peace today. However, you've been the gainer in self-respect as well as in my respect for you, and I know you respect me, so I consider that the relationship has been vastly improved."

"You may be right. I do want to mention, though, that I never needed this trip to gain my self-respect. I always had that, Chester. I always will."

"Well, it's a good thing to have, if you think you deserve it."

In spite of the mutuality of respect between them, Robert knew that something had gone out of the relationship and that it probably had gone forever. If, as Zilph Millhouser maintained, a quarrel cleared the air, it also cooled the air, and the knowledge that Chester could be deliberately so remote while living in the same studio, and for so long a period, had presented to Robert a choice of two patterns of behavior: he could attempt to placate Chester, which would have been an act of insincerity; or he could meet silence with silence. The choice he had made turned out to be effective, in that Chester had made his apology and notwithstanding the incompleteness of it or the admitted ulterior reason for it. The week of silence had been a disillusioning experience for Robert, but it contributed to a fuller, more accurate understanding of the man he still so greatly admired. At the same time, he was learning to be self-sufficient—relearning, possibly, for he had never actually depended on anyone but his father.

The long Philadelphia phase of the friendship was a novelty for Chester and for Robert, and its novelty had kept it going. A senior, and a senior whose scholastic accomplishments were so outstanding that his airs and eccentricities were accepted with good humor on campus, had taken up a freshman whose sole campus accomplishment was to achieve membership in Delta Psi. There were other students who were nice-looking, unobtrusive, well dressed, financially well fixed, and eligible to membership in Phi Kappa Sigma, Delta Phi, and Delta Psi. There were many more whom Chester Calthorp might have taken up for their interest in the fine and the liberal arts, and

115

whose admiration of Chester Calthorp was as open as Robert Mill-houser's. But Millhouser was Calthorp's choice, and the friendship continued to grow after Calthorp left the campus. Robert still had no all-inclusive explanation for Chester's interest in him, but in Paris and in Rome he sometimes thought of the London conversation in which Chester had praised the practice of following the instincts. If that philosophy guided his life, an instinctive reaction to Robert Mill-houser would have been enough for Chester. It was an easy answer, and Robert Millhouser, who did not always believe in the easy an-swers, was not so foolish as to reject them merely because they were easy.

In the time remaining before the di Cattaneo luncheon Chester re-fused to be rebuffed by Robert's calm. Once again he was in a state of jollity that equaled his mood in London. "I have looked them up," said Chester. "The count is the son of a duke, no less. The only son, with four older sisters. They are enormously wealthy. Land every-where, banking, steamship lines. The duchess has gone to heaven. They've only just come out of mourning for her. She was a Peruvian, of an Italian family that settled in Peru a hundred years ago, and wealthy in her own right. The duke is a friend of the new Pope's but he was also a friend of the one that just died, and I'm told that that's an extraordinary state of affairs, since the old one, Pius, and the new one, Leo, didn't like each other. I'd somehow rather hoped that Popes would get along better than the rest of us, but apparently not. They must wait for heaven, even as you and I, Robert."

"Interesting, but—"

"Let me finish, please. I want to see how much I've picked up. The duke, as I say, got along well with both Popes, but the real test is going to come. The new Pope didn't like it when the Church lost all that property, and who's to blame him? And the chap that gave me all this information thinks the new one, Leo, may try to get it back. In that case, the duke may be in an embarrassing predicament, hav-ing to choose between the King and the Pope. But from all I've heard, he'll probably come out of it none the worse. He'll manage." He gave Robert a warning look against another interruption. "The duke was married twice. The first duchess was exhausted after giving him four daughters, and our friend, the count, is the child of the duke's final vigor, to put it one way. There were no other children by the second duchess, although I gather there could have been others, not necessarily by the duke. There, I've summed it up for you, but you still have a question."

"Yes. Why were we invited for lunch, a couple of strangers on a train?"

"That fascinated me, too, but I suppose I'm not as mystified as you'd be."

"Why not?"

"Oh—I'm better with strangers than you are. The nobility likes flattery, too, you know, and I paid him the compliment of noticing him and remembering him."

"He remembered you, too."

"Yes, he did. That often happens to me. Douglass Repperton and I, for instance. And you and I, too, if it comes to that. Not to mention my pickpocket friends, and my medical students at home."

"But you're not a friendly man, Chester."

"Heavens, no. But I read people quite well." Then he added: "Some people."

The black carriage with the yellow wheels was sent to fetch the Americans. "I didn't expect this," said Robert.

"I did. I wrote the count a polite note while you and I were observing silence. He wrote me and said he would send the carriage. You miss a lot by not speaking to me."

The carriage took them through the gateway of the duke's town house and they descended in the courtyard. Di Cattaneo greeted them on the doorstep and led them inside and up a winding staircase past the staggered paintings that filled the wall. On the second story they walked down the hall to the library. "My father is indisposed, but he has asked me to bring you to him," said di Cattaneo.

The old man was seated near one of the ceiling-high windows, and he slowly turned his head as they entered, but he did not speak until they had been introduced. He was a large man, dressed in a gray frock coat with gray satin inserts in the lapels. In Italian he asked his son if the Americans spoke Italian, and when his son answered, he nodded. His speech came thick and slow, in both languages. He did not offer his hand. "I am sorry I never visited United States of America," he said. "My brother visited. New York has more people than Rome. Many Italians leave the homeland to work in United States of America. They do not remain at that place. They have more dollars, but to eat, to have a house is costing more dollars. Italian men who visit United States of America do not think. They are without intelligence." He spoke again in Italian.

"My father asks the names of your cities, where you live," said the son.

"Philadelphia," said Chester.

The old man nodded.

"Lyons, Pennsylvania," said Robert.

The old man frowned.

"The town is so small that I also give the name of the state," said Robert.

"Thank you," said the old man, with a slight bow.

"As though he were to say, Torino, Piedmont," said Chester.

"I understand," the duke said, curtly.

"You will excuse us now, Father? Gentlemen?"

The old man bowed, then looked away from them and they left.

In the hall Chester said, "Your father has been very ill, has he not?"

"Yes. He is in pain, and he knows he is going to die. He does not wish to die, but he wishes for death to end the pain."

"He'll have the second wish very soon," said Chester.

"Ah, you are a physician?"

"No, but I have spent a lot of time with them. Your father has his pain down below? Between the legs?"

"Yes. It is sad to see him so, he was once so strong."

"There is nothing to be done. Let him do anything he wants to do, give him everything he asks for."

"You are kind, very kind," said the young man. "But he wants most a grandson, from me."

"I'm afraid he won't live long enough to see that, even if you were to marry tomorrow."

"Even if, yes," said the young man. "Even if." At that moment, and for the first time, Robert saw the astonishing resemblance to Emily Hartung. He had not seen it on the train, nor in the library with the old man; but in di Cattaneo's rejection of the possibility of giving his father a grandchild there was unmistakable feminine petulance. Di Cattaneo actually pouted and from it Robert got a quick picture of the scenes that must have taken place between the old duke and the son on the subject of marriage and an heir.

The only other member of the family in the palace was one of the four sisters, who was acting as hostess. She was taller than her half-brother, dressed in black silk and lace, and wore no adornment except a gold cross on a thin gold chain, and a wide, heavy wedding ring. The chain and cross lay on her chest, which was covered with lace that was sewn to a wide lace choker that covered her neck. But the lines of her figure were not concealed. She had large breasts and a waist that had thickened with the years, but she had once had a superb body. She was about twice her half-brother's age. She was, it developed, the widow of a Belgian baron, whose children were all married, and she was in Rome to be with her invalid father. It was plain to see that she did not enjoy the task of hostess to her half-brother's friends. The conversation, such as it was, was carried on in

118

French, and there was so little of it that Robert understood most of it, although at no time did he attempt to introduce a topic. Indeed, there was no topic. The weather, the Americans' visit and the length of their stay, the antiquity of the palace, the remoteness of America, and the inconveniences of travel sufficed to break the silences, and when the meal was ended the baroness excused herself to go to the private chapel on the other side of the palace.

"Could it be that your sister doesn't like Americans?" said Chester.

"She doesn't like Italians, if they are friends of mine," said the count. He commenced ticking off with his fingers. "Friends of mine. Protestants. Jews. Living painters. Peasant priests. Germans. Dutch. The entire middle class of the world." He pretended to whisper. "The new Pope. She knew him in Belgium, I think. She goes to pray now because she has sinful doubts. She has sinful doubts that the new Pope can be infallible, and that is heresy."

"Well, I'm relieved that we're not alone in her displeasure."

"Francesca is the alone one. She is in mourning for my mother, who was her stepmother and whom she did not like. She is in mourning for the old Pope. And she is in black because it is Lent. When my father dies, she will be completely alone. I have a naughty friend who would like to be her lover. A very naughty boy. He says if he can ever weep on her bosom she will be his mistress in five minutes. But that will not be. She would not permit herself to be alone with a friend of mine. Oh, he is naughty, this friend. I say to him, 'You will be like Boccaccio. Naughty now, and penitent when you grow old.' Yes, he agrees with me. But he does not write. He lives all the stories Boccaccio wrote. Oh, naughty, but so charming. You must meet Gianni. But you will not believe what I tell you when you look at his face. What innocence!"

Di Cattaneo continued to speak of his naughty friend, relating escapades that Gianni had experienced and was planning. The stories were directed at Chester, with at first a courtesy glance at Robert, but after a while Robert was virtually ignored. It was impossible not to be annoyed at the exclusion, and suddenly Robert looked at his watch and announced that he had some letters to write for the next boat. Di Cattaneo was shocked back into his good manners and tried to insist on sending Robert in the carriage, but Robert declined and Chester said: "Robert is a determined fellow, and I'd like to stay and speak Italian, if I may."

Robert found his way home without difficulty, and got out paper and pen, but there was nothing he wanted to write to anyone. He was overcome with homesickness that he could not put into words to his

119

mother, to Moses Hatfield—to anyone. It was not homesickness for Lyons or the house or for the people he knew. And slowly he realized that it was not homesickness at all, as such, but the first full realization that he needed someone who would need him. What he had called homesickness was made to seem so by his surroundings; the overwhelming unity of a great city in which he had no one. The city became for him a collection of people, hundreds of thousands of individual men and women who were too busy needing and being needed, in houses and streets and in a language they all knew and that he did not know. At home, at least, he could get a new start in his search for someone whom he would take into his life for the future. Vaguely he understood that he never had wanted people but had been comfortable and even happy in the familiarity with the places and with the people who lived in the places. Now he wanted someone who would live with him in the familiar places. He now thought of Chester with disdain, the brilliant companion who could be so easily entertained by an effeminate young aristocrat's admiring stories of a dreadful little pimp.

It was for Robert a new look at Chester, who had deceived him with his versatility and agile mind and speech, but who betrayed his virtuosity by his choice of entertainment. Chester was like an aristocrat who preferred the company of whores. Di Cattaneo was a whore, Douglass Repperton was a whore, and so were the regular visitors to Spring Garden Street. And inevitably Robert saw that he, too, was a whore. He was the intellectual inferior of Chester Calthorp, and he saw plainly that Chester had tolerated him because he was the most placid whore of them all.

He reduced his homesickness to this appraisal of his relationship with Chester Calthorp, and when he saw a way out, a practical way out of his present misery, he felt better. He would go home; that was the practical way out. He immediately felt an affection for Chester that he had not felt during most of their European trip, and he was grateful for the amusing times they had had during their friendship. He would show his gratitude by showing nothing; he would prepare Chester for his departure, do nothing abruptly, and leave Chester undisturbed by any maladjustment of their friendship. He not only owed Chester that much; in his relief at finding a solution to his unhappiness he was pleased that he could go away without any damage to his friend. In a matter of minutes Chester Calthorp had become a friend of his youth and a memory of his future.

It did not surprise Robert that in the weeks that followed the palace luncheon, Chester totally neglected his painting and was away from the apartment sometimes for days at a time. Once during those

120

weeks Chester spoke of his absences: "I can see you've been hard at work. That does wonders for my conscience, you know. But you have missed me, haven't you?"

"Shall I be truthful and rude, or untruthful?"

"You've answered my question, and rested my conscience all anew. Well, just so long as I know you're happy."

"I guess I could call myself that. I'm a happy, fourth-rate dauber, as you once said."

"No, third-rate, close to second. But you're staying on, aren't you?"

"Not the full year, Chester."

"You're not? Is it money? I've been winning fabulous sums at cards. Alfredo and his friends are reckless, and when I sit down at cards I can't help using my brains."

"It isn't only money, although that's a consideration. It's my conscience attacking me from two angles. I know I'm not a good painter and never will be. That's my artistic conscience. The other—my mother and I've never been like most mothers and sons. But maybe for that very reason I've been bothered by filial conscience. I ought to start doing something for her, instead of her doing it all for me."

"But she's given you the full year."

"I think I'm going to give some of it back."

Chester considered. "Has this decision anything to do with me?"

"It may have, but I don't think so. I don't know how to answer that truthfully," he said, untruthfully. "But even if it has, something to do with you, I'm afraid I don't feel at home in Europe."

"Well of course not! You didn't come here to feel at home."

"No, but I considered myself more of a cosmopolite. I was wrong. I'm a Pennsylvanian. Upstate, at that."

"You're nothing of the kind, Robert. Whom can you talk to in Pennsylvania?"

"Whom do I talk to in Europe? It isn't only a question of the languages. I've never felt, even with the English, that anything I said made the slightest difference. And it shouldn't. I'm a listener and a reader, never a talker or a—"

"Or a what?"

"Well, an entertainer. You're a talker and an entertainer."

"I should hope so. I try hard enough."

"And you're very good at it."

"Fairly good. But this is all news to me. You'll have to let me think it over."

"Why? I've just about decided to go home in May. I might even go in April."

"Well, you wouldn't go if I opposed it very firmly, would you?"

121

"I'm afraid I would."

"I'll still have to think it over. I can't now. My Romans are much too entertaining. But I may decide to try to change your mind. I could, too, Robert Millhouser. Don't think I couldn't."

"I'd rather you didn't try. It wouldn't be very good for our friendship."

"May I be slightly cryptic? You may never know the depth of this friendship, and if you don't, you may thank your Lutheran God."

"How can I thank Him for—"

"Cryptic, I said." He put his finger to his lips. "Silence."

Robert arranged for passage at the end of April, so that in the next conversation with Chester he would be able to announce definite plans. With the tickets in his desk drawer, the Roman weather improving, and a work schedule keeping him busy, he lived from day to day in a state of comparative euphoria. And then one afternoon he had a visitor.

Robert was alone, and windows and doors were open to allow a cooling breeze to circulate. There was a gentle knock on the open door and a tall man in a black cassock said: "May I come in, please?"

"Of course. Come right in, Father."

"You are very kind," said the priest. He looked at the unfinished painting on the easel before Robert. "Ah-ha, yes. May I sit down, please?"

"Please do. May I offer you a glass of wine?"

"No thank you, very much."

"Seltzer and lemon? That's what I'm going to have."

"I would like that."

Robert prepared the drinks and set them on the table and seated himself across from the priest. The priest took his glass, raised it and bowed to Robert. *"À votre santé."*

"And to you, sir."

They sipped their drinks and the priest put his glass on the table. "You make a difficult task less difficult, but by so doing, you make it more difficult." The priest spoke with a French accent. "But I shall at least try to make it less difficult for *you,* my dear sir. As an American, you prefer the direct approach, and I shall respect the American custom. What is it you say? Laying the cards on the table. I have been chosen, I believe, because I have been acquainted with American customs through my residence in the city of New York and the city of Philadelphia. I was a teacher at Fordham University and at St. Joseph's College."

"I see."

122

"I believe that you attended the University of Pennsylvania, a splendid institution."

"Yes, I did."

"I was acquainted with Professor John W. Stanhope, the distinguished philosopher, and with Professor Darius M. Perkins, the equally distinguished mathematician."

"I studied under both of them."

"Yes. You see, the Society to which I belong takes a somewhat more liberal attitude toward fraternizing with scholars of other faiths."

"Yes, I understand."

"But I am not living up to my promise to respect the American custom, am I? Then let me, as you say, come out with it. My dear sir, as a man whose father has long since gone to his eternal reward, you cannot be expected to appreciate the desire of a father to see his son, as you say, settled down. Married, and settled down."

"Well, my father never said much about it to me."

The priest made a muscular smile. "I should think not. You were much too young when he died."

"I suppose so."

"In any event, my dear sir, regardless of conversations you may or may not have had with your father, I am sure that if circumstances had so permitted, you would have been encouraged to marry a suitable young woman and assume the responsibility of raising children for the greater honor and glory of God. Will you not, then, try to understand that just as it would have been your own dear father's wish, had he been able to express it, so it is the wish of the father of a young man with whom you are acquainted. I shall not mention names."

"Oh, but I think we'd better mention some names."

The priest held up his hand. "No! Please do not. I have come to ask you to abandon your attachment to a young man, and to ask you even more. To—"

"Now wait a second, Father. Please. First of all. What is my name?"

"Your name, sir? I think I have shown already that I not only know your name, but that I have considerable information concerning your personal history."

"Nevertheless. What is my name?"

"Very well, sir. Your full name is Chester Sterling Calthorp, and you were born—"

"My name is *not* Chester Sterling Calthorp."

"Then it is Sterling Chester Calthorp."

"No. My name is Robert Millhouser."

The priest was silent, then he spoke aloud to himself. "I asked the woman downstairs to direct me to the apartment of Mr. Calthorp. Mr. Calthorp is a painter. A gentleman. The University of Pennsylvania. Stanhope and Perkins. Sir, who are you?"

"Robert Millhouser. I live here with Mr. Calthorp. I am trying to be a painter. I think I'm a gentleman, and I went to the University of Pennsylvania and studied under Perkins and Stanhope."

"Is your father living?"

"He died when I was fifteen."

"I have made a serious mistake. And the mistake was entirely mine. I apologize to you, sir. I beg you to forgive me. Yes, you even tried to stop me when I had already said too much, but I blundered on." The priest took a sip of the lemon-water. He took a deep breath and looked steadily at Robert. "Have I said anything to you that is damaging to your friend, in your eyes? Have I given you any information you did not have before I entered this room?"

Robert hesitated. "No, I don't think you have."

"You knew, then, that an unhealthy situation exists?"

"Unhealthy. Well, I don't know about that."

"You do not consider it unhealthy. Perhaps that is a point of view. You do not look upon such a situation as unhealthy. Is that, then, because—and you will not shock me, Mr. Millhouser. I am not easily shocked—is that because you are a member of the same clique, you and your friend?"

"My dear sir, now you're making it difficult," said Robert. "Mr. Calthorp is a friend of mine, obviously. We came over here together, and we've lived together in London, Paris, and Rome."

"You help me. 'Lived together.' As lovers?"

"Jesus Christ, what are you saying?"

"I am asking you to make it clear to me why you do not consider the situation an unhealthy one. And I ask you as a gentleman to respect my habit. Please do not be blasphemous."

"I've respected your habit enough. What are you accusing me of?"

"I accuse you of nothing if you do not accuse yourself."

"Will you get out of here?"

"Leaving things as they are?"

"Just get out."

"Mr. Millhouser, I must save something from this wreckage. I have blundered badly."

"Yes, you are a stupid man. And so clever. It's no wonder people hate you, all of you."

"Yes, I am a stupid man. And I have made you hate me. I shall go, but before I go, one word. I believe, on instinct alone, that the implication of my question regarding the relationship between you and Mr. Calthorp—was unjustified."

"Where was your God damn instinct when you *asked* the question?"

"Yes, where was it? But it's alive now, Mr. Millhouser."

"And have you anything else to go on besides instinct when you make these accusations about Cattaneo and Calthorp?"

"There, sadly, I have more than instinct."

"I'd like you to tell that to Calthorp."

"But that, my dear sir, is why I am here. If you had been Calthorp, you could deny nothing. And would not. Calthorp parades his sin in the very streets of Rome. If you had been Calthorp you would have known why I was here, and I was stupid because I did not see that. Stupid and clever, because I thought you were Calthorp and flaunting your cleverness for me. The young man whose name I have not mentioned, he is not a nobody. His sin is compounded by the sin of giving scandal."

"Then you talk to him about it. He's one of your people."

"Will you talk to Calthorp? He's one of *your* people."

"There you go, clever again. You and Calthorp would get along like two thieves."

"I deserve anything you say. But not your hatred. I pray that you will conquer that."

"You're going to be on your knees a long, long time."

"I am on my knees most of the time, Mr. Millhouser. It is when I am not that I make my worst mistakes. There remain two things I must say to you. First, I shall return to speak to Mr. Calthorp. Second, if you have any influence with Mr. Calthorp, you will be doing him a kindness to persuade him to leave Rome."

"Now you want me to do your work for you."

"I put it on a basis of your friendship for Mr. Calthorp."

"Make a threat, let's hear you."

"Very well. In French, you know, we have the word *menace* that corresponds to threat. But menace means something slightly different in English, does it not? Yes. The menace to Mr. Calthorp is Mr. Calthorp himself. You may tell him I said that. As a priest I do not wish to carry threats to Mr. Calthorp. But someone will carry them, Mr. Millhouser. Or worse, no one will carry them. His young friend is not a nobody, and already your embassy is twisting—*wringing*—its hands over this unhealthy situation. Do you know that Mr. Calthorp amuses himself as a pickpocket? *I* know that, Mr. Millhouser. And the pickpockets and their friends know it. You see, I

125

have not made a threat? But I have told a friend of Mr. Calthorp's that Mr. Calthorp is a menace to himself. God bless you, sir." The priest straightened his cassock, picked up his hat, and was gone.

And so there it was; the fetid orchid, the cadaver incised from neck to scrotum, the horse left rotting on the cobblestones, yesterday's feast become excrement. And in the desperation of his confusions Robert had a clear recollection of the many signs that he had ignored, the warnings he had rejected. The worldly priest had asked the question, but so many others had not bothered to ask; they had looked, and they had passed their judgments. Alice Sterling and her contempt. I. Goldberg and Canon Lovelace, in their separate ways treating him as though he had forfeited any right to expect respect. And his mother, with her annoyingly insistent questions. For six years he had been stimulated by this man, laughed with him, admired him and probably emulated him in at least his own judgments on men and things. The flashing and slashing methods of Chester Calthorp's attacks on banality and the commonplace were too quick and sharp for Robert to copy, but how much had they affected his judgments even when Chester Calthorp was not present to instruct him? He had chosen Chester Calthorp as his friend, practically to the exclusion of everyone else; now how many members of his world—small, but his own world—had shared the same judgment as the priest, as Alice Sterling, I. Goldberg, Canon Lovelace? And how many were there, if there were any, who had wanted to ask the questions his mother had asked? And how many, or how few, had no suspicion at all?

So much of his thinking was clear; but the confusions were in control: in the midst of a return of his homesickness came a revulsion against painting because painting had been one of the symbols of Chester Calthorp's influence. The city of Rome, the whole of Europe, likewise became unhealthy—and he was shocked to notice how quickly that word came to mind. At another time, in years past, he would conceivably have said that he loved Chester Calthorp, with the same connotation that he might have said he loved Moses Hatfield. But now love, as a word, belonged with the fetid orchid, the cadaver incised, the putrefying horse, the nasty mess that had been a hearty meal. And love, at this moment, was no more than a word.

And yet—and this was another confusion—so fixed was the need of Chester's good opinion that Robert could not hurriedly pack and go to a hotel. He would not be called a coward by this man. Once, and finally, he would have to stand up to him.

It was impossible to tell when Chester would return, and after an hour Robert went for a walk, a tiring walk up and down the thousands of steps of Rome. He stopped once and had a glass of wine,

126

and again for a glass of wine and some bread and cheese, and by the time he returned to the studio the lamplighters were on their patrols. It was dark in the studio and he thought he was alone, but immediately he smelled cigar smoke. Chester was sitting at the window in one of the high-backed chairs.

"Will you light the candles, please?" said Chester.

"It's not Nicolena. It's me."

"I know. Will you light the candles?"

Robert put the taper to the fat candles.

"And now will you sit down somewhere?" said Chester.

Robert seated himself in the nearest chair, and Chester stood up and looked at him. "I know about your visitor. He came again and just left. I'm glad you didn't have to see him again, and I'm glad we can be alone." He paused, but remained standing. "I am not staying here tonight. You stay. I have several places where I can go. You stay, do your packing, and you can be gone when I come back late tomorrow. I shouldn't imagine you'd have to stay in Rome very long. There must be a steamer from Naples at least once a week, if you'd like to go directly to New York or Philadelphia. You can exchange your other tickets, they'll accept them here for credit. And you have your letter of credit. Do you need any money? I can lend you as much as you need."

"No."

"Then there isn't much else to say. You can move to a hotel tomorrow, and if I find anything you've left behind, I'll ship it to you. So much for those details. As to the other. Lest there be any doubts in your mind, let me dispel them. Everything the priest said or implied is true. I am what he says I am. I have never been anything else since I was a boy. I think I told you once that I was a cripple. That's what I meant. That was the first time I tried to tell you, and then I couldn't, I forget why. But I know why I wanted to tell you. I wanted to warn you. In the five or six years that I've known you we'd never spent a night under the same roof until you came to my house last September. Since then we've been together almost daily and, practically speaking, every night. Sooner or later I would have, as they say, molested you. I'm glad now that I never did. I was glad in Paris. Do you remember when I accused you of having an assignation with that diseased model? I'd never known until then, at least I was never quite certain, how innocent you were. But that didn't make it easier for me. We—men like me—are no respecters of innocence. *I* haven't been, I admit that. And so it wasn't your innocence that protected you. It was your simple, unsophisticated, faith in me. The only human being I've ever known that knew me at all well, and yet saw no evil in me. Innocence is often mere ignorance. But you knew me, you saw that I was interested in many things that don't interest most men. But you didn't question my tastes, the way I lived, my friends. You did not see in them, as so many men would see, other implications. There are men who look at me and know instantaneously what I am. Alfredo. Douglass Repperton. Servants. Ship stewards. Men of business. That priest today. But you never knew, and you didn't know, because the only other man you were ever close to was your father, and your father could do no wrong.

"You told me about a teacher at your school. The man that hanged himself. He saw in you the same blind faith that I saw, and rather than abuse that, he hanged himself."

"I don't believe that."

"You'll have a long time to believe whatever you like, so let me speak. I am trying to let you go away in full possession of the facts. I am repaying you for your faith in me, the last time I will. When I leave here, in another five minutes or so, I do not expect to see you ever again. I am going to stay abroad for at least five years and quite possibly for the rest of my life.

"I have a few things to say. First, give up your painting. Give it up now before you put too much of yourself in it. Take it up again if you like, but for the present, give it up. You have no career as a painter, but you may get some pleasure as an amateur. The next thing I must tell you, take a mistress. Lyons, Pennsylvania, is not well suited to such an arrangement, but so much the better. Have one in Philadelphia. Other men have. See her when you want to, and then always go back to Lyons. But stay a bachelor. Never get married. Women will want to marry you. You are a good catch. But don't give in. Why? Because you have come this far without loving a woman, and marriage is not essential to your happiness. Therefore if you marry you will make the woman unhappy and she will do the same to you. You are not like me, my kind of cripple. You will take pleasure in a woman, various women. But you are not a husband.

"Finally, don't let your disgust with me turn into pity. Although I call myself a cripple, it is not self-pity that causes me to say that. I do not apologize for myself or my actions. This is my life, and not yours or the priest's or the old duke's or Wendell Banning's. I am a cripple only because I lack the instinct for women, but my life is complete without that. It's you, you know, you that have the instinct for women, that deserve pity. You try to remake the woman to suit yourself, or the women try to remake you. And whether you succeed or fail, in both cases someone is the loser.

"Now I take my departure. Bon voyage, Robert. Oh, leave the

cuff links and studs, will you please? You probably would have in any case, but since they will give you no pleasure, I want to give them to someone who will appreciate their beauty."

"Beware of pickpockets, Chester," said Robert.

Chester laughed. "Thank you for the warning. I'll miss you." He went quickly. Uncharacteristically he left a dead cigar, that had the same acrid pungency as all dead cigars.

•

I am going to quote from one of Robert Millhouser's weekly dispatches. The passage I quote almost verbatim is more straightforward than his previous accounts of his trip abroad, and I do not believe I can further improve upon it.—G.H.

My mother was ill when I returned to Lyons. The illness, I was informed by Dr. Willetts, was neither more serious nor more trivial than we had a right to expect at her time of life. She had passed the fifty-year mark and Dr. Willetts disclosed that she was undergoing "the change" at a later time than most of his patients. I knew so little about this phenomenon of the opposite sex that I was embarrassed to confess my ignorance to Dr. Willetts. However, he saw through my "knowing" questions and was extremely helpful. Mama had begun to display the first symptoms shortly after Chester Calthorp and I embarked for England. She was subject to moods of depression and listlessness, two of the characteristic manifestations of the phenomenon, as well as one other of which I shall speak presently. Dr. Willetts said she had appeared pleased when I first wrote to tell her I was coming home, but that during the interval between my letter and my actual arrival, she had developed a feeling of hostility toward me to such a degree that she remarked to Dr. Willetts: "Why does he have to come home now?"

Upon my arrival she greeted me affectionately but her searching glances prepared me for the question she asked after I had been home less than a week. "What went wrong?" she asked. Knowing her as I did, and prepared by her questioning gaze, I needed an explanation that was strong enough to justify my return (and the effects of the disillusionment that must have been apparent to this woman who knew me at least as well as I did her). I pretended to be, and of course actually was, evasive in my first answers, leading up to an admission that I felt was strong enough to account for my return and the differences in my behavior. "I had hoped to convince you that I came home because I had remorse of conscience over leaving all this responsibility to you," I said.

"I was reconciled to your absence," she said.

"Yes," I said. "The truth of the matter is that Chester and I had a falling-out."

"So I surmised," said she.

"It came to a head in Rome," I said. "In London and in Paris he had never touched brush to canvas. He refused to take either his own or my work seriously and seemed to prefer the company of people who lived the life of artists but used it as an excuse for loose living without having any work to show for it."

"And you refused to participate in that life?"

"I did. I had only so much money and therefore only so much time. I persuaded him to leave Paris for Rome, and for a few weeks he painted in earnest but then things got worse in Rome than they had been in Paris, if possible, and when I remonstrated with him he told me that I lacked the talent to whitewash a fence, that I could never hope to be as much as a fourth-rate painter, and that I was a very dull companion. After that there was nothing to be gained by staying. So I arranged for passage home."

"Was his word enough to convince you of your lack of talent?"

"Yes, because it had been his word alone that had encouraged me to believe that I had any talent."

"He made no effort to apologize?"

"Chester never apologizes."

"And he wasn't upset, or regretful?"

"Not to any degree. He even asked me to return a present he had given me. We did not part on the friendliest of terms."

"I am still somewhat mystified by his asking you to go with him in the first place. Perhaps he thought that life among the Bohemians would teach you to enjoy life in general."

"You seem to be on his side," I said.

"My loyalty is to you, but I confess that I had hoped the trip would bring you out of your shell. The expense was worth that, even if you had no talent whatsoever. It's foolish to ask, but I'll ask it. Did you fall in love over there?"

"No, I did not."

"That's what I mean. I'd hoped something of that sort would happen to you. Your father was a man of deep feeling. Why can't you be more like him?"

"I'd give anything to be like him. Perhaps I'm more like you."

"Ha! Little enough you know about me, and God knows I see little enough of myself in you."

The conversation had taken a turn that I had not foreseen; I was willing enough to appear to be the loser in a quarrel with Chester

Calthorp and to admit that my trip had been a failure; I was ready to devote my time and energy to the estate and to relieve my mother of its burdens. But it was distressing to be told, in effect, that I was a man without feeling and a bit of a prig besides. I almost wished that I could boast of a succession of mistresses and a squandering of time and money in riotous living. I wanted to protest her harsh, unfair judgment of me and I was tempted, for the briefest of moments, to lay bare the facts of the debacle. Only an instinctive feeling that she would side with Chester and thereby ruin my relations with her kept me from telling her the ugly truth. It was strange to be so instinctively sure of her reactions in advance, while at the same time to have made no progress toward a more typical mother-and-son relationship. It was difficult to accept as a fact the impression that my mother did not like me. She was a woman, a fine woman, and I could count on her love, but if I had had any hope that my return to Lyons would improve our companionship, I now abandoned it.

Nevertheless I stayed, in spite of my first impulse to leave her. Every day I systematically learned about the estate; the farms and timber lands and the securities. It was as well that I had that to do. The managing of the estate had keenly interested her and so long as we kept our two-hour daily meetings on that subject, we avoided friction. Two hours was the limit. Longer than that tired her, and she would begin to accuse me of having paid no attention to details that actually she had not yet disclosed. I made my own sets of notes on each of the farms and timber leases, and for the time being I made no effort to master the portfolio of securities. To my surprise, I apparently had inherited from both my parents some sense of business. There was a great deal of detail, especially in connection with the farms, and no two farms were alike, even in size. My father and, later, my mother had bought and sold acreage without regard to the forty-acre section scheme. They had sold (or bought) pieces of land when it suited them. They would, for instance, trade ten acres in order to obtain one acre that contained a fresh-water spring, or give up pieces of land for a desirable right of way. Whenever possible my father had seen to it that each farm had access to a minimum of two roads, township or county, and my mother continued that policy. Consequently, the result showed itself on the crude maps of the farms, and almost immediately I decided to spend some of our money on surveying, in order to bring the maps up to date. I did not mention my intention; it would have seemed like a criticism of my mother's management of the estate. I also decided, and informed her, that I would personally visit the farms that spring. So far I was only a "paper" farmer; I had little personal knowledge of the human element, the farmers and their fam-

131

ilies, and even less of the condition of the livestock and the true condition of the land.

By degrees, with the increase of my information, my own interest in the farms became an enthusiasm that I was careful to mask. I am not sure why I controlled my enthusiasm; a natural reticence is the partial explanation, but I also was afraid my mother might resent my taking over the management too abruptly, leaving her with nothing to do. True, she had once urged upon me the necessity of taking over at some future time, but her obvious pride as she acquainted me with farm details and deals she had made warned me to be cautious.

Those first weeks were like being at school again. In the latter part of the morning I would have my meeting with Mama; we would stop for lunch, and before sitting down I would go to the post office, come home for lunch, and in the afternoon I would go over the information I had obtained in the morning. Usually I would find that questions would arise and I would make note of them for the next day's consultation with Mama. The days were quite full and they passed quickly. My visits to the post office invariably meant some conversation with local friends and acquaintances; Mr. and Mrs. Fred Langendorf were the only Lyons people who had been abroad, and I could have chatted endlessly with my post office acquaintances. But fortunately they became accustomed to my presence again, and the questions they might have asked were indefinitely and then forever postponed.

After dinner Mama would retire early and I would try to catch up on my reading. In Europe I had read very little in English; I was so anxious to improve my French and Italian that I had forced myself to spend some time each day with a French novel or with the Italian newspapers—the appropriate dictionaries within arm's reach—and the pleasure of reading did not there exist for me. Home again, among familiar books and authors, I resumed the custom of taking down a volume of fiction or poetry after dinner. But the habit did not immediately return. My thoughts would wander back across the sea and I would attempt to overcome the bitterness of my disappointment in my friend.

That there were men and boys who indulged in certain acts among themselves as a substitute for the pleasures of the opposite sex was no new revelation to me. Both in school and college it had been common knowledge that certain boys had allowed their friendship to deteriorate into taking physical pleasure with each other. But they were, or became, "marked men," and I believe that at some time during every year of my school and college career at least one student was shipped home in disgrace. Among my college friends for whom I had any admiration, it was a strongly held belief (to which I myself subscribed)

132

that a man should approach marriage no less virtuously than the girl with whom he intended to spend his life. At the University there were those students who would boast of their experiences with prostitutes, but I regarded them as muckers. At an earlier age, in Lyons, Leonard Vance had been accosted by a young woman who was herself so ugly that she made sin ugly. Her ugliness, however, had not repelled all my Lyons contemporaries. They would laugh among themselves at M.M. and the "thrill" she provided, which, with some of the boys, became a habit that was unbreakable. At first she would offer them candy in order to gain power over them, but after they had succumbed she played upon their weakness and demanded certain attentions to herself which even now cause me to shudder. Eventually she was committed to the insane asylum, but not before she had corrupted an incredible number of my contemporaries. I escaped her clutches because she was so ugly that I ran away from her every time I saw her. Leonard Vance accepted candy from her, but when she revealed her true purpose, he took to his heels and carefully avoided her thereafter. I am also inclined to believe that in accosting Leonard she was unaware of the standing of the Vance family, or that Leonard was a member of that family. That, I am convinced, was my protection.

So much for my innocence and virtue. It was a condition that existed through my own choice, and you may put it down to fastidiousness or an abhorrence of ugliness. I am quite sure that if I had met a Juliet in Lyons and love had been awakened, or that if I had known an Héloïse in Philadelphia, romance in the form of passionate experience would have entered my life—not, I trust, with the consequences visited upon poor Abélard! Instead I had been made to appear the toady and the fool in the eyes of uncounted men and women who had formed their own ugly suspicions of the relationship I had had with Chester Calthorp. Most discouraging was my own mother's implied rejection of my version of the quarrel with Chester. If I was not fooling her, she was not fooling me; with nothing to go on, she was yet cynical of my friendship with Chester, and her lack of faith in me was more distressing than I have ever admitted to anyone until I wrote these words.

Mind you, Gerald, I was not soft. I was hard, with the hardness of self-reliance that had grown in me as I matured. Perhaps self-sufficient would be a better word, but it does not convey or imply my need of someone to love that my mother did not recognize and did, in effect, deny. I had come this far loving my father, my mother, and no one else. You have noticed in my letters, I am sure, that except for Moses Hatfield, Leonard Vance, and Chester Calthorp, I have scarcely mentioned anyone else with affection. That, I feel sure, was what might be called my personal chemistry; and Nature, which I am told compensates for deficiencies in one's makeup, made me self-sufficient or self-reliant, therefore hard or strong. In Nature's own good time she would supply me with someone to love for the rest of my life. I cannot truthfully say that I believed that at this time, but I do recall being conscious of my strength. In fact, I felt my strength sufficiently to enable me to oppose my mother in her attitude toward me, her unspoken accusation regarding my friendship with Chester, and her outspoken charge that I was cold and unfeeling. A few weeks of living with her in that atmosphere reshaped my attitude toward her and eventually toward the whole of life. I began to understand that this woman, my mother, who had great charm, wit, agility of mind, passion, bitterness, an amused cynicism, and the body of a female, was in all respects save the last a great deal like Chester Calthorp. I repeat: I *began* to understand; it was months before I could see the whole resemblance. But when I did, and when I realized that I could count on my mother's love and faith no more than on Chester Calthorp's, I was as strong as I have ever been.

Her "indisposition" meanwhile continued, and here I return for a moment to the new habits I was forming. As I have said on an earlier page, it was difficult for me to concentrate on my evening reading, and occasionally I would leave the house for a stroll that usually took me to the drug store, where I would buy a cigar, exchange a few pleasantries with "Doc" Brown, and return to the house. I did not join in the group of Doc Brown's friends who sat with him in the rear of the store; they were older than I and in their own way an exclusive club. But they were friendly enough and so was I to them, and I mention them as a single item in my discovery of the town. On the night of payday at the collieries most of the stores stayed open until nine o'clock, but on other nights there were only three arc lights left burning on Main Street after the post office closed. Doc Brown stayed open until nine every night; the other stores literally barred their doors with padlocked iron straps. I often walked home from Doc Brown's without seeing another human being, although the hour might be short of nine-thirty. Then I made a new friend, as a result of Mama's indisposition. Dr. Willetts's office, which occupied the two front rooms of his residence, was a block beyond Doc Brown's, and I knew his office hours were six-to-eight. I dropped in one evening, to talk about Mama.

Dr. Willetts was in his forties, smooth-shaven, with a long, large nose that extended out and down over his upper lip. His clothes were old but good. In the office he wore soft-leather Congress boots, but in the knee-hole under the desk I could see the thick-soled workman's shoes that he put on when making his calls. He was not a Lyons man, but his wife came of a Lyons family. He had been a contract surgeon with the Union Army and had set up practice in Lyons after the war.

He told me to take a chair, then went to the front office and blew out the lamp and came back, closing the door behind him. "That won't keep them from hammering on the door," he said. "But it may discourage the drug salesmen." He gave me a cigar and sat back in his chair with his pipe. "Your mother's going to be all right. It's something women have to put up with, as we have to, too, while they're going through it. However, it seems to cause more trouble with women of well-to-do families than with the lower-class women. A lot of them look upon it as something to be grateful for. No more children. The poor go through life dreading children, but having them anyway. The upper-class women, who can afford children, want something more out of life. Attention. Keeping their figures. When they start having the change, they think it means the end of their lives, the romantic side, to put it one way. Well, that isn't true, physically. But it just so happens that men are usually older than their wives, and they're of an age when the old tool doesn't stand up as much as it used to. So it's the men that ought to worry more than the women. Mind you, I can give you a lot of exceptions, but generally speaking, the woman could go on cohabitating if the men could. Your mother will be all right, I think."

"Why do you say, 'I think.' "

"Well, I've known you for about ten years almost, and I wouldn't say this to everybody, but you've been raised differently and you've been out in the great wide world. If your father were alive I'd talk to him, or I wouldn't even have to talk to him. But he died a long time ago. Now. One of the things that happens to women during the change is that some of them think they're pregnant. They're not, but they convince themselves that they are, and sometimes I have a hard time believing they're not. Would you have any reason to believe, any reason at all, to believe that your mother could possibly have grounds for thinking she was pregnant?"

"No."

"Are you sure?"

"Not unless you did it, Doctor."

"Well, I don't have to worry about you. You have your sense of humor. All right, now I'm going to ask you that question again, and I don't want you to answer so quickly. Does she see any men at all? When she goes away, for instance. Now I'm not saying that one of them made her pregnant, but if she has a friend, a man, who got into bed with her, it's possible that she had some reason to believe she was made pregnant."

"At her age?"

"Yes, at her age, and past her age."

"I can't think of anyone she sees that that might happen with."

"Well, one of her hallucinations is that she's with child. She's not. But she worries about it, and I'd like to know whether she's manufacturing the whole thing, or what. I'm a doctor, Robert, not a minister. I'm not going to pray over her and ask the good Lord to forgive her sins. I just want to know whether she's imagining the whole thing, and if she is, then you may have to be very patient with her for a couple of years. On the other hand, if she had relations with a man, just once, in the past year, it isn't all imagination and I'll know how to treat her."

"I see."

"Women in that state can even have what they think is a miscarriage. And if you want to know what I think, just between the two of us, I think your mother did sleep with a man. I'll tell you why I think so. First she was pretty glad you were coming home, then she wished you weren't. 'Why does he have to come home now?' That was part of her imaginary pregnancy, but based on an actual getting together with a man."

"Do you want me to find out?"

"Sure. But I wouldn't want the job of trying. You're not going to find anything out by asking questions. Women going through the change are the worst liars in captivity. About everything. And when it comes to matters that occur between the knees and the shoulders, you can't believe a word they say. Even to a doctor."

"Well, I'll try."

"Do your best. It'll help you understand your own wife when you get married."

Shortly after the preceding conversation I engaged a surveyor and the two of us made a tour of the farms, an interesting experience for me. Each of the fifteen farms had its own character, subject to the personalities of the farmers and their families, and even today I could write a book about those farmers and their farms, practically from memory. At one time or another I had met all the farmers, but now I was in a different position toward them, and they, of course, treated me differently. Now they were my employees, I was their employer. But I also had my own, secret mission: I studied each farmer carefully, looking for some sign, any sign, that would indicate that he had been my mother's lover. I came away satisfied that if Dr. Willetts's theory had any substance, the fortunate man was not to be found among our farmers. When I returned to Lyons after my two weeks' trip I so reported to Dr. Willetts. He was greatly amused, as well as pleased.

"All right," he said. "We've eliminated them, although I should have told you that I didn't want to know *who* it was. Just whether or not there was someone. Don't feel that you have to tell me who it was if you do find out. I'll keep your confidence if you do tell me, but don't feel it's necessary.

"Now, since you've been honest with me, I'll be honest with you. Sometimes during this change period, women get so distressed that maybe one in five hundred of them will commit suicide. In my years of practice I've had two that did, but one of those was dying of cancer, so she isn't a typical case. There's a whole hell of a lot about the human mind that we don't know. The effect of mind over matter, we call it. People get sick for no reason. Others get well when by all the signs they should die. A woman going through the change is a perfect specimen for us to study, but unfortunately nobody has the time and the women either can't or won't tell the truth about what's going on inside their minds. I'm just a country doctor and I never get enough sleep as it is, but sometimes when I'm driving along with old Betsy swinging her tail at the flies, I think to myself how much I could do if we had forty-eight hours in the day instead of twenty-five. I always tell Mrs. Willetts there's twenty-five hours in my day. I add on the extra hour for the times I go to sleep with my eyes open while my patients tell me for the third or fourth time what ails them. But if I had the time I'd like to keep records of the cases where the mind makes a liar out of body chemistry, just the cases that have come under my care. I guess every doctor gets that idea. But the most fertile field that I can think of is women undergoing the change. The pause of the menses. The no-men pause, we used to call it in medical school. Babies without intercourse. Intercourse that never happened. Swelling of the belly. Sensitive breasts. Miscarriages. You wouldn't believe what the imagination can do to women at such times. Jealousy to the point where a woman will accuse her husband of having relations with a young daughter. And murder. I'm satisfied that that woman up in Johnsville two years ago. What was her name? Cut her husband up with a hatchet two-three years ago. I wasn't called in on the case, but I saw her at the squire's office. Forty-eight or -nine years of age, she was. Healthy-looking woman. No reason whatsoever to hack up her man. But she chopped him up in his sleep and didn't remember a thing about it. She couldn't believe it when they arrested her. What was the matter? She was an extreme case, but I bet you she had these hallucinations from the change. Didn't keep them from putting a rope around her neck, but I don't think she was responsible. Well, I don't want you to think you have to lock your door when you go to bed at night. But it's a difficult time for your mother, and you have to be patient with her. She's as fine a woman as we have in this town . . . Tell me about Rome. I always wanted to go there. You know the Italians are great doctors."

I tried to persuade my mother to go to the seashore for the hottest part of that summer, but that was a mistake, and I should have known that it would be. Once a year, in November, she spent a week in Philadelphia, buying clothes and Christmas presents, attending the opera, paying duty calls on relatives, and seeing her few friends. My well-intended suggestion that the seashore might be a welcome change from the heat of the dog days was spurned. "Why are you trying to get rid of me?" said Mama.

"I'm not trying to get rid of you. If that's all I wanted to do, I'd go myself."

"Then why don't you, pray?"

"The farms. I want to be there for the thrashing."

"They all thrash at the same time. You can't be at all of them."

"They don't all thrash at the same time. The same week, but I can visit a lot of farms in a week."

"If you're trying to show me that you're a better manager than I was, I'm sure it's little enough I care. But if you want to get rid of me, don't invent such a transparent device, Robert. Say so and be done with it."

I held my tongue. Dr. Willetts, whom I now called on two or three nights a week, believed that her condition was not worsening and therefore could be considered as improving. He was an enjoyable man, good company in spite of the difference in our ages. He seemed to think that my years at school and the University and my few months abroad had made me more a man of the world than I thought I was, and I know that he looked forward to our evening chats almost as much as I did. He once said that he conversed intimately with twenty to thirty men and women a day, but that hardly a single person ever so much as asked him how he felt, let alone what he thought, the inference, of course, being that I did ask him or at least display some interest in him as a human being. Sometimes when I stayed later than usual his wife would serve us cocoa and buttered toast, or lemonade and cookies, and on several occasions I waited up with him until midnight when he was waiting for the summons to a confinement case.

"Did you ever have any leanings toward this?" he asked me one

138

night, waving his hand toward the glass-fronted medicine case and the examination table.

"No, never. Why?"

"I wondered. If you did, you're not too old to start. I had a friend who went to normal school, then taught for three or four years, saved his money, and he was in my class in medical school. Good doctor. Practising in Williamsport. I hear from him every now and again."

"Do you think I'd make a good doctor?"

"Well, no, Robert, I don't. Not the usual kind of doctor. But I'll tell you what you could have been. You remember my telling you about keeping records of cases that showed the power of mind over matter?"

"Yes, I do."

"Well, the thing that would keep you from being a good doctor in the way that I'm a good doctor—you'd spend too much time on a single patient and you'd never get your work done. But that would be a good thing for another kind of doctor. There's always that matter of earning a living. I couldn't stop now, with a wife and three children and an aged mother. But you could set yourself up as a sort of specialist. However, I guess you'd have your share of troubles doing that. Some doctors wouldn't help you. It's an odd profession. Every patient we see is an experiment, in a way. Either he's got the classic symptoms and responds to the usual treatment, thereby confirming past experiments. Or he's unusual, and we have to try all we know. But the profession doesn't like to think of doctors experimenting, and that's what you'd be. An innovation. We have never been very receptive to innovations or innovators, if there is such a word. Which is unfortunate for the people who've suffered and died without, say, chloroform. But on the other hand, the innovators have to be watched. If there aren't some restraints on them, they'd be all over the place and doing a lot of harm. The worst harm they'd do would be to undermine the confidence of the people. People will go to quacks and evangelists and priests and won't hold it against them if they fail. But when a man goes to an M.D. he has a right to have confidence in him and in conservative methods. So, as usual, there are two sides to the question. Still, I'd like to see some young fellows with zeal and money get into the profession. Not you, though, I guess. You haven't got the zeal, have you?"

"I'm afraid not."

"Then stay where you are. You could do yourself a great deal of harm, as well as the medical profession. You'd die of a broken heart, and you'd make it very hard for the innovators that believe in what they're doing. It isn't the same thing as trying to be an artist. If you fail, no harm done except to yourself."

"I suppose not."

"You could be a surgeon. You have the hands for it. But I've seen men with hands like yours that were very clumsy with the knife. The hands of a surgeon are overrated, if the rest isn't there. The heart, the knowledge, the control."

"I know exactly what you mean. A painter friend of mine told me the same thing about painting. The interesting thing about him was that he knew a lot about medicine."

"Did he? Then he probably told you that he was a painter instead of a surgeon because he realized that a clumsy painter can thumb out his mistakes. But it isn't very pretty to see a man bleed to death because you were clumsy with the knife."

"No, he didn't tell me that."

"Well, maybe he didn't give it much thought. He's better off a painter. And so's the world."

I took a strange comfort from Dr. Willetts's criticism of Chester Calthorp, and as I did I became aware of the distance in miles and in time that now separated me from Chester. What with my mother, the farms, and Dr. Willetts himself, I had so filled my life that if there had been a wound to touch, I could have touched it and felt no pain. It was now almost exactly as long a time since I had seen Chester as the length of my trip abroad. Soon it would be a year since we had left Philadelphia, the most crowded year of my life thus far. Intuitively, briefly, but almost completely I admitted, or perhaps claimed, or perhaps conceded, that I was a happy man. Here was where I belonged, the better for having been elsewhere; and with a new hope that was not born of desperation and loneliness I could look to the future, patiently ready to love and be loved.

•

In the next several batches of material Robert Millhouser filled nearly 300 pages of the legal notepaper with Lyons reminiscences, descriptions of the farms and timber lands, and details of the transactions that supported his belief in himself as a businessman. From his accounts there could be no doubt whatever that he was alert and shrewd, and the figures showed him to be successful, in that he added to the earnings and the holdings of the estate. On my first reading of this material I thought that he might be writing about business at such length because he was proud of the fact that he had duplicated his father's success. The reader will recall that Henry Mill-

houser, despite a late start, had re-established the family fortune in spite of its chaotic condition after the murder of Judge Peter Mill- houser. But in this 300-page report, which also covered a period of about five years, scarcely any mention was made of Robert's rela- tions with his mother, and I wrote him a note in which I spoke in com- plimentary tones of the material he had sent me, and asked him if it would be convenient to interrupt his story with a letter that would com- plete that part of his report on his mother. I frankly suspected that he was subtly leading me away from that part of the story, and my note, as the saying goes, drew blood. He replied quite coldly that if I reserved the right to handle his material as I saw fit, he too reserved the right to tell the story in his own way. "However, since you specifically re- quest that information, I shall oblige. My mother regained her health completely and while I cannot say that our relations were cordial, the mutual respect and understanding made for a workable arrange- ment between us," he wrote. "But I must ask you in future not to im- pede the free flow of my story as I tell it." It was not a satisfactory reply, and I wrote a second note in which I said as much, but I tore it up. It was apparent to me that Robert Millhouser, however candid he might be in self-revelation, was increasingly reluctant to say more than he had to about anyone else. I therefore returned to the fictional method which I have used earlier. It made my job more difficult, since it often meant plowing through hundreds of pages of irrelevant material to unearth a single essential fact, but obviously my curi- osity (if not my somewhat dwindling "compassion") was greater than my impatience. I now continue, following the fictional method.—G.H.

In the autumn of that year (1878) Robert Millhouser was pleased and surprised to be invited to serve on the board of directors of the Johnsville Fair. The invitation came too late for the inclusion of his name on the Fair stationery or for him to take an active part in the preparations, but it had sentimental value because Henry Millhouser had served on the original board prior to the Civil War, and the Fair was only just being revived after seventeen years. Moreover, it was a token of recognition of the position Robert could be, and was, expected to occupy in the area. The Fair was dominated by Johns- ville men, and the representatives of the neighboring towns were carefully selected from the ranks of the leading business and pro- fessional men. Robert Millhouser was at least ten years younger than any other director, but obviously he had created a good impression in the short time he had spent in Lyons. "Did you have anything to do with it?" he asked Dr. Willetts, who was another director.

"I certainly did," said Dr. Willetts. "I said at a meeting, this was a *country* fair, intended to give the farmers a little something to look forward to, and why didn't they put a real farmer on the board, instead of storekeepers and lawyers and doctors."

"Oh, I see."

"No you don't see. There've been other farmers discussed. And all I did was suggest you. I couldn't have elected you all by myself. The other fellows in Lyons agreed with me. You're getting to be pretty well liked in town, Robert. Maybe because you haven't tried to be. Just going along and minding your own business."

"Well, I admit I like to be liked, but I want to go on minding my own business. I don't want any public life."

"You mean like politics."

"Yes."

"The politicians won't bother you. Just give them their contribution and let them do the dirty work."

"I haven't even given them a contribution so far."

"They'll be around to see you one of these days."

"Well, I appreciate being elected, but this is the last public thing I'll ever do."

"Public thing, but you ought to take an interest in church matters, and I know the bank wants to ask you to be on their board. If you vote your own stock and your mother's, you'd be pretty strong there."

"Later, maybe. But as far as church goes, that's like politics to me. I'll give them a contribution if they'll let me alone."

"Well, there're all kinds of things you could get mixed up in if you showed the slightest interest. You're a college graduate and well-to-do. You won't be able to say no to everything, and you shouldn't. This is your town."

"The Fair and maybe later the bank. Otherwise, no."

"I'd like to see you in the Masons."

"I don't know very much about the Masons, but I don't think I'll ever join. My father was a Lutheran."

"But there are Lutherans Masons."

"Not the kind of Lutheran my father was. No Millhouser was ever a Mason. I know that."

"Well, I'll say no more about it."

"I don't mean to offend you."

"I'll never mention the subject again, and I understand your feelings," said Dr. Willetts. "Pretty soon you ought to be thinking about getting married."

"I do think about it."

"Haven't found the right girl?"

"Haven't found any girl, right or wrong."

"Well, I guess there aren't as many right ones in town as there are wrong ones. Right for you, that is. Nothing against their morals. Your father went all the way to Ireland to pick one, and he picked a good one."

"He didn't have to go to Ireland, though. He met her in Philadelphia."

"Well, after harvest you can see if you have the same luck. Plenty of time then."

"I've been thinking of doing that. By the way, how is my mother?"

"Coming around nicely. She's got rid of that imaginary baby. It just evaporated, and the hired girl, Margaret—well, you don't want me to talk about female matters, but your mother's going to be all right. Haven't you noticed an improvement?"

"I have, but I didn't rely on my opinion."

"You've handled her the right way. Patiently, but you didn't spoil her." He was silent. His pipe had gone out and he tapped out the top ashes and relit it. "There *was* a *man,* Robert."

"There was? How did you find that out?"

"Well, I had to do some detective work."

"I wasn't very successful, was I?"

"I didn't think you would be."

"Who was it?"

"Oh, I wouldn't tell you that even if I knew."

"But if you tell me anything I could pretty nearly figure it out, couldn't I?"

"Not the way I'll tell you. I'm not repeating gossip. I'm only telling you so that you'll be easier in your mind about your mother and her mind."

"Is it a Lyons man?"

"I don't think so, but I'm not going to answer any more of those kind of questions. But to relieve your mind, she had intercourse with a man just about a year ago, not quite."

"I wonder who the hell it was," said Robert.

"Well, now that you know that much you could probably find out. But why do you want to find out?"

"I don't know."

"I'll tell you how I found out. I was sure, you remember. I was always sure. So I went ahead and I said to her one time, I said to her, 'How soon after your period did you have relations with this man?' And she said without thinking, 'Four or five days.' Then she realized I'd tricked her. I didn't mention it again when I saw her the next time, but the second or third time I asked her the same question. 'I told you before,' she said. 'It was about four or five days.' So then

I acted natural and I said, 'Yes, but was it only the one time?' And she said yes, it was only the one time and she hoped it would be the last. Well, I had to ask her certain other questions and she answered them. Normal. No nervousness. And she was telling me the truth."

"I wonder who it was. I wonder where it was."

"Well, I don't know who it was, but I guess it was right in your own home. Somebody that happened to be there when she was ready for it. I think that's the way it happened, Robert, and you just remember, you're not her husband. You're only her son. Don't you go bothering her about it. Don't you ever let on you know. She's alone in the world except for you and she's been a good mother to you. That's a lonely life she's had, you know."

"I know that."

"Furthermore, I'll give you some medical advice that I won't send you a bill for. If she ever shows any interest in a man, you do your best to encourage it. With the right man she could have a lot of good years left. And I'm not saying anything your father wouldn't say if he could speak. There was a big difference in age there, and yet I don't think another man existed for her while your father was alive."

"No, I guess not."

"You don't have to guess. You know."

"I do," said Robert.

Now and then in their conversations Dr. Willetts would speak semi-paternally, semi-professionally, as in this meeting, and Robert found that he liked it when the doctor assumed the fatherly role. Robert's good education and polish usually put the young man and the middle-aged physician on an equal footing, but in matters pertaining to his life work the doctor spoke *ex cathedra,* and at such times Robert recalled his father. The men were unalike, but there was a little something of Henry Millhouser's quiet conviction in Dr. Willetts's pronouncements and *obiter dicta.* In so short a time Robert had found so disparate a man and ideas to take the place of Chester Calthorp, and Robert did not fail to appreciate the significance of the fact that Dr. Willetts had not changed, Chester Calthorp had not changed; the change was going on in himself.

The Johnsville Fair was a modest endeavor and in spite of the support of some leading citizens of the Valley, there was opposition from church people, who objected to the wheels of chance, the harness racing, and the sale of beer. The clergy were restrained from preaching against the Fair, since the prominent men on the Fair board were the highly respectable parishioners of the more prosperous churches. Nevertheless the ministers and their most active vol-

144

unteer assistants withheld their blessings and stayed away.* Robert Millhouser asked his mother to accompany him to the opening day, and when she declined he remarked that he hoped she was not frightened by the Reverend Emil Betz.

"Frightened by that creature? How dare you say a thing like that!"

"Well, he's one of the anti-Fair crowd."

"Then I'll be pleased to go with you," said Zilph.

"If we had a high-wheeler I'd enter the gray."

"Would they let a director race?"

"I wouldn't drive. I'd have Moses drive."

"How much does a high-wheeler cost?"

"I know where you can get one for seventy-five dollars."

"Buy it."

"Do you mean that?"

"Of course I mean it. We won't win, but we'll show the church people where we stand. Next year I'll put up a trophy in your father's memory."

"They'd like a purse better."

"Very well, then, a purse. Fifty dollars?"

"Oh, that'd be more than enough."

The gray, driven by Moses Hatfield, did not finish in the money, but the race was for Zilph the high point of her afternoon at the Fair. It was a hot Indian-summer day and Robert was concerned for his mother; the only shelter at the Fair was under the exhibition tents and the sun was as strong as in August. But Zilph seemed not to mind, and in spite of the poor showing of the gray she was so enthusiastic that people near her watched her instead of the race.

"I coulda beat them horses," said Moses. "But I didn't want to kill my horse beating a lot of nobody horses."

"You did well, Moses," said Zilph. "Next year we'll win everything in sight."

"No ma'am. I aint gonna ask this gray horse to go that fast again, never."

"I wasn't talking about the gray horse. Mr. Robert is going to find us a winner."

"Am I? I guess I am."

Zilph's appearance at the Fair, and the quickly spreading rumor that she planned to establish a racing stable (it did not stop there; the Millhousers were said to be planning a sixteenth farm as a breeding establishment), had the predictable effect of reviving some of the

---

* In later years there was a change of heart; many of the Valley congregations had tents on the Fair grounds where meals were served.

antagonism against her. On the other hand, she and her son had now taken an active part in a community enterprise and overnight they ceased to be the remote, self-sufficient pair who literally looked down on Lyons from their big house on the hillside. Zilph was asked to be a patroness of the Lyons Assembly, and she accepted; Robert had inherited his membership from his father, although his father and mother had never attended an Assembly. It could hardly be said that Lyons was undergoing a complete social transformation, but the town was now getting close to a hundred years old, its character was set; it had progressed from a way-station on a stagecoach highway to a terminus of two railways, the banking and marketing center for the collieries and farms, and the site of several small factories. Two of the one-story false-front buildings on Main and Market Streets were being replaced by a two-story and a three-story false-front buildings. There were several third-generation families in the town and at least a dozen men in the town owned full-dress. The Langendorfs were the town's oldest family, but the very fact that they were so thoroughly Lyons people, and totally lacking in points of contrast with other Lyons families, made them ineligible for the position that became open to the Millhousers. That position was open or already occupied in hundreds of towns and cities between the Hudson and the Mississippi in the Middle Atlantic and Middle Western States. The possession of money was a basic requirement, but the imaginative spending of money on luxuries was the factor that set certain families apart from others that possessed money, lived comfortably, and did not set any style. Lyons in the late seventies discovered that the Millhousers were the only family in town that could be compared to the fabulous Caldwells of Fort Penn, who were said to be so much the leaders of Fort Penn society that every new governor made sure to have the Caldwells to dinner during the first week of his administration, then waited—sometimes forever—for the Caldwells to return his invitation. The Caldwells were richer than the Millhousers and more firmly established in Fort Penn than the Millhousers in Lyons, but the comparison was a fair one. Indeed, there was even a little bit of the exotic to the Millhousers that operated in their favor where style and dash were concerned: Zilph was a foreign-born woman, not an immigrant, who was reputed to be the daughter of a Sir John Somebody. (The reputation was inaccurate; Zilph's maternal aunt was the lady of a knight, and the rumor originated in the post office, where Zilph's letters addressed to Lady Somebody in Belfast did not pass unnoticed. It would not have mattered much if the Lyons men and women had been told that Zilph's Sir John and Lady Somebody were an extremely undashing elderly couple who

146

owed the knighthood to Sir John's abstruse findings in the field of astronomy; no one else in Lyons, or probably in Fort Penn, was so closely connected to a Sir John and Lady.) Robert Millhouser likewise had acquired, without earning, a reputation as a figure in European society and artistic circles. He owed this reputation to Margaret Dillon, to whom Zilph occasionally had read parts of Robert's letters from abroad.

And thus it was that Zilph and Robert Millhouser were precipitated into the position of acknowledged style-setters for Lyons and the Valley. Zilph and Robert had not changed; the change was going on in Lyons itself. That is not to say, however, that Zilph and Robert could ignore their new status. They could not pretend that they were not pleased and amused by the invitations that came to them. Zilph declined the invitations, as she always had, but Robert put in an appearance at an Assembly or two, attended the annual dinner of the bank directors and their wives, sat on the platform for the dedication of the new G. C. & L. depot, and practically by acclamation was sent to Fort Penn to represent Lyons at the inauguration of a new governor. All these activities, covering a period of three years, made life somewhat more agreeable for Robert. As to Zilph, she responded to the town's bows and smiles that for so many years had been only bows; at MacMahon's and the other town shops she would engage in small talk with the customers as well as with the clerks who for so many years had been her principal conversational contact with the town. She still did not want the town women in her house or in her confidence, but the new cordiality expressing the new admiration was agreeable to her also. "It's a mistake to tell a whole town to go to hell, indubitably," she remarked to Robert. "But *they* put the chip on my shoulder when I came here to live. Now if they want to gently lift it off with their best kid gloves, I'll give them a smile and pretend I don't notice what it is they're taking off. That they put there in the first place."

Robert refused to take part in church activities or in politics. At bank meetings and meetings of the Fair directors he volunteered few suggestions but he asked such questions as were necessary for his understanding of the affairs of the bank and Fair. Consequently his suggestions were favorably received, and since they never involved serious changes of policy, they were acted upon and were successful. "Gentlemen, do you know who ought to be on this board and isn't, and he's our biggest competitor?" he asked the bank directors one Monday afternoon. "Jeremiah MacMahon."

"Jeremiah MacMahon? Our biggest competitor?"

"Jeremiah MacMahon has the best of the miners for his customers.

147

A miner runs up a bill at MacMahon's store and on payday he goes to MacMahon's first thing. But not only to pay what he owes Mac-Mahon. MacMahon has them saving money and they save it with him. They trust him. Some of them are saving money with MacMahon until they have enough to bring the wife over from the old country. They trust MacMahon, and they don't even know us."

"MacMahon is a depositor of ours. Where does he keep this money?"

"I don't know. In his safe, probably. But these are men that MacMahon has taught the habit of saving. Every one of them should be a depositor here."

"How do you know all this?"

"From my mother. We even have a maid that saves her money with MacMahon instead of depositing it here and drawing interest."

"Well," said a director. "That's up to Fred."

Fred Langendorf was the bank president. "I have nothing against Jerry. Competitors don't make us enemies. To my way of thinking there isn't a better man in the town than Jerry MacMahon."

"Yes, but do we want a Catholic on the board?" said another director.

"If we don't, we're liable to see a Catholic bank in town and Jerry the president of it," said Langendorf. "I'll hear a motion we elect Jerry to this board, and another motion commending Robert Mill-houser."

The election of Jeremiah MacMahon was followed by the opening of more than fifty new accounts in one week and nearly fifty more in the course of six months. "Robert, this is the nicest thing that's happened to me since I opened my store, and I know you did it," Mac-Mahon told Robert. "Fred Langendorf gives all the credit to you. Yes, in fact Fred told me it was your idea to have him invite me, and that's nice, too. I'll never forget this, not as long as I live."

In those years was created the opinion of Robert Millhouser that lasted into the next century: a man who could have lived anywhere, and chose to live in Lyons; a shy man, who could change in an instant from his reserved manner to courtliness; a good son to a spirited mother; a successful businessman who was not a penny-pincher; a man whom it was safe to copy in matters of social usage; and finally a man who was an eccentric because he was not like anyone else in town, and yet defied every effort to be classified as queer through any evidence of appearance, speech, conduct or history. It was the town's first opinion of Robert Millhouser in maturity, and such opinions do not as a rule change. Lyons had changed its opinion of his mother, but to many of the citizens she was still a newcomer and would so remain, regardless of the low or high esteem in which she might be held. And meanwhile the Millhousers went along, living their lives, less and less amused or concerned with their place in the Lyons social scheme, occupying themselves with their own daily routines, making adjustments when necessary and trying to avoid the necessity of making adjustments. They had been fitted into a place that was more or less their own creation, and without the subtle disturbances that not fitting in would have caused them, they could forget about Lyons and Lyons, slowly, could forget about them. Once classified, they ceased to be a problem to Lyons, and Lyons ceased to be a problem to them. But there were problems of the Millhousers' own.

Long after Dr. Willetts had reported his discovery to Robert Millhouser, years after, Robert had the troublous problem of his curiosity over his mother's love affair. Weeks and months would pass without his consciously attempting to penetrate the mystery, but then she would say to him: "I've told you it's rude to stare."

"Have I been staring?"

"For ten minutes, and it's even ruder to stare without looking. Is it the mystery of the sphinx you're trying to penetrate?"

"I'm sorry. Put it down to that. I was thirty miles away, at the Lindemuth farm."

"I'm all for your thinking about the Lindemuth farm, but I'm not a rick of hay."

But if she could not bear to be stared at, she would as often do the staring. Many times when he was on his way out of a room he would suddenly remember something and turn about and she would be caught in an open expression of perplexity. He was, he told himself, generally happy with her except when she would accidentally remind him that even the best of relations with her was necessarily incomplete and that if there was to be any solution to that problem, it had to be his own. He did not, therefore, resent her staring because it was "rude" or even because it betokened her bafflement; his uneasiness was due to her unintended reminder of his celibate state.

It was not unusual for a man in his situation to remain unmarried. In the upper classes especially there were bachelors who took pride in their bachelorhood, as though it proclaimed a series of victories over individual women and all of womanly guile. Leaving out the monstrously unattractive men whom no woman would want, there were many men, upper and middle class, who preferred what they called single blessedness, their pipes and cigars and whiskey, their households run for their own comfort, their freedom to come and go, and their freedom to enjoy the company of women and to terminate the pleasure at will. So Robert Millhouser said to himself many times.

149

But in the black darkness of truth, alone with the truth, he admitted that the men in their thirties—and he was now nearing his thirties—who spoke of their freedom, fell into two groups: the men he believed, who had women along with their pipes and cigars and whiskey, and the men whom he did not believe, who did not want women. In Lyons there were a teacher of the piano, a paperhanger, a dry-goods clerk at Langendorf's, a bookkeeper at the bank who also earned a modest pittance by writing name-cards and invitations, who were in their thirties and forties and wifeless. They were also the only men in Lyons who called him Bob, and the piano teacher even called him Bobby. (A few of the girls he had grown up with, and their mothers, sometimes had called him Bobby, but at home he had always been Robert, and Leonard Vance, the last contemporary who had called him Bobby, was long since dead.) They were the men who did not want women, and he knew that without asking them. He had never thought of them as a homogeneous group until a few years after his return to Lyons and the beginning of his mother's disturbing perplexity. When he sought to justify his bachelorhood in her cold eyes, he found only a piano teacher, a paperhanger, a dry-goods clerk, and a Spencerian penman in one group of bachelors, and a night constable, a railway brakeman and a crapulous horse-doctor in another. He knew that his mother would place him in the first group, but he wanted to be placed in neither. Indeed, he wanted to be in no group at all, but one Monday afternoon, after the weekly bank meeting, the bookkeeper said to him: "Walking home, Bob?"

"Yes, I am."

"I'll walk part of the way with you."

For three successive Mondays the bookkeeper waited for Robert. Normie Vogel, the bookkeeper, was a stout man in his late thirties who lived with his mother and three sisters in the built-up section that ended a block away from the Millhouser place. He was carefully inoffensive during the forced conversations and Robert set such a fast pace that Normie was out of breath when they parted, but not so winded on the third Monday that he could not invite Robert to come in and take a look at some scrollwork he had just completed for the Grand Army encampment. "It's on real genuine parchment and it took me over two months," said Normie. "All that work and nobody'll ever take notice to it hanging on their wall."

"Afraid I haven't got time, Normie."

"Oh, let her wait. It'll do her good to wait once in her life."

"Who?"

"Who? Your mother. I stopped my mother bossing me. Now did I hurt your feelings saying that?"

150

"Deeply."

"I better shut up before I say too much."

"That's a *very* good idea, Normie. Good day."

Normie was not waiting the next Monday, and Robert noticed that the piano teacher, the paperhanger, and the dry-goods clerk avoided speaking to him thereafter. His sense of relief was enough to warn him of the depths of his fears; Normie Vogel had not acted on impulse on that first Monday; he and the others had been quite convinced that Robert belonged with them and would respond to the slightest beckoning. For the first time in several years he thought of Canon Lovelace and I. Goldberg and those Philadelphia friends of Chester Calthorp's.

Robert Millhouser's only intimate friend now was Dr. Willetts. Their meetings after office hours were a fixed custom, and in addition they would take Moses Hatfield and Dr. Willetts's hound dog and go gunning in the fall, and largely out of friendship Robert would accompany the doctor on a trout-fishing day in the spring. It was a friendship that would not have been predictably successful, but paradoxically almost everything was in its favor. Robert's hours and unmarried status made him available during the only time when Dr. Willetts was in a relaxing mood, and by instinct they were men who preferred limited companionship to the gregariousness of the lodge or the saloon. The esoterics of medicine made professional talk impossible, but there was enough going on in the world, in and out of the Valley, to supply conversational topics. Dr. Willetts got around, saw people and things that Robert Millhouser did not see; Robert Millhouser took the Fort Penn newspapers, which the doctor did not have time to read. Consequently, Robert would learn that the upper Johnsville bridge was washed out, and the doctor would learn that a big new hotel was going up in Fort Penn—things neither would have known about without the other. Once or twice Robert volunteered to go with the doctor on a night call, but the doctor said: "What would you do? Sit in the cutter and freeze to death, or sit in the kitchen with the family?" Since Robert had no desire to help in reducing a fracture or disposing of placenta, the area of companionship was limited to the doctor's back office and the uplands during the fall. Robert was therefore surprised one night when Dr. Willetts said: "What are you doing week after next, toward the middle of the week?"

"Week after next? Same as usual."

"Not going down to the farms?"

"No, not that week. I'll be right here."

"Well, the reason I'm asking is because that's the week I usually take two or three days off every year. The County Medical Society has its annual banquet that week, and I go to that. And I own a little property in Fort Penn that I take a look at once a year. Mrs. Willetts always went with me before, but this year she wants to work on Mary's graduation dress. Would you like to take the trip with me? It'd be a change."

Robert did not regard a trip to Fort Penn as much of a change, but he sensed that the doctor wanted his company, and so they agreed that two nights away from Lyons would be a break in the routine.

In Fort Penn the doctor attended one afternoon meeting of the Medical Society, came back to their hotel, put on his full-dress, and departed for the banquet. Robert, a non-resident member of the Fort Penn Club, dined there alone, watched without interest a game of three-ball billiards, and returned to the hotel and went to bed, having spoken to two club servants and declined a polite invitation to join in the billiards match. An overpowering attack of loneliness lasted long enough for him to regret the impulse that had caused him to take this trip; his friend was enjoying himself with other doctors, while he lay in an uncomfortable bed in an ugly room, without his books or a hearth-fire. Dr. Willetts had a room across the hall and Robert did not hear him come in and did not see him until breakfast. In spite of his misery, Robert had slept well and was even surprised when the doctor said: "I don't know what's the matter with me. I don't think I was very considerate, leaving you alone like that. What did you do?"

"I was all right. I did what I said I'd do. I had dinner at the Fort Penn Club and watched them play billiards."

"Did you have a good dinner?"

"No, but there aren't many clubs where you do. At least the waiters are friendly, even if they don't know you."

"You're a funny man, Robert. Why do you belong to the Fort Penn Club?"

"Because my father was a member and my mother's lawyer put me up when I was twenty-one. When I was twenty-five I was elected and last night was the first time I ever went there on my own."

"Does Fred Langendorf know you're a member? He's been trying to get in for three-four years."

"He's never mentioned it to me, but I'd be glad to do anything I could. As I said, I was put up by Conrad Isaminger. My seconder was a man I didn't know very well, Ben Rosebery, a fraternity brother of mine, a few years ahead of me at Penn."

"Well, if you'd say a good word for Fred he'd be very grateful. That is, if you have no objection."

"Far from it. I'll go around and see Ben today. But how about you? Would you like to join?"

"With me it's a question of finances. I'd like to be a member, anyone would, but it'd be a sheer waste of money. But thanks for suggesting it."

"Well, if you ever change your mind. They must have a city directory downstairs. I'll find out where Ben Rosebery has his office and we can go around and call on him."

"You do it while I go have a look at my property."

Ben Rosebery's office was only a block away. He looked up from his desk as Robert entered and he called out to him. "Robert Millhouser! Come on in and shake the coal dust off your feet." He was a large, hearty man with a cavalryman's moustache. He and Robert quickly looked at each other's watch-chain and the Delta Psi charm and smiled.

"You know, I've been meaning to write you a letter," said Rosebery. "There's a man up your way that's been put up for the Fort Penn Club. He's been up for three or four years and I often wondered why he didn't have a letter from you."

"That's what I dropped in to see you about. Fred Langendorf."

"That's the man. I thought perhaps they might have asked you to write a letter for him and you didn't want to."

"I never knew he was up."

"Don't you read your mail?"

"Not from the Fort Penn Club. I pay my bills and I don't pay much attention to the rest."

"That's a hell of a fine attitude to take. If everybody did that the club wouldn't be worth a damn. Well, what about this Langendorf fellow? Is he all right?"

"Well, he's not pushy, that's obvious, or I'd have known about his being up. He's a good man. I've known him all my life, and our families have been friends. I see him every week at bank meeting."

"Delta Psi?"

"No. I wouldn't vote against him for Delta Psi, but there's a lot of difference between Delta Psi and the Fort Penn Club. You know that better than I do. I'd vote for a man for the Fort Penn Club that I might hesitate to vote for Delta Psi."

"So would I, and have. Well, it's a good thing you spoke to me. I'm chairman of the committee and we were going to pass over Langendorf for the third time. Next year we'd have to ask his sponsors to withdraw his name. I'll put him through on your say-so. And now the hell with him. Can you have dinner with me? I have to be in court in half an hour."

Dr. Willetts, Rosebery and Robert had dinner at a rathskeller owned by a man named Fritz Gottlieb. Rosebery was a man who made up his own mind about other men, but he would accept a friend's appraisal of a man if the friend had met Rosebery's requirements. He had already accepted Fred Langendorf on Robert Millhouser's say-so; he now accepted Dr. Willetts for the same reason. After two drinks all around, Rosebery knew all he needed to know about Dr. Willetts for a sociable evening, and since he was an affably dominating man, they ate and drank everything he ordered and followed his conversational leads. He had a way of hesitating for a fraction of a second before letting go with a laugh, which created a sort of suspense over the cause of the laughter and, when he let go, made the laugh itself an event. It was impossible not to be affected by his laugh, and he laughed with such thorough enjoyment that men and women who heard him were usually cheered up.

"Are you married, Mr. Rosebery?" said Dr. Willetts.

"Am I married?" He let go with a laugh. "I'm the most un-married man in the Commonwealth of Pennsylvania. As long as they don't shake a lassoo at me, I love 'em. Would a wife let me come here to Fritz's every night? I don't, but I want to be able to if I feel like it. What made you ask that question, Doctor?"

"Because I thought I knew the answer, but I wanted to make sure."

"No, I'm like our friend here. A couple of artful dodgers, we are. I'd wager a case of bonded whiskey the good ladies up in Lyons have their traps set for Robert, but no success. You *are* married, of course, Doctor?"

"Oh, yes. Very much so."

"So much so that, uh, you wouldn't come along with us later in the evening? I'm going to take Robert to a place I don't think he's ever been to, because it only opened this year."

"Are you? Where am I going?" said Robert.

"No hurry. You'll see. They know we're coming. Let's just eat and drink now and be merry later. You wouldn't want to come along, Doctor?"

"I'm getting past the age."

"Oh, if that's all that's keeping you. Some of the politicians that go there are old enough to be your father. Truthfully. Come and have a look anyway, Doctor."

"Well, I don't see why not."

Not a sliver of light showed at the windows of the house they went to, and downstairs in a reception room four men were sipping whiskey and smoking cigars. They all nodded to Rosebery, who waved to them and said: "Gentlemen." A pretty mulatto said: "Mr. Ben, gentlemen, rest your hats and coats, please?" They moved to the second floor front and were greeted by a stalwart woman of sixty, whose face and neck were thickly covered with rice powder. "Good evening, Ben," she said. "Gentlemen, come with me?" They proceeded to a tiny room where they could hear the music of a violin, cello and viola coming from a closed room across the hall.

"This is Dr. Willetts and Mr. Millhouser," said Ben. "Gentlemen, this is Mrs. Jones."

"Pleased to meet you. That's Dr. Willetts and Mr. Millhouser? Right the first time. Well, Ben, I hear you got that woman off. She was guilty a mile, and you know it."

"She isn't now. She's as innocent as you are, of that particular crime."

"I was gonna say, if she was as innocent as me, they oughta take her out and shoot her."

Ben let go one of his laughs. "Ah, you, you're a great woman, Jonesey."

"Don't call me Jonesey. Mary is the name, or Mrs. Jones. But I don't like Jonesey. It's too familiar. You're just a customer here, Ben."

"A damn good customer, though."

"I'll give you that much, but it don't entitle you. Gentlemen, will I have them bring up a bottle of wine? Champagne?"

"We'd better say yes. Yes, bring up a bottle of champagne but also a bottle of good whiskey," said Ben.

Mrs. Jones went to the speaking tube and gave the order. "Now, all three wish to be accommodated this evening?"

"Well, you have to show these gentlemen the livestock," said Ben.

"You keep talking like that and you can bet your sweet ass you're not gonna be welcome here. I mean it, Ben," said Mrs. Jones.

He laughed again. "You're always threatening me, but if I stopped coming here you'd die of a broken heart. I'm your favorite boy and you know it."

"You must be or I wouldn't let you carry on the way you do. But my girls don't like it."

"If you kept me out I'd open up across the street in the same line of business," said Ben.

"You think that's all there is to it, eh? It looks easy to you. Ah, here we are. Just put them things on the table, Jim, and see who's busy. Three."

"Three, yes ma'am."

Presently the three women appeared and were introduced as Pearl, Dottie-May, and Zaza. They wore evening gowns and fake jewelry, and they served the drinks, which gave them an opportunity to move about and display their décolletage. They were all young but had little else in common. Pearl was enough like Mrs. Jones to be her daughter; Dottie-May was on the stout side, with large pendulous breasts; and Zaza was short and blond and fully aware that she was unmistakably younger than the others.

"All right, girls, thank you," said Mrs. Jones. The girls left. "Well, gentlemen? Did you come to any decision? I have seven other girls but you may have to wait a while to see them."

"Doctor?" said Ben.

"Well, I don't know why I should have first choice, but I liked the one named Pearl."

"Pearl is a wonderful girl," said Mrs. Jones. "You'll like her. Mr. Millhouser?"

"Well, I liked Zaza."

"All the young fellows like Zaza," said Mrs. Jones. "There's one young fellow, if I told you his name, he wants to marry her. I have to keep him out of here because his father's one of the few men that could close me up."

"That's the truth," said Ben. "I know that for a fact."

"Ben can tell you. Ben, you're gonna have to wait if you don't wish Dottie-May."

"I'll sit and talk to you."

"Not all night. I was up till all hours with those doctors. I guess you're here for the banquet, Doctor? Surprised I didn't see you last night."

"You almost did."

"Well, that's a good recommendation for my place, not that I need it. Another drink, gentlemen, or any time you're ready."

"I'm ready," said Robert. He was more than ready; he was in a state of excitement that he was sure Dr. Willetts could detect in his breathing. The mulatto girl escorted him to a room upstairs where Zaza was smoking a cigarette, still in her evening gown and relaxed in an armchair. The mulatto girl left them and Zaza smiled. "You got my wink. I was afraid you wouldn't get it. You can hang up your clothes in the wardrobe."

"What about you?"

"Me? This comes off quicker than you can untie your necktie. Unless you rather I took my time."

Robert undressed awkwardly, and finally sat naked on the edge of the bed. "Now watch how quick this comes off. Br-r-r-r-r, and there we are."

"Beautiful," he said. "Beautiful. Now get in."

"First I want to have a look at you." She inspected him, and said: "You're all right, but we better get in quick."

All the visual pleasure and anticipation were denied him by his urgent haste.

"Mister!" she said. "How long since you had a woman?"

"A long time," he said.

"Are you always fast like that?"

"I guess so."

"How long was it? A couple years?"

"Do we have to talk about it?"

"No. I just as soon you were quick as slow. I'd sooner. But I'm supposed to be for your pleasure and you don't get no pleasure in that short a time. Or maybe you do. I guess you starded getting horny downstairs."

"Uh-huh."

"I'll be back in a minute," said Zaza.

When she returned, wearing a flannel bathrobe, he pretended to be asleep. She lit a cigarette and sat in the armchair, and every tiny sound in the room—every time she changed her position in the chair, or blew smoke into the air, or softly whistled a tune—was so magnified that in his concentration on sound and silence he did actually fall asleep. When he awoke she was lying in bed with him. "Wake up," she said. "You been asleep over an hour. Can I do anything for you?"

"You are," he said.

"I want you to have a good time."

"I want *you* to have a good time."

"All right. Give me a good time," she said. She teased him until he was close to violence and then she accepted him and he was proud. He lay back with an arm around her neck.

"Thank you," he said.

"That's all right," she said. "You know, I shouldn't ask you this. Maybe you'll want to punch me one. But did you ever have a woman before?"

"No."

"Is that the honest truth? How old are you?"

"Twenty-seven."

"Twenty-seven. God, six years older than me, and you're not a fairy. How come you never had a woman before? At least I don't think you're a fairy. Are you?"

"I couldn't be if you don't think I am, could I?"

"Listen, everybody's different. There's no two the same. Where I worked before I came here, I used to have an old buzzard he'd always ask for me, and then you know what he'd do? Sit and talk for an hour. He was an old fairy but he didn't want to let on. Covering up, that's what he was doing. No, I don't think you're a fairy but maybe you are. A person can be both. But I hope you're not, because if there's one son of a bitch I hate it's a fairy."

"Why?"

"Why? Because I was married to one, that's why. He was a pretender, but I was no sooner married to him than I found out what he was. A pimp. I coulda had him arrested."

"No you couldn't."

"Not for pimping. I know that much about what the law says. But he had another wife. Bigamy. I could testimony against him for bigamy. Dirty son of a bitch took every nickel I earned. You don't live here in town, do you?"

"No."

"Come around and see me the next time you're in town. You know, some girls say it's very lucky to get a virgin. Others say it's bad luck. I think good luck. The only other time I had one was here, and that was good luck. A young fellow's old man ga' me a hundred dollars to get rid of the kid. At least Mrs. Jones ga' me the hundred. I don't know what the old man gave her. Well, that's lucky. How many times do you get a hundred dollars that easy?"

"Not often, I guess. I'll give you a hundred dollars."

"Yeah? What for?" she said. "I'm a straight girl, so far. I don't have to do anything I don't want to do. Yet."

"I'll give it to you for luck. For giving me a good night's sleep."

"I don't know. That sounds fishy. You could get me into trouble with the old lady."

"How?"

"I don't know, but it sounds fishy. You come and see me the next time you're in town and maybe give it to me for a tip. But if it gets around you ga' me a hundred dollars, the old lady's liable to think what did I do for a hundred dollars? There's hundred-dollar girls, but believe me they earn it, and I aint ready for that yet."

"You're too suspicious, Zaza."

"Too suspicious. Listen, if I wasn't too suspicious I wouldn't be in a high-class house like this. I'd be down by the freight yards for two-bits a hustle. That son of a bitch of a fairy's the one that made me suspicious. Maybe you can sneak me the hundred the next time you're in town, but thanks for the offer. Only don't say nothing to the old lady, nothing. She gets thinking I'm a hundred-dollar girl and that's what I'll be and I'll be old before my time. You know how it is, you get to be a hundred-dollar girl and the old lady won't let you work for less. Why should she let a hundred-dollar girl work for ten or five? So all you do is wait around for some rich senator and you start borr'ing money from the old lady. No. Well, just as long as you had a good time. You can tell her *that*. You can tell her I was the best little piece of tail you ever had, and that wouldn't be lying, would it? What did you say your name was?"

"Robert Millhouser."

"All right, Bob. I guess our time is up, unless you want to stay all night. You have to talk to the old lady about that. She don't like men going out of here in broad daylight. I hung up your suit while you were asleep. It was gettin' all wrinkled. Say, do you like this gown? I think it's too old for me. I told the old lady I said, listen, Mrs. Jones, the younger I look the better. And she said yeah, and then it gets around she has fifteen- sixteen-year-old girls working for her and some preacher gets up in church and yells bloody murder and the police have to raid us. She's pretty clever, I guess. You have to give her credit."

"Are you coming downstairs with me?"

"No, I'm suppose to wait till the old lady sends for me."

"Well, goodbye, Zaza."

"Goodbye, Bob. Don't forget the next time you're in town. Maybe next month? Sooner than that, maybe?"

"Can't tell."

Downstairs, in the little room, Mrs. Jones said: "Did you enjoy a good time?"

"Yes, I did. Thank you."

"Ben said to say goodnight to you. The doctor went home about a half an hour ago. And take your hand out of your pocket. Ben said it was his treat."

"A little something for you?"

"No, if Ben found out he'd be sore. Next time, if you feel like it. I hope there'll be a next time. I think Zaza took a shine to you. Wonderful little girl. Did you ever see such a slender waist on a girl? She's the envy. Well, goodnight, Mr. Millhouser, come see us again when you feel like it."

Robert lay thinking of the simple act that until now had kept him apart from the race of men, the transaction between his body and a woman's that had really started with a little more whiskey than he was accustomed to and that had ended simply with a conversation with an ignorant girl. He was sorry that it had occurred without love; in the presence of love and its tenderness there would be so much more of the delights of touch and sight, and in the afterglow there would be, he knew, the peace of exhaustion from an excitement

159

shared. And yet he was grateful to this ignorant girl for caring so little; her casualness would mean that when there was love in the act it would be complete for the first time. Now it was enough that he had wanted this girl and responded to her, the excitement of her mystery and the sight of her body. It was enough for now, even if it would not always be enough. He fell asleep.

In the morning he awoke instantly to the knowledge that he was different from all he had ever been, and then remembering he thought of the girl and could only be glad that he had bought her, or that she had been bought for him. He quickly made excuses to avoid seeing Ben Rosebery, but he could not avoid Dr. Willetts. He wished that he could go home alone, without having to talk to the doctor, but in a little while there was a knock on the door. "I have to catch the nine-forty train," said the doctor. "But you don't have to."

"It'll only take me ten minutes. Yes, I have to be back this afternoon."

The doctor put down his grip and sat in a chair near the window. "You ever been to one of those places before?" he said, as Robert lathered up for a shave.

"Not like that. I've been to cafés where there were whores."

"It pays to go to the best. In the long run it's safer. I just wanted to tell you to be sure and have a good look at your privates the next couple weeks. If you notice anything unusual, come to me right away."

"Do you think there's any danger I might have caught something?"

"There's always that danger, and you more or less got into this through my doing, so I feel responsible. I don't want to worry you, but I don't want you to get careless, either."

Neither then nor on the train did the doctor offer any excuses for himself. Robert had expected some, and when they did not come he invented them, and in so doing realized how little he knew about this man of whom he had grown so fond. Mrs. Willetts could not have been a beauty even in her youth, and now the doctor chose not to share his few hours of relaxation with her. As much of their conversations as Robert had heard was no more than was necessary for the running of the house and the raising of the children. But of the doctor's romantic life Robert knew nothing. He never spoke of that, if it had ever existed. And yet he could speak of other matters with passion; of the cruelty of life for the poor, of the relentlessness of disease, of the inhumanity of parents toward their children, of the futility of his profession and the ironies of God. It was preposterous to suppose that the same man had not at some time felt great love for a woman, and it was incredible that the woman was now his wife.

160

There was love in their relationship; he was gentle with her, and she was sweet with him. But Robert Millhouser was convinced that the other woman had been someone like his own mother. (And how little he knew her, with all of her first marriage, her first love, her first tragedy a locked memory, and her last affair a medical secret.) Robert's gradual idealization of his friend had created the necessity for the present excuses, and the doctor's perfunctory assignation with the whore was best explained by the colorless wife and the frustrated husband, the woman without imagination and the man with his dreams, the doctor's compromise with banality and defeat.

Not then or ever did the doctor ask the question to which the answer could not be given without the question. Robert would not, could not voluntarily say that Zaza had been his first woman, although he was ready to reply truthfully if the question had been put. But question and answer were all implicit in the doctor's feeling of responsibility toward the younger man, and in the succeeding weeks the secret they shared became more immediately real than Robert's lost chastity. Five times a year Robert visited the farms, and for two years he took advantage of the trips to pay a visit to Mrs. Jones's establishment. He never again went there with the doctor, and if the doctor went there during his annual trip to Fort Penn, no mention was made of it. Nine times in two years Robert went to bed with Zaza; on his tenth visit he was told that "Zaza isn't here any more." He received the news with relief rather than regret; she had become greedy and complaining, and once when he saw her from a distance in the Fort Penn depot, obviously soliciting, he stood behind a pillar until a police officer sent her away.

•

ONCE AGAIN I was faced with the problem of a voluminous manuscript that for my purposes was hardly more than skeletal. Robert Millhouser covered in detail more than twenty years of his life after the first visit to Mrs. Jones's place, but of the two items that interested me the most, only one of them appeared in Mr. Millhouser's manuscript. I obtained the other through intuition and stealth. The item in the manuscript I shall deal with later on; the other concerns Zilph Millhouser and the reader will soon see why I am compelled to report it in the first person. I was shocked by my discovery, not really so much by the item itself, although it is tragic and repellent, but by my own stupidity, since I had handled the material twice over and had missed the significance of it both times.

The reader has already observed that I concluded the previous section of the Millhouser story without revealing the circumstances of Zilph Millhouser's final "romance." I can only say, with embarrassed regret, that at least half the fault is my own. Robert Millhouser had not explicitly stated those circumstances; he had been un-co-operative in that respect. But neither had I had the wit to notice what was there and to pin him down with the right questions. I decided to pay another visit to Lyons and Robert Millhouser, and did so in the spring of 1927, announcing to Millhouser that I missed the atmosphere of the town and especially of the Millhouser place. Somewhat to my surprise—for our relations had been slightly strained —he welcomed my visit. "I'm glad you came," he said. "It doesn't pay to get too far away, to be too objective, does it?"

"No," I said. "I'd like to go all over the whole house."

"The whole house? Why?"

"To try to get the feel of living here thirty or forty years ago. How it must have seemed to you and your mother."

He smiled. "Well, I don't envy you your task, trying to imagine yourself as me or my mother that long ago, but you're welcome to try. And I must say you're thorough."

"Thank you. It isn't that I'm so thorough, but I need the stimulation, if that's the right word. I never have trouble re-creating those times when I'm in this house."

"True. It's changed very little."

"That's what I mean. Tell me, Mr. Millhouser, did your mother keep a scrapbook? I know that she kept a sort of journal."

"But she stopped keeping the journal, you remember. No, she had no scrapbook, but I think she meant to start one and never did. If you'll look in her room you'll come across one of those cardboard business files, unmarked. It's half full of newspaper clippings and Fair programs and things like that, the kind of thing you save to put in a scrapbook."

"That's just the kind of thing I'd like to have a look at."

"Why?"

"Because even if she didn't paste them into a book, they show what interested her at the time she saved them. And I imagine most of the things have the dates on them."

"I don't remember. The programs would."

"Well, if you'll excuse me, I'll go up and have a look."

"Let me know if you find anything interesting."

The file was in the warped bottom drawer of her desk, which I had trouble forcing open, and even the newspaper clippings were in good condition, although there was no semblance of chronological order, and I had a feeling amounting to a suspicion that the box had been gone through by Robert Millhouser.

I shall not burden the reader with a catalog of the contents of the file. I spent most of three days reading every single item. I learned that Mrs. Henry Millhouser had apparently bought a horse which she named Ulster Boy (it surely had not been so named by the Pennsylvania breeder), that Ulster Boy had won more races than he lost, and that he was followed by Ulster Boy II. Moses Hatfield had driven Ulster Boy in all his races. Mrs. Henry Millhouser, I read, had presented the ribbon and a purse of $50 to winners of the Henry Millhouser Memorial Race for horses bred in Nesquehela County (a condition which automatically disqualified Ulster Boy). And so on, through programs and clippings that covered a ten-year period, whereupon Mrs. Henry Millhouser apparently retired from racing. Most of the items concerned Robert Millhouser and were repetitious in that year after year his name would appear on the same committees of annual civic events. But in 1890 the newspapers of Lyons, Fort Penn and Philadelphia reported the announcement of Robert Millhouser's engagement to Miss Esther Baumgarten, daughter of Mr. and Mrs. Karl Baumgarten, of Fort Penn. I could tell from the Baumgartens' street address that they were well-to-do, and Esther had gone to Miss Holbrook's, which was and is Fort Penn's fashionable school for girls. A few months later there was a Fort Penn clipping announcing the termination of the engagement "by mutual consent." When I spoke of these findings to Robert Millhouser he nodded. "Telling you all about that, not next week, but either the week after or the week after that," he said. "By and large it's rather dull stuff, don't you think?"

"Not to me. I'd meant to ask you about your mother's interest in the Fair, whether it continued."

"The racing was all she cared about. Stayed with it for about ten years, then she got out of it when Moses told her that he'd been offered a bribe. The Fair was going on, but she took a can of paint and a paint brush and painted over Second Boy's name on the stall, withdrew from the races, and personally led Second Boy off the grounds in front of a thousand people. Caused quite a stir, as you can imagine. Mrs. Henry Millhouser, high heels and all, leading her horse by the tie-strap, and Moses tagging along after, pulling the sulky and the harness. She refused to speak to anybody about it."

"Even you?"

"Oh, she spoke to me. She told me about the bribe and I naturally said I'd resign from the Fair. 'Like hell you will,' she said. 'Like hell you will. Not before you have that scum ruled off for life.' "

"Did you?"

"No. There were too many mixed up in it, Valley farmers, most of them. So then I did resign. But the word got around and the next year the principal culprits were quietly told their entries wouldn't be accepted, and I went back on the board again. But as far as Mama was concerned, the harm had been done. The church people had won. Everybody in the Valley knew about it. It was the only time I ever saw Mama cry, the only time. It meant a great deal to her, you know. She loved horses, and having Ulster Boy and then Second Boy— Second Boy was our name for Ulster Boy II—gave her a lot of pleasure and kept her busy. I've always been of the opinion that half the fun for her was thumbing her nose at the church people. And when she found out about the cheating that was going on, that's why she cried. It gave people like Reverend Betz the chance they'd been waiting for."

"Oh, yes. They could openly oppose the Fair *and* racing."

"And did they! Not the Fair. The Fair was catching on. The women in the Valley showed their fancy-work and preserves and so on, and there were plowing contests and feats of strength for the men. But I think you'll find one clipping that caused quite a stir. The Reverend Betz denouncing horse-racing from the pulpit. He'd always been afraid to come out in the open, but—well, you find the clipping. I'm sure it's there."

It was, and as I read it I acquired a respect for the Reverend Mr. Betz that had not been part of my impression of the man. His sermon was printed in full, which indicated that he had given a copy to the Lyons weekly. My new respect, I should add, did not include admiration except as one can respect and admire sly tactics on the part of an unpleasant person. His sermon was an inspired, masterful piece of work, probably his masterpiece. He never once mentioned the Fair or Zilph Millhouser by name, but he gloated over the scandal that had "even soiled the skirts of one who has innocently given support to this devil's pastime in the mistaken belief that horse-racing could exist without the temptation to gamble." He concluded by asking all to join him in prayer for the innocent victims of the scandal as well as for the guilty parties, and since the obvious innocent victim, in the singular number, had been Zilph Millhouser, I asked Robert what he had done next; had he paid a call on Betz?

"I wanted to horsewhip him, minister or no minister, for talking so about Mama, but she pleaded with me not to see him or speak to him or anyone else. It made us very close, that I reacted that way. She was very pleased. Well, she was my mother, and if she didn't have me to defend her, who was there?"

164

"Yes, I imagine she was proud of you," I said, and meant it sincerely, for I had come to love Zilph Millhouser as one can love a character in a novel who becomes a part of one's company of living acquaintances.

I returned to Zilph's filing case and the nineteenth century in Lyons, reading everything conscientiously, often amused to see names that I recognized, including those of Mr. and Mrs. Jeremiah MacMahon and the grandparents of my Lyons friends. But I do not deny that some of it was tedious work and late in the second afternoon I was about to give up for the day when I picked up a clipping which I reprint in full:

REV. EMIL BETZ
FOUND DEAD

Rev. Emil J. Betz, pastor of the Lyons Lutheran Church, died suddenly at his home on Main Street Monday last. The body was found by a member of the family. Private funeral services were held Wednesday, with burial in the Lutheran cemetery. There were no pallbearers. Rev. Betz was called to the local pastorate about 20 years ago, having served previously as pastor of several congregations in Adams, Lancaster and Nesquehela counties. He was a graduate of the Lutheran seminary in Philadelphia. He is survived by three daughters, his wife having preceded him in death several years ago.

I held the clipping in my hand for ten or more minutes. I knew from the wording of the story—"died suddenly" was a standard euphemism in small-town Pennsylvania newspapers—and from its brevity, that Betz had been unmistakably a suicide. If there had been any doubt, the editor would have inserted the line: "Death was due to natural causes." But it was not the report or even the fact of Betz's suicide that fascinated me. It was the sudden silence of this room. It was the kind of silence that occurs after one has been told a long and long-withheld story, which ends with the narrator's saying, "Now you know." I do not mean to say or to imply that I had a vision of Zilph Millhouser and that she was the one who was saying, "Now you know." But the room said it; no single object in the room, but life that had lived in the room and was leaving something behind, perhaps that silence. The room and the silence had a voice that was as real to me as would be the voice of my mother, my wife, my children, or, at that moment, the old man downstairs. I knew, I knew, I knew that in this room Betz had raped Zilph Millhouser. I wished that I could go to Dr. Willetts with my discovery, but he was many

165

years dead. And I found myself wondering if at just that moment Robert Millhouser could be waiting for me to come down and ask him the questions that he did not want me to ask. Yes, for a few minutes he was waiting for me, of that I was sure; but if I did not go to him, now, his remote apprehension would pass and be forgotten. It was not kindness that kept me from going to him; it was the anticipation of his lie. If he knew what I knew, he would lie as he had been lying across hundreds of pages of yellow paper. And I did not want to listen to his lie. Zilph Millhouser deserved more than a lie; she was too good for that. It was one thing to keep her secret; for her to keep it, for her son to keep it, for Betz to keep it; but I had come upon the truth, and now a lie was not good enough for her. And I could not now believe that her son had a good, unselfish reason for the lie he would tell. Who would be shamed by this ugly discovery? Not Zilph Millhouser. Betz had been shameful past endurance and had flaunted his shame in a sermon and in the last act of his life. Then who remained for shame?

I got up and walked around the room. The bedstead was a great, elaborately carved walnut piece, matching two of the chairs in the carving and approximating in color and finish the washstand and the desk. The only pictures were two large chromo-photographs of Henry and Zilph Millhouser, in walnut and gilt oval frames, and a smaller photograph of the young Robert Millhouser. The pillows and mattress on the bed were covered by a single spread of heavy dark green muslin flecked with gold. The wallpaper was not paper; it was a cloth that resembled the bedspread in color and like the spread had thin, more widely separated stripes of gold. It was a corner room, with two windows cut through each of the exterior walls, but it was not a room for day living. It was dark and unfeminine, with latticed shutters inside and out, the outside ones permanently open, the inside ones as permanently closed. The north windows commanded the same view of the town that could be had from Robert Millhouser's present bedroom, and to the east and south I could see the distant collieries and the Johnsville road, below the populated area of Lyons. The sun had gone around to the other side of the house and the room was ready for the darkness that seemed to me its natural condition. And in the gloaming I was ready for my conversation with Zilph Millhouser.

As a boy I had often carried on conversations with invisible people, who of course were real enough to me and, my mother said, to her. I had an invisible friend named Frank, according to my mother. As far as she could make out he was a grownup, who could do wonderful things; he could be in two places at once, he could fly like a bird, walk through closed doors, escape from closets, and con-

166

verse with me. But I never saw him. My mother told me that she had often listened to me in my conversations with Frank; she told me this when I was quite grown and did not remember Frank at all. She asked me to describe Frank, but I could not, and my only recollections of him are hers. I would sit on the floor in her sewing-room and I would say something to Frank in my natural voice, and the answer would come to me and I would utter the words of the answer in a lower pitch. Once when I was naughty she threatened to tell Frank, and I looked at her coldly and said, "You don't know Frank." I was sixteen or seventeen when my mother first told me about my invisible friend, and I believe that she would not have told me about him if a neighbor had not reported to my mother that she, the neighbor, was worried about her young son's similar conversations with an invisible person. My mother was a little afraid of the First Commandment, and by her standards she might well have been, for I spent many hours trying to recall Frank and my conversations with him, and my failure to resurrect him disturbed me. My mother was a literal-minded, although superstitious, woman, who could not have invented such an elaborate fiction as my friendship with Frank; and I therefore was disturbed because Frank had so completely vanished from my memory. As an older boy, ten to fifteen, I would talk to myself when I was crying from a whipping or the loss of a treasure, but at such times I was only pouring out my unhappiness to an unlistening world and I was much too old to have a Frank.

Now I say these things to the reader in the hope that he will better understand my conversation with Zilph Millhouser, for once again I spoke with an invisible (but once real) person. Our conversation did not occur in dialogue form, but as I sat there in her room she answered the questions that were in my mind. Yes, she told me, Betz raped me in this room. He came to see me when he heard I was ill, and we were alone long enough for him to rape me. He had come to rape me. You must understand (she said) that I submitted to him rather than make a fuss. He pulled down the bedclothes and up with my nightgown and I lay there while he burned my insides with his thing. When he finished with me he got off me and cursed me but I pretended to have fainted. He had hurt me and the pain was bad, but I was afraid that if I so much as moaned, he would kill me. I could hear him breathing and muttering to himself. Finally I got an unexpected sharp pain and I could not pretend any longer, and opened my eyes. He put his hand over my mouth and told me that if I ever said anything about this he would kill me. And then he left. I never looked at him again, but he would look at me and I knew how he looked; desperate and terrified and dying. From week to week he could see the doctor's buggy at our house and I know he must have looked at the doctor, to see how much the doctor knew. And then one day he took his own worthless life.

That was what I learned from Zilph Millhouser, that came from her as I sat in her room. I wanted to comfort her and I tried, but I had no feeling that I was succeeding, and it did not matter. It was intended that I, someone who loved her, should be drawn to this room, read the clipping; and because a young man who loved her had touched the clipping, she told him what he needed to know, and when that was told the stillness of the room changed. It was quiet, but it was not silence. And I could not tell how long I had been there. I had read the clipping, I had got up and moved about and I had sat down, but then I had got up again and between my fingers still burning was a cigarette that I had lit while reading the clipping. I searched the room, but there was no other cigarette. How many seconds had it taken me to look out the window, to register my impressions of a room with which I was already familiar, to sit down and get up again? The cigarette had the answer: as long as it had taken the cigarette to burn less than one inch. In other words, the clipping, my movements about the room, my conversation with Zilph, had all been within a space of three minutes.

For that space of time I could have blacked out, even with a cigarette in my hand. It was late in the day, the tedium of reading the contents of the box was as bad as the previous day. So I argued, for I disliked having to resort to supernatural explanations. But I took out my watch and saw that it was 5:44, and I wrote the time on an envelope as a precaution against another blackout, if there had been one. Then I returned to my chair and read the text and advertisements of a high school play program and when I had finished I tested my memory on the program and again looked at my watch. The time was now 5:56, and I had not again blacked out. I was, you see, easing my way back to normal. There was only one difficulty: all that I had been told by Zilph Millhouser was as real to me as any of the printed facts in her filing case.

The old man was having his dinner and I joined him on the sun porch. "You look tired," he said. "Let me offer you a glass of whiskey."

"No thanks," I said. "I have a date tonight and I don't want to start drinking too early. I wanted to ask you—did the Reverend Betz commit suicide?"

"The Reverend Betz. Yes he did. He hanged himself in the attic. It didn't surprise me, or anyone else for that matter. The story was— now let me see. Yes. We never had anything to do with him after that

168

sermon. Paid our church dues for another year, then Mama changed back to Presbyterian. She didn't go there any oftener than she went to the Lutheran, and I didn't go to any. But naturally you hear things, and the last few years of his life Betz was acting very strangely."

"How, for instance?"

"Well, now let me think. I'll give you one example. One day he was in Langendorf's store and over on the dry-goods side of the store they had kind of a form to advertise corsets, women's corsets. Had neither head nor arms, but it had a bust. Not separate breasts, but a bust. And it was no question about it a woman's form. Well, Betz carried a cane, and he swung that cane one day and knocked the form on the floor and told Fred Langendorf that he ought to be ashamed to have such an indecent thing up where everybody could see it. Well, he was a minister, and Fred knuckled under. Then there were two or three other incidents like that, all having to do with the female form divine. And finally I understand the Synod was told about it and the bishop told Betz to stop making a public spectacle of himself. They were getting ready to send him to a sanitarium when he saved them the trouble. I think he must have been the only man my mother really despised."

"On account of the sermon?"

"On account of the sermon, but I told you he proposed marriage to her and she laughed him out of countenance."

"Yes."

"Well, there was something else that she never told me. What it was I could never guess, but she told me once she could never bear to look at him."

"What?" I felt physically ill.

"Yes. She couldn't stand to look at him or the way he looked at her. Gerald, are you all right?"

"Let me have a sip of your water," I said. "I'll be all right."

"You oughtn't to be cooped up in this musty old house on a day like this. You ought to be out in the fresh air. Take a day off tomorrow, play some tennis."

"No, I'll be all right tomorrow. I want to come."

"Well, whatever you say."

The Johnsville girl that I had a date with that night would not have thought of herself as an angel of mercy or of anything else. She had the same *quid pro quo* arrangement with me that she had with other young men. At eight o'clock I picked her up at the corner, a block away from her house, and we drove fifty miles to an island in the river near Fort Penn, where Jean Goldkette was playing a one-nighter. We danced until midnight and between us drank a pint of rye and returned to her house. We lay down on the sofa and finished off our evening exactly as we had known it would be finished. "When am I going to see you again?" I said.

"That's up to you."

"I'll be back again in July."

"All right. Phone me. You gotta go now. Goodnight, Ger'."

"Goodnight, Naomi."

"Don't make any noise."

"No. Goodnight."

"Goodnight."

I wondered about Naomi. I was never allowed to call for her at her house, always met her at the corner. But after we had been out for the evening I was permitted to park the car in front of the house and we would quietly go inside and make love on the parlor sofa. I never saw either of her parents, and whenever I made a date with her I had to telephone her during noon hour at the public school in which she taught third and fourth grades. She liked to dance, to wear pretty clothes, to get a little tight, and to make love. For the last she used the regional word coother or cuther, with the soft *th*. I had not come across the word in Old English and had no idea of its etymology; its meaning was anything from soul-kissing to conventional sexual intercourse to special perversions, but it was considered a funny, not a naughty or dirty, word. At the dance that night, for example, she had said: "We can't stay after twelve if we want to do any coothering. I have school tomorrow."

On the way back to my grandmother's, in the spring night with the top down and my hat hanging on the emergency brake, I was grateful to Naomi for an extra reason that I could never explain to her. Everything about her was real: her Djer Kiss perfume, her nicely cut suit, her silk stockings, her shirtwaist, the black cord on which dangled her steady fellow's gold basketball, her little rascals in fourth grade, her Pennsylvania Dutch singsong, her vitality. "Oh, sweetheart, you do me so much good," she would whisper in the early stages of coothering. And then, "I popped. Did you pop?" I could think of her and prolong thinking of her, standing at the doorway in her stocking feet and her shirtwaist untucked, her bobbed hair uncombed, and a pleased, oddly maternal half-smile on her pretty face. So long as I could think about her reality, her tangibility, her recently loosed vitality and her nice smile, I could keep my mind occupied until the whiskey and the night air and the day's and night's exhaustions put me to sleep. I was not afraid of what I might dream, but I did not want to think of Zilph Millhouser. I wished that I had never heard of Zilph Millhouser.

170

I got undressed and brushed my teeth and went to bed with the light on. I went to sleep very soon and had a dream about a man named Frank who was faceless part of the time and part of the time was interchangeable with Robert Millhouser. The first roosters woke me up and I turned out the light, wondering how I had happened to leave it on. And then I could not get back to sleep until the six o'clock colliery whistles filled the Valley. After the colliery whistles the town always made early-morning sounds; more than half the people in Lyons began to stir then, and I was reassured by familiar noises, predictable, known noises that signified the living, who were suddenly my dear friends. It was only in that barren silence between the first roosters and the six o'clock whistles that my grandmother's house was as still as Zilph Millhouser's bedroom, when I thought I could look out the window and the world would be empty and dead and forgotten, with the deserted look of a George Luks landscape, and me unable to speak to anyone because I had done the terrible thing of speaking with the dead, and the living were hiding from me.

Even now, so many years later, I am tempted to say that in a few days I came down with typhoid fever. But I must tell the truth. A fever would explain so much so easily, but why must I explain with an untruth? No one would ask me to explain the millions of facts that were material things, living people, witnessed acts in one day of my life. I could say that on that one day the temperature was seventy degrees Fahrenheit, and I would be believed; that Robert Millhouser wore a blue necktie; that Moses Hatfield brought the mail, and so on. I could say so many factual things and be wrong about all of them, since I trusted to my memory, and yet I would be believed. But the biggest fact to me on that day was that for a matter of minutes I had spoken with Zilph Millhouser, and the only way I can make that credible is to offer "factual" evidence that two or three things I first learned in my conversation with Mrs. Millhouser turned out to be true. Robert Millhouser told me that his mother could not bear to look at or be looked at by Betz, and there we have a fact that I had learned in the conversation and that was retroactively confirmed. I decided to make one more attempt to have such confirmation of the facts in my conversation with the dead woman, and regardless of success or failure to make the conversation a permanent fact of my own. I asked Robert Millhouser for permission to talk to Margaret Dillon.

"She's quite old," he said. "You mustn't upset her."

"Why would I upset her?"

"I must remind you, Gerald. She's been through a lot with me."

"But she wasn't here when you shot your wife."

"No, she wasn't. She'd quit about a year after I was married. Didn't like my wife. But then she came back when I went to prison."

"Oh, I see."

"The other women quit, but Margaret Dillon came back. She and Moses ran the house until I was set free."

"Well, I'll try not to upset her. Where does she live?"

"Here in town. Moses will take you to see her."

Robert Millhouser had a Dodge sedan, a two-door black model with wire wheels that was especially popular with people who could afford a much better car but refused to spend the money. Moses was the worst driver I have ever known but he never took the car out of town and the citizens were on the alert for him. "Wuffor you wanna see Margaret?"

"Just to talk with her."

"You get plenty of talk. You sure get plenty of talk, you talk to that old woman."

Margaret lived with a younger cousin who was presumably glad to get the money for Margaret's room and board, and who probably was not unmindful of Margaret's savings. "Cousin Marg, it's Mr. Higgins to see you."

Margaret, leaning on a cane, took a chair in the front room and arranged herself before speaking to me. "Well, well. I never would of recognized you," she said. "You grew like a weed. Can I offer you anything? Join me in a nice cup of tea."

The cousin, who had been told that I was coming, brought in the tea and would have lingered, but Margaret sent her away. "They tell me Grandma'd a hard time getting through the winter. Is she poorly?"

"No, she's all right."

"Doesn't want to be bothered by people."

"I hope *I* don't bother *you*."

"Well, if you do, you'll know soon enough. What's this book you're writing about Robert Millhouser? It's a crazy notion if I ever heard tell of one. A book about Robert Millhouser, and him *wanting* you to is the strangest part of all."

"Everybody has a book in them, Margaret."

"Too true. Well, he said I was to help you if I could, so go ahead and ask me questions."

"All right. Do you remember—"

"I remember everything, but that ain't saying I'm telling everything."

172

"Well, do you remember, and can you *tell* me, about the time the preacher preached that sermon—"

"Criticizing Robert's mother. Indeed I do. There was a man wasn't fit to go around loose, and daring to criticize that dear woman. Oho-ho. Speaking of remembering everything and telling nothing. There's a case for you."

"Well, I don't want you to tell me anything you feel you shouldn't."

"I wouldn't know how, it's so awful, so frightful."

"You mean about Reverend Betz?"

"Reverend! He finally put a rope around his neck, his conscience was plaguing him so, but it took him years to do it. I just hope he didn't expiate his sins in this world and leave nothing to be punished in the next. The torture he inflicted on that dear, lovely woman."

"Oh, the sermon wasn't all that bad, Margaret."

"The sermon! Would anything that hypocrite could say hurt my darling? Sermon? It's little enough you know, Gerald Higgins. It's little enough anybody knows, and that goes for her own unfortunate son. There's a book, all right, but it'll never get written."

"You mean that it's just as well that it won't?"

"There's no one alive today could tell it, with the exception of yours truly and one other."

"You and Robert Millhouser?"

"Me, and *not* Robert Millhouser."

"You mean there's some secret that you know and only one other person knows."

"Me, and one other person. Now. There was two others till a few years back, then one of them passed away, may-his-soul-and-all-the-souls-of-the-faithful-departed-through-the-mercy-of-God-rest-in-peace-amen. Oh, this is an odd one. You askin' me these questions. You of all the people that could be askin'. Ah, well, there's only the two of us that when we pass away the terrible story will go to our graves with us."

"Well, that's as it should be."

"You never said a truer word, Gerald."

"She must have been a wonderful woman, from all I've been able to ascertain."

"A lovely spirit. A fine, lovely, decent spirit. When her time came and she knew she didn't have long to live I was sittin' there trying to keep back the tears and it was her comforting me and not the other way around. 'Come, Margaret, don't be sad,' she said. 'I'm ready.' And I knew if there was ever a gentle soul headed straight for heaven

—a short while in purgatory at the most—it was her. But I said to her could I send for the priest, with her permission? And she looked at me with the coldest look I'd ever seen on her dear face. 'No!' said she. 'No priest nor preacher will I have.' And no wonder, with the outrage committed against her by the wind-sucking goat that she trusted."

"You mean Betz."

"I mean no one else. I took her be the hand and said, 'You'll soon be with your dear one, think of him,' and I said some prayers under me breath and in a couple minutes she was gone. Thank our dear Lord she had her last thoughts on Henry Millhouser."

"Where was Robert Millhouser?"

"Downstairs. He come as soon as I called him, but it was just her and I there at the last. Just her and I." She nodded her head. "I wonder would it be a good thing if I was to tell you what I know."

"No, Margaret," I said, now almost sure that the garrulous old woman could not be prevented from telling me. "If it's something as awful as you say, and only the one other person knows it. Will the other person keep his mouth shut?"

"If it was *his* mouth, but it's *her* mouth. It's a woman that knows besides me. She's a good woman, mind. But I'm wondering to myself at this very moment, I know the story straight. I was there in the house, whereat and whereas the other woman got it from her husband that got it from me. Now says I to meself, what if in her old age the other woman loosens her tongue and starts telling the story all wrong? Meaning well, mind, but with her insufficient ignorance telling the story so wrong that my dear lovely Zilph Millhouser is made to look bad."

"I see what you mean, I think. You'd rather tell me and have the story straight than risk having it told wrong by this other person. Then if I know the story straight from you, I can correct the other person if she tells it wrong."

"Maybe you don't even know the other person."

"Probably don't, except that you gave me a feeling a minute ago that I did. You know, you said it was odd that I of all people—"

"I know what I said. I'll need a minute to think," she said. Her minute was a silence lasting about twenty seconds, then: "If I was to die before this other woman, that would leave the story with her and nobody else, and the good Lord only knows what distortions and contortions she could make out of it. See is that door shut, and if it aint, pull it to."

I closed the door firmly.

"The walls have ears, they say, and some people have ears as broad as a wall," said Margaret. "I oughtn't to be talking about such matters to a single man, and me a single woman as well, but a body can tell a sinful story without taking pleasure in it, and that's where the sin is, you know from your catechism. Taking pleasure in it. You remember your catechism."

"Oh, yes."

"Different though it was to the catechism I was taught."

"But essentially the same."

"Oho, essentially. Holy Mother Church don't skip about like some will o' the wisp. If it's true in Ireland it's true in Lyons, Pennsylvania, only you don't come from Lyons, but never mind. Essentially the same is true the world over. Oho, yes.

"Long before you were born and even before your dear little mother come into this world, the man Betz fastened his sinful eye on Mrs. Henry Millhouser. Henry Millhouser was still warm, as they say, when Betz come strutting into the house and as much as told the young widow that if she didn't marry him, she was going against God's will. To her everlasting credit she refused him and sent him on his way."

"You must have been very close to her for her to tell you such confidential things."

"I was close enough, but it wasn't as if she told it to me all at once and altogether. I insinuated it out of her and then after a bit she admitted it. But I said to her, 'Look here, me girl, watch out for that one. He's cracked in the head.' I didn't say 'me girl,' but I give her the warning, and I was right. Forever after he was all the time gazing at her like a wolf ready to pounce. And that, Gerald Higgins, is exactly what he did do.

"One day, one afternoon, I let him in to call on her because she was poorly, and had taken to her bed. I didn't trust him no more than I would a serpent, but he was there masquerading as a minister of God and it wasn't my place to stay in the room with him. I only wisht I had."

"What happened?"

"As shameful a disgraceful outrage as ever happened to a proud and virtuous woman."

"Is it what I think?"

"If you're thinking the worst imaginable thing for a proud and virtuous woman . . ."

"What they call in the newspapers, assault."

She nodded. "I was in the kitchen, but my thoughts were on the second story. 'I oughta be up there this minute,' I said to myself. 'I oughta be within call.' Finally I could stand it no longer and I started on my way up with some made-up excuse, and I met him coming down. I take me oath the saliva was pouring out of his mouth. He pushed me out of the way and out of the house he went and I hurried to her room and looked in, quietly. She was lying on the bed, crying so softly I with my keen hearing could scarcely hear her. I went in and took her in my arms and tried to comfort her. 'Henry, Henry,' she kept muttering to herself. Or was it 'Harry'? No, it was 'Henry.'

"We'd guns in the house, all shapes and sizes, and if I'd of been sure of the operation of them I'd have snatched one up and made the best use of it on Betz. But I'd never handled one in me life and the noise of them frightened me. And what good would that've done anyway? It was a secret, and shooting off guns is no way to keep a secret, let alone putting a bullet in a man."

"Did she tell you all about it?"

"What was there to tell I didn't know with one look?"

"Yes, I suppose so," I said. "But did she talk about it, ever?"

"Did she give me shameful detail after shameful detail? Zilph Mill-houser was a lady, not one of your short-skirted ragtime moving-picture heroines. Bit by bit I found out all she could remember. Not by questions I asked her so much as questions she asked me. Did I ever hear of a similar occurrence in the old country? I did. Was there certain consequences? There was and there wasn't. Did the people think the less of the poor woman? All them questions she asked me, one by one, till I very soon didn't have to ask her any. And we'd a fine man a doctor in the town, Dr. Willetts by name, the one now's father, and he asked me a roundabout question or two himself. It was almost as if I'd been there meself to witness the whole unsavory episode, but I was at least spared that."

"Were you frightened of Betz?"

"A madman? And to be sure I lived in mortal terror of him, not for meself, but for her. At home a poor girl was victimized by one like him and scarcely was he out of prison before he went looking for her again, the very same girl. Only this time her brother bashed his head in with a stone as big as you could lift."

"So what did you do?"

"The only thing I could do. I couldn't ask the black man Moses Hatfield for protection. He worshipped the ground she walked on and'd of cut Betz's throat ear-to-ear. Instead I told Jeremiah Mac-Mahon, swearing him to secrecy."

"Grandpa? What could he have done if Betz had come around again?"

"It wasn't what he could do then. If Betz'd come around I'd have

176

done something, I don't know what, but something. But I wanted Jerry to know. If worst come to worst and my poor lady and I were done in, Jerry'd at least know who to suspect. But I always thought Jerry did more. I think one way or another he put the fear of God in Betz's black heart. Jerry could do that easily."

"How?"

"How? Well one way would be if he just went and said in so many words, don't go near Zilph Millhouser or suffer the consequences. That would worry Betz. And you only remember your grandfather when he was older. Jerry MacMahon as a younger man had the reputation for being as brave a soldier as they had in the entire Union Army. Didn't you know that about your own grandfather, then?"

"Oh, sure."

"Meade. General Meade raised him to a leftenant for his bravery at Gettysburg. You knew that, surely."

"I knew he was promoted."

"Well, be proud of him, lad. You don't have to act like it was every family'd as brave a soldier as Jerry MacMahon."

"I'm very proud of Grandpa and I was very fond of him, too."

"Huh. For a minute there you sounded very English to me."

"Did I? In any case, Margaret, he took care of Betz, didn't he?"

"Whatever he done, if it was only a look or if it was a word to the wise, Jerry MacMahon's the one I give the credit for protecting Zilph Millhouser from further molestations and outrages."

"Then when Grandpa died, that left only you and Grandma that knew the story."

"That wasn't hard to guess, was it?"

"No."

"One more question, did Mrs. Millhouser ever know that Grandpa and Grandma knew about Betz?"

"Holy Mother, no. The first I knew that Jerry told your Grandma was after they buried Zilph Millhouser. Your Grandma's never one to sit tongue-tied during a conversation, but one word from Jerry and a secret was a secret. Ah, there was a man for you. Straight and true as an arrow. And not one of your loud-mouths. I wisht I'da been there to hear him order his troops into battle. I can depict him on a fine black stallion, with his arm stretched out and his sword in his hand."

"He was in a mortar battery, Margaret."

"A motor battery, and what's that?"

"A mortar is a little cannon. It lobs grapeshot at the enemy. Grandpa was made a lieutenant because all the other officers were killed."

"What's the difference? He'd a horse, didn't he?"

"I suppose he had."

"Well, what else do you want to know?"

"I can't think of anything else at the moment, but I appreciate what you've told me."

"Well, you can show your appreciation if your Grandma takes it into her head to spread any stories about Zilph Millhouser. She's a good woman, your Grandma, but always a little tiny bit jealous of the laughin' and talkin', innocent, when Jerry would wait on Zilph Millhouser at the old store. He wasn't a jokester, Jerry MacMahon, but the women of the town would walk in the rain to see his face light up with a smile. Give me an Irishman over all comers when a smile is needed."

" 'Sure it's like a morn in Spring.' "

"Now that's the first decent human thing you said all afternoon."

"Well, I'll take my gloomy self away, Margaret. Thank you very much. God bless all here."

"You don't sound right saying it, so don't say it."

"God save Ireland!"

"You sound better saying that, although only the dear Lord knows why."

"Up Wexford! Down with Cromwell!"

"Teasin' me will only make me angry, Gerald. Go on with you. Oh, there's dear old black Moses, bless his heart. Ask him can he still count to ten in French."

"Est-ce que vous avez appris à compter en français?"

"Oui."

"So long, Margaret."

"Fooled you, didn't I?"

Thenceforth I made no further inquiries that would give factual support to my belief in my conversation with Zilph Millhouser. I had the rudimentary explanations: as a child, as a boy, I undoubtedly had heard a word here, a word there, that formed the mass of fact that I converted into a conversation. I did not have to invent an attack of typhoid fever or to effect a compromise between reality and the supernatural. Best of all, I was no longer frightened. All the world could have the sensible explanation that it might demand; I was left untroubled now in the belief that I had had a conversation with Zilph Millhouser. I had never doubted it, but I had doubted my ability to supply the factual evidence for the factual world and in that weakness lay my fright. If the world could defy me to offer proof and I had none that was acceptable, I would remain subject to my doubts on the world's terms. But now I had the answers that the world would have to accept, and I could believe what I truly believed.

178

I was again ready to go on with Robert Millhouser's story, after having extricated myself from being more seriously, dangerously involved with its people than I would have thought possible. As Penrod I had been in love with Marjorie Jones, as Amory Blaine I had been in love with Rosalind Connage—indeed, I was more in love with Marjorie than Penrod had been, and less in love with Rosalind than Amory had been. Creatures of the imagination were so real to me that I measured flesh-and-blood people against the fictional prototypes and shared the imagined anxieties, joys, hopes and sorrows to a degree that was, I think, uncommon. It was therefore not a totally new experience for me to associate myself with ghosts. An author's creations and God's partook of the same animate unreality once God's creatures were no longer in this life and provided that the author had given life to his. And so it was with so many of the people in Robert Millhouser's story, who were not in this world during my lifetime. Zilph Millhouser, Dr. Willetts, Moses Hatfield's father, the blind soldier after Gettysburg were no less real to me than Fitzgerald's Rosalind or Tarkington's Marjorie, and Robert Millhouser was already more truly alive in his past than he was now or ever since "for where no hope is left, is left no fear." So, at least, it seemed to me, and so it must have seemed to him.

I must say these things at this point in Robert Millhouser's story because it must be apparent to the reader that I, Gerald Higgins, had begun at this point to realize that I had so filled my life with the life of another man that much of the time I was Robert Millhouser. I would read the reminiscences he sent me, and it was *I* reliving his life. It was as though his notes were stimulating *my* memory. Sometimes I could hardly wait to see what I would do next, and I believe that during those days I would have answered to his name. Now it is true that in my telling Robert Millhouser's story, from the very first and every succeeding word, I was aware of what the future held: it all, all the words, went in the direction of the great fact that he would (and did) murder his wife. I was surely affected by that knowledge. Consciously or subconsciously my telling of the story was governed by that knowledge—but so too was Robert Millhouser in his notes to me. He filled in the details of a story to which we both knew the ending and the details fascinated as much of my own personality as I continued to retain. This was no relationship of biographer to subject. It was becoming (and I knew it) an absorption of biographer by subject; I was still so young that my smaller life was fitting into his larger, sometimes as though my life were like those surgical stitches that become part of the patient's flesh. I must remind the reader that I had begun to write Robert Millhouser's story when

179

I was at about the same age as Robert when he went to Europe with Chester Calthorp. The fact that at twenty-two I was more worldly than Robert Millhouser—about women, for instance—grew increasingly less important as I continued to write. And I saw in that diminution of difference one of the first signs of the absorption of the smaller personality by the larger. Concurrently with my recognition of the signs, I experienced a gradual decrease in my admiration of Robert Millhouser which I daresay is easily enough understood. But I could not halt the loss of my own personality unless I gave up the whole project, and for that I did not have the courage. I could not say to Robert Millhouser that I was abandoning this thing we had begun; I was dominated by the larger personality, in a way that was, at least partially, recognizably similar to Chester Calthorp's domination of Robert Millhouser. The circumstances were not the same, and the latent or dormant homosexuality that was a factor in the relationship between Chester and Robert was not the strength of Robert Millhouser's unconscious domination of me. More than anything else, I think, I was fascinated by his age. Every day I would grow a day older, but Robert Millhouser was almost exactly fifty years older than I, and single days added to our ages were unimportant. All that was momentous in his life had happened by the time I was four years old, before anything momentous had happened in my own life. This man, wearing the present-day suits of a good Philadelphia tailor, the gold pin in his collar, the shoes that I could not afford, was to me a speaking monument of another time. To me, for instance, Sigmund Freud was new; but to Robert Millhouser he was only *another*. Charles Darwin had been new to Robert Millhouser; to me he belonged with the ancients, a face to be remembered in a marble bust. I could look out at the Millhouser stable and see a Dodge sedan, but Robert Millhouser had stood there one day while the Union cavalry attempted to seize his father's horses. In the entablature of some Lyons buildings there were the raised figures that told the date of construction, buildings that were old and old-fashioned; but Robert Millhouser had already been to Europe and back before those buildings were erected. He was alive when Dred Scott and John Brown were alive and his grandfather could have known Benjamin Franklin and the Marquis de Lafayette; while I would be thinking of Marshal Foch and Frank B. Kellogg. I was just old enough to realize how little a history I had, how enormously much there was before my birth; and Robert Millhouser was my guiding companion into the great past, my intermediary with some of the heroes and scoundrels of the previous century and even of the century before that. Robert Millhouser quite properly belonged with the

180

horse and sail, the means of travel and conquest that sufficed equally for Robert Millhouser's father and for the ancient Egyptians; and if I did not see Robert as an anachronism in my century, he nevertheless belonged to a time in which *his* immediate predecessors, the men and women to whom he paid respect and who brought him up, dispelled the darkness with the light of candles and before snuffing out the candles put their powdered wigs on little pedestals. Somewhere I had seen a reproduction of a portrait of the aging Aaron Burr* that was a ruthless picture of that unfortunate man; bent, cold, crafty and not far from death. I had no hatred of Burr, since I had no fondness for Alexander Hamilton, and the truth or unfairness of the portrait had not concerned me so much as the painter's terrifying economical, stark depiction of old age. Robert Millhouser did not resemble Burr in features, but during the years when I saw him most frequently, and especially when I would see him after a lapse of months, he almost seemed to be growing into that portrait of the aging Burr, without losing his hair or the straightness of his nose. I suppose that the point of resemblance was in the general timelessness of the Burr portrait—it could have been an aging Roman senator as easily as a man who died in 1836—and in the particular aging of this man whom I had come to know so thoroughly. My grandfather, older than Robert Millhouser and already dead, had never symbolized any time but my actual own; he was my grandfather and as alive as his presence. He had never existed for me until I became conscious of him, and when he died he was my deceased, well-loved grandparent. For that reason he was the only major character in among the men and women in Robert Millhouser's story who was almost completely fictitious to me. Jeremiah MacMahon, who turned into my grandfather, was simply another person than the man I knew.

As for my father—since the question inevitably arises—he was not a very interesting man. I loved him automatically for his generosity and for the simple pride he took in my mother's good looks and style and in my small triumphs at school and college. But during the winter he played volleyball with the businessmen's class at the Y.M.C.A., golf in summer; poker one night a week with one group of men, bridge one night a week with a group of men and women, and on Saturday nights he and my mother went unfailingly to the country club dance and danced with the men and women at their own table. Once a year he and my mother and another couple drove the Peerless to Easton or South Bethlehem for the Lehigh game, and at less regular intervals he and a party of men would attend the heavyweight championship prize fights. He considered himself a

* The original is owned by the Century Association, New York City.

181

hard-working businessman, and he made money. But he had inherited his father's lumber yard and planing mill, which expanded
with the times and the town, and the extra money he made was on
investments that he was let in on because he was a good fellow: an
amusement park, a dyestuff plant, an ice cream plant, and the building and loan association. I sometimes suspected that he was bored
but would not admit it to himself because for him any life outside
the one he lived was a trackless waste, full of unimaginable perils.
As a younger man he had coached the high school football team for
two successful seasons; photographs of him and his teams were the
last that showed him with a single chin. He spoke in a fashion that
was not quite a stammer. He would say, "I was gonna say, I was
gonna say . . ." and "Why do you wanna do that, why do you
wanna do that?" He parted his thin hair in the middle and wore his
fraternity pin until he was past forty years of age, when the hair
could no longer be parted and I joined Zeta Psi, a better fraternity.
He was a nice man and a good husband and father, but he was just
not very interesting to anyone but my mother and people who considered him a go-getter. From the time I was sixteen we had
practically nothing to say to each other that did not concern either
sports or money, and when I announced that I wanted to teach I
know he was secretly relieved because it meant that he would remain in command at the mill, with no threat to his ability or his
authority. The only time I ever hurt his feelings was when I came
home for Christmas, freshman year, and backed away from his kiss.
"Well, you're not a kid any more, you're not a kid," he said. But I
had hurt him and I am sorry. Nobody ever should have hurt my
father, as nice a man as that.

Let us now proceed with the story of Robert Millhouser.

•

ONE AFTERNOON in December, 1889, Robert Millhouser came home
from a two-day business trip to Fort Penn. He was met at the depot
by Moses Hatfield in the Stanhope. He took the reins from Moses
and asked the usual question: "Anything happen while I was away?"

"Sumpn happen."

"Good, or bad? Bad, from the way you say it."

"Bad."

"My mother? Did something happen to her?"

"Not you' mother. You' friend, Dr. Willetts. He dead."

"He can't be! I saw him the night before last."

"You never see him no mo'."

182

"How did it happen?"

"You' mother tell you."

Zilph Millhouser saw at once that Moses had reported the news of Dr. Willetts's death. "I wanted to tell you myself, but I knew Moses would. I've been to call on Mrs. Willetts. The doctor had been to see a patient last night at about ten o'clock. A farm out on the Johnsville road. He finished whatever he had to do and the farmer saw him get in the carriage and drive away. Somewhere between the farm and his house he had heart failure and died. The horse brought him home and stood outside the Willetts's barn for a while and then began pawing the ground, and Mrs. Willetts went out and there was the doctor slumped down in the carriage."

"He died alone," said Robert.

"I thought of that, too. All the people he comforted when their time came, and when it was his time there was no one. A horse that wanted to go home. All the babies he helped into the world."

"How is Mrs. Willetts taking it?"

"That poor woman. I've hardly known her, but she said to me, 'But Mrs. *Millhouser,* what am I going to *do?*' As if I knew the answer. She wasn't weeping, no hysterics. Just 'What am I going to do?' And I muttered the things one does mutter at such a time. The children. 'Yes, the children,' she said. As though she were thinking of them for the first time."

Suddenly Robert wept, and almost as suddenly he stopped. "Excuse me, I didn't know I was going to do that," he said.

"Excuse you? I don't think I'd have forgiven you if you hadn't. I've done my share of weeping for the man."

"I wouldn't have forgiven myself, but I didn't have to let go in front of you."

"Are we that far apart, that you can't mourn a friend in front of your mother?"

"I'm thirty-five years old."

"What in God's name has that got to do with it? Crying is for children, but weeping is for men. Jesus wept."

"Yes, Jesus wept. I forget why."

"I think He did for all of us."

"I guess so. I was weeping for Dr. Willetts, and the things he never did. If you see me weep again, Mama, it won't be for all the good he did. They'll all be weeping over that. But I'm sad for the things he wanted to do and didn't. That I knew he wanted to do and nobody else knew. Oh, yes, and my own loss. I'm not unselfish."

"Who is, in this world? Will they need money?"

"No, I don't think so. The older boy gets out of medical school this year. The doctor told me five or six years ago that he could retire but he wanted to keep the practice going till the boy could take it over. He never spent any money on himself and he's probably worth thirty or forty thousand dollars. At least that, if he could retire five years ago. I'll find out. He had some property in Fort Penn, and he was a director at the bank. That income goes on, so she'll be all right. But I'll make sure."

Robert was a pallbearer for his friend. It was what was always spoken of as a good turnout. Valley farmers and their wives came in buggies and spring wagons and some men rode in the Kentucky saddle that every farmer seemed to own. The G.A.R. fife and drum corps, with muffled drums and the funeral beat, led the cortege from the Willetts house to the Episcopal chapel and thence to the cemetery. The matched pairs of the well-to-do brought citizens from Johnsville and the larger Valley farms, and there was hardly room in the chapel for the assortment of men and women from "all walks of life." Even Trapper Bill, a guide who lived the year round in a Second Valley cabin, had mysteriously heard the news and was there in his squirrel hat. The Millhousers provided beds and meals for five out-of-town physicians, and a most surprising visitor from Fort Penn was Ben Rosebery, who invited himself to the Millhousers' for lunch with the doctors. "I read about it in the paper," he told Robert, almost apologetically.

"It was darn nice of you to come," said Robert.

"Well, I thought about it," said Ben. "I only saw him that one time, but he had an effect on me. I remembered him, where I have a hard time remembering fellows I spent four years with at college. Which reminds me, Robert. I ran across a friend of yours in Philly a while back. Chester Calthorp. Never any friend of mine. Too much of a willy-boy for me, but he asked me if I ever saw you."

"Where did you see Chester?"

"At Bookbinder's. He was leaving as I was going in. I was with one of my slightly tarnished lady friends and he was with a party of four or five young fellows. We didn't stop long. In fact I wouldn't have spoken to him if I could have helped it. If he hadn't been a member of The Hall, and just between the two of us, he wouldn't have been that if I'd had my way. There were four of us voted against Chester, you know, on the first ballot. And I was the last to withdraw my objections. I didn't give a damn for all the Calthorps and the Sterlings. In fact on the first ballot one of the four against Chester was a Sterling."

"You embarrass me, Ben. I only got in through my cousins, I'm sure of that."

184

"We all got in through cousins. But there wasn't the same objection to you as there was to Chester."

"How do you know? You weren't there. You were an old alumnus by that time."

"You were an altogether different kind of man, and I don't think I have to go into details on this solemn occasion. Come in and see me when you get to Fort Penn again. You haven't bought me a meal in damn near a year, and I know you've been in town. I get my reports on you every once in a while."

"Mrs. Jones talks too much."

"She does. She's getting careless, too sure of herself. Those Pittsburgh politicians are giving her delusions of grandeur. She can't do us much harm, bachelors, but in her line of work it doesn't pay to run off at the mouth. She didn't use to be that way. I see you have my fellow townsman, Dr. O'Brien, for lunch. He wouldn't be here if he'd known Dr. Willetts was a Jones patron. Well, I don't want to keep you from your other guests. But don't you come to Fort Penn without dropping in on old Ben."

The life and death of Dr. Willetts was all over in time for the four o'clock Fort Penn train. The out-of-town people scattered to depots, to the local hotels and saloons and private residences, and by the time the evening mail was being sorted, the doctor and his final ceremony were part of the vanished light of that day, not even much talked about. Death had been sudden and sent forth a shock, but it had been neat in a community where neatness was not always a characteristic of sudden death. He died all in one piece, above ground, and the manner of his death had not endangered others. Where coal is mined the people of a town can never wholly ignore death-in-quantity, no more than it can be ignored by the people of a fishing village. The colliery and the sea provide their livelihood, but miners and fishermen leave home forever whenever they go to work, and if they return alive from that one time, the next time out will be the same; they are not going to work in a chocolate factory or a silk mill, where death is a negligible presence. And so the men and their wives and the older young children must always look at the colliery and the sea and at death and life with the disciplined eyes of all those who are never far from the ultimate unforeseeable truth. A neat, single death can never have the same force in a Lyons or a Gloucester as in a town where the place of livelihood is not itself a hazardous situation. Affection for Dr. Willetts was genuine and universal, but there was also a contradictory gratitude to him for being the one who died: for the time being, death was satisfied with one, and not four or forty, but four or forty there might be tomorrow.

Now there were more miners and members of miners' families than any other class or group in Lyons; more miners than storekeepers and clerks, more miners than factory workers, more miners than the combined forces of storekeepers and clerks and factory workers and railroad men. Thus the miners' attitude toward a single death was felt even if it did not also represent the attitude of the others. An attitude so formidable had to be noticed by the others. Consequently there was private, individual sadness in the town, but largely the town was back at work the next day without keenings and further interruption of its regular ways. In the morning Robert Millhouser, whose friendship with Dr. Willetts was known to all, went to the post office, the barber shop, and the bank with never a word said to him about the death of his friend. He came home to lunch and said to Zilph: "They're a cold lot in this place."

"They are that," she said.

She understood, and he knew that she understood, his reason for his comment. "It's a *small* town, Robert," she said. "But I daresay all small towns are small. I've only lived in city and country, aside from this place. Until I came here I had no in-betweens, so I wouldn't really know. But the minute a place is no longer a village, with the pigs outnumbering the people, the town partakes of the city ways while holding on to some of the village. Despite all the years I've lived here I can go into the town and see a lot of strangers. That's the city way. The village way is where one stranger would attract attention and be gawked at till he explained himself and his unwanted presence. Here they don't like strangers—the village way. But they have to have them—the city way."

"I thought you might explain why the place is so cold."

"Maybe it isn't. It's the day after a funeral, remember. And a funeral doesn't bring out the jollity in a person. Don't bring up the Irish wake, either. The wake without the whiskey is a discouraging event. Bad enough with the whiskey, if you don't happen to be drinking along. I don't know, Robert. I suppose I'm of two minds about Lyons. I can't deny the smallness. That's there and nothing will change it. But I wonder if they're cold. I'll charge the town with smallness, but coldness—I may be wrong there. Coldness is another matter, where you have to take into account all the people, but one by one, not as a generality. What we call coldness may be merely bad manners, indifference. A man can be cold-acting without being cold."

"Well, I'm glad to hear you say that."

"It is an admission for me, isn't it? But how long has it been since I accused you of it?"

186

"I still never know what you're thinking."

"Well, if you were cold-acting I believe you've thawed out."

"When did you decide that?"

"Not when you wept for Dr. Willetts. A long while ago. Although I may say, since we're speaking of Dr. Willetts, he seemed to thaw you out where I never succeeded."

"Well, you never tried."

"Then *I* was cold-acting, and I'm sorry. And since we're talking like two sensible people, have you taken a mistress?"

"No."

"I'm sorry I asked the question."

"Why?"

"Because it leaves me with only one other that I've no right to ask."

"Well, I'll answer it. Yes. I buy women."

"If you expect me to be shocked, I'm not. For many men that's the solution, and it's better than others I can think of. Do you like going with whores?"

"Yes."

"Don't you miss love? For example, were you ever tempted to marry a whore, or to set her up for your own exclusive pleasure?"

"Several times. I never considered marrying one, but if I'd been rich I'd have kept one."

"And what happened to her?"

"Oh, there were two or three I would have kept, at different times, I mean."

"Then I don't think you'll ever marry, will you?"

"I might. Would you like to have a grandchild?"

"I would love to, but that isn't my first concern. It's you. I've had love, Robert. A great love with your father, but I loved my first husband, too. He was my first love, my girlhood love. With your father, all the meaning of the word came true for me. I don't want my son to miss that. I don't want your father's son to miss that. I outlived your father, but the love is just as alive and true today as thirty years ago. It's in you to have that, and I hope you find it."

"I hope I do, too."

"Then will you listen to some advice from a woman?"

"Of course."

"Give up your whores for a while and give love a chance. All you give to the whores is money, but the pleasure you get with them keeps you from being dissatisfied with your life."

"I know that," he said. "But if I'm dissatisfied will I be more likely to fall in love?"

"You'll look on women differently. And if you have none at all, there may be one you prefer above all the others."

"That seems artificial."

"You're thirty-five and have had women. You're not going to be a schoolboy in love, whatever happens."

"No, I guess not."

"That's gone forever. But a man's love is still open to you. You can still have that, and without the agony that schoolboys go through. You're a good-looking chap and a pleasant one, and your father'd be proud of your manners. I think you could make almost any woman fall in love with you if you wanted to."

"Thank you. I'm not used to such compliments."

"Not in the company you're keeping these days. But if you'd move about in polite society—"

"Not Lyons, surely."

"Fort Penn I'm told is very gay in the winter. And eligible bachelors are always scarce, everywhere. Fort Penn, Philadelphia. Try New York, if you care to."

"Fort Penn is far enough to look. I'd never get a New York or Philadelphia girl to settle down here."

"Your father got me, and I was happy."

"My father was a lot of things that I'm not."

"I don't know. When you were growing up it was very easy for me to see your father in you. Until he died I used to think that you as a child and a young boy were the living image of your father. Not so much in appearance as mannerisms, liking the same things, and *dis*-liking, too. Quiet and reserved, but enthusiastic, too. The Henry Millhouser that I'd missed knowing, he was you."

"But then I changed, eh?"

"Maybe I was the one that changed. Sure, you changed. At fifteen, sixteen, you'd have changed anyway—"

"But became very different from my father, that kind of change."

"Yes. But then maybe you never were like him. Maybe I was only forcing the resemblance."

"I've always been fond of him, but I never thought I was much like him."

"Why?"

"Why? Well, offhand that's hard to say."

"It shouldn't be so hard. Why weren't you like him, in what particulars?"

"That's just it. It wasn't the particulars. In fact, I tried to be like him as much as I could. But I *wasn't* like him, and maybe I do know why."

188

"All right, why?"

"Well, you. The two of you were so close that the one without the other was incomplete. Even when I'd spend a day with my father, I'd always know he was going back to you."

"Yes, but why not? I was his wife."

"No, Mama, you were more than his wife. I've seen a lot of husbands and wives that didn't ever become the one unit that you two were."

She nodded. "It's too bad we didn't have more children. An only child feels that about his parents, that they're together and he's outside. I lost two children before you were born. A pity. You would have been the youngest of three if they'd lived, and you wouldn't have grown up so alone."

"I wonder what they would have been, my brothers or sisters or whatever combination. I mean, what it would have been like to grow up with them."

"Oh. I can tell you what they were. They were a brother and a sister."

"Which was the older?"

"The brother, then the sister, then you."

He laughed at himself. "Thirty-five years old, and all I can think of is how nice it would have been to have had an older brother and sister to play with."

She looked at him in what he took to be a horrified expression.

"What's the matter?" he said.

"I was thinking what a terrible loneliness you've had, and I never really knew it before, God forgive me. If I'd known I'd have made more of an effort."

"I'd have seen through that, Mama."

"Probably, but I could have tried."

"And I'd have resented it. I'd be much worse off now if I'd known you were pitying me."

"I don't know. But now I feel that I've let your father down. He adored you, and I neglected you."

"How old are you, Mama?"

"Sixty-two."

"Well, don't start having regrets for your thirty-five-year-old baby. I'm not even a young man any more. In five years I'll be forty."

"In five years you'll be thirty-nine. You're not yet thirty-five."

"Well, don't *you* be coy about my age. Whatever you and I are toward each other, the die is cast. I was miserable sometimes, but I'm not any more, and don't you start creating trouble for yourself. I shall go looking for a wife and in due course you'll have a grandchild to

189

worry over. I'll have three grandchildren, so that none of them will grow up like me."

"I wish I knew how to take that."

"I wish I knew what made me say it."

"Oh, we know that, Robert. Your bitterness, your loneliness. Not to mention your dislike of me."

"Now, Mama. Caution. Stop fretting yourself. I'm all right. You know how it is with some jailbirds. They come out and they don't know what to do with themselves, so they commit another crime to be put back where they can feel at home."

"And why? Because their spirit died in prison."

"That's if they had any spirit to start with."

But in spite of the impossibility of their having a prolonged conversation without some asperity, Zilph and Robert Millhouser maintained mutual respect that was not simple politeness. They did not automatically oppose each other for the sake of animosity and stubbornness. In the present instance, Robert a few days later mentioned to her his intention of participating in Fort Penn social functions. "Rosebery, the fellow that was here to lunch that day, knows everybody in Fort Penn, and he's the kind of fellow that I can say to him I'm looking for a wife."

"My impression of Mr. Rosebery was that he'd take you to some other man's wife."

"True, but what if I *should* fall in love with another man's wife and want to marry her? Would you object?"

"It's not likely to happen if you stay away from those others we spoke of. A married woman would give in too readily, and you'd stop wanting to marry her."

Ben Rosebery at first acquiesced, then for his own amusement he co-operated more whole-heartedly in Robert's venture. "I'm more accustomed to leading my married friends astray, but this promises to be quite a novelty. I'll start you off with a dinner party, people I've owed for two or three years. They'll be older people, older than you or I, but the wives will very craftily put you down as a prospect for their daughters. You wait and see. You're going to have to lie a little. Make them think you spend more time in Fort Penn than you do, and you'd better rent a mailbox at the club. That's where they'll send invitations later on. It's too late for this year, but next year you ought to have your name in the Blue Book. I'll arrange that. If you want to do it up brown, you ought to have a horse of your own. You're a horseback rider, aren't you?"

"Yes, but why do I need a horse?"

190

"It's one of the best ways to get a virgin off by herself, without mama. It isn't absolutely necessary."

"Then I'll do without the horse, but I'm lost in admiration. You know all the tricks."

"You bet I do. I learned to dodge them, too. But as the fellow says, it's your funeral."

"Wedding."

"No. Funeral. A good man leading himself to the slaughter. You've asked me to help you and I will, but I'll always be ready to entertain a motion to dismiss. Unfortunately, Robert, I'm afraid you're going to have to give up Mrs. Jones. Some of the fathers would be understanding, but not the brothers. I can hear some of them say, 'You stay away from my sister, you nasty reprobate.' I have absolutely no use for anybody under thirty years of age. Male, that is. Noisy, quarrelsome, know-it-all pups."

Under Rosebery's sponsorship Robert Millhouser was introduced to Fort Penn society, and he was amazed at the extent of its activity and the quiet splendor of the parties. There was a hidden string quartet at nearly every formal dinner, and champagne was served throughout the evening. Robert learned from Rosebery that each of the dinners was an annual event for the hostess, who virtually owned her third Wednesday in January, second Thursday in February, or fourth Friday in March, year after year. (Lent did not figure in their calculations, in this Protestant, Low Church city.) The money was older than Pittsburgh's, and Philadelphia was by-passed for New York when the women shopped out of town, although the men who had not gone to Yale were frequently University of Pennsylvania alumni, among a sprinkling of Lafayette and Franklin & Marshall men. Political power as such was not recognized, and an assemblyman from Tioga County who had gone to Yale was more likely to be invited than a self-made man who controlled 100,000 votes. Robert met men who remembered his father chiefly as a name on the roster of the Fort Penn Club, and he also encountered a man who had been a law partner of the late Conrad Isaminger, but all the others were total strangers. His qualifications were adequate for a moderately friendly acceptance of his presence at the parties: he appeared to be a gentleman, a friend of Rosebery's but quite unlike roistering Rosebery; a second-generation member of the Fort Penn Club, a member of Delta Psi, and landowner in several nearby counties. Robert was by no means "in." He turned up at three dinner parties, which was an achievement for a first-year man-about-town, but he had not yet been judged by the husbands. They had not even bothered to express an interest in his activities in Fort Penn. There was a certain way of saying, "You live in Lyons, ah yes," that revealed the speaker as a stockholder in a colliery or a railroad; and when a man said, "You don't farm this land yourself, do you?" Robert knew that the speaker was making a quick but probably accurate guess as to the part of Robert's income that was dependent on farming. None of the older men expressed any desire to take lunch with Robert, although when they saw him at the club they bowed and spoke to him. "I don't seem to be getting very far," he told Rosebery. "I haven't met anybody that will ever see forty-five again."

"Patience, my son," said Rosebery. "Progress has already been made. Can you be in Fort Penn next Sunday?"

"No, I'm teaching my Sunday School class, you know."

"Your what? Oh, pulling my leg. Well, next Sunday afternoon I've been asked to have tea at the Baumgartens' and to bring that interesting Mr. Millhouser if he's in town."

"Is that progress?"

"Decidedly. In the first place, I've never been invited there for tea, never, although I'm distantly related to the Baumgartens. In the second place, there won't be many people there *over* forty-five. The Baumgarten Sunday afternoon teas are generally considered to be Fort Penn's slave market. Beautiful young white women are on display there every Sunday, also some of the plainest Janes in captivity. Jennie Baumgarten, Cousin Jennie, has had a great success with her teas. She has five daughters, and I've heard more than one mother say that Jennie was able to marry off three of the girls for the cost of a few cucumber sandwiches. Esther is the present candidate. There's one younger sister, fourteen or fifteen. She won't be there, thank God."

"Well, that is progress."

"Yes, after this Sunday you'll be invited every Sunday. And to tell the truth, there are some pretty youngsters in this town, and they all go to the Baumgartens'. Esther's a pretty girl."

Esther Baumgarten *was* a pretty girl, as distinguished from non-pretty girls, but she would more accurately have been called handsome, with large brown eyes, dark brown hair parted in the middle, calmness at the mouth and a nose that completed an Italianate face.

Rosebery's implied warning that the girls at the Baumgarten teas were there to attract husbands did not apply to Esther. She seemed content in her present situation, and as co-hostess she allotted her time in equal shares to all her guests, individually or by groups. There was friendliness and exactly no more in her greeting and few words with Robert Millhouser.

"Your cousin was the pick of that basket," he said to Rosebery as they walked back to the club.

"Esther? You could do worse. Jennie's brought them up very strictly. Karl Baumgarten is a namby-pamby, married Jennie for her money and if it'd been up to him she wouldn't have much left. He got her into some bad investments that cost her about fifty thousand dollars before her brothers stepped in. They got him a job up at the capital where he couldn't do much harm, and now he's retired and goes to the Public Library every afternoon because it makes him feel important. He's on the board of trustees. They meet once a month, but he's there every day. I think he goes there to take a nap in the trustees' room. Jennie raised the girls. I suppose Karl trims the Christmas tree, and he's always there to give the daughters away. I wouldn't mind Karl so much if he didn't act so damned superior to Jennie."

The formal dinner season ended after Easter, and without a fixed program to rely upon, Robert Millhouser faced a spring and summer in Lyons. Looking back he realized that Ben Rosebery, acting as his social counselor, had been a substitute for Dr. Willetts. He had no affection for Rosebery, since Rosebery had no affection for anyone else or true interest in anything but his work and his appetites; but so long as Robert Millhouser was being guided by Rosebery, the absence of Dr. Willetts was not so keenly felt. Now, with the coming of spring, Robert had no good excuse to spend so much time in Fort Penn, and he missed Dr. Willetts and fearfully anticipated a long period of missing him. In this mood he went to a Baumgarten Sunday tea for the first time without Rosebery.

Esther looked over his shoulder and saw that Ben Rosebery had not accompanied him. "You came alone. How nice," she said.

"I almost didn't."

"But I told you to. At least I *asked* you to. The first day you were here, I told you you were always welcome. We've never sent out invitations to these parties. That's the nicest thing about them. Our friends only come here when they want to, not because they've been invited. That's the way it's always been, for ever so many years. It's how my mother married off my three older sisters, although I suppose I shouldn't say that. It calls attention to the next on the list —me."

"You don't need anything to call attention to yourself. You're all I ever see."

She was startled, and looked away. "Oh, am I? Excuse me. Some people—"

"Wait. I'm not going to apologize. I'm going to make it worse."

"Please don't. You hardly know me."

"Shall I go? It would be very noticeable if I left this minute."

"No, don't go. But please don't say anything like that again."

"Esther, almost anything I say is going to be like that. I'm not a boy. I'm thirty-five years old."

"All the more reason for being careful what you say."

"Very well. I'll be extremely careful. Now listen. Esther Baumgarten, will you marry me?"

"That's unforgivable. I thought you were a gentleman."

"It would be unforgivable if I didn't mean it."

"What if I were to stand up this very minute and say, 'Ladies and gentlemen, Mr. Millhouser has just asked me to marry him, and I have accepted.' "

"That *would* be unforgivable—if you didn't mean it."

"That's easy to say. You're sure I won't do it."

"Then I will," he said, and started to rise.

"Wait, wait, wait. Please, please?" she said. "Come with me." She led him to a small room on the other side of the hall and closed the door. She faced him. "I don't know what to say. If I'd stayed there I don't know what I'd have done. The blood is all rushing to my head." She put her hands to her cheeks. He took her hands and placed them around his waist. He kissed her and she did not protest.

"That's all I needed. A kiss," she said. "I'm all right now. We can go back."

"And tell them?"

"There's nothing to tell. It was all my wanting you to kiss me."

"That's not all it was for me. I want you to marry me."

"No, I'll never marry you, Robert. We're not right for each other, but I do enjoy your kissing me. Will you again?"

"Now?"

"Right now. And hold me as close as you can."

He kissed her and she pressed herself against him and when he moved his body she moved in unison with him. Then she abruptly drew back her head and breathed deeply, and less abruptly moved her body free. "I think I'll always want you to kiss me, every time I see you," she said.

"Do you want me to speak to your father?"

She smiled. "I like you enough to kiss you, but I'm not going to marry you, Robert."

"Why not? I'm sure you're not in love with someone else."

"I'm not, and never have been. But I'm not in love with you, either. And you're not in love with me. Shall I be your mistress?"

"Do you know what you're saying?"

"Not exactly, but I can guess. No, I wouldn't like that, either. But I do like to kiss you and have you kiss me. Let's go back or I'll have some explaining to do."

Their absence had been noticed. The quick silence as they re-entered the sittingroom, followed quickly by a hum of forced conversation, made everyone in the room aware of their absence and of an awareness of their absence. On an impulse Robert Millhouser went to Karl Baumgarten, who was sitting with one of his married daughters. "May I join you?" said Robert. The daughter immediately had to be going home.

"Sit down, Mr. Millhouser."

"Thank you. Mr. Baumgarten, I've asked Esther to marry me and she has refused me."

"They have minds of their own, all of them. Are you asking me for permission to try to make her change her mind?"

"Yes."

"Well, all right. You're certainly old enough to know your own mind, and enough of a man of the world, if you don't mind my saying so. You have my permission."

"Thank you, sir."

One month later the engagement was announced. It followed a courtship that was disappointingly brief for conversational purposes in Fort Penn and consisted of a few picnics, canoeing on the Nesquehela River, Baumgarten Sunday teas (at which the prospective affianced were made more and more self-conscious), and once-weekly evening calls. Esther changed her decision during an evening call. "I *will* marry you, Robert," she said, as soon as they were alone.

"What a pleasant surprise," he said.

"In spite of our not loving each other."

"But I do love you."

"Please don't say it. *I* don't, and you *shouldn't*. Can we be truthful with each other on that?"

"On everything," he said.

"Ruth says I will love you."

"Your sister Ruth?"

"Yes. And she's told me some other things, particularly about marriage. I haven't been fair to you, but that was because I didn't know. Now I do know. Ruth and I are very close, and now I know certain things that I never knew before. You know them because you're older and a man. Do you know what I'm talking about?"

"Yes, dear, I do. You're lucky to have Ruth."

"Hereafter I won't kiss you. I don't want to as much since Ruth told me these things. It's made it all different, Robert. I didn't know anything before and Ruth frightened me and made me cry, but now I know what to expect and she says I'll love you. She said I didn't know what love was, before."

"Good for her. When can we be married?"

"September?"

"The sooner the better."

Now began a strange period of great tenderness between them, in which they belonged to each other without passion and as though they were guarding something precious that would not come into their possession until some future time. It was love that they were guarding; they had been promised love and they both believed in both the promise and the love. They agreed that they had not been in love, and they solemnly refrained from giving the name love to their present tenderness. One consequence of their reverence of the promised future happiness was the selflessness of what they now felt and an unselfish acceptance of a trust imposed; each was protective of the other's hope in the eventual achievement of love, and this protectiveness of their hopes functioned as a safeguard against the irritants and vicissitudes of explicit romance. Alone in the night Robert would say, "I love you, Esther, I know that I do," and in the calm of the love that they denied he was for the first time in his manhood at peace.

There was no regularity to the occasions of their meetings after the engagement was announced. They would be together for three days, and then a week would pass before they met again. Because it was summer and so many of her friends were away, the pre-wedding parties were being postponed until September. But they could not postpone Esther's visit to Lyons and Zilph Millhouser. "You and your father and mother come for the night, then Mama can visit you a couple of weeks later. I wish it didn't have to be in August, though. Mama feels the heat during the dog days."

"You're nervous, aren't you?" said Esther.

"Yes, I am. I wish my father were still alive."

"So do I, but he's not, so we have to make the best of it. One night isn't very long."

"Aren't you nervous, too? Meeting your future mother-in-law?"

"More curious than nervous, I guess."

The Baumgartens arrived on the noon train and were met by Robert Millhouser and Moses Hatfield in the surrey. The program was to be lunch, naps, tea, changes of clothes, dinner, and early retirement; then the next morning, breakfast, strolls, lunch, and the Baumgartens' departure on the two o'clock train. The company was restricted to the immediate families, three Baumgartens and two Millhousers. All went stiffly but well until after dinner, when the women were upstairs and Robert Millhouser was left alone with Karl Baumgarten. Baumgarten in a white linen suit was waving a palm fan and smoking a cigar and he and Robert were sitting on the side porch in the twilight. "Quite a nice place you have here," said Baumgarten.

"My father built it when he was getting ready to marry my mother."

"He was fortunate to be able to do that, although if she had changed her mind at the last minute, would he have still lived here? I don't suppose you'd know the answer to that."

Robert Millhouser tried to be agreeable. "No, sir, I don't think I do."

"I'm a pessimist. I never would have built a house for my wife until after we were married. Not that I was able to. As a young man I didn't have much money, and Mrs. Baumgarten and I had to live with my parents the first few years. Then I began to do rather well and I built our present house. I hope you're planning something like that, Robert. It isn't good for a young couple to live with the parents of either one. No house is big enough."

"Oh, Esther doesn't feel that way."

"That's what she'll tell you now, but a year from now it may be very different."

"Not much different. My mother is planning a trip to Ireland, and she won't be here much during our first year. We'll have it pretty much to ourselves."

"But she'll be back, your mother."

"Of course."

"Then you'll have the same problem a year from now that you have now."

"If it is a problem, only I don't think it is, and Esther doesn't."

"I know better. You see, I've spoken to Esther, and she's perhaps a little more candid with me than she is with you."

"Do you really think that, Mr. Baumgarten?"

"Yes, I do. Esther would much rather you lived in Fort Penn. So would her mother and I, but I'm not thinking of us as much as I am of Esther. Lord knows you could run your affairs from Fort Penn as easily as from here."

"I'm afraid I don't agree with you, sir."

"Some of your farms are actually closer to Fort—"

"I wasn't thinking of the farms. I was thinking of where I want to live, and I know. It's right here."

"And have a young girl give up her family and all the friends she grew up with, to live in—"

"We're only two hours by train from Fort Penn. My mother had a sister in Philadelphia and all the rest of her family were three thousand miles away."

"But she didn't have to live with your father's mother."

"No."

"Then I suggest that you'd better discuss this with Esther, and make her tell you the truth. Mrs. Baumgarten and I will retire early and you and Esther can have a chance to talk."

"When did you and Esther have *your* talks?"

"Well, we had one this very afternoon."

In due course the three older people retired and left Robert and Esther in the summer house. "I've had a rather—well—disconcerting talk with your father," said Robert.

"He shouldn't have said anything to you. You mean about our living here?"

"Yes."

"I could never live with your mother, Robert. She doesn't like me."

"How can you tell a thing like that in no time? That's rubbish, Esther."

"It's not rubbish. It's rubbish to say she likes me."

"I haven't said that. I wouldn't presume to say she liked you or disliked you on such short acquaintance."

"Then you force me to say what I don't want to say. *I* don't like her."

"She's accustomed to that."

"Then you surely don't want us living in the same house?"

"Mama is going to Ireland in October and may be gone a year. We'll have this house to ourselves while she's gone."

"Then we'll have the same problem a year from now that we have now."

"You and your father did have a talk, didn't you—except that I think he did most of the talking."

"I don't know what you mean by that, or your superior smile."

"Esther, I don't like your father, but I'll put up with him, as long as he doesn't interfere. He's a confounded liar, with his talk about making money to build the house you're in. Your father had to be restrained from squandering your mother's money in bad investments."

"And your mother entertained her lovers in this house! I don't want to live here, where things like that went on. Yes, she's accus-

198

tomed to people not liking her. What did she expect? If my mother knew any of that we wouldn't be here this minute."

"Therefore it was your father who told you this lie. Well, I said he was a liar."

"My father is a gentleman. He wanted to persuade you to make our home in Fort Penn without mentioning what he knew about your mother. But now it's out, and I only wish there was a train tonight."

"I was thinking the very same thing."

"Here is your ring. I'll tell my mother that you and I have broken our engagement because I wouldn't live here. You can tell your mother whatever you choose to. But please don't either of you attempt to say goodbye in the morning. I don't want to see your mother or you, ever again."

He looked at the ring in the palm of his hand. "The worst of it is, what you're doing is exactly right. If you believe what you believe."

She touched his shoulder with the tips of her fingers. "And so are you, Robert. You have to stand by her."

"Goodnight, Esther."

He watched her on the brick walk on her way to the house, and he had a fierce impulse to call to her, knowing that each sharp click of her heel on the brick was a telegraphed invitation, not to a reconciliation but to the desire that for both of them had taken the place of the long calm protectiveness. But when her slippers came down on the porch steps and the sound of her footsteps was a hollow one, and an announcement to the people upstairs that she was on her way inside, she was gone in all ways and in all ways he was alone.

In a while he walked around to the other side of the house. There was no light in his mother's room or in the rooms that had been assigned to the Baumgartens. In the thick stillness of the house any voice would be heard by the sleepless ones on the second story. He went inside and wrote his mother a note.

The Baumgartens left on the morning train, without seeing Zilph Millhouser or Robert, who remained in their bedrooms.

"Your mother'd like for you to see her in her room," said Margaret Dillon. The wording was exactly what it once had been when Robert was young and needed a talking-to.

Zilph was fully dressed and seated in the rocking chair near the window. He kissed her forehead. "Have you had your breakfast?" she said.

"Not yet."

She touched the teapot. "Still warm. Have a cup of tea."

"The Irish answer to everything, isn't it? And the English. A nice cup of tea."

"The answer to nothing, but it smooths the way. For a man that's just broken his engagement you seem chipper. I take it it *is* broken. Your note didn't say so, but ordering me to stay in my room till our visitors left . . ."

"It's broken beyond repair."

"What did I do? Now no use denying I had a part in it. Everything was all right till they met me."

"You married my father and gave birth to me."

"Yes, and?"

"Esther didn't want to live here."

"With me. Hadn't you discussed that prior to their visit?"

"We had, but not very much. But she told me that she suddenly realized what it would be like, coming to a strange town, giving up her family and friends, and having no one but you."

"She didn't like me."

"No, and you didn't like her."

"Yes, I did, but there'd be no convincing her of that if she didn't like me. Did you tell her I was going abroad?"

"That would only have postponed it, she said."

"She's right. It would only have postponed it. Just as at this very moment you're postponing telling me the real reason why you're not getting married."

"Can you think of a better reason?"

"Whether I can or not, it's a sufficient reason. Was that little fox-mask of a father in on it?"

"Oh, of course. He backed her up."

"If backing her up was all he did. He may have decided we didn't own half the county and she could do better elsewhere."

"If that entered into it it was on his part, not hers. She's not like that."

"You love her, don't you?"

He hesitated. "It will pass."

"The Garden of Gethsemane."

"No, Mama, not as bad as that. If we'd married, I think it would have been all right. But she said from the beginning she didn't want to marry me."

"And yet you could still have her. I feel that. Do you?"

"Truthfully, yes."

"But you don't want her enough to try again?"

"No."

"I must be honest with you, should have been sooner. My intention was to go to Ireland in October, that you know. But I never told you what else was in my mind. I was never coming back."

"You were going to stay in Ireland?"

"Yes. The girl Esther has every reason to want a home of her own, and she was going to have it, but I wasn't going to tell you that because of the kind of man you are. You never would have looked for a wife if it was going to mean sending me away. Your feeling for your father would have been too strong for that. But now I think you ought to make another try, Robert. Tell Esther that I'm going to Ireland and not coming back. The place is hers and yours. When you've a grandchild to show me, come to Ireland, the three of you, and I'll be more than content. Give it a few days, then go see the girl."

"It's all over, Mama."

"You're sure of that?"

"I'm sure of it."

"You really want it to be?"

"Yes."

"Then there's another reason that you're not telling me. You can say yes or no to that, can't you?"

"Yes, but don't ask me what it is."

"I won't. It's not for me to know."

"And it has nothing to do with you. It's between Esther and me."

"That could be many things," said Zilph. "And now what? Of course it's much too soon to say."

"What am I going to do?"

"Yes."

He smiled. "Well, I'm not going to go *looking* for a wife. If you hear of a good one, let me know."

"I admire you, Robert. You're putting on a good show. More distressed than you're letting on."

"There's no use trying to bluff you. I don't like losing Esther. But she's gone, and she'll never be back."

Margaret Dillon appeared in the doorway, bearing a tray of tea things and toast. "I thought you'd want your tea while you're talking," she said.

"Thank you, Margaret. It's the Irish answer to everything, isn't it?" said Robert.

"It is that. There's very few complications and situations that aren't the better for a good cup of tea. And a man's never his best starting the day on an empty stomach," she said. "And, uh, they caught their train all right. Moses is back from seeing them off."

"Thank you, Margaret," said Zilph.

"I'll just take your tray if you're done with it," said Margaret.

"Yes, and I'll have a full report for you later on," said Zilph.

"A full report, ma'am?"

"On Mr. Robert's broken engagement."

"Oh. Is that so? Well, very considerate, ma'am, and then I'll make my own report, as well. I've been having an interesting chat with Moses."

"I might have known," said Zilph. "Go on."

"The young lady, Miss Baumgarten, I'll say this for her. She had spunk. The father commenced an oration on how glad he was to be getting away from this house, meaning this house, and the daughter up and said, if there was another word said she'd get out of the surrey and go on foot, and it wasn't home she'd go to. She'd go and stay with Ruth, whoever she is, and never come home again. That Baumgarten, he had the face of a ferret. We're all glad we've seen the last of him."

"Well, thank you, Margaret."

"You'd at least think he'd have the decency not to say things in front of Moses," said Margaret. "That was no gentleman. Well, we're still all together is one way of looking at it."

"And a very nice way to look at it," said Robert.

"Yes. Come down when you're ready and we've some sliced banahnas and nice thick cream for you."

"Thank you, I'll be down in a minute or two," said Robert.

"Take your time, take your time," she said, and left.

"Sliced bananas and thick cream," said Robert. "I'll bet the Baumgartens weren't served that."

"Stale toast and tepid tea, I should imagine," said Zilph. "Never mind, it's nice to have a Margaret Dillon, that never believes anything but the best of us. It's something to live up to." She saw that Robert was not listening.

"They start thrashing next Monday," said Robert. "They'll have nearly twice as much oats as last year, more than we can use. I'm going to sell about half, and we'll have no trouble getting rid of the straw. I talked to a fellow in Fort Penn, he belongs to the Fort Penn Troop, and they'll buy it all if it's baled."

"Are you going to be gone all week?"

"Yes. Why?"

"Nothing. Enjoy yourself."

"Mama, don't worry about me. This had to happen, and it could have been so much worse. Ten years ago I might have been heartbroken."

"Ten years ago, yes, I guess you would have," said Zilph.

202

I have tried very hard, in writing this chronicle, to keep faith with the reader. Since this is, and will be, my sole venture in the field of the biographical novel, I have had no experience to guide me; and this experience will give me nothing to profit by in a future enterprise. At this stage of the writing I avail myself of what may be the last opportunity to point with some pride to the fact that I have frequently, and, I believe, completely resisted every temptation to take advantage of the reader. Specifically, I have disdained the opportunities to create false suspense by withholding information. I admit that the temptation was often strong, but I did not set out to write a mystery novel. (I am not the kind of snob who says he never reads mystery novels, any more than I am the kind of snob who says he never reads anything else.) This is largely the story of Robert Millhouser, using the facts as he told them to me, and editing and rewriting them in my own fashion without changing factual content of anything that was told me. It may even be said that I have been over-conscientious in my method: I have set down very nearly all the facts (certainly all the important ones) either in their chronological order or in the order in which I came upon them. An experienced novelist might argue that I could have legitimately postponed certain revelations without having had to resort to the device of the deus ex machina. *But once I had determined my policy and method, I adhered to them, and the reader has known almost from the beginning not only that Robert Millhouser fatally shot his young wife, but that Millhouser considered that that act put an end to his own life in every sense save literally. At the same time I have scrupulously and in detail presented "characters" and events and even objects that later have had or still later will have their place in the story. In brief, I have held out nothing that in a mystery story might be designated or recognized as a clue to the future developments. Moreover, in my effort to be fair with the reader I have to the best of my ability revealed my characters (myself included, for obviously I have intruded myself as a character in this chronicle) in such a way as to acquaint the reader with their spiritual and emotional realities and potentialities, thus in some cases making their later conduct subject to anticipation by the reader, and in all cases, I trust, making their conduct credible and psychologically consistent insofar as there can be limits to the consistency of human behavior.*

As I said earlier in this annotation, this may be my last opportunity to call attention to my efforts to play fair with the reader. In return I shall ask the reader's co-operation. I shall ask the reader if presently he will pause in his reading for a minute or two and, from what he has learned of Robert Millhouser, to imagine Robert Millhouser's life between 1890 and 1902. I resort to this unusual request because I myself have diligently examined Millhouser's own account of those years, and it is singularly unrewarding for a journal that is so exhaustive and so personal. The imaginative reader, now acquainted with Robert Millhouser, his mother, the town of Lyons, and the barest outlines of contemporary history, can almost surely supply his own version of the uneventful life of Robert Millhouser from age thirty-five to age forty-seven, and I assure the reader that his version will be close to the truth. Robert Millhouser attended to his business affairs, he withdrew from participation in the social life of Fort Penn, he satisfied his sexual needs at a house that was operated by a successor to Mrs. Jones, he made no effort to find a successor to Dr. Willetts, and while neither he nor Zilph Millhouser ever put it into spoken words, they knew that the routine into which they settled was to be their mode of life until the death of one of the two terminated the routine. I am on safe ground when, in a manner of speaking, I give the reader freedom to devise his own conception of the next twelve years in the life of Robert Millhouser. And since I am being so straightforward with the reader, let me add that my reason for asking his co-operation is not to shirk my own task, but rather to give him a moment or two in which to contemplate the life of Robert Millhouser, so orderly, so uneventful, as it might have continued but for the death of Zilph Millhouser in 1902.

If the reader will now pause a moment to consider those quiet years, I shall then proceed with the Robert Millhouser story from a point in the third year of the new century.—G.H.

•

IN LYONS things were bad. The strike that was called in May, and joined in so hopefully by the men at the collieries, was now nearly two months old and some of the men had already begun to lose faith in the judgment of John Mitchell, their Maytime hero. Why, they asked, did Johnny the Mitch' call the strike at just that time, when the mine owners had had four prosperous years and could afford to live off their fat? The loyal admirers of Mitchell would explain that he knew what he was doing: the mine owners were in a better mood to listen to Mitchell than if they had been losing money for those four

204

years. He is too young, the grumblers would say; the owners were all older men, and Mitchell was only thirty-two. But the answer to that was that whatever his age, Mitchell, and no other labor leader before him, had unified and not merely unionized 150,000 men, who had hitherto remained divided by a dozen languages and Old Country animosities and by the three great religious traditions of the Roman Catholic, the Greek Orthodox, and the Protestant. There were still more supporters than critics of the intense, frock-coated little Presbyterian, but as their savings dwindled and coal stayed uncut in the mines and the sun of the dog days kept above-ground activity at a minimum, some of the miners' hopeful spirit of May disappeared. There was nothing to do but pitch quoits, stay in the shade, circulate rumors, and avoid the wives and their worried looks and their sharp tongues.

In the middle, between the miners and the owners, were the Lyons businessmen—and as in every town in the anthracite region, their position was misstated. It was not so much that they were in the middle as that they were pushed by the one faction to the extreme of the other. A Lyons storekeeper was acquainted with a Lyons miner and the miner's family, and he was not acquainted with J. P. Morgan and George F. Baer. A Lyons storekeeper knew the hat size and shoe size of a Lyons miner and the corset size of the miner's wife, and he also knew when a Lyons miner had another mouth to feed. His sympathies were more likely to be, and in most cases were, with the miner, and yet the miner, to whom the storekeeper could give or suspend credit, soon regarded the storekeeper as the enemy. The Monday meetings of the bank directors ceased to be pleasant get-togethers. The directors stopped saving jokes for the Monday meetings; the weekly statement told the dismal story of steady withdrawals, no deposits, and called loans. Late in July it was unanimously agreed that the directors would no longer collect the $2.50 gold pieces that were by custom their fee for attendance at the meetings. Industry was somewhat more diversified in Lyons than in towns to the east and northeast, but coal was still king, and every Monday brought new rumors that certain regional banks were barely hanging on.

"October, September will tell the story," said Robert Millhouser to his mother. "The farmers. Generally they've had a good year, and by the first of October we'll know how good, when they start coming in to pay off their loans. We're not going to burn any mortgages this year, you can be sure of that, but on crop loans we'll get some money. Farmers don't like to pay interest between harvest and spring planting. The question that we're waiting to see answered is whether they'll leave their money on deposit with us, or take it home and hide it in their milk crocks. If they decide to leave their money with us, fine. We won't have to worry about a run on the bank if the farmers have enough confidence in us and the future. We can thank God for the farmers, and the tap-and-reamer, and the box factory. The Collieryville bank closed its doors Friday morning. They couldn't get any more help from the Gibbsville banks. We don't like to hear that."

"Why?"

"Well, the larger Gibbsville banks are very close to Philadelphia and New York. They're so close that they're not going to go under. But when a Gibbsville bank is advised not to help a Collieryville bank, the fellows today all said that that was the handwriting on the wall. Philadelphia and New York are determined to win this strike."

"How awful," said Zilph.

"It's business, Mama."

"What are we doing about it?"

"About the Collieryville bank? Nothing."

"I wasn't speaking of the Collieryville bank. I wanted to know what you and I were doing."

"Nothing."

"We should be doing something. I'm Irish, you know, and we don't like the absentee landlord. That's what New York and Philadelphia are."

Robert laughed. "That's what you and I are. It's precisely what we are, Mama."

"It's not the same thing. We own land in other counties, true. But you yourself supervise. You know what every acre is in, whether it's in potatoes or timothy or whatever."

"Well, what would you like us to do? All we can do is wait. You sound a little bit like Jerry MacMahon."

"Tell me about Jerry MacMahon."

"Well, he said last Monday that he'd go broke with the miners."

"Did he, now? How would he do that?"

"He said that as long as he could get credit, he'd let the miners have credit."

"Good for Jerry MacMahon!"

"No. I don't agree with you. And Billy Williams certainly didn't agree with you."

"Billy Williams is the superintendent and he has to take the side of the operators. That's why he's a director. Why don't *you* agree with me?"

"Well, you won't like this, but I think it's just as bad for one director to be on the side of the miners as it is for another to be on the side of the owners."

"Neither one of them, Williams or MacMahon, is using bank money."

"Not bank cash, no. But Billy Williams is honor-bound to report to his boss that one of our directors is carrying the miners."

"What if he does?"

"What if he *does?* The coal company keeps a lot of money in our bank."

"As much as the miners?"

"More."

"But it's one or two coal companies against over a hundred miners, and most of the miners are depositors because Jerry MacMahon persuaded them to be."

"It isn't a hundred miners any more, Mama. It's less than fifty. We had a hundred and seventy-four depositors that were members of the union. Now we have about forty-five. It's been a gradual thing, not a run, but you must remember that some of those accounts were for less than a hundred dollars."

"I can very well imagine that they were. But they were accounts, nonetheless, and a hundred-dollar account now will be a thousand-dollar account ten years from now."

"Would have been but for the strike, but there *is* a *strike*."

"I've heard of it, thank you. Has Jerry MacMahon started giving credit?"

"Oh, yes."

"Has he a telephone?"

"He has that one at the store, yes."

"Ring him up and ask him to come see me."

"Now?"

"He'll still be there."

Jeremiah MacMahon called on Zilph Millhouser after dinner.

"Jerry MacMahon, this is the first time you've ever been to call on me, and I had to ask you."

"Yes, you had to ask me or I'd never have come at all. I've never seen you in my house, either, Mrs. Millhouser."

"Oh, there you have me. Well, if the MacMahons and the Millhousers ever change their ways, let's exchange visits."

"All right. I've been to your house, now you come to ours."

"Agreed. I'm told that you intend to go broke with the miners."

"I told her that," said Robert Millhouser.

"I hope it won't be necessary, but I'm going to carry those that are on my books. Some of them have been for a good many years.

Whatever I have, I owe mostly to the miners, and Henry Millhouser."

"You're an ungrateful man. What about Zilph Millhouser? *I've* been dealing with you for over thirty years."

"I included you with Henry," said Jeremiah MacMahon. "Do you object to me carrying the miners?"

"No, I don't object, and I'm sure it wouldn't make the slightest difference if I did. But it happens that I'm with you."

"I'm glad to hear it."

"Why are you doing it, aside from appreciation?"

"It's good business to, it'd be very bad business not to. I'm taking a chance, to be sure. I *can* go broke. If this strike lasts—well, through the winter—my business would fail. On the other hand, I look at it this way. Fred Langendorf, a man with much more capital than I have, can also go broke without carrying the miners. Fred doesn't owe as much to the miners as I do. He's never had as many of them for customers as I've had, so there's no particular reason why he should carry them. But if he can go broke not carrying them, I might as well go broke carrying them. The only difference is that I'll go broke first."

"How old are you, Jerry?"

"I'm fifty-nine."

"And you'd be willing to start all over again?"

"I wouldn't be starting all over again. I've sent my children to the best schools, the boys to college, the girls to finishing school. I wouldn't like to work as hard as I did when I was first starting out, and I couldn't ask my wife to work that hard again. But I could start all over again if I had to. I have friends in town and in the Valley. I've always been straight with them, I think most of them would be straight with me."

"Do you hate the companies?"

"The coal companies? Of course not. I don't hate anybody. I must admit that George F. Baer and J. P. Morgan are beginning to try my patience. Mitchell is a very reasonable man and in my opinion he's doing the right thing. You can't ignore the wants of 150,000 miners, most of them with families, and Teddy Roosevelt isn't going to let them. George F. Baer saying God put the operators in charge—I don't like that. A lot of priests of my faith are with John Mitchell, and he isn't a Catholic. But if those two little fellows would sit down together and talk sensibly like two human beings, they could settle this thing. They're both fighters. George F. Baer was with the 133d Pennsylvania Volunteers. I think I could talk to him. I saw him once when he was in town a couple of years ago on an inspection. Not any taller than I am, if anything a little bit shorter. But a clever brain. First he licked the Coal & Iron, then they got him on their side. No, I don't hate the companies. The only man I ever hated was a Confederate sharpshooter. He picked off two of my officers from up in a tree. Then I took aim and shot *him*. But do you know, I never even saw what he looked like. I saw his musket fall out of the tree, but he must have had himself lashed to the trunk, and I didn't wait around for him to fall. I had to take charge of our battery. But I didn't come here to talk about the war. Not that war, at any rate."

"There's always *some* war, isn't there?"

"Somewhere, I guess. We had a good many years of peace, and I don't like to see it all go to waste in a strike, but this had to come, Mrs. Millhouser. And now that it's here, well, if I have to go with one side or the other, as Robert says, I'll go broke with the miners. If I have to."

"All I wanted to say I can say in a few words. If you *should* need financial help, you can count on me."

"Thank you very much. I appreciate your kindness."

"Well, I guess you can count on me, too, Jerry. But not for the same reason as my mother's. Mine is business. My mother's is sentimental. She hates the absentee landlords, meaning Morgan and Baer."

"I may need all the help I can get—as a loan. I wouldn't take it otherwise. And being a loan, I can ask you now how much you'd be willing to let me have."

"Ten thousand dollars?" said Zilph.

"Five, from me," said Robert.

"Fifteen thousand dollars? That just about takes all the risk out of it. But I may need it, and if I do, I'll remind you. I'm not going to say anything about this to anybody, except my wife. No use you creating hard feelings. If it has to come out later on, but for now I won't say anything."

When he had gone Robert Millhouser said to his mother: "I had no idea you intended to go into this to that extent. Ten thousand dollars. I thought five hundred."

"Would five hundred get him started again? It would *take* ten thousand," said Zilph. "Jerry MacMahon means it, you know. He'll go along with the miners all the way."

"Well, just as long as you realize that you and I'd both be giving up capital."

"I did realize that. But looking at it from your point of view, wouldn't you rather invest your capital in Jerry MacMahon than in the Pennsylvania Railroad?"

"Any day," said Robert.

"I'm weary," said Zilph. "I'm off to bed."

"Every year I tell you—"

"I know," she said. "And next year I'm going. I'm not certain whether it'll be the seashore or the mountains, but this is the first year I've really had trouble breathing. Stifling." She rose.

"Would you like me to help you upstairs?"

"Oh, no thanks. I'll go slowly."

Some time in the night she died. Margaret Dillon went prattling in with the morning tea, but she knew at once that Zilph Millhouser was dead. She knelt beside the bed and prayed, and then called to Robert, who was having breakfast on the porch. "Mr. Robert, it's your mother."

"I'll be right there," he said. He did not go on eating, but he did roll up his napkin and put it in the silver ring. Margaret Dillon had spoken in words and tone that she would reserve for only one occasion.

He looked at his mother so everlastingly dead, and he uttered Stanton's words without immediately remembering their origin: " 'Now she belongs to the ages,' " he said.

"That's beautiful, Mr. Robert," said Margaret Dillon.

"I wasn't the first to say it, Margaret," he said. "I don't even know who did. Yes, now I remember. Mr. Stanton said it when Abraham Lincoln died. But she does, doesn't she, belong to the ages?"

"I'll remember this, but it's not the way I'll remember *her*," said Margaret Dillon.

"No, we won't remember her this way. This isn't the way she was."

Margaret Dillon whispered: "I always wonder, can they hear us? It's wrong to think that. I know her soul left her body, but God forgive me, I wonder can she hear me?"

Robert Millhouser covered his mother's face with the bedsheet. "I'm sure you've prayed, haven't you?" he said.

"Yes, and what's to stop *you?*" Margaret Dillon put a hand on his shoulder, gently pressing downward. "She'll be none the worse if you get down on your knees. If you don't know a prayer to say, repeat after me."

He knelt beside the bed and said after her: "May her soul—and all the souls—of the faithful departed—through the mercy of God— rest in peace—amen."

"You'll want to be alone with her," said Margaret Dillon.

"No. I won't do that," he said.

There were two married nieces in Philadelphia and two first cousins in Belfast to be notified, perfunctorily. Jeremiah MacMahon, Fred Langendorf, young Dr. Willetts, Billy Williams, and Ivor

Brown were chosen as the Lyons pallbearers, and Christian Kimmel, the oldest of the farmers and the one for whom Zilph had had the most respect, was the sixth. The service would take place in the Presbyterian church, and burial would be beside the grave of Henry Millhouser in the Lyons Lutheran cemetery. Robert Millhouser was downstairs, making these arrangements, when Margaret Dillon came in. "Who's going to tell Moses? It's too much for me, and he'll be back from the mail any minute."

"Send him in to me," said Robert Millhouser.

Moses appeared and Robert told him to have a seat.

"Have a seat? Wud I do now? I do sumpn wrong?"

"No, but it's unpleasant, what I have to tell you."

"I knowed it was unpleasant when you say sit down."

"Unpleasant for all of us. My mother died last night. We found her this morning. The doctor's on his way out, but he's sure to say it was heart failure." He wanted to keep talking, to engage Moses' attention and distract him at the same time.

"She finally give up," said Moses, calmly.

"Yes, she finally gave up," said Robert in surprise.

"She had to raise you, she had to do that, but the year 1870, they wasn't much for her after the year 1870. She was just waitin', sittin' here and waitin'. I'm sorry for you, Mr. Robert. Everybody be sorry for you, that's the truth."

"Thank you, Moses."

The little Presbyterian church did not have room for all the citizens who turned up. The townspeople seemed to realize that Zilph Millhouser had stood for something worthy of their respect, even if it was to many of them only her forbidding, self-respecting independence. With the few who were closer to her there was another word: integrity. It was a quiet gathering, with little said in the small groups that collected before and after the ceremony. They were the simplest of people, making a living and a home, and not quite knowing why they were there, but knowing that they wanted to be there. Being there was to express something felt and not understood or expressible, one to another, in spoken words. And yet by being there they revealed that the dignity that was in them responded to the dignity in her, and perhaps for some of them the independence they could not afford responded to the independence in her that in her lifetime they feared.

When the hearse turned the corner at Market and Main the idle miners on the four corners removed their hats, and most of them made the sign of the cross. So soon had the word spread among them that this woman's last worldly gesture was to help the man who was

211

helping them. Billy Williams, the super, was riding in the second carriage, and there was no one from the Union, but Jerry MacMahon was in the carriage, too.

In the late afternoon, after the last of the callers had left the house, Robert Millhouser was sitting on the porch and having a cigar with Ben Rosebery, who was waiting to depart on the evening train. The whiskey and the women and the long hours at Fritz Gottlieb's Rathskeller had begun to tell, and so had the efforts of the day.

"Why don't you spend the night?" said Robert Millhouser. "It's bad here, but I'm sure it's much worse in Fort Penn. I'll give you a corner room and you'll get whatever breeze there is."

"No thanks, Robert. Have to be in court, first thing in the morning."

"Now, Ben. There's no court in session in August."

"Well, you're right, there isn't. But I was thinking as soon as I get off the train I'm going right out to my boathouse and I don't care who's around, I'm going to take off every stitch of clothing and jump in that river."

At that moment there was a clap of thunder, followed by the splatter of the first large raindrops, and in a minute the rain came in a steady downpour. "That's a good honest rain," said Ben Rosebery.

"If we'd had it a few days ago I think my mother would still be alive."

"I wonder. From what you've told me, Robert, maybe she'd have had a few more days, but not much more than that."

"Maybe not, but I wish she could have had one more nice day, instead of this damned heat. I wonder if it's raining down-country. We don't want too much rain before the grain's all in, especially here in the Valley. It's going to make a lot of difference in this town, I can tell you."

"On account of the strike?"

"Yes. If the farmers don't have a good year this is going to be a terrible winter for a lot of people. It's bad enough now. There's talk of a soup kitchen starting next week, and the miners hate that. Miners are proud men, and they're not going to like having their families standing in line for a bowl of soup."

"They're going to be standing a long time, Robert. This Mitchell made a wrong guess."

"How so?"

"Well, the way I hear it, he thought the operators would be more kindly disposed because we've had some prosperity, but he's not dealing with men that have to worry about where their next meal is coming from. J. P. Morgan isn't going to go broke even if the mines don't work for two years. And by the same token, he's not going to get that much richer if they do work. What he's fighting is the Union, the Union and Teddy Roosevelt. Men at the club have told me that Morgan has passed the word on to T. R. that he'd better keep his nose out of it. In other words, if T. R. wants a fight, he'll get it."

"Then Mr. Morgan's going to have to stand up to the whole country. At least we hear that sentiment is in favor of the miners."

"Maybe it is, but I wouldn't count on it. And I'm not so sure that sentiment is in favor of the miners. Teddy's popular, and Morgan isn't, but if Teddy puts the government on the side of labor and against all employers, you just watch Teddy's popularity go up in smoke. These years of prosperity we've been having, they've made capitalists out of a lot of people. Every son of a bitch that owns a share of stock is going to think twice if Roosevelt goes after the corporations. Personally, I think Teddy's the biggest God damn show-off in the history of the country. I don't think he cares any more about the working man than Morgan does. But I'm not saying he isn't one of the smartest politicians we've ever had, too. I'm with politicians every day of my life, smart ones. They don't like Teddy, but they'll admit privately that he's smarter than most. He's got this big suit on against the Northern Securities people. All I can say is he'd better win it, because if he loses, if the government loses, then all the talk about Wall Street running the country will turn into an actual fact. Morgan, Harriman, Hill and the rest of them will own every stick and stone in the country inside of ten years. The Sherman Act will be as dead as the old gray goose. On the other hand, if Knox wins this suit for him, and Mitchell wins this strike, that'll be the start of socialism."

"Socialism?"

"Socialism. In ten years, maybe twenty, you're going to have to ask the government's permission to blow your nose. And you're going to have to share your handkerchief with somebody else. It won't *be* your handkerchief. It's true that there is public sentiment against Big Business, as Roosevelt calls it, and they've invited trouble. But I'm a lawyer, and maybe I know a little bit more about what we lose when a law is passed. Every law, good or bad, strengthens the government, and nearly every law stays on the books no matter what party is in power. Meanwhile, you and I, the individual citizen, have lost some liberty. The trouble is, of course, every new thing means new laws. For instance, this Italian that I always call Macaroni, the wireless telegrapher. A young fellow in law school should start specializing in wireless telegraphy, and by the time he's thirty-five years

213

old he'd be a millionaire, because wireless law is going to be a specialty like maritime law, railroad law, medical jurisprudence and so on. You know, it's cooling off, and speaking of railroad law, I've missed my train."

"Good, then you'll have to spend the night."

"I'd like to. I've been thinking while I was talking, you oughtn't to spend tonight all by yourself. When my mother passed on I was a few years younger than you are, but not much, and being alone in our house the night after she was buried, I never put through such a night. And you were closer to your mother. Tonight you ought to have company, even if it's only me. I hope this rain isn't too heavy for all those flowers out at the grave. They must have thought a lot of your mother in this town."

"You deliberately missed your train, didn't you, Ben?"

"Well—I guess I *could* have given you my lecture some other time. Yes, I did. I'm the lonesomest son of a bitch in the world, myself. If I'm not working I've simply got to have people near me."

"I never would have thought that."

"Uh-huh. By the way, Esther Parkinson, Esther Baumgarten that used to be, she asked to be remembered to you. Now what did she say, that she wanted me to get straight. Please tell Robert that she never believed that story about the hunters. That's what she said. Do you know some people named Hunter?"

"I know what she meant. How is she?"

"I can't honestly say. I never see Esther. She called me on the telephone when she read in the paper about your mother. Parkinson's a doctor, I believe he's a friend of the Dr. Willetts that I saw here today. They have three or four children, but I never see Esther and I hardly know her husband."

Ben looked at his cigar, quickly at Robert Millhouser, then again at his cigar. "You were almost my cousin," he said.

"No, Ben. I never really was. Esther and I did get engaged, and for a few weeks we were in love, but from the very beginning she'd said we shouldn't marry."

Ben popped out a mouthful of smoke. "I don't know why she said that. You stayed away from me for quite a while after the engagement was broken. I understand why. But I almost came to see you. Esther wanted to marry you. She came to see me at my office and told me the engagement was broken. I'd more or less got you two together and she felt she owed me an explanation, but she didn't have any explanation."

"Yes she had. She didn't want to live here."

"That was for the benefit of the public, but I broke that down in

214

no time, and I didn't have any trouble making her admit that she still wanted to marry you. She said you didn't really want to marry her. Why would she say that?"

"I don't know, Ben. Maybe it was true. We believed in love, but weren't in love."

"Then Esther was right, I guess."

"The proof that she was right is that she seems to be happy today."

"The two of you are so polite about each other, it seems a shame. She may have been right at the time, but it might have worked out all right. Something happened here when they all came to visit, and my deduction, from all I've seen in the courtroom, is that it had something to do with those people, the Hunters, or your mother."

"Both," said Robert.

"I was sure of it, plus some monkey business on the part of Karl Baumgarten. If we're going to have new laws all the time, I'd like to write one that establishes a new custom. Let a young couple go off and live together as man and wife for two or three months. If I'd had that idea when I was younger I might have gone into politics. Six wives a year and no strings tied to you. Paradise, my friend. Paradise. Wouldn't do anybody any harm at all. Only true love would survive."

"There would be a lot of little bastards resulting."

"Wards of the state. Socialism. Put the boys in the army and navy. Teddy would like that, he's so fond of the Navy. And the girls, well, now I wonder what we could do with all those girls? We'd have to find another word instead of prostitution. What would we call them, Robert? What would be a good name for them? Nurses of some kind. Nurses. The Florence Nightingale Brigade. That would be a dignified name. Every city in the country would have a Florence Nightingale Brigade. I could be persuaded to give up the law and take charge of a training school, even at my age. 'Young lady, afraid we can't give you your certificate. You're going to have to tutor under General Rosebery.' "

They had some wine at dinner and Ben talked continually until nearly eleven o'clock and Robert began to fall asleep in his chair. Ben shook him lightly. "Go to bed, son," he said. Robert made an effort to apologize, but Ben shushed him. "Just go to bed. I'll see you in the morning."

At breakfast Ben refused to listen to apologies. "I can put anybody to sleep. I've done it with juries. A very valuable trick, on occasion. I got a mistrial one time by calling the judge's attention to the fact that Juror Number Five had been sound asleep for twenty-five minutes, by my watch, and was *still* asleep. And I don't know how many

215

times I've used the trick at Fritz Gottlieb's. You took longer because you have good manners, but I'll bet you slept pretty soundly."

"I did. You're a gifted man, Ben. Many-sided."

"And I like to talk. I like to hear those words rolling out, especially when there's no God damn district attorney interposing objections every two minutes."

Robert drove him to the morning train and as they shook hands Ben said: "I like to see a gentleman once in a while, Robert. Most of my cronies are not. So come and see me. Use my house as your headquarters."

"I'll do that, Ben. And thank you for everything."

Robert Millhouser drove from the depot to Jeremiah MacMahon's store. The mare he was driving had never taken to the tie-strap and would not stand at a hitching-post, and Robert signaled to Mac-Mahon to come out to the sidewalk. "This animal is skittish or I'd have come in," said Robert.

"Oh, I know her. This mare's worth any two that will stand. What can I do for you, Robert?"

"I just wanted to tell you that the bargain we made still holds good. My mother's estate will be tied up for a while, but you're not to worry about that. It's still fifteen thousand."

Jeremiah MacMahon stroked the mare's rump. "Do you think you had to tell me that, Robert? Do you think I didn't know that as well as I know my own name?"

There was a silence, and then Robert said: "How is everything?"

"Bad. Bad. This very morning I went to the Company office and advised Billy Williams to stay off the street. On foot, that is. I don't want him walking in the midst of those men at Market and Main."

"Is it that bad?"

"One or two trouble-makers, and Billy himself. In the cab yesterday, sitting next to Billy, he took something out of his hip pocket and put it in his coat pocket. A pistol. 'There's no need for you to carry that, Billy,' I said to him. 'There isn't, isn't there? Well, I've been threatened already,' said he. And I guess it's not only the threats, Robert. The Company always has spies, and I guess Billy's been tipped off."

"Shall I speak to Billy?"

"What could you say? In his position I'd carry a pistol. Look down the street, at the Four Corners. Not even ten o'clock and I'd guess there are sixty men there, fifteen to a corner. This afternoon there'll be a hundred. Most of them peaceable, but watch out for those trouble-makers."

"Then there's nothing we can do."

216

"Not unless you have influence with George F. Baer."

"Good Lord," said Robert Millhouser. "Well, good morning, Jerry."

He proceeded on Market Street to the Four Corners and turned to his right into Main. Suddenly the mare screamed and bolted and galloped toward home, virtually out of control most of the way.

Moses was at the stable and he looked at the mare and said: "Why you in all that hurry in this hot weather? All this lather on this little mare. *Say, she bleedin'.* She got a cut on her ribs."

"Is it deep?"

"Aint deep, but deep enough."

"Well, let's unhitch and cool her out a little and I'll get the ointment. Somebody threw a stone at her and she damned near jumped out of the shafts."

"Who done that?"

"I don't know. We haven't got time to talk," said Robert. He brought out the gelding, the other half of the pair, and harnessed up while Moses was busy with the mare. "All right, put her in the stall and come with me."

"Where we going? You mad at somebody?"

"You let me off at Main and Market and then go down to the bank and wait for me there."

"You better not go amongst them strikers without a gun."

"I haven't got a gun."

"Yes you do too," said Moses. He went inside the stable and returned with the Colt Storekeeper that Henry Millhouser had purchased for Ryan in the last year of the Civil War.

"That old thing," said Robert Millhouser.

"Old, but not rusty."

"All right, get in."

They drove to the Four Corners and Robert got down and Moses drove away. Robert went to the group of men from whom he knew the stone must have come. "Somebody here, some filthy coward threw a stone and cut my horse. Who was it?"

There was silence, total silence except for the sounds of men from the other corners coming to join the group.

"Who was it? Are you all cowards?"

A tall, black-moustached man in an undershirt and the trousers of a suit slowly came forward. "Me name is Pat Brennan."

"I know you, and you didn't throw the stone."

"And I didn't throw the stone. The one that trun the stone aint here. If it's any satisfaction to you, Millhouser, he got his punishment, all he deserved. He'll throw no more stones at harses for a day or two, according to my guess. Now if I was you I'd be satisfied with that, and don't come chargin' into us looking for trouble. If there's a bill for the harse we'll make it up to you. Send it to me, Pat Brennan. Now good day to ye, Mr. Millhouser." He turned his back on Robert Millhouser and pushed his way through the group. They likewise turned their backs, and Robert walked around them and on to the waiting Moses.

He took the reins and headed the horse for home, at a walk. At the Four Corners there was not a word, not a whisper.

In Lyons the situation worsened so that the same incident a month later could not have had the same outcome. Robert Millhouser would have died under their feet. Whenever he drove through the Four Corners intersection there was a distinct cessation of conversation; when he was on foot they moved out of his course in a way that was insolent rather than respectful or accommodating. "You're in some danger, Robert," said Jeremiah MacMahon, a few days later.

"Do you think so? Why?"

"I don't know that I can explain it. There isn't a man among them doesn't know your offer to me. I let the word get out when your mother passed away. I wanted her to have that little respect from them. And they admired your spunk, the day the mare was injured. It was very embarrassing to Pat Brennan I can tell you, because he didn't know, nobody could have known that five minutes earlier you'd just been renewing your offer."

"Pat Brennan behaved very well. I'm afraid he behaved with more dignity than I did."

"If they were all like Pat, but they're not. In another month they won't be listening to Pat. They're going to listen to the first hothead that wants to burn down the breakers. That will probably be Tim Brennan, Pat's younger brother but always jealous of Pat since they were boys."

"And the very same man who threw the stone at my mare."

Jeremiah MacMahon stared coldly at Robert Millhouser. "Is that a guess?" he said.

"Is it a good one?"

"It's too good. Yes, it was Tim threw the stone, and Pat that gave him the beating for it. But was it a guess, Robert? On your word of honor was it a guess and no more?"

"On my word of honor. Why?"

"Because if it was more than a guess—information from Billy Williams—this would be the last time I could come to your house. I wouldn't take your loan, I wouldn't even want you to deal at my store. Robert, these men have to have somebody they can trust, and

218

they trust me. Some of them wish they didn't have to trust me. I'm a director at the bank, to them I'm a rich man, but they know I'm with them. But if you were getting information from Billy Williams, Billy has his spies, but they have theirs. Here's how it is. If they thought for one minute that I was giving you information, they'd kill Pat Brennan tonight in his bed. Maybe they would and maybe they wouldn't kill me. Would, I guess. I shouldn't have made the remark about Tim Brennan, and the dear Lord knows I should never forget that you're half Irish. You know our ways."

"No I don't."

"You think you don't, but you do. Half, anyway."

"Well, maybe I do without knowing it. But you think they'd murder Pat—"

"Because you were extracting information from me that Pat gave me in secret. And then you were passing it on to Billy Williams."

"No."

"No what?"

"No, I don't know your ways. I'm not that good at intrigue. If I were Tim Brennan I'd never suspect that of Robert Millhouser."

"If you were Tim Brennan, the dear Lord forbid, you'd suspect everybody of everything. It isn't always this bad, Robert. You must take into consideration what these men are going through. Do you know what was in the collection last Sunday, the total for three Masses?"

"No."

"Eighteen dollars and some cents, nearly all of it pennies. That's to support two priests, the six nuns and the reverend mother, the school expenses and the expenses of the church. When school opens in a couple of weeks many of the youngsters aren't going to be there. They won't have shoes."

"Well, God damn it, I'll see that they have shoes."

"Shall I tell that to Father Laubenstein?"

"Certainly. No child is going to be kept out of school because he hasn't got a pair of shoes. I'll pay for them."

"Why? You've never been interested in children, have you?"

"No, and I'm not now. But it just seems so nasty to have them suffer. I don't know, Jerry. Children staying home from school because they haven't got shoes—it's so wrong. Tell Father Laubenstein that I'll guarantee payment."

"What about the children in the public school?"

"The same for them. I don't want you to think I only care about little Catholic feet. It has nothing to do with religion, or the miners. It's just suddenly struck me that these youngsters that can't help themselves are paying too much. Who's head of the school board? Tom Lloyd? Is he still in?"

"Till next election."

"You tell him whatever you tell Laubenstein. But don't tell either one of them that I'm paying the bill. I don't want any thanks, and I'll never do it again. How much do children's shoes cost, and how many children are there?"

"Well, you can go all the way up to two dollars for a pair of good high-laced boy's shoes. In the district, including parochial, about three hundred children. But not all of them will need shoes. Father Laubenstein will find out from the nuns and Tom Lloyd will get his information from the teachers."

"Well, just so that no child has to stay out of school for such a stupid reason."

"It's time for me to be going," said Jeremiah MacMahon. "Take care of yourself. And don't lose your temper."

"I didn't know I had one till Tim Brennan hurt my mare. What did my mare ever do to Tim Brennan?"

"Forget that name. You don't know who hit your mare."

"All right."

"And don't you be the one that starts the bloodshed. You very nearly did, and it wouldn't have stopped there. We're like living in a mine that's filled with gas. Someone lights a match and away goes everything. Robert, it isn't enough to have good intentions. A man out of work can think today that Robert Millhouser has shown his good intentions, and tomorrow the same man can think your mother and you—I don't like to put it in words."

"That we were only protecting ourselves."

"Yes. The men are ready for trouble, but you have to remember, they've had trouble since May. There's another thing, too."

"Yes?"

"If trouble comes it isn't George F. Baer that'll die. It isn't even Johnny Mitchell. It's good men like Pat Brennan and some farmer lad that joined the National Guard for the fun of it. I don't want to see any of that here. And neither do you."

"I have an uneasy suspicion that you're trying to tell me a lot more."

"I am."

"But you can't."

"No, I can't. Make another guess if you want to."

"Is it about—"

"No names!"

"Well, I won't leave town, if that's what you're hinting. And that *is* what you're hinting. A certain party is liable to come at me because his brother gave him a beating. Well, I'm staying right here, and hereafter I'm not sending Moses for the mail. I'll go myself, on foot. But I'll be armed."

"Then it'll commence with two dead. You're willing to start the bloodshed."

"Jerry, I'm forty-seven years old, and I have nobody left in the world. I'm absolutely alone. And if I can't walk the streets of my own town, where is there for me to go? Let me tell you a story about my father, that I know you never heard." Robert Millhouser then related the incident of the cavalry lieutenant whom Henry Millhouser defied. "Don't get into the habit of running away from fights," he concluded.

"I've been in battle many times, Robert, and I always wanted to run away."

"Before the battle started, maybe, but not after, not while it was going on."

"Well, I guess that's true. Not while it was going on. But your battle hasn't started."

"Yes it has, my battle with myself. The temptation to go away. But I'm not going. A bad man, and a coward at that, that would throw a stone at a dumb animal, he's not going to drive me into a hole or frighten me away. No matter what the consequences. If the men can't control *him*, then *he* has taken control of the *men*, and I owe them nothing."

"I've killed men. I've taken life. But I put you down as a man of peace. Yet you could leave this house with a pistol in your pocket, knowing that less than a half a mile from here you're liable to meet a man and kill him?"

"A man who attacks me first? Yes."

"On your part it's still cold-blooded, Robert."

"Because I go armed?"

"Because a man of your intelligence knows what's liable to provoke that kind of a man, and you stand on your rights, and you go armed. It isn't only the going armed. It's all three."

"So it is, and it isn't my rights as a citizen of the United States. It's my rights as one human being threatened by another human being. Slowly, gradually, this is getting turned around so that I'm in the wrong and he's in the right. Oh, no, Jerry. It won't do."

"All right. But while we're sitting here, maybe weeks before you meet this man, you can make your plans to shoot him."

"If that's the way you want to put it, yes. Just as he's planning to do me harm that may cost me my life. When you were a soldier, did you ever get a report that the Confederates were ten miles away?"

"Many times."

"What did you do? Sit around the campfire singing songs, or did you perhaps plan to take them by surprise? Let them walk into an ambush? At least you didn't do anything that would put you at a disadvantage."

"Not if we could help it, but that was war."

"I'm at war, and I'm alone. I *am* a peace-loving man, as you said, but I'm alone. My life may be worthless to everyone but me, but as long as I have any desire to live, I have to be prepared to do whatever is necessary to go on living. I have to feed myself, provide shelter for myself, and watch out for whatever threatens my life. In this case, *who*ever. You're pleased to call it cold-bloodedness, Jerry, and you're not the first one. But you don't understand what it is to be alone most of your life. And I have been."

"You're the man that a minute ago wanted to give shoes to school children."

"Yes. You bet I did. A child is alone, too. He is every bit as much alone as I've always been, as long as he is dependent on his parents. All the helpless are alone. Your miners are alone. You don't see that, I'm sure."

"There you're wrong. I do see it. A soldier going into battle is alone."

"Ah, you do see it! A child that's old enough can steal a pair of shoes, and should. And I can kill Tim Brennan."

"You must excuse me now, Robert."

"Yes, I know. Goodnight, Jerry."

"Goodnight to you, Robert."

His troubled friend walked down the brick path and Robert Millhouser heard the snap of the thumb-latch as Jerry MacMahon opened the gate, the click of the latch as he closed it. Whatever happened, things would never be the same again with Jeremiah MacMahon. They might be better, but more likely they would not be as good. Jerry now stood alone between the men and those who were not with them, and the least that could be said for his position was that it was awkward; at its worst the position was mortally dangerous, and Robert Millhouser was sympathetic and apprehensive. But in Jeremiah MacMahon's solitary position Robert Millhouser did not see, refused to see, a man alone as he himself was alone. This was temporary solitude, and not truly that, for Jeremiah MacMahon was husband, father, grandfather and, so to speak, advocate. He stood to lose through the capricious treachery of the people he defended, but until treachery occurred, Jeremiah MacMahon was far from alone. Thus Robert Millhouser, separating himself from his friend and, quite possibly, anticipating some such action on Jerry's part. "Maybe I want to be alone," he said, but that was a lightly cynical comment that he would not develop; it would have cheapened the unhappiness of all the years since the death of his father, and to renounce that unhappiness now would also have meant the abandonment of hope, for his hope and his unhappiness were never far apart.

The death of Zilph Millhouser had been a sadness but in no sense a tragedy. She had been a stimulating companion, with a dutiful interest in his welfare that passed for love, to which he responded in kind. Very few of the thousands of words that passed between them gave any expression to their understanding of each other and of their rather well-defined relationship. On no day but in some season, some year, the relationship was achieved and thereafter remained constant. In it there was humor and there was respect, as well as an acceptance of an antagonism that they kept safely within bounds. So long as they both were alive, he was necessary in her life, she in his. The existence of the one demanded recognition by the other, and neither could reject the other. But of love there was nothing, and if love for a third party had come to Zilph or to Robert, the relationship, such as it was, would have collapsed. As Moses Hatfield instinctively knew, she died of weariness, of waiting, and her death was a relief to her son. It simplified his own life by taking away the companionship which was a dreary substitute for the love he had yet to experience. And part of the relief, as well as part of the simplification, was that her death put an end to the nonsense of his blaming her for his unhappiness. In moments of impatience he would think of Zilph as an interfering mother, and at other times as a responsibility he could not shirk. None of this was true, he well knew, but when he needed a temporary excuse a helpless or a dominant Zilph would serve. Now that she was dead—certainly powerless and certainly beyond help— he was alone with his judgments of himself; harsh, fair, or whatever they might be, but all self-contained. The parting with Chester Calthorp, the death of Dr. Willetts, the fiasco of Esther Baumgarten, the death of Zilph Millhouser, and now the scene with Jeremiah MacMahon, were not brought about by Robert Millhouser or even by forces he could control; but each of the events had left him once more alone except for Zilph, and with her death the pattern, whether or not of his own making, was for the first time complete, perfected. He now had a freedom that he had never had, or that he had never claimed, and he fully realized that whatever he made of his life henceforth was truly his own doing. He could not honestly accuse himself of enjoying his mother's death, but neither could he deny that her death had given him opportunities that he must accept.

On the very next day he went to a closet and took out an easel and the boxes that contained his brushes and paints. But the paint was hard and crumbly and the bristles were hopelessly curled after so many years. Some day soon he would order everything new. He then remembered that he had told Jeremiah MacMahon of his intention to walk to the post office. He looked at his watch; it was too late to stop Moses; but he could invent other excuses for the walk to town.

He put the Colt Storekeeper in his hip pocket and set out for a visit to the hardware stores. They would have catalogs of house paint manufacturers and might have the addresses of artists' supply houses. Then he remembered that there was a vogue for "painting" among the ladies of Lyons; china painting. The stationery store would have the address he wanted.

He was within a few yards of the Four Corners before he remembered the pistol in his pocket and the defiant secondary purpose of his expedition. He realized that in his present buoyant mood there was almost nothing that the men could do that would cause him to draw his pistol. The pistol was a heavy weight in his pocket and not a weapon. But he could not turn back or otherwise avoid walking through the groups of men at the two corners on his course. "Let him pass," he heard someone say. "Give him room." The men fell back and he was safely though both groups.

He had been light-headed with fear, not so much fear of an attack as fear of his temporary inability to fight back. In the stationery store he wiped his forehead and face with a handkerchief. The woman who owned the store had once been his teacher in fifth grade. "Are you all right, Robert? Do you feel shaky?"

"Could I have a glass of water?" He sat down and she went to the back of the store, which was curtained off. He heard the water in the sink, and the next thing he knew was the vapor of spirits of ammonia in his nasal passages and Ivor Brown standing over him.

"You're all right. You had a fainting spell," said Ivor Brown. "Maybe a little heat prostration."

"I've never done that before," said Robert Millhouser. "I'm very sorry."

"They carry people in my store every day, last couple weeks. We sent for Moses. I guess he'll be here any minute," said Ivor Brown.

"I want to walk home."

"I wouldn't if I were you, Robert," said Ivor Brown. "Go home and lie down, pull down the shades, and don't go in the sun for a couple of days. That's what it is, it's the sun. From about nine o'clock on till about ha' past two in the afternoon, it's murderous. Here's Moses. You got the bumbershoot on the carriage, Moses? We don't want him in any more sun. Here, Robert, you take this bottle, spirits of ammonia, my compliments."

The men did not customarily gather at the Four Corners at evening mail-time, and therefore no defiant gesture was to be made by going through them again. But in the morning he put the pistol in his pocket and proceeded to the post office, half-hoping that one of them would provoke him to shoot. But as he approached he heard the same order: "Let him pass. Give him room," and he knew the voice was Pat Brennan's.

Twice daily thereafter he walked through the groups at the two corners, and so it continued until late October and the settlement of the strike. That night, with dishpans and dinner pails and anything else that would make noise the men serenaded Jeremiah MacMahon. At the post office the next evening Pat Brennan stood beside Robert Millhouser and in a low voice said: "Ye can put your pistol away now, Millhouser."

"I already have, Pat," said Robert Millhouser. "Last night, when I heard the good news."

"The good news, was it? But twicet a day you were ready to turn this town into a slaughterhouse. I wisht I never had to lay eyes on you again, the murderous calculating son of a bitch that you are." Then he walked away.

Lyons entered one of its periods of prosperity almost immediately, upon settlement of the strike. As soon as the mines were inspected and called safe, work was resumed, with a great deal of overtime and frequent double shifts; there was money for meat, there was money for Christmas—both Christmases, the Roman and the Russian. Christmas had once been the climax of Robert Millhouser's year, when as a boy, an only child, he was the center of attention for his father and mother and three servants; then in college years it was a holiday that included a change of scene from the uninviting prospects in the University section of Philadelphia, as well as a brief period in which his Lyons contemporaries tried to look their best and behave as well as they knew how. But after college, Christmases seemed to follow Christmases too soon, and his chief pleasure on the occasion was in the almost shocked pleasure of his mother on receiving his gifts. He did not stint on money or imagination in his presents for Zilph. A casual remark in May that she liked a certain parasol, a piece of silverware, a bit of porcelain, a set of books—and

225

sometimes it was a remark she had made to Margaret Dillon and not in his presence—enabled him to lay aside the necessary money, and nearly always her instantaneous reaction on first seeing the present was an expression close to fear, as though she suspected him of powers of divination that penetrated her secret mind. "How did you know I wanted that?" she would ask, for days after Christmas. "I didn't know I wanted it myself." Sometimes he would torture her slightly by answering that it had seemed exactly right for her, which he well knew would only add to her alarmed bafflement. It had always been, in a sense, a form of revenge, especially during the years when she could not fully hide her contemptuous estimate of his relations with Chester Calthorp. But that game ended, and in the final ten years of her life his Christmas presents to her had been lacking in the element of surprise, since they had all been discussed a month ahead of time and since the objects themselves were usually as commonplace as a dozen silk handkerchiefs.

On this Christmas of 1902 he could not expect her usual gifts of some small, moderately expensive article of jewelry and a large cheque; she had died too soon to buy the scarf pin, and the money was now all his own. He received almost no presents: a basket from Mr. and Mrs. Jeremiah MacMahon, containing jars of guava jelly, candied dates, tinned sardines and anchovies; a box of cigars, surprisingly, from Ben Rosebery; another knitted scarf and mittens from the kitchen; a seven-foot rattlesnake skin tacked on a polished walnut board, from Moses Hatfield, which was almost surely the only gift in Lyons for which the giver had risked his life. As tribute from the world-at-large the collection, he conceded, was as much as he deserved, but it was not much to show for forty-seven years as a human being.

He distributed the gold pieces that he annually gave to the servants and cheques in the amounts his mother was accustomed to give. Then he sat down to a fine dinner of roast goose, ate it rapidly so that the women could finish in the kitchen, and took a bottle of port and Ben Rosebery's cigars to the little room, where he fell asleep in front of the fire without having lit his cigar.

He was awakened by the doorbell, which was set in one of the front doors and operated by hand. He got to his feet and went to the door. At first he could see no one through the lace curtains, but he opened the door and saw a small freckle-faced boy holding a large package wrapped in tissue paper and tied with red ribbon.

"Thisfromthesistersmerrychristmas," said the boy.

"What? I can't understand what you're saying, son."

"This, is, from, the sisters. Merry Christmas."

"The sisters? You have the wrong house."

"No I don't. The sisters sent this to you, Mr. Millhouser-in-the-big-house. It's a *pre-sent*. Here, take it."

"Well, I guess you must be right. Just a moment. Here. Merry Christmas to you." He handed the boy a silver dollar.

"Is this for me? I don't have to give it to the sisters?"

"It's yours. Thank you very much, and Merry Christmas to you."

He closed the door and took the large but light package to the little room. There was an envelope, with *Robert Millhouser, Esquire* written in a proudly florid script, and on the enclosed card, in the same script, *May the Infant Jesus Bless You on the Feast of His Nativity,* and on a separate line, *From the Sisters of St. Joseph.*

He opened the package and spread on his chair a "throw," done in exquisite needlepoint and depicting in precise detail the southern elevation of the house in which he lived, complete to the trees in bloom. He made a quick calculation; they had accomplished this work in about two months, probably less, since he had made his offer to shoe the shoeless, and at that time the trees had been almost bare. He was suddenly overwhelmed by the day and the years, the proudly florid script and the thought of those faceless women, chattering like birds as their task progressed. With no one to hear and no one to see, he could weep, and did.

The servants were gone for the day and overnight and for the first time in his life he was literally alone in the house. It may even have been the first time since the house was built that only one person occupied it overnight. Now he was alone *in* the house and *with* the house: there was a note on the kitchen table with instructions for his preparation of his supper, and a postscript to remind him to fix the furnace for the night. Margaret and Theresa had lived in the house for many, many years, and he thought of it as their home; but when they were given the opportunity and wanted to enjoy themselves they spent the night with families in Lyons. It was a new thought for him, that they did not consider this their home. Moses Hatfield had his family, went home every night to them. But Robert Millhouser had never thought of Margaret and Theresa as having any other life outside this house, although he was aware vaguely that they had their friends in town. He refused to see himself as a character in one of Mr. Dickens's novels, and yet he was the owner of fifteen farms and tonight he would not be welcome in any of them; in two wards of the town he could surely find poverty to match anything Mr. Dickens described, but no matter how much they would welcome his money, they would not want him to be with it. In the more comfortable houses it would be the same; there was a great deal of casual visiting among the well-to-do on Christmas night, but a single man, aged forty-seven, could not now participate in a custom he had always ignored.

As soon as darkness came he went about and turned on a light in every room on the first floor. No one would come, but someone might. Then he thought how silly he would feel if someone should come and find him all alone in an overlit house, and he went about again, turning off lights in the diningroom and the parlor. Next he remembered that every evening Margaret would go about closing the inside shutters and lowering the shades, so that only the front hall light would show from outside. He closed the shutters, lowered the shades, and although he was not at all hungry he made a small pot of tea and ate the sandwiches that Theresa had wrapped in wax paper. He rinsed out the pot and cup and saucer and smoked a cigarette. Then on an impulse that was not all kindly he put some sugar lumps in his pocket and went down to the stable and fed them to the horses, his only living companions on the whole place. He was even tempted to bring a piece of cheese for the rats, but Moses would not have liked that. He stood in the yard in the cold clear night and looked out on the town, in which each house had some light. It was so clear that he could see a maintenance man's lantern moving from one shanty to another at the Outerbridge Colliery, and he could hear a yard engine making up a coal train farther up the Valley. But for the moment he could not see a living person. His watch in the moonlight showed the time to be ten minutes short of eight but for him the day was over.

He went back to the house, surprised when the warmth of it was so pleasing, but the pleasure did not last. The lonely years seemed only to have been leading up to this loneliest night of all, and he knew that this would be the rest of his life if he did nothing to change it. But he recognized that there was hope so long as he could want it changed. On that hope, and not much more, he lived for three more years.

•

IN AN American town the respectable citizens are supposed to stay put: they are born in the town, spend their lives there, and when they die they are buried in the family plot. It takes a full generation for a newcomer's family to settle in the town, just as it takes the town a full generation to relinquish possession of a native family that has moved away. But there are certain permissible exceptions to the rule that temporary residents do not acquire respectability. Scarcely any clergymen are native to the towns in which they serve, and they are subject to orders or calls that will summon them to other, distant parishes. School superintendents and principals are likely to be nomadic during their early professional careers. The station agent hopes for promotion to a more important post in the railway system, and bank cashiers, factory managers and hotel executives belong to a town's floating population. In all these cases the job confers respectability on the holder of the job, and the novelty of a new school principal or minister is a pleasant part of small-town social life. The newcomer is guaranteed to be a reliable addition to the town, and usually turns out to be just that. In Lyons, as in other mining towns, there was always a new civil engineering graduate; young, unmarried, and gaining experience. When the mines were at work on major construction projects, the engineers were often married men who brought their families and became residents of Lyons on a semi-transient basis. One such man was Edward Steele, who rented a house in Lyons in 1905 with the assurance that he would be living there at least three years.

Ed Steele was about ready to settle down. He was forty-two years old, a graduate of the University of Wisconsin, and he and his wife Ruth had lived and brought up their two children in a dozen of the United States and in Mexico, Chile, and Canada. During some of the jobs Ruth had had to remain in Milwaukee with her children at the home of her parents; at other times the Steeles had lived the life of army officers' families, with social obligations that they could not afford in spite of the construction companies' allowances. Thus at forty-two Ed Steele had saved little money, his son would soon be going to college, and he knew that Ruth was finding it increasingly difficult to adjust to new towns. Three years in Lyons, he told her, and he would then take the best job that offered a permanent home, but he cautioned her that he was out to make a good showing on the Lyons job so that he would have it to recommend him in the negotiations for the permanent post. The Lyons job was not the biggest he had worked on, but it was to be his biggest personal responsibility to date. He would be in complete charge, answerable only to the general manager of Wadsworth & Valentine, Incorporated, the construction firm for which he had now worked ten years. The contract involved the rebuilding and modernization of the exterior (non-mining) properties known as the Outerbridge Colliery and Outerbridge Number 2, locally called Outer Two. The Outerbridge collieries had expanded in slapdash fashion and were inefficient, and both the Union and the Bureau of Mines were constantly reminding the owners of the minimum safety requirements. Since the operation was profitable in spite of the obsolescent equipment and its inefficiency, the owners had no

229

trouble in finding new money and the improvements were ordered. The work was to cost more than $1,000,000.

As representative of two million dollars (the figure arrived at by Lyons gossip), Ed Steele would have been well received if he had turned up with a slatternly wife and two cretinous offspring. In reality Ed Steele was spare, bald, blue-eyed, soft-spoken, with large strong teeth and a sudden smile that contrasted with his customary air of abstraction; Ruth Steele was thin-faced, large-busted, quick-moving and watchful. Their son Lars, sixteen, was a physical reproduction of the father, and in fourth-year high school had already mastered differential calculus under his father's sporadic tutoring. The daughter, seventeen, was a small beauty, a quick throwback to her mother's completely Swedish ancestry, who wore her nearly white hair in two braids pinned up and around her skull. She had always been in the same grade as her younger brother, and she might have fallen behind him if her parents had not exerted some influence over the many teachers that had taken some part in the children's irregular education. Hedwig Steele had a quick impatient mind, unretentive of the matter to be found in books, but in her wide travels with her mother and brother she was always the first to be able to speak the Spanish and French languages as they were spoken by the Mexicans and the Canadians; always the one to attract helpful strangers when there was a luggage mix-up; and always, in ships and on trains, she was staring at the fellow-passengers and neglecting the toys and picture-books that were supposed to alleviate the tedium. Lars would read, and fall asleep; but Hedda would stay awake and watch the men and women, and sometimes when Ruth and Lars had dozed off, Hedda would make friends with the men and women and often Ruth would have to compel the child to go back to the nice people and return the coins they had given her. As the child grew older Ruth Steele was more insistent on her staying in her own seat, but Hedda was a disobedient young girl and there were frequent scenes and slappings. In 1904, on a train from Mexico City to Vera Cruz, Hedda slapped back.

The entertainment program for the newly arrived Steele family was on Lyons's highest level, the kind of activity that had all but originated with Robert and Zilph Millhouser rather than the church-supper and ladies' "500" parties that were quite sufficient for a school superintendent and his wife. Neither Ed nor Ruth Steele had ever been to Europe, but they were very different from the young couple who had left Wisconsin twenty years earlier. There was a polish, there was a manner, an air, and Lyons could not offer the Steeles a chicken-

and-waffle party, as though Ed Steele were the new station agent, transferred from a town twenty miles down the line.

A banquet was arranged in honor of the Outerbridge reconstruction and the man in charge of it, Ed Steele. Eli W. Wadsworth came all the way from New York to attend the banquet and he made a humorous, somewhat noncommittal speech. Common Pleas Judge Matthew R. Holland came from nearby Johnsville and his speech was humorous and optimistic. Billy Williams, superintendent of the competing collieries, managed to get up and sit down without saying anything that might detract from the good-fellowship of the occasion. John J. Lanagan, union leader of the district, was vulgar, long-winded, and disputatious, and attacked both Wadsworth and Williams for delaying settlement of the strike that had been settled in 1902. He ended his speech so abruptly ("And that's all I got to say") that it was obvious that he had not yet finished, and Fred Langendorf, toastmaster, stood up in the midst of the murmurs and delivered an unintentional coup de grâce with the remark that he was "sure that all present would remember John's speech." Ed Steele read a speech prepared in New York, and Robert Millhouser, chosen by the bank and the Merchants Association, presented to Steele a "black diamond" inkstand made of anthracite. Robert Millhouser's slight witticism was to the effect that the stand contained a patented feature which prevented the stand from holding red ink.

Steele made one *faux pas:* he went home without taking the inkstand, and Robert Millhouser covertly retrieved the forgotten souvenir and on the following morning took it to Steele's office.

"Good morning, Mr. Millhouser," said the secretary, a Lyons girl. "He has somebody in there with him now but she'll be right out. It's his daughter, asking him for some money."

"Well, I'll just leave this package," said Robert Millhouser.

"Don't. I know what it is, and he feels awful about it. It's his present, isn't it? The black diamond inkstand? Oh, he came in this morning and he said to me how could he get in touch with Mr. Millhouser, and I said if I know Mr. *Mill*houser, Mr. Millhouser'd see to it that— here's Mr. Millhouser, Mr. Steele."

"Good morning, sir," said Steele. "Ah, this is my daughter Hedwig, nicknamed Hedda."

"Good morning," said Robert Millhouser. "Good morning, Miss Steele."

"Is that for me?" said Hedda.

Robert Millhouser smiled. "Well, why don't you wait until you see it, then if you like it I'll get you one."

"My daughter is trying to show some profit this morning. She hasn't been very successful so far. All right, run along, Hedda."

"I want to see what's in the package. May I stay for that?"

Robert Millhouser undid the package, speaking as he did so: "This is a present for your father, welcoming him to Lyons."

"And he forgot it, didn't he?" said Hedda. "As usual."

"Yes, I did. But not as usual. I don't get that many presents."

"There we are," said Robert Millhouser.

"I think it's the homeliest thing I ever saw," said Hedda.

"Hedda!"

"It is, too. But I like it."

"Then I'll send you one. They come in a smaller size for a lady's desk."

"What do they call that stuff?" said Hedda.

"They call it black diamond. But your father will tell you that it's pure, polished anthracite. In other words, coal."

"Well, it's the same thing as diamonds. Carbon. Isn't that all diamonds are?" said Hedda.

"I'm agreeably surprised that you knew that."

"I'm agreeably surprised when you're agreeably surprised, Poppa."

"Well, there it is," said Robert Millhouser.

"Telephone, Mr. Steele," said the secretary. "Outer Two."

"I'll run along," said Robert Millhouser. Steele shook hands and retired to the inner office.

"Can I go with you?" said Hedda, outside.

"I'd be honored. Would you like to pick out your own inkstand?"

"What else have they got besides inkstands? I never write letters."

"Don't you go to school, or college somewhere?"

"They're trying to send me away but they're having trouble getting me in. I'll probably go to high school here. I've been to nine schools so far and I haven't even finished high school. One year I went to three schools. Three schools in one year. Do you live here?"

"All my life."

"You don't look as if you did. Where is your house? Are you married? *You're not.*"

"No, I'm not, but does bachelorhood show so much?"

"No, but I know you haven't got a wife. You didn't answer me. Where do you live?"

" 'Way at the other end of town. Out that way."

"Show it to me."

"You can't see it from here."

"I meant take me there. Is it a big place, with lots of horses? Have you got an automobile?"

"Two horses. No automobile. It's in between, not big, not small. Are you a rider?"

"I can. I don't like it very much but I can if I have to. Do you ride?"

"Not any more. I used to, when I had to. When I was your age there were a lot of places you couldn't get to unless you rode."

"How old are you now?"

"Fifty."

"Eight years older than Poppa, but Poppa's young. Isn't he?"

"Yes, I supppose he is. Yes, I see what you mean."

"Very young."

"Quite true," said Robert Millhouser. "I'm eight years older than your father, but I'm in no way young."

"Not in the same way Poppa is. He reminds me of a boy. You remind me of a *little* boy," said Hedda. "Do you know what you remind me of? An altar boy. When we lived in Mexico."

"Excuse me, Miss Steele. Are we headed toward my house?"

"Well, aren't we?"

"I guess so."

They chatted on until they reached Robert Millhouser's house. She looked at it and said: "You live here all alone, don't you?"

"Two servants."

"But no relations."

"None."

"Everything is so spick-and-span. Who is that, your butler?"

"Coachman. We haven't got a butler."

"Who is we?"

"My mother and I, the household, the house and I."

"When did your mother die? She did die, didn't she?"

"She died three years ago."

"And you didn't have any brothers or sisters?"

"No."

"Aren't you going to take me inside?"

"I'm afraid it wouldn't be proper."

"Why not? You have two maids in the house."

"It still wouldn't be proper, Hedda. You know that."

"Yes, I know. They're probably looking at us from behind the curtain."

"I'd bet anything they are."

"Wondering if you're going to take me inside. Let's go and look at the horses."

They went to the stable. "Such beautiful carriages," she said. "They look almost new."

"Moses does that. Here he is. Moses, Miss Steele has just been admiring the carriages."

"I said they looked brand-new. Can you bring out the horses for a better look?"

"Yes ma'am," said Moses. He went to the stalls and led out one of the animals.

"Oh, I like this mare," said Hedda. "But what happened here, this thing on her coat?"

"Someone threw a stone at her, three years ago."

"I hate people that do that. Or clap their hands. In Mexico you could shoot a man that did that. Let's see the gelding."

Moses brought out the gelding.

"The mare's more beautiful. May I ride them sometime? I can really ride."

"Have we still got the side-saddle?" said Robert Millhouser.

"Yes sir, in the trunk, laid away if the rats didn't get at it," said Moses Hatfield.

"You could tell that quickly enough. If the rats haven't chewed a hole in the trunk. I don't think Moses *wants* me to ride."

"I wouldn't worry about that," said Robert Millhouser. "Let's have a look at the trunk. Moses? I said we'd like to have a look at the trunk."

"Trunk's up on the second story behind the cutters. I can't get it out now lessen I move them sleighs."

"Then let's go up and see for ourselves," said Robert Millhouser.

"You got a key to that trunk?" said Moses.

"No, I haven't, but I'll just take a screwdriver and break open the lock."

"No," said Hedda Steele. "I don't want you to do that. I don't want to break anything."

"But I do," said Robert Millhouser.

"But *I don't*," said the girl. "I must go now."

"Wait two minutes and I'll drive you home. Moses, hitch up the mare, and be quick about it."

"Thank you, but I haven't time to wait."

"If you haven't time to wait, you certainly haven't time to walk. Don't stand there, Moses. Put the mare in the trap and bring it up to the house. Miss Steele and I will be on the side porch."

The girl walked beside him but did not speak.

"He's getting old, I guess. But I won't have him behaving that way," said Robert Millhouser as they reached the porch.

"You're only making him dislike me more. I saw him look at me when we got to your house."

"Pay no attention. Would you like some iced tea? Or lemonade? Let's have some iced tea."

"We won't have time."

"Why won't we have time? We have all the time in the world."

"Have we?"

"Well, haven't we? Or are you going to have to be somewhere at a certain time?"

"That isn't what I was thinking, and you know it."

"What *were* you thinking?"

"Never mind. Yes, I'll have some iced tea. I want to see what the maids look like."

He went inside and called Margaret. "Some iced tea, Margaret."

"Tell her it's for two, or she'll bring one."

"Let's see what she does," said Robert Millhouser.

Margaret appeared with two glasses of iced tea. "Good morning, ma'am," she said.

"This is Miss Steele. Her father is in charge of the Outerbridge work."

"I took notice to Miss Steele Saturday, shopping. Welcome to Lyons, ma'am."

"Thank you."

Margaret left them.

"You see?" said Robert Millhouser. "She was friendly."

"She was clever," said Hedda. "There's the carriage. He *isn't* clever. He's an ape. And the first thing I'd . . ."

"The first thing what?"

"Never mind."

"Young lady, it seems to me that you're somewhat lacking in respect for a man my age, older than your father."

"Let's not pretend, Mr. Millhouser."

"I see," said Robert Millhouser. "It might be better if we did. It might be much better. It would be better."

"All right, then, try it for a while."

"Did you say you were going to high school this year?"

"Yes, that's what I said."

"There are so many questions I'd like to ask you."

"I know there are. And I know what kinds of questions they are, too. But I'm not going to help you. You have to ask them yourself."

"Then I think I already have some of the answers."

"How nice. Then you won't have to ask the questions."

"There's one question I know the answer to, don't I?"

"Do you?"

"Don't I?"

"I don't know."

"Was it a Mexican?"

"Was what a Mexican, Mr. Millhouser?"

"If you looked at me, this same way, and said, 'Was it a Mexican?' you'd expect me to know what you meant, wouldn't you?"

"If you have a question to ask, ask it. If you're afraid it's the wrong kind of question to ask, maybe you'd better not ask it at all."

"I'm almost sure. Everything else that I've learned about you in one hour's time. You're without a doubt the most interesting young woman I've ever met."

"Fuff."

"Is that a Spanish word?"

"It isn't a word. It's just *fuff*. It's what I say when I'd really like to say something else. I used to say it when grownups talked to me as if I were a child."

"But now of course you're a woman."

"Oh, Mr. Millhouser, do you have to stoop to a trick like that? 'Now of course you're a woman.' I didn't really want this iced tea, and I do want to walk home."

"Would you like to ride my horses sometimes?"

"As I said to you before, I can ride. I don't like it very much but I can if I have to."

He walked with her to the driveway where the mare was being held by Moses. Suddenly and very seriously the girl said: "Moses, you may take the mare back to the stable."

"Yes ma'am," said Moses.

The girl looked at Robert Millhouser and laughed gaily. "He learns quickly," she said. "I may keep him after all. *Hasta la vista.*"

She did not look back, but he knew she was smiling at him, and if her smiling contempt was part of the bargain, he would accept that too.

•

TWO WALKS TOGETHER in the world of a small town, and Robert Millhouser and Hedda Steele had created a sensation. The second time they walked together Robert carried a package, a dress she had bought at Langendorf's. The meeting, a week after their first, was accidental: Robert was on the men's side of the store, buying collar buttons, and two aisles away he saw Hedda, raised his hat, was rewarded with a smile, and joined her. *"Como está Usted*—but don't answer me in Spanish, because that's all I know," he said.

"It's all you'll need, in Lyons," she said.

"May I carry your package?"

"It's not a bit heavy."

"So much the better, at my time of life," he said.

"Charge it, please, to Mr. Edward Steele, my father," said Hedda.

"I know," said the saleswoman. "Good day, Miss."

"Good day," said Hedda.

"Buenos días," said Robert.

"Are you studying Spanish?" said Hedda, as they left the store.

"How did you know? I'm not studying it, but I bought a dictionary."

"Where would you buy a Spanish dictionary in this town?"

"I wouldn't even try. I bought mine in Fort Penn."

"I'm surprised they'd even have one there."

"Fort Penn might surprise you in many ways. It's an interesting city, the capital. Don't forget, this State is as big as some kingdoms."

"I've only been to Fort Penn to change trains."

"By the way, are you going to boarding school?"

"Yes. To Pinewood Seminary. Did you ever hear of it?"

"Yes. It's near Lancaster. Local girls go there, always one or two."

"Will you miss me?"

"Why do you say that, Hedda? You know I'll miss you," he said. "I met your mother the night before last."

"She told me you did."

"What else did she tell you?"

"That I was never to go to your house again. That I was a foolish, headstrong girl. As careless of your reputation as I was of my own."

"Did you tell her you'd been to my house?"

"Yes, luckily. Someone else already had. My mother makes me account for every minute. She doesn't trust me."

"Then my walking home with you now isn't such a good idea, is it? Will you be punished?"

"I don't know about punished. A talking-to. I know more about you now than I did."

"For instance."

"That you're rich, and you're supposed to have a woman in Fort Penn. Somebody you were going to marry one time and didn't, and now you see her whenever you can."

"Well, that's something new. It's not true, by the way."

"I wouldn't mind if it was true. I'm not jealous."

"Have you ever been?"

"Oh, yes. I didn't say I couldn't be. I just said I wasn't now," she said. "Is it going to be like this for three years? Living in a gossipy town?"

"You forget something."

"What?"

"The town is right. You and I covered more ground in one meeting than some people do in years."

"But they don't know that."

"They don't know it as a fact, in our case, but it's what happens. Usually small-town gossip is too quick. This time it was quick, but we beat them to it. Didn't we?"

She smiled. "Yes, I guess we did. We didn't *lose* any time. We're always talking about time."

"So it seems."

"Would you give me the money to run away?"

"Where would you go?"

"Don't answer a question with a question. Would you give me the money?"

"No."

"I didn't think you would."

"I'd be doing a terrible thing if I did. They'd find you and bring you back, and God knows what might happen to you before they found you. Have you a friend you could go to?"

"No. I just want to run away."

"And it wouldn't take a Sherlock Holmes to discover who gave you the money."

"Are you afraid?"

"Not in the way you think. I don't want anything to happen to you."

"Why don't you just say it?"

"What?"

"That you're in love with me."

"I would if it were true. If I were sure of that I'd say it and act accordingly."

"How, act accordingly?"

"What does a man usually do when he's in love with a girl?"

"Question for a question again."

"Well, answer my question for a change."

"Well, they usually get married."

"I don't know that they usually get married, but the man tells the girl he loves her and hopes she loves him. You couldn't possibly be in love with me."

"I'm not, but I could be."

"You don't like to ride, but you can if you have to. Something like that."

"Something like it, but nicer."

238

"Here's your house. I used to play here when I was a boy. My best friend lived here."

"Mr. Vance? Was he your best friend?"

"Not the one you know. His older brother, died many many many years ago. Younger than you were when he died. Which is your room?"

"On the second floor, that corner."

"That was my friend's room."

"Then I guess I sleep in his bed. What was his name?"

"Leonard Vance."

"Did you love him? You did."

"I guess I did."

"Well, I guess I'm sleeping in his bed."

"I've slept in that bed, too, Hedda. Carved wood? A large oval in the middle of the head of the bed?"

"Yes, and what's in the middle of that?"

"In the middle of that?"

"Something that looks like one of these." She put her finger over her left breast.

"Yes! That's what we used to think, too."

"Thank you for carrying my parcel."

"Thank you for letting me walk home with you. I hope you don't get a talking-to."

"If they knew how little I cared. Goodbye."

"Oh—the saddle's all right, if you want to ride the mare. I'll have Moses lead her over any time you want."

"We'll see," she said.

Their second walk had begun in one of the town's principal centers for the exchange of gossip, the ladies' side of Langendorf's Emporium, and continued part of the way on the two busiest shopping streets and one of the main residential streets. Due note was made of the fact that the girl and Robert Millhouser chatted together in a foreign language, a reliable indication that the walks in public had probably sandwiched-in less public meetings. To this was added the widely circulated report that the girl's parents were moving heaven and earth to get her into a boarding school before a real scandal came out in the open. The girl had already been asked to leave several schools and had even been heard to boast of it, *on dit*.

"There's nothing to it, and stop talking about it," said Fred Langendorf to his wife.

"Are you two going to confession this Saturday?" said Jeremiah MacMahon to his wife and daughter. "Don't forget to tell what you've been saying about Robert Millhouser."

"What is the meaning of this?" said Ed Steele to his wife. He handed her a scrap of lined paper on which was drawn a picture of intertwined hearts over the legend: "Robert loves Hettie."

"Where did this come from?" said Ruth Steele.

"It came in my mail. A Lyons postmark. No name on the envelope, of course. Who is Robert?"

"Mr. Millhouser."

"You're crazy! Robert Millhouser? He's older than I am. What have you known about this?"

She told him what she knew, and what she had done, which was to forbid Hedda to see Robert Millhouser.

"What kind of a crazy town is this? Or is there more to it than you've told me?" said Ed Steele.

"I'm sure she's only seen him twice, but I'll be glad when she goes away to school."

"Then there *is* more. What is it, Ruth?"

"Ed, I've been holding this in till I think sometimes I'm going to explode. Sit down. I've got something to tell you that I've kept inside me for over a year. You're not going to like any of it, you're not going to like me, you're going to hate Hedda."

"Speak up, speak up."

"I will! But for God's sake, Ed, she's my daughter as much as yours. It's made me old, and sick of moving from place to place, trying to bring up two children as if they were—circus animals or something. And I've had to sit there and listen to how wonderful it's been to have them see the world."

"That's all over. This is our last move."

"I'm not blaming you. I'm blaming myself," she said, and took a deep breath. "The first thing was four years ago."

"Four years ago? In Canada?"

"Yes, when we had the house in Quebec. You remember, she used to walk to school every day with the girl next door, the Dawson girl, Sheilah Dawson. But one day I noticed Sheilah at her house, and Hedda wasn't home yet. I asked Hedda why she hadn't walked home with Sheilah and she said she'd had to make up some work after school. That was a lie. And when I caught her in it again I threatened to tell you if I didn't get the truth out of her. And I got the truth, God help us I did. There was a stableman, a groom, at one of those big places near the river. He made her do things to him."

"What kind of things?"

"Touch him. Fondle him."

"What else? Did he pay her? Give her presents?"

"No. I took her to the doctor and had her examined. She was—all right. I mean she was a virgin. Then I went and saw the man."

"Why on earth didn't you tell me?"

"You were at the mine, where you always are. I had to do all this myself. I went and saw the man and my first thought was that Hedda had lied to me. He was a nice man, older. English. He knew why I was there. He was married and had grown children and to tell the truth he was—you could call him handsome. Dignified. He broke down and said he had taken to drink after fifteen years because of what had happened. She was the one that started it. One day she came wandering in through the gate and watched him curry-combing the horses, and they became sort of friends and he got used to having her drop in. Then one day when he was lying down on a chest, half asleep, she came in and felt around him—and he didn't stop her."

"And never did stop her."

"No. He knew he should have the first time, and never let her come back again. That's what he should have done. But once he had let her start the first time, the harm was done. There was nothing ahead but disgrace to himself and his family. And *I* said there would be worse than that if he ever saw her again. But he took care of that. The morning after I'd been to see him they found him hanging in the stable. I read about it in the paper."

"What effect did that have on Hedda?"

"I never told her."

"You never told her at all?"

"No. If there was any hope for her it would have been lost if I'd told her she'd caused a man to kill himself."

"And she doesn't know to this day?"

"No."

"Good God."

"She never went near the place again, and she never read a newspaper. And she knew I had my eye on her."

"You said this was the first thing. What else was there?"

"In Mexico City, last year. I'd practically never let her out of my sight, but she had an affair, a real affair, with a Mexican boy."

"A boy, this time."

"Yes. Her own age exactly. Johnny Villareal."

"Johnny Villareal? He was even younger than she was."

"No, not in years. The same age."

"And very religious."

"Huh. Religious."

"If they had a real affair why didn't she get pregnant?"

241

"You can get those things in Mexico as easily as any place else. I found a box of them hidden behind a picture in her room."

"How did you find out about it?"

"Because I discovered a stack of photographs, the worst things I ever saw in my life. I couldn't even tell you about them, they were so awful. I made her tell me where she got them. Johnny. And the rest came out slap by slap. Johnny'd come over the wall in his bare feet, and climb a ladder to her room."

"And that's why you got sick in Mexico City."

"It was real enough, my sickness. I took her to the American doctor and told him the whole story, and he advised me to do anything in the world that would get us out of there."

"And that's what we have for a daughter," said her husband.

"She's ours, wherever she gets it."

"Ruth, I don't mean anything by that. Please understand that."

"I know you didn't," she said. "Now it's out I don't feel any better. I thought if I could only tell you, but I have, and nothing's better. Ed, there may be more that we don't know about. There probably is. I can remember a man on a train one time, going from Omaha to Denver. I just remember his face. I never spoke to him and he never spoke to us, but he walked up and down the aisle and he'd always look at us in our section. Maybe it was nothing. And one time when we were staying at my parents' she came home with a $2.50 gold piece that she found on the sidewalk. Did she find it? I don't know. She always attracted attention, wherever we went. She's beautiful, God knows, and her coloring."

"There's nobody like that in your family or in mine."

"Oh, how do we know? And what if there isn't? One thing, I don't want you to say a word to her."

"I'm going to have to, now. This Millhouser business."

"No, don't. The one thing that will make her obey is the threat to tell you everything. You're the only person she looks up to, and if she thought you knew, I wouldn't have anything to use as a threat."

"She'll sense it."

"Not if you're careful. You go on being preoccupied about the job. I'll take her to school and deposit her there, and I've arranged for a special weekly report on how she's getting along. I guess I do feel better, being able to talk to you."

He sat on the arm of her chair and put his arm around her. "I haven't been a good husband *or* a good father."

"You've been both, but you've been away too much."

"What shall we do about Millhouser?"

"If I told you what I'm hoping, you'd think I was crazy."

"You're not crazy, even if you must have come close to it. What are you hoping?"

"I wish Millhouser would marry her."

"A man that age—well, of course that objection is foolish, isn't it?"

"Yes. Millhouser is strange, too, you know, and I think she's fascinated by him. She all but told me so. She said he was the only man or woman in Lyons that interested her the least bit. She said all the rest were like people she'd known before."

"But you've forbidden her to see him."

"But I haven't forbidden him to see her. He's never been married. Came close to it once, and now I understand that he's got a woman in Fort Penn that he sees, but Hedda thinks he's smitten with *her*. Smitten. He'll try to see her, I think, and if he does, I'm going to be very old-fashioned. I'm going to tell him that I don't think it's suitable for a man his age to take up a young girl's time."

"I liked Millhouser, what I've seen of him. But I don't see him as a husband for Hedda."

"I didn't like him, but I do see him as a husband for her. He isn't manly, but he's older and experienced. I wouldn't be surprised if he understood Hedda better than anybody does. I think they're birds of a feather."

"But don't count on Millhouser. A man that's stayed a bachelor this long isn't liable to fall for the first pretty face he sees."

"Hedda's more than a pretty face, and a man like Millhouser knows it. He lived in Europe for several years, trying to be an artist."

"You know more about these people than I will when we leave."

"That's my part of our life. Meeting the people, entertaining. Entertaining? We can invite Millhouser here when we start paying back invitations. We don't have to wait for a bachelor to invite us."

"Hedda will be at the seminary."

"I don't care. I'd like to talk to Millhouser. And Hedda will be home for Thanksgiving."

"If she stays that long," he said. He stood up and went to his pipe rack and seated himself with pipe, pouch, and matches. His wife knew that if she came back in an hour the pipe would still be empty of tobacco, that he would be unaware of the length of her absence. He could sit this way for hours when he had a problem.

•

BEN ROSEBERY, the man of appetites, evolved to the status of friend of Robert Millhouser; he had not been chosen as Robert had chosen and been chosen by Chester Calthorp and Dr. Willetts. Ben had been

243

almost a convenience, and he certainly had not promised intimacy and warmth and stimulation and reliability, the pleasures of friendship that Robert Millhouser had got from his associations with Chester Calthorp and the doctor. Ben, the lawyer and the libertine, was a pragmatist himself, subject to sentiment only in his dread of loneliness while yet refusing to make the sacrifice of his liberty that might have been the one effective means of dispelling his fear. He, too, used men and women as a convenience and their value to him was based on their usefulness. Therefore he understood that he was being used as a convenience long before Robert Millhouser made the secret admission to himself, and in that respect Ben Rosebery was more honest about their relationship. Robert Millhouser was a gentleman, most of Ben's companions were not, and occasionally Ben liked to be with a gentleman. The association evolved into friendship largely as a result of Ben's having more time for the company of a gentleman as his appetites became less demanding. He was getting old.

He was seen oftener these days at the Fort Penn Club and less often at the whorehouses and whoring parties. Unfortunately the gentlemen at the common table at the club felt compelled to greet and treat Ben as a gentleman-roué, when he would have preferred to forget that side of his nature. "Over there's a fellow," he said to Robert Millhouser. "He has a judgeship that I turned down ten years ago. He wasn't even next on the list after I turned it down. But now I come in this club and he looks down his nose at me. He wants me to talk about cunt, and I don't. He thinks that if he can get me to talk about cunt it'll make him more respectable. And when he feels respectable he can forget that I could have had his job. He doesn't want me to forget that he's a judge and I'm a hell-raiser. Of course it doesn't make him love me any more, the fact that I've had about five cases before him that were reversed on appeal. Five in ten years, one every two years, it averages. And he looks down his nose at me."

This meeting took place in the autumn of 1905, and Robert Millhouser had arranged it in the hope that Ben would say something, anything, that would invite confidences. Robert now regarded Ben as more friend than convenience, and the Fort Penn Club was more frequently the scene of their meetings than Gottlieb's Rathskeller. Robert wanted to talk about Hedda Steele, and he was eager for some sign from Ben that would demonstrate Ben's trustworthiness and sympathy in advance. "Does it bother you when people look down their noses at you?" said Robert Millhouser.

"Yes. No. That's a hell of an answer for a lawyer to give. If it's somebody I respect, it doesn't bother me. But when it's somebody I know is my inferior, yes. I waste a lot of good time devising ways and means to put him in his place. Occasionally I envy you your life, that comfortable house and good servants to take care of you. Work that you like, and not too much of it. But most of all, something in your character. It's always been there, as far as I know."

"In my character? What?"

"It's the ability you have, to live quietly in a town like Lyons. Early to bed, early to rise. Read your books, I suppose. Not dependent on other people. You always had that ability. It's close to thirty years, isn't it, since you came home from Europe and settled down?"

"Twenty-seven."

"And look what happened to Chester Calthorp. It took him all those twenty-some years to arrive at approximately the same point. Although I guess you wouldn't call it quite the same point, would you?" Ben grinned. "No, I guess hardly."

"Don't tell me Chester's married."

"Married? Don't you know about Chester?"

"Not a thing. I don't know where he is or anything about him."

"You mean to say I'm the first to give you the news? Oh, my friend, sit back and prepare yourself for a shock. You didn't know that we're never going to see old Chester again?"

"Why? Is he in prison?"

"Worse than that. He's in a monastery."

"What?"

"That's what I said. A monastery. How long is it since you've known anything at all about him?"

"Oh, it must be several years. I guess the last time was when you ran into him in Kugler's."

"Bookbinder's. That was long ago. Don't you ever get to Philadelphia?"

"Very seldom."

"Well, then I guess I have to give you the whole background. I must have taken for granted that you knew it all better than I did, since you were a friend of his and I never was. Let me see. Two years ago, three years ago, I'm not sure which, Chester turned Catholic."

"Where? In Philadelphia?"

"Yes, in Philly. They have these Jesuits there. You know what they are?"

"Yes, I know."

"Then you know they have them every place, all over the God damn world. Well, one of them turned up that Chester'd met in Europe. Rome, or Paris. I don't know. I didn't know Chester spent much time with priests over there, but he knew this one. And I don't know how they got together in Philadelphia, but they did. And our

Philadelphia Quaker friend turned Catholic, before anybody knew what was happening."

"And then he became a Jesuit?"

"Oh, not so fast. Not right away. For a year or so he made kind of a nuisance of himself preaching the Catholic religion to all his friends. You know what chance he had with *his* friends, that artistic bunch of rich Bohemians. But he got one convert. A woman. Now let me see if I can remember her name."

"Let me guess. Was it Alice Sterling?"

"That's exactly who it was! Alice Sterling. I knew her name was either Sterling or Calthorp. She's older than Chester, and related to him somehow. Alice Sterling. He got her to join the Catholic church, but he didn't get anyone else. I gather she was an old souse that knew her way around. Did you know her?"

"Met her. She didn't like me."

"Maybe it's just as well, or you'd be a candidate."

"I hardly think so. Don't tell me she became a nun?"

"No. I don't know what happened to her. I just happened to hear about her in connection with Chester. It was at a St. Anthony's dinner I heard all this. See, that's what you get for missing those dinners. You don't hear what's been happening to your fraternity brothers."

"I'm sorry I missed that one, anyway. Go on about Chester."

"Never fear. I intend to. Well, I guess he was so disappointed at getting only one convert that he decided to become a missionary. Maybe win over the heathen Chinee. But they didn't want him. I mean the missionaries. They only want healthy young fellows, on account of the climate, and Chester Calthorp never took a day's exercise in his life except to take the cork out of a bottle. I'm an Olympic runner compared to Chester, you know that. And his age. He was around fifty when he saw the light. Also, and this is only my idea, but they may have thought the conversion wouldn't last. But there I'd of been wrong, and so would they. Wait till you hear the next part.

"Chester was so determined to give up all his past life that he scoured around until he found a what do they call them, an order that would accept him. Don't ask me the name of it, because I don't remember. But it's a monastery. They have their, uh, monastery in the mountains over near Lebanon. Good Lutheran country, by the way. They take vows of obedience and poverty. He hasn't got a nickel. They get up around four o'clock in the morning and pray on their knees for a couple of hours, and then they do manual labor. I don't know what. Some of them farm the property, and they saw wood. Nobody seems to know very much about what they do, except

246

pray. They never see anybody. Nobody, absolutely nobody. And they're not allowed to write letters or receive them. In fact, somebody said they don't even talk among themselves. I can understand that part. I don't know what the hell they'd have to talk about under those conditions. They're on the earth, but not in the world. They wear sandals winter and summer, no socks, and some kind of a robe with a hood on it. And they never get to be priests. Always monks, working and praying, praying and working. When they die the immediate family can come to the service, but they're buried right there on the property. Oh, and they give up their names. Chester is Brother Something, and the other brothers don't know his real name. Now, aren't you glad you invited me to lunch? Isn't that worth seventy-five cents? I think it's worth more. I'm going to have a Benedictine, in honor of the occasion. How about you?"

"Go ahead, have one," said Robert Millhouser. "It's as if he were dead and I hadn't heard about it."

"Yes, it is a little, isn't it? It must be pretty hard on a man that's lived his kind of life. Especially all that manual labor."

"It saddens me. I was very close to Chester. I feel as if I were partly responsible."

"What for? Look at it this way, he's doing what he wants to do. You and I wouldn't want to do it, but he must know what he wants. God knows he always did. He never denied himself anything. He was a millionaire several times over, and he lived like one."

"I wish I'd had a chance to say goodbye to him."

"Well, if he'd wanted to say goodbye he could have. He had to take a long time to make up his mind, and I'm told these monasteries are very strict about who they let in. They don't want fellows going and then finding out the life is too severe. Chester could have let you know. But maybe he was afraid you'd remind him of the good times you had. I'm sure it's all a mystery to me. Personally, if I wanted to get out of this world I'd know how to do it pleasantly. I'd just drink a bottle of brandy every night and in about two weeks' time I think my troubles would be over. Less, according to my overanxious, overpaid sawbones."

In shock and confusion Robert finished his lunch with Ben, forgetting the original purpose of the meeting and eager to get away to be alone with his thoughts. It would be futile to ask Ben any more questions: Ben obviously had told as much as he knew, and his answers would be only frivolously disparaging comments. At long last Ben had to leave, and Robert retired to a quiet corner of the club library, where conversation was forbidden and the only sound was snoring.

It was true, he reflected, that the news had affected him as though it had been news of a death; it was saddening, and he wished he had had a chance to say goodbye to a man he had not seen or heard from in twenty-seven years. He now realized that the goodbye he had said in Rome had never been, in his mind, of a permanent character; that throughout the years there had been a lingering hope that Chester would some day break the silence. Chester Calthorp had been so comfortably disposed of—so long as that hope lingered—but now Robert felt deserted, slighted, chastised, and as he sat in the club library that hope of which he had not been aware turned sour and nasty. Chester Calthorp had deliberately punished him by allying himself with a foreign religion, a renunciation of pleasure, the adoption of an austerity that was a rebuke to their friendship. In rejecting the philosophy and *modus vivendi* that had made him unique, Chester Calthorp was performing a *calculated* act of repudiation of their friendship, and had made doubly sure that its implications would not be lost on Robert Millhouser with his failure to say a word about his intentions or make a gesture of farewell. There was the weakness in Chester Calthorp. He had been afraid to say farewell. It was not much comfort at this moment, but Robert considered that Chester's silence could be regarded as a victory. If Chester was afraid to say goodbye, it was because the one man he could not face was Robert Millhouser, the one thing he could not face was Robert Millhouser's skepticism. The conversion was incomplete and unsure, and for the first time in his friendship with Chester Calthorp, Robert Millhouser knew himself to be the superior man. His anger and sadness subsided into a contemptuous tranquillity.

"Are you going back on the afternoon train?"

Robert Millhouser turned and saw that the whispered question came from Bart Vance.

"Yes, are you?" said Robert.

Vance nodded. "Good. I'll meet you in the smoking car."

Robert Millhouser had taken himself so far away from his early unhappiness over the Calthorp news that he was even willing to have Bart Vance as a seatmate. Bart was the only member of the Vance family who still maintained connections with Lyons. The Vance sisters and Chauncey, the other brother, lived in New York and did not even have a financial stake in Lyons. Bart's share of the Vance Estate included mineral rights to various parcels of Valley land as well as royalties from leases of the original Vance Tract, now being worked by the Outerbridge collieries. Robert Millhouser had simply never known Bart Vance; they were friendly acquaintances, separated by ten years in age, joined by the mutual interests of one rich

248

family with another rich family, and sentimentally attached by the fact that Bart Vance's brother Leonard, whom he did not remember, had been Robert Millhouser's boyhood playmate. But the Vance family had moved away from Lyons during the seventies, when Bart Vance was in his early teens, and he did not begin to pay his semi-annual visits to the area until he came into his inheritance. He was seldom in Lyons for more than three days at a time, and in truth he never needed to come at all. His presence neither added to nor detracte⌐ from the profitable management of his holdings, and there were people in Lyons who said Bart only came back to feel important.

No one else in Lyons would have sat beside Robert Millhouser without being asked, but Bart Vance was a man who had gone through life always sure of his welcome, never questioning it. He put his valise on the luggage rack and flipped the back of the seat ahead and put his feet on the seat. "How've you been, Robert?"

"I've been well, thank you, and you?"

"Have a cigar. You'll find that a lighter leaf than the Fort Penn Club's. Oh, I'm in no mood to complain. I've been after the Outerbridge people for years, to get them to spend some money on the collieries, and now they've gone ahead and done it and it ought to be worth a mint of money to me. I don't get royalties for coal they keep in the ground. I get paid at the tipple, you might say. Actually of course I have my own men in the weighmaster's offices, watching the tonnage. What do you think of Ed Steele?"

"Personally, very nice. I don't know anything about him otherwise."

"I think he's the man for the job. If he isn't we'll soon find out."

"Are you in on the contract with Wadsworth & Valentine?"

"Well, no. The Outerbridge people did all that, but I'm keeping an eye on everything. I expect to be in Lyons once a month till the reconstruction's finished. Very inconvenient for me, but after all, I own the coal, don't I?"

"Yes. So I understand."

"Chauncey wanted me to sell out, you know. Couple of years ago. But I held on and I guess I'll have the last laugh when tonnage is doubled, three years from now."

The conductor held out his hand for Robert's ticket. "Mr. Millhouser, Mr. Vance," he said, and passed on. Vance did not even nod at the conductor.

"I had a little trouble with that fellow one time. He told me to take my feet off the seat and I said to him, 'I travel this road on a pass because the company thinks my business is worth a lot of money.' Of

249

course I don't pay the company a penny. The Outerbridges pay the freight, but I always get a pass every year. So I said if the company thought enough of my business to give me a pass, they wouldn't mind if I made myself comfortable. Never had another word from him after that. I don't see why you fellows in Lyons don't insist on a Pullman chair car. It'd be so much nicer for the women and children than these day coaches."

"There's talk about it every once in a while. Do you think you'll ever move back to Lyons?"

"Not in a thousand years! My wife wouldn't hear of it. She thinks New York is bad enough to bring up the children. My boy's at school at Groton and my daughter is going abroad next year."

"School in Switzerland?"

"Oh, Lord, no. She's going to live with an English family. They see to it that she meets the right people, rides to hounds. It's a sort of a p.g. arrangement. The man's a retired brigadier and his wife was formerly a lady-in-waiting to the late Queen. We heard about them through friends of ours. It's the way to do it if you want to have your daughter presented at Court."

"I've never met your wife. She's from Chicago, isn't she?"

"Cleveland. No, you haven't. But you never come to New York, do you?"

"Never."

"I must say Rhoda has a natural gift for the social life. She's brought it down to a fine art. We entertain a lot, and when you have the money to do it, I think you ought to. Not *my* money. We couldn't do it on that scale on my money. Rhoda has her own, and if that's what she wants to do with it, suits me. I have no objections. But you can easily see I'd have one hell of a time persuading her to move to Lyons, even if I wanted to, which I don't. I like New York. God, when I come to Lyons I go from the hotel to the collieries to the lawyers' office and back to the hotel, and I don't see a single woman that I'd want to take to bed with me. What do you do, if you don't mind my asking? Fort Penn? Is there much here?"

"It's a pretty big town."

"And I guess you'd have to be pretty careful in Lyons. Not that you can flaunt it in New York. Rhoda knows damn good and well that I must be getting it on the side, but I don't flaunt it. There *is* something I'd like to have a little try at in Lyons. This fellow Steele has a daughter. Have you seen her?"

"Oh, yes."

"She may be only a kid, but she's had experience. You can always tell by the way a girl walks. It gives them away every time. The last time I was in Lyons I saw her walking down Market Street. I met her once, so I knew who she was. You knew they rented our old house?"

"Yes."

"So I saw her walking down Market Street and her little ass, a real Swiss movement. Ball-bearing. You couldn't see it, but the way she walked made you want to keep watching. And she knew it. 'Here it is, boys. First come, first served.' If I'd seen her when I rented them the house I'd have stayed on as a boarder. And no doubt got myself into all sorts of trouble, so it's just as well I didn't. That's the damned trouble with Lyons, you see? In New York I could take a few afternoons off and investigate. But you know how it would be in Lyons. However, they've rented the house for three years, so maybe I'll start collecting the rent in person. The mother has her good points, too, but I think she's staying pretty close to Poppa. I never got the same impression from the mother that I got from the daughter."

It could have been a more agonizing journey if Robert had not still been preoccupied with his thoughts of Chester Calthorp, and if Bart Vance had not been so garrulous that he needed no encouragement. Bart Vance talked from Fort Penn to Lyons, recklessly involving himself and the men and women in his life. He was almost a harmless fool, but the harm in him kept him from being a fool, and Robert Millhouser's second judgment of him was that he was a harmless fool except to anyone who would confide in him, trust him, make love with him, or arouse his interest or curiosity, and to all those he was dangerous. He was particularly dangerous because he was a fool who did not deviate from the truth. He had taken up twenty-five minutes of the journey with the story of an adventure with a woman whose name, which he did not fail to mention, symbolized fashionable charity work, one of the few New York society names that was recognizable everywhere. Vance dwelt on her peculiarities in bed with such offhand authority that Robert Millhouser believed every word, the more so because there was neither malice nor pride in the telling of the story. It was a true story, and it was there to be told. And there was a kind of naïve implicit revelation running through all of Vance's stories: the unmistakable truth that Vance's wife despised him, the strong probability that she had a lover, and the fact that Vance was aware of neither the truth nor the probability. Moreover, Vance was so fantastically reckless with his own reputation and the reputation of others that a less perceptive and sensitive man than Robert Millhouser would have disbelieved one story and then disbelieved them all. The buttons of the rattlesnake.

They parted company at the Lyons depot, where Moses was waiting in the trap. "When are you going to buy an automobile?" said

251

Bart Vance. "When you decide to, let me know. I know all about them."

"I'm sure you do," said Robert Millhouser.

For a few days, whenever the conversation with Bart Vance came back to him, Robert would think of Hedda as though she were standing on a block while Bart Vance took off her clothes and pointed to the places on her body that would be sources of pleasure. From the beginning Robert had only sought confirmation of his instinctive suspicions of Hedda, and she had at least kept the suspicions alive. But if the same suspicions occurred to a man like Bart Vance, the need for subtlety with Hedda would seem to have passed, for it was not mere lecherous desire that Vance had expressed: it was desire based on conviction based on the crude knowledge of experience. To the same degree that Robert believed Vance's story of the society woman, he recognized the cogency of Vance's estimate of the girl. In about six weeks she would be home for Thanksgiving, and in that time Robert would devise his strategy for the seduction of Hedda Steele. To his astonishment he was greatly assisted by Hedda's mother, who could not have fallen in more neatly with his plans if he had asked her to.

Ruth Steele invited him to dinner, along with some others who he knew had entertained for the Steeles. By this time—it was October— some of the Steeles' souvenirs of their travels had been unpacked and were decorating the parlor, sittingroom and hall. It was impossible not to distinguish between Vance possessions and Steele additions, and everything the Steeles had installed was a conversation piece.

"This, I suppose, comes from Chile," said Robert Millhouser.

"No, this we bought in Mexico, although I've seen some like it in Chile," said Ruth Steele. The object under discussion was a polished mahogany statuette, a head of an Indian.

"I thought Chilean because I think of Chile as having more pure-blood Indians than Mexico," said Robert. "Not that I know anything about either place."

"Oh, there are lots of Indians in Mexico, but they're the last people you meet. They live in the mountains and keep very much to themselves. They have their own languages, dialects, I guess you'd call them, and they don't welcome visitors."

"Speaking of which, are you pleased with your welcome to Lyons? I should think you would be."

"Yes indeed. Ed and I understand small towns. We were both born in small towns in the Middle West, so we know what they can be like to strangers. But Lyons has certainly been nice to us."

252

"I imagine that's been your experience everywhere, though. Certainly a *comely* family."

"Well, thank you. Most of that is concentrated in our Hedda, needless to say."

"She's a little beauty."

"Coming from you, that's high praise. Didn't you use to paint?"

"I never painted anyone like Hedda."

"Do you still keep it up?"

"I gave it up entirely, then a few years ago I had another try at it, but I haven't been very pleased with what I've done. I haven't worked hard enough. A friend of mine once said I'd never be anything but a fourth-rate dauber anyway."

"That's too bad, because I'd like to see a portrait of Hedda at this age. She takes a good photograph, but the camera will never capture her coloring the way a painting would."

"A *good* painting. I wouldn't want to do a bad one of Hedda."

"Would you do one at all, if I asked you to?"

"I would certainly try."

"One that we could keep, even if you weren't satisfied with it. One that the family could keep. And I know Hedda would love to have you do it. You're the only person in Lyons that she likes to talk to. Have you ever talked with her about painting?"

"No."

"She knows you used to paint, but sometimes Hedda doesn't talk about what's uppermost in her mind. She's a strange girl, Mr. Millhouser."

"She's an interesting girl."

"And she's never been a typical young girl. She went from childhood to young womanhood. She's seventeen, almost eighteen, but she has the poise of a woman of thirty. I'm afraid she's missed something by going from one age to another and skipping the one in between. Do you know what I mean?"

"Well, perhaps I can sympathize with her. I went from boyhood to middle age, I think, without the in-between stage. In some respects I was already middle-aged when I was at the University. I was set in my ways, as they say. Of course that's not what's happened to Hedda."

"No. But it doesn't with a pretty girl, does it? Whether she's eighteen or thirty, the only thing that will make her set in her ways is marrying the right man. I hope she finds him soon. I would like to take her away next summer, where she'd meet some Americans. Or she may make friends at school. One of her troubles is that even boys of college age don't interest her for long. It's easy to see why.

Most of them are really quite young in the ways that matter to a girl like Hedda."

"If I were of college age I'd be tongue-tied with Hedda. I might be enraptured by her beauty, but I'd think it was way beyond me, and her mind is so quick that I wouldn't be able to keep up with it."

"That's just what *has* happened. She enjoyed talking to you, but where does that leave her when she's with college boys? Ed was my first beau, and we were married the year I graduated from college. The same month, in fact. But except for Ed I'd never known anybody but other Swedes. I was born in Minnesota and when we moved to Wisconsin we Swedes huddled together like cattle in a snowstorm."

"That's where she gets her coloring?"

"Oh, I'm pure Svenska. But Ed's blue eyes and blond hair—he's English extraction—make her more Swedish than the Swedes. Her hair will get darker soon. *Will* you paint her portrait?"

"I'd be delighted to try."

"You could do it here, in this house. Then there wouldn't be talk in Lyons. Oh, there'd be some. I know that, and so do you. But much less."

"If you and Hedda are willing to risk it, I have no qualms."

"It would be worth it to me, and I'm sure to Hedda also."

"And your husband?"

"In such matters the husband always has the final word, Mr. Millhouser. But I have most of the words that come before the final word. As a bachelor you must have noticed that."

"You are a very clever woman."

"Yes, but don't tell anybody."

In the time remaining until Thanksgiving holiday Robert worked at least two hours every day that he was in Lyons, with oils, with charcoal, with plumbago, and with ink. He sketched a great deal, as rapidly as possible, rarely completing a sketch but always writing a criticism on the side or the bottom of each sketch. He let it be known that he was at his "hobby" again; he set up his easel in the front yard, and he even drew a quick picture of Langendorf's delivery wagon and team and driver, which Fred Langendorf put in one of his show windows, which accomplished what Robert had intended it to: it prepared Lyons for less of a surprise than otherwise would have been the case. The picture in Langendorf's window was written up in the Lyons newspaper and Robert Millhouser permitted mention of the fact that for several years he had been indulging in painting and sketching of local subjects. He did not deny the rumor (which he had started) that he was considering painting a portrait of Fred

Langendorf and presenting it to the bank. He got in two sittings with Fred Langendorf before the Thanksgiving holiday, and the instantaneously circulated news that he was painting Hedwig Steele, at her house, at her mother's request, was never recognized as the culmination of a campaign to disappoint the citizens of Lyons.

Robert was delighted with his new penchant for intrigue and the experience of planning a seduction. In a matter of weeks Lyons had become for him as exciting as the court of Louis XIV, and in these plainest of surroundings he could see himself as the Sun King. He was leaving to circumstances the details of the seduction, where and how it would take place, but that it would take place he never doubted. The age of the girl was right, and so was his own age, and because of what he had guessed about the girl, that Bart Vance had in effect confirmed, he was not troubled by conscience or fear of consequences. He was even convinced that the excitement would stimulate him to paint a good portrait.

The first sitting was on the Friday morning after Thanksgiving Day, and it was the first time Robert had seen Hedda since their second walk together. Moses Hatfield dropped Robert with his painting equipment, and Ruth Steele opened the door for him.

"I hope Hedda had a good night's sleep," said Robert.

"I'm afraid not. There was a dance for the young people, but she's had her breakfast and she's putting on her dress, the one she wore last night. It's quite old for her. A new dress, but not a young girl's dress. She insisted on it. If it's not right, you say so and make her change. But I think it *is* right."

The dress was red velvet, much too old for any young girl but Hedda, strapless and off-the-shoulder in the prevailing fashion of evening gowns. "Good morning, Hedda. I almost said 'good evening,' " he said, as she swept in.

"On account of my dress? Good morning, Mr. Millhouser. It got me a lot of black looks at the dance."

"From the girls, but not from the boys."

"Oh, these boys," said Hedda. "Would you like me to stand, or sit?"

"I'll leave you now," said Ruth Steele, and closed the door behind her.

"This was a wonderful scheme," said Hedda. "Do you mind if I sit down for a while?"

"Do sit down. I have to get things ready."

"Are you really going to paint my picture?"

"Of course I am."

"Did you ask to do it or did my mother?"

"Your mother asked me to."

"Oh, then it wasn't such a wonderful scheme. I thought you wanted to be able to see me alone."

"I do." He kept occupied with the easel and paint box, and did not look at her.

"But you didn't think up the scheme."

"No, but I'd have thought of something. It happened to work out this way."

"You're not going to be able to do much in two days, are you? Don't pictures take weeks and months?"

"I don't intend to finish this in two days."

"I wish you could get them to let me stay home from school. It's only three weeks before Christmas vacation. I hate that school. I hate all schools, and I don't learn anything. There's only one man teacher and he must be eighty. He looks like Henry Wadsworth Longfellow."

"The author of *Hiawatha*."

"What made you say that? If there's any poem I hate it's *Hiawatha*."

"I knew a painter that used to recite *Hiawatha* to put himself to sleep."

"I didn't sleep much last night. I didn't get home till twelve-thirty, and at school we have to be in bed at nine."

"Then you should have been exhausted and gone right to sleep."

"Not after a dance. The music keeps me awake for hours, the songs."

"Now, Hedda, if you'll stand over near the fireplace, facing this way, I'll see how the light is."

"You don't want to paint me in daylight, in this dress?"

"Yes, I do."

"I thought you'd want it all dark except for the electric lights on me."

"No, I want to try to get your own natural coloring, and daylight's best for that. Sunlight."

"I don't want to be in sunlight."

"But that's what your mother wants, too."

"I don't *care* what she wants. If you want me in sunlight then I'll take my clothes off and you can paint me nude. But don't put me in sunlight with this dress on. This red will be awful if you have my face in the sunlight. Look and see for yourself." She went to the window and exposed her face to the sun, and she was right; the glaring sun on her white skin and blond hair flattened out her features and her coloring, and the red dress only accented the damage.

"You are entirely correct. How did you know that? You've never painted, have you?"

"They didn't teach it to me at that awful school. Do you know what you ought to do?"

"From now on I'll listen to you. What?"

"You ought to paint two pictures. One for them and one for yourself."

"You're not serious."

"I would be if we could lock the door. No, I'm not serious, but that's what you want, isn't it?"

"Of course it is."

"Oh, then paint any old way you want to and they'll think it's wonderful. And we can talk."

"I don't want to do a bad picture of you, Hedda."

"Well, you're going to, so let's enjoy ourselves. Have you got a cigarette?"

"Luckily, I have. I don't always carry them."

"Will you light one and let me smoke it?"

"Of course." He did so, and she sat down.

"All you have to do is paint something that looks like me and they'll be satisfied. And I won't have to stand up all the time."

He smiled. "So much for my lofty aspirations."

"I'd rather pose for a statue anyway. You're not a sculptrist, are you?"

"No. I'm not even a painter, if it comes to that. I'm a dauber."

"Some day while I'm still young I'm going to pose for a sculptrist."

"Sculptor."

"I thought it was sculptrist."

"I don't think so. Haven't you ever posed at all?"

"No. And I've never painted or sculpted. I would like to be a sculptoress. But only men. I'd love that. Would you pose for me?"

"If you wanted me to. It might present certain difficulties."

"Yes, it might. But you don't mean you'd be embarrassed."

"That isn't what I was thinking of, but I might be embarrassed to pose in the nude for you. That's what you had in mind, isn't it?"

"Not in a toga. Of course in the nude. You'd be embarrassed in front of me? I wouldn't be in front of you."

"Is that on the theory that we're going to be some day?"

"I don't understand that question."

"Well, the idea doesn't embarrass you because some day you expect to be in the nude with me."

"I would be now if we could lock that door. Where can we go?"

"I don't know."

"Haven't you thought of some place?"

"I've thought of a hundred places, but there are objections to all of them."

"There's one place that I thought of."

"Where?"

"Your house."

"There are two objections there all the time. The cook and the maid."

"What time do they go to bed?"

"About ten o'clock."

"Not before that? If you have dinner early wouldn't they go to bed before ten?"

"Nine-thirty, maybe."

"My mother and father are going out tonight."

"What about your brother and your maid?"

"The maid will be here, but her room's in the attic. My brother will think I've gone to bed. Will you leave your door unlocked? I'll be there at five minutes after ten. I know the way without going up on Main Street, and I'll go right upstairs and you leave the light on in the room where you want me to go."

"Are you sure of all this?"

"I thought about it in school, and then when I heard my mother and father were going out tonight . . ."

"I see. The main objection is having you on the street after dark."

"I'll wear a shawl and an old coat of my mother's."

"It would be a wonderful adventure."

"That's why I like it." She came to him and he kissed her. "Before my mother comes back. Put your hands lower. Hold on to me. That's right. Oh, Millhouser. Just you wait."

In the evening he waited and she did not come. He sat in the darkened parlor until ten-thirty, and then soundlessly made a circle about the house, but on instinct alone he knew she was nowhere near.

Again in the morning he was greeted by Ruth Steele. "You left a cloth over the painting, so I haven't looked at it. Are you pleased with it?"

"I'll never be pleased with it," he said. "But I'm not going to give up. We haven't much time, but maybe we can finish it at Christmas."

"Hedda will be right down. I ought to warn you, she's in a bad humor. Nothing to do with you. Woke up grouchy, the way they do sometimes."

"The way we all do, I suppose. Here she is."

"Good morning," said Hedda. To her mother she said: "Are you going out?"

"I'm going to the butcher shop. Why?"

"You have your hat and coat on, and it's just something to say."

"Oh, now, young lady. I'll be back before you leave, Mr. Millhouser." She closed the door and the girl stood still until they heard the front door closing.

"They *stayed home* last night. They never went out at all. She watches me, you know. They were supposed to go to somebody's house but the people came here instead. Let's do something now, before she gets back. I have nothing on underneath this." The girl was in a fury of hatred. "I don't care if she does come in. I wish she'd come in while you're doing it to me." She lay on the floor for him, impatient until he was inside her, and the passion continued to be hatred, as though the quick, short movements of her hips were capable of stabbing her mother. "That was good," she said, and immediately began to cry. "They hate me. They watch me. Take me away from them." He made an effort at tenderness and tried to comfort her, but she was not appealing to him for help nor was she speaking to *him* as distinguished from anyone else who might have been there to share her hatred. Presently she sat up and looked at him. He was sitting on the floor, resting on an elbow and facing her.

"Why are you sad?" she said.

"Do I seem sad? I don't want you to be unhappy."

"I'm not. But I was. They do that to me all the time. They say they're going to do one thing, and then they do something else. We never thought it would happen this way, did we?"

"No, we didn't."

"Help me up," she said, reaching out a hand. "Did you hate me last night?"

"No, I knew you wanted to come. I was worried, though. Something could have happened to you on the way."

"My brother went out and the maid went to bed early, and I kept waiting for *them* to come up and say goodnight to me. Then I heard the doorbell ring and those other people. Oh, how I hated them all. The people stayed till after twelve o'clock. I smoked one cigarette after another. When she came in this morning she asked me if I'd been smoking and I said *yes,* and that's all I said to her." She grinned. "I'll be punished for *smoking* today. Ha ha ha. If she only knew."

"How does she punish you for smoking?"

"Different ways. Today she's going to make me polish the silverware. She doesn't know it, but I *like* to polish the silverware. My father's catching on. He says I do it too well for it to be a punishment, but she hates to do it herself so she thinks I do too."

"How would she punish you if she knew what we just did?"

"Are you trying to find out something?"

"Yes, I was."

"You were trying to find out whether she'd ever punished me for that."

"Yes."

"Don't do that again. Don't you start watching me, trying to find things out the way she does. I'll hate you if you do. I will. I'll really hate you, and I'll do something to *you.*"

"Forgive me."

"This time, but not again."

"I wish I could paint you now."

"Well, I guess you might as well try. This is your last chance."

"Not tomorrow?"

"Tomorrow's Sunday. Don't you go to church?"

"No."

"Neither would I if I didn't have to, but we all go, all four together. Lars doesn't go because he wants to, but he has to too. He and my father have arguments about it. I don't argue, I just don't believe any of it."

"Then is this the last time I'll see you till Christmas?"

"Unless you come and take me away from that school."

"Stay till June, then I'll take you away."

"You mean you'll marry me?"

"I didn't say that."

"But it's what you meant. You wouldn't take me away unless it was to marry me. But I'm not sure I want to marry you."

"Why not?"

"Maybe I do, I don't know. It has its advantages. *Enamorar.* Did you find that word in your dictionary? *Enamorar?*"

"Something concerned with love?"

"To make love. When you're married you can make love whenever you feel like it, and with your clothes off. Let me look at you? Yes, you are all right. Am I?"

"Let me see. Yes."

"Are you sleepy?"

"I could go to sleep."

"So could I. That would be nice, if we could go to sleep and wake up and make love again. What shall I call you?"

"You'd better go on calling me Mr. Millhouser."

"I guess I will, but now it's going to seem funny. Hello, *Mister,* shall we get on the floor again?"

"Hedda, I think I do love you."

"Well, you ought to. And do you know what *I* think?"

"What?"

"I think you will. But I don't want babies, *Mister*. Don't marry me for babies. I don't want them till—oh, till I'm twenty-five."

"Well, eight years from now."

"If I'm not having one now. That would be a joke on us, if we had one from today."

"When will you know?"

"Next Wednesday."

"As sure as that?"

"Yes, always, but I don't like to talk about that. I've never talked to anyone about that, not even my mother. Well, I did talk to her about it, but I didn't want to. And don't jump at conclusions. It was because in the high altitude it affects some women."

"But you'll write me next Wednesday."

"Well, I'll say yes or no. But I don't like to write letters."

"How will I know what yes means?"

"Yes will mean that it happened. No that it hasn't happened. You're right. Yes will mean no, won't it? Well, I'll write and say that it has happened, or that it hasn't happened."

"And if it hasn't happened we can be married at Christmas."

"All right. There's the front door. *Paint!*"

The sadness Hedda had seen was real. It was the sadness of guilt but it was also the sadness of love come late and the sadness of pity for this girl. And it was the sadness of the gentleness he wanted to show her and of the hopelessness of what he wanted to do for her, which was to give her the life that could only be given her by a young husband who would love her without understanding her. And above all there was the sadness of knowing that he would not now give her up. He had planned to seduce her, and the seduction had not taken place; circumstances had seduced them both; but he had become a man who was capable of deliberate seduction, and this capability, this suspension of conscience, had insinuated itself into his code of conduct, so that he would resist all opposition to his possession of Hedda, whether it came from Lyons, from her family, or from Hedda herself. His lifelong loneliness changed into an angry thing, a historical thing that had been angered, and without considering the causes of the angry loneliness or the reasons for it, he was determined that for a while it would cease to exist. There was something he wanted—Hedda—that would eradicate loneliness, or anaesthetize it, and this was his last chance. And that was in the sadness. Pity, guilt, the last chance to be *with* someone; and the person was Hedda, who was a treat to so many of his senses. He knew all about love, from not having had it; what it was supposed to be and when it was supposed to be. This was not what or when it was supposed to be, and therefore may not have been the love that he had missed, but he could call it love, speak of it as love, and convince her of its genuineness. The time would come when someone would *be* love to her, and when that happened she would not consider such matters as its genuineness. She would go with the new man and the difference between the new man and Robert would be precisely the difference between complacence with Robert and passion with the new man. Robert had no thought that the love for the new man would be happy or right or lasting, but that was where pity re-entered his contemplation. This creature had already experimented with ecstasy and embraced it with her thighs and her hands, her eyes and her lips, and she had the power of her knowledge that would take her as far as the man whom she would love and who would love her for a while. And then she would be destroyed by love, because love would not tolerate equal standing with the loveless experiments in ecstasy. She had learned this, she had learned that, in loveless embraces (as he had done with the whores); she had even learned something about loneliness; and his pity for her was deeper than his pity for himself because he knew what had to happen, and she could not know it until it happened. She could fight her mother in the stabbing movements of her hips and she could call it good because it was good enough. She could do so many things with her body, and surely had, but when she wanted it for the pleasures of love, it would be unable to respond except as it had responded to hatred and itches and curiosity, not uniquely and finally to love. Robert wished that he could keep her forever, to protect her from the disaster of love, but perhaps she would be gone from him before love came to her and showed her her life. But until then he would be good to her, with no more gratitude than his pride would let him show, and with as much domination as she would endure.

She was not pregnant. She discovered the fact on Wednesday, but did not mail her one-line report—"Yes it happened"—until Saturday, by which time he was already rehearsing the scene with Ed and Ruth Steele, notifying them of his intention to marry Hedda. He was pleased that she was not with child; she would not be a good mother or mother-to-be, and whatever chance he had of a few years of happiness with her would be lost. She wrote no more until Christmas vacation was about to begin.

Dear Mister—
We are getting off the Sat. before Xmas. My mother wants you
to finish the picture but wait till you hear from her.

Sincerely,
"H"

The portrait of Fred Langendorf had been, predictably, a huge
success and Robert agreed to do one of Fred's wife and Jeremiah
MacMahon's daughter May. As to the latter two he said: "I won't
be able to get started until after Christmas. That's the only time I'll
have to paint Ed Steele's daughter."

He took his paraphernalia to Hedda's house, and when they were
alone she kissed him happily. "Oh, Millhouser, I'm so glad to see
you."

"You're very happy. Are you liking school any better?"

"Don't mention the place. No, I'm just glad to see you."

"I'm glad you are, but there must be some reason."

"There is. They're going away for two nights. They can't play any
tricks, because I'm not supposed to know it. But I read a letter that a
lady in Fort Penn wrote my mother. They're expected to spend two
nights at her house. My father has to go to some civil-engineer meetings and my mother's going with him. The only one here will be my
brother, and he likes a girl in town."

"I still have the two servants in my house."

"No. You come here. As soon as my brother goes out and the
maid goes to bed. I'll turn out all the downstairs lights and start running the water in the tub. That way, if the maid hears anybody
moving around she'll think it's me. Next Monday and Tuesday,
they'll be away. But don't you forget to get those protection things. I
don't want any babies."

He went to her house and stayed for an hour on Monday and
Tuesday nights. "Is this the same bed?" she said. She pointed to the
carving and to her breast.

"It's the same bed. I've slept in it many times."

"But always with a boy. Come, get in, Millhouser."

She was more interested in him than in his efforts to make love to
her. She was completely naked when she opened her bedroom door
for him, and everything that she did was from her fascination with
him as the male in whom she would take pleasure. She kissed him,
caressed him, and then when she was ready she led him inside her,
closed her eyes, and quickly brought herself to the climax. He had
not actively made love to her at all. On the second night it was al-

263

most the same, except that she enjoyed the longer time it took him to be ready for her. It was a curious thing that with so beautiful a body she did not demand or expect more from him. Both times, when it was over she lay with her eyes closed, then suddenly opened them and said briskly: "You have to go. Don't make any noise." As he was leaving on the second night she said: "I'll think about this till the next time. Goodnight, Millhouser." She let him be guided by the light from her room, and when he was closing the front door he saw that she likewise closed her door, shutting out all light in the hall and on the stairs.

On Tuesday morning and Wednesday morning she kissed him and felt him between his legs possessively, but she did not speak of the previous nights. She talked less while posing and not at all of love or marriage. But on the last day of the holidays, when he told her that he would finish the picture at his house within the week, she became angry. "Damn that school! I'm going to run away."

"Wait till June, I told you."

"If you make me wait till June there'll be somebody else."

"Have you someone in mind?"

"Yes."

"Who?"

"I won't tell you."

"Well, I won't try to guess. It's probably the gardener, or the school dentist, or that man that looks like Longfellow. But I'm not going to coax you to wait, Hedda. If you can't wait, I won't. Let's have that understood now, so that I won't wait."

"You have that woman in Fort Penn."

"I have no woman in Fort Penn. But I'll find one."

"You're nasty to me."

"You know better than that. In June I plan to ask your father to give you permission to marry me."

"Why do you have to wait till June?"

"I'll tell you why. If I asked him now he'd be so surprised, and alarmed, that they'd probably send you to an even stricter school. We have to wait till they get to know me better, or at least longer. They've only known me three or four months."

"You're older than my father. Why do you have to ask him anything?"

"Because he *is* your father and he has charge of you. You and I can see each other at Easter, and then in June I'll tell him."

"What if he says no?"

"I'll have to convince him. And so will you. He's going to ask you what you want to do. What are you going to tell him?"

264

"I don't know."

"Then you need time to think it over, too. Maybe in June you won't want to marry me."

"Come here, Millhouser."

"No."

"Mister? Señor?"

He laughed. "Do you want to kiss me?"

"More than that. Shall I get on the floor?"

"No. There are people moving about."

"Then come here and kiss me."

"No."

She laughed. "Millhouser?"

"What?"

"You want to."

"Of course I do."

"I would like to do something to you."

"We can't."

"Not on the floor. Just stand close to me."

"We'd have to stand too close. It'd be just as bad if they saw us that way."

"I have to just touch you."

He went to her, carrying palette and brush, and she touched him and stared at him, watching his face until at last she smiled. "There," she said.

"Did you enjoy that?" he said.

She nodded. "I like to watch your face. Your eyes get so blue."

"I must sit down, now, Hedda."

"Are you sleepy?"

"Yes. Very. But I must put my things away and go home before I do fall asleep."

"I'll help you."

"Will you? That would be nice."

"I love you, Millhouser. I'm sure I do."

"Will you wait till June?"

"If I can see you at Easter, I'll wait."

"Why do you love me, Hedda?"

"Because you're nice to me most of the time."

"As good a reason as there is in God's world, I guess."

•

It has just occurred to me that there will be no place later on where I can interrupt Robert Millhouser's story with an annotation. At least there is no place where an annotation would not seriously distract, and probably annoy, the reader who has come this far. As the reader will have anticipated, the next, penultimate phase of this chronicle deals with Robert's marriage to Hedda and the proliferating tragedy that is caused by their union. I feel that it would be fairer to the reader (and to myself as a chronicler with a natural desire to hold the reader's interest) to present Robert Millhouser's marriage as a cohesive whole, and all that will remain after that has been told will be a few concluding remarks of my own. Those remarks, by the way, will be my only statement that does not in some way originate with Robert Millhouser.

Now the purpose of this annotation is to reply to a question which has arisen in the minds of the only two persons who have read what I have written. Those persons are George Kevorkian, who was my roommate and close friend in college, and Matthew R. Holland, Junior, my attorney. They have read this manuscript at my request, and independently of each other they have asked the same question: will the reader know that the manuscript in its present form is the final version, rewritten and edited in 1948, or twenty years after my consultations with Robert Millhouser? Kevorkian's point is that the reader should be told that I, Gerald Higgins, am forty-four years old, not twenty-four. Matt Holland's point, that of the legal mind, is that the reader should be informed that I have observed the term of my agreement with Robert Millhouser which required me to wait twenty years before submitting this work for publication. I accepted $5,000 from Robert Millhouser (at his insistence, I may add) with that understanding. Kevorkian's and Holland's are good points. Kevorkian, although a historian, is often praised for the literary merit of his Civil War lectures at Harvard, which have been collected and published in three volumes. He does not wish to have me appear to claim for myself at twenty-four the maturity of a man of forty-four. Matt Holland simply wants it on the record that I did not violate my agreement with Robert Millhouser.*

Accordingly, I repeat for the record, that the story in this its final form represents my treatment of the facts provided by Robert Millhouser and by my own observation, as I wish it to leave my hands at the age of forty-four.

Let us now take up Robert Millhouser's story as of June, 1906.—G.H.

* *War: the Catalyst,* by George A. Kevorkian, Ph.D. (University of Oklahoma Press; 1947; 3 vols. $30.)

•

"I CAME TO SEE YOU because I want to enlist your support," said Robert Millhouser to Ruth Steele.

"My support? Gladly. I can't think of anything you'd want me to do that I wouldn't like to do," said Ruth Steele.

"I won't hold you to that till you've heard what it is."

"Of course you wouldn't, Robert. I know that much about you."

"Unfortunately there are some things you don't know. Unfortunately, because now I have to take the cold plunge. Ruth, I want to marry Hedda."

"Do you?"

"That isn't the way I expected you to take it. Aren't you surprised?"

"Not as much as you may have expected. When you said you wanted to enlist my support, what else could I support you in? I've seen you look at Hedda, Robert. And I guess you've managed to see her when we didn't know about it."

"I'm rather ashamed of that part."

"Don't be. In a place like Lyons you had to do it that way, and there was something between you two from the first day you met."

"There was indeed."

"And the gossip started right away. I don't blame you for being cautious. I suppose I could have made it easier for you, but it wasn't my place to."

"You did, quite by accident."

"Getting you to paint her portrait?"

"Yes."

"Well, yes, if that was an accident. I don't know what my real intention was. I may have been wanting it to end before it started, or I may have been lending a helping hand. I honestly can't say. I can't treat Hedda the way other mothers treat their daughters."

"I know. I remember a conversation you and I had."

"I remember it well. I told you I wanted to take her away somewhere, to meet some American boys this summer. That's interesting."

"What is?"

"I told her at Easter that her father and I'd decided to go to a place on Lake Michigan. It's a big hotel, lots of young people. Dancing every night. I thought it would appeal to her, but now I remember what she said. 'A lot of things can happen between now and the summer,' she said. Did that mean you'd spoken to her then, Robert?"

"Yes. I'd spoken to her."

"Then when you say you want my support, you're asking me to— what is the word?—intercede with her father?"

"I'll speak to him, but I'd like to know beforehand whether I can count on you, Ruth. You didn't bring up the obvious objections, but he will. The most obvious, of course, being that I'm older than *he* is."

"There's one thing about Ed. He's always backed me up in whatever I thought was best for Hedda."

"Do you think this is good for Hedda?"

"For Hedda, yes. I hope it's the best thing for you, Robert. But you've thought that out, haven't you?"

The wedding took place at the home of the bride and there were no attendants, no guests, no reception. The Episcopal service was used, but in all other respects it was scarcely more than a civil ceremony. The bride-to-be came home from boarding school and was married two days later and only the Steele family were in on the secret.

The new Mr. and Mrs. Robert Millhouser were in Atlantic City before anyone in Lyons knew what had happened. Robert even kept the secret from Moses Hatfield and Margaret Dillon and Theresa O'Malley. A carriage was hired in Betzville, six miles away and the next stop on the railway, and Robert and Hedda were driven there to catch the afternoon train, thus avoiding people at the Lyons station. The conspiratorial aspects of the wedding delighted Hedda. "I'll never forget Lars' face at breakfast," she said, on the Fort Penn-Philadelphia Express. "He asked me what I was going to do today and I said I was going to get married, and what was he going to do? And he said he was going to play tennis. And I said I hoped he'd be home in time to see me get married. The only thing that made him believe I *was* getting married was my father staying home from work and going around in his best suit."

"What did Lars say when you told him you were marrying me?"

"He said, 'God help him.' "

"Not shocked or anything like that?"

"Oh, he wouldn't show it even if he was shocked. He's like my father. They never show anything that goes on inside them. My mother's the one with the temper. Just think, I'll never have to ask her for permission to do anything, or go anywhere. And those terrible, smelly teachers at school. They smell as if they never took their

268

clothes off. Almost like the Indians in Wisconsin. Have you ever got that close to an Indian?"

"Of course. We had Indians in Lyons. A few."

"Indians? In Lyons? I never saw any."

"Well, I did. Over in Second Valley. They were trappers, and guides."

"That must have been a long time ago."

"Not so terribly long ago. There were still quite a few around after the Civil War."

"Do you remember the Civil War? You weren't *in* it, were you?"

"No, but I remember it. I remember the wounded coming home after the battle of Gettysburg."

"How old *are* you?"

"You know how old I am. I'm fifty-one."

"When was the Civil War?"

"Between 1861 and 1865. It ended forty-one years ago, when I was ten years old. What are you thinking?"

"Grandpa Steele was in the Civil War. The Wisconsin Volunteers, some name like that. When was my father born?"

"I guess he was born about 1863."

"That was during the Civil War, then?"

"Yes," said Robert. "Does that make it better? It does, doesn't it? I don't seem quite so ancient."

"For a minute I thought of you and Grandpa Steele."

"I knew that, all right."

The first of the inevitable "your daughter" incidents occurred on the second day of their wedding trip. They had gone for a ride in a rolling-chair and at the end of the ride, in front of their Boardwalk hotel, the Negro who had been pushing them said he would be glad to meet the gentleman and his daughter at the same time next day. The second such incident, also occurring on the second day a few hours after the rolling-chair attendant's *gaffe,* was in the diningroom. Robert ordered the meal, and the waiter volunteered to provide a glass of milk for "the little lady."

"That makes me mad," said Hedda. "You'd think they'd notice my ring."

"He's old, that waiter. He meant well."

For the two weeks of their stay in Atlantic City she was insatiable. She expected to have intercourse every night, and it was accomplished, and when it was accomplished she expected no more until the next night. But her insatiability was not so much a matter of complete intercourse as the curiosity of her hands. She wanted to touch him while they were riding in the rolling-chair, under the table at mealtimes, in the Boardwalk shops when the clerk's back was turned. He began to understand that it was not always a conscious act, certainly not always a deliberately exciting gesture. She touched him in much the same way that she would use words to express her first full freedom. They went bathing in the sea every morning before lunch, and then she would seek the shade and gaze at the other people on the beach. "Look at that tiny little man with that big wife," she would say. "And that big man with that teeny wife. They ought to trade. But maybe the little man has a bigger one than the big man," or, "How could you ever put it in a woman with such a big breadbasket? You'd have to have one that was a yard long."

"Hedda, I'm sure a lot of these people haven't thought of it in years."

"I don't believe that. Even if they're ugly and old, I'm sure they think of it. Women as much as men."

"I guess it's about even."

They got through the two weeks at Atlantic City without a quarrel or even a minor dispute. She seemed content to be with him day and night and not in need of any other company. But on the way to the Camden train she said: "Do we have to go to Lyons? I don't want to spend the night in your house."

"It's our house now, Hedda."

"It'll never be my house."

"It will be after tonight. You'll feel differently."

"I want a room by myself."

"Why?"

"Because it's your house and the maids belong to you. And that Moses."

"That doesn't explain why you want a room by yourself."

"It would if you weren't stupid."

"Well, I don't think I'm stupid, but suppose I am. Tell me why you want a room by yourself."

"Because I always have had one."

"What has made you change? We've been together every night for two weeks."

"It's something I don't want to talk about."

"Oh, I think I know. But that only lasts for a few days."

"I don't care. I'm not going to have those women know every time it happens, so I'm going to have a room by myself *all* the time."

"All right."

270

"May I? Do you mean it?"

"Of course I mean it. But I'll miss you."

"I'll miss you, too. But you can come to my room and I can go to yours. We can love each other, but I just want a room by myself."

They took a seat on the afternoon Fort Penn-Lyons train, at the rear of the coach because Hedda did not want to have people staring at the back of her neck. It was their third train of the day. "Two more hours and we'll be home," said Robert. "A bath is going to feel good."

"Will I have my own bathroom?"

"Yes. Quite a good-sized one."

"That's one thing I've never had, my own bathroom. Do you have gas, or electricity, in your house?"

"Both."

"Is there a gas heater in the bathroom? I like a bathroom that's warm and bright. You should have seen some of the places I've taken a bath in. In Mexico I used to take a bath in an iron tub. The woman would bring in the hot water in big jugs this high but it didn't stay hot very long. It gets cold there, you know. As soon as I finished my bath I'd get out of the tub, and I like to lie in a tub."

"I noticed that."

"I like to lie there till my fingertips get crinkly. I wouldn't be surprised if I fell asleep and drowned some day."

"Take an alarm clock with you."

"It wouldn't wake me up if I was dead."

"There you have a point. Oh, good Lord."

"What?"

"Do you know that man? You do, don't you?"

"I can't tell when his back is turned."

Bart Vance had boarded the train and was walking through their coach, presumably on his way to the smoker. "Keep going, keep going, keep going," Robert whispered. But halfway up the aisle Vance halted and inspected the passengers. He saw Hedda and Robert and came back to them.

"Good afternoon, Miss Steele. Robert, you can't have this pretty young lady all to yourself."

"So it would appear."

Vance swung the back of the forward seat and sat down. "You been shopping, Miss Steele?"

She laughed and looked at Robert. "Yes, I did some shopping."

"She has some new charge accounts," said Robert. "Under the name of Mrs. Robert Millhouser."

"What? You're pulling my leg."

"Not pulling it, pushing it. I'm trying to push it out of the way, as delicately as possible."

"Excuse me. But what was that about Mrs. Robert Millhouser?" Hedda held out her left hand, palm down.

"The whole shooting match. I didn't know you were engaged, let alone married."

"We got the engagement ring today, in Philadelphia. I've had the wedding ring for two weeks and one day."

"For God's sake. Well, Robert, envious congratulations to you. And Mrs. Millhouser, all the happiness in the world. Two weeks? You're newlyweds, so I'll leave you. Yes, I can see it now, Robert. You've changed, for the better, of course." He stood up. He was flustered and embarrassed and, Robert knew, was recalling the conversation on this same train during the previous autumn. "You're going to live in Lyons, aren't you? Hope to see you."

"Thank you," said Robert.

Vance moved on to the smoker.

"He followed me one day," said Hedda. "Before Christmas. I had a feeling someone was following me, and I saw who it was. Every time I'd stop to look in a store window, he'd stop a little way behind me. I pretended I forgot something and turned around and took him by surprise. He almost bumped into me."

"It doesn't seem to've annoyed you."

"I could hardly keep from laughing."

"You don't *like* him, do you?"

"Oh, he's conceited. He's one of those men that think they're handsome."

"Do you think he's handsome?"

"Well, he is, to some extent. I don't like his mouth very much. His lips are too thick. But he's handsome in a way. He likes the girls, you can easily tell that."

"Yes, *he'll* tell it, too."

"You mean he says things about girls?"

"He says everything about them."

"Did he ever say anything about me?"

"He talks about all women."

"What did he say about me? When was that?"

"I don't really remember, Hedda. He'll say anything that comes into his head about any member of the female sex."

"Try to remember what he said about me."

"Just some idle talk. I honestly don't remember."

"When did he say it? Around Christmas time?"

"No. Before that."

"Long before?"

"It might have been several weeks, or months. Why?"

"I just wondered whether the day he followed me was the first time he ever noticed me."

"It wasn't. But why should you care when he noticed you?"

"Well, if he just followed me on the spur of the moment. But if he'd been wanting to before. Sometimes men will follow you on the spur of the moment, but other times you'll get so used to the same man following you every time he sees you."

"Are you used to having men follow you?"

"I'm used to it, yes. *I* know I'm pretty. I've been told it often enough ever since I was six years old. Or five. Or three. And if you're pretty, men will follow you. So will women. Some rich woman in Milwaukee wanted to adopt me when I was ten. She didn't have any children, but she bought a pony and cart so I could drive it. *You* think I'm pretty or you wouldn't have married me."

"I think you're beautiful. But I don't think I'd have followed you on the street."

"Maybe not, but . . ." She did not finish the thought.

"But what?"

"Nothing."

"Come on, say it. But what?"

"You wanted the same thing, even if you didn't follow me."

"Yes, I did. And that makes me as bad as those that followed you."

"I didn't say it makes you bad, or *as* bad. It's just that one person will think it and follow you, and another person will think it but not follow you. If nobody could have seen us you'd have taken me in your house that day."

"I know."

"I'd have gone, too. You didn't follow me, because we were walking together. But you did the same as follow me, asking me those questions. Why does somebody follow you? Because he wants to find out what he can do and what you'll do. *You* tried to find out by asking me questions."

"I love you, Hedda. I've never known anyone like you."

"I love you, too. You don't get cross when I say these things to you. Most people would get cross because they don't like to face the truth. My mother's always so strict with me, but I've heard her and my father. She gets him to where he's insane before she'll let him, you know."

"I'm learning more and more about your mother."

"I'm glad somebody is. Everybody thinks she's so moral, as if a kiss would make her faint. But she teases my father till he can't stand it, and then he's sorry for what he did, but she makes him do it because that's what she likes. I know. I've heard them. And the same thing's going to happen to Lars. The girl he has a case on, she even looks like my mother. Sara-Frances Lloyd. She'll ask him to play tennis, and then when he goes to the tennis court she won't be there. And he has a scholarship to two universities. Just like my father, all over again."

They were met at the depot by Moses Hatfield and the pair in the surrey, and incidentally by the citizens who usually met that train: the station agent, the driver of the hotel dray, the driver for the Adams Express Company, the boy who took the bundle of newspapers to the stationery store, one of the undertakers and his driver-assistant, Constable Tommy Fenstermacher, a clerk from the coal company for the company mail, an assortment of grade-school boys, several railroad pensioners checking the arrival time, the engine hostler, the Lyons postmaster; and two Lithuanian girls from the paper-box factory, a Valley farmer with a fine pair of mules meeting his sailor son, Mr. and Mrs. Billy Williams meeting her sister, two nuns meeting two nuns, a Chi Phi from Franklin & Marshall meeting another Chi Phi who carried a tennis racquet and a calabash mandolin, a middle-aged woman in mourning meeting a middle-aged man who was speaking to the undertaker, and a man in overalls and straw hat who was meeting a crate of pigeons.

Bart Vance stopped only long enough to raise his hat and mutter a few parting words. The Williamses waved to Robert but decided not to bring their visitor over to be introduced. The Lithuanian girls whispered to each other and studied Hedda. The visiting Chi Phi smiled and winked at her. But all the others who recognized Robert looked at him and at Hedda in sullen curiosity. It was fortunately an hour during which most of the women in the town were busy in their kitchens, cooking, serving, or washing up after supper. Moses Hatfield was sweating in his winter livery and square bowler. "Welcome home, Mr. Robert. Ma'am. Pleased to welcome you home," said Moses. If he retained any resentment for being left entirely out of the wedding, it did not show; but neither did his dignity permit him to make any display of loyalty or affection. The mare had worked up a lather and she shook her head and a puff of froth came to rest on Robert's sleeve.

"May I take the reins?" said Hedda.

"You don't want to sit in back, in style?"

"No, I'd rather drive."

"Then Moses, you get in back."

She extended her arms so that they were out at full length, but she

274

kept the pair under good control at a brisk trot until they reached the carriage gate at Robert's house. "You take over," she said. "I'm not sure I can get through the gate."

"Good girl," said Robert.

"Were you worried?"

"No, you handle them quite well, but it *is* a narrow gateway if you're not used to it. Very sensible."

"You look at them gateposts you see where a lot of *men* don't judge them right," said Moses, in a tone that was a compliment to her decision. "I show you how to go thoo that gate tomorrow, maybe. They's a mark in the gutter, you just keep you' off-front wheel straight over that mark and you get thoo nice and easy. Don't you bother about nothin' else. Just that wheel over that mark."

"I never knew that, Moses. What mark?"

"Inside you' head."

The hoofbeats and the rumble of the surrey had Margaret Dillon and Theresa O'Malley at the porte-cochere. Margaret was in her black uniform with the white lace trim and apron; Theresa was in her white-striped blue uniform, with her apron rolled up to her waist. "This is Margaret Dillon, whom you've seen before and who's seen you before. This is Theresa O'Malley, whom you have not seen before, but undoubtedly has seen you from one vantage point or another." Margaret dipped in a curtsy, and Theresa wiped her right hand on the rolled-up apron and came forward. "We hope you'll be very happy in your new home," said Margaret.

"Very happy," said Theresa.

"Thank you. I hope we'll all be very happy," said Hedda S. Millhouser.

"Mrs. Millhouser is going to have the guest room across the hall from my room."

"Yes sir," said Margaret. "I'll be a couple minutes getting it ready instead of the corner room."

"You can do that after we've had our baths."

"You're not going to use the corner room at all?"

"No, I'll be in my same room, across the hall from the guest room. Got it all straight?"

"Yes sir."

"Eight o'clock for dinner, Hedda? Would that be about right?"

"How much time does that give us?"

"About an hour and a quarter. Let's make it eight-thirty. It'll be cooler then."

"I'd like to go upstairs first," said Margaret Dillon.

"What for, Margaret? Did you leave the place in a mess as usual? If there's one wrinkle in the counterpane Margaret thinks the place is a mess."

"Well, it isn't any wrinkle in the counterpane. It's the flowers we put in the corner room I want to put in the guest room."

"Oh, I spoiled your surprise," said Robert.

"No you didn't," said Hedda. "Thank you, Margaret. We'll wait downstairs till you're ready."

"Thank you, ma'am."

Robert and Hedda went to the den to await Margaret's return. "I might as well smoke a cigarette," said Hedda. "They're going to know I do, and they might as well know it now."

"Right. Don't yield an inch now or it'll be that much harder later. That's why I was glad you didn't want dinner at eight. Nothing's been changed much here in thirty-five years, since my father died. You're going to want a lot of things changed, and the time to start is now. Just be firm with Margaret. Theresa won't be as difficult."

"I've never had a servant of my own, but we've always had at least one, and sometimes five."

"Then you know."

"Well, enough to keep them from getting the upper hand."

"Good for you. On the other hand, there's no reason why you shouldn't get along together."

"No. Not as long as she understands that I'm your wife, not a schoolgirl. I can cook, you know. I can do a lot of things you don't know about."

"I like what I do know about."

"I'm glad now that we never did anything in this house."

"So am I," said Robert.

Margaret tapped on the open door. "Your room is ready now, ma'am."

"Thank you, Margaret."

Robert and Hedda went upstairs together. "Here's your room."

"Oh, that's a nice big bed," said Hedda. "I was afraid it might turn out to be one of those single beds, and then I'd have had to tell them to move a big one in."

"This was a guest room, room for two. How do you like the flowers?"

There were four cut-glass vases of peonies and red and white roses.

"Pretty," said Hedda.

"Here's your bathroom. You're not going to need the gas heater, but there it is."

"And the corner room. Was that your mother's room?"

"It was my mother and father's room. After my father died my

276

mother moved to another room on the other side of the house. The corner room is the best bedroom in the house, but it's practically never slept in. You might like that for your room later on."

"I may, but I like this room now. Look at the view. You can see the whole town, nearly. Why, look. I can see Outerbridge and Outer Two from here. I wonder if my father's home yet."

"We can ring them up later."

"Later. Where do the maids sleep?"

"One flight up and over in that direction."

"They don't use these stairs, do they?"

"No, they have their own. And their own bathroom."

"Where did your mother die?"

"In her room. Her own room. My father died in the corner room. At least I think he did. Maybe he died downstairs? Why—I've never known where he died. Think of my not knowing that. I was away at school, and I always took for granted that he died in the corner room."

"Well, I never knew him," said Hedda.

"But you never knew my mother, either. And yet you wanted to know where she died."

"There's more of your mother in this house than there is of your father. Anybody could tell that this house was run by women."

"I could take umbrage at that, but I suppose it's true. My mother was here all the time. She never traveled. Once a year to Philadelphia to buy Christmas presents."

"She decided the way she wanted things in the house, and Margaret did them."

"Yes, she decided everything but me. Are you going to change things much?"

"Would you care if I did?"

"Far from it. I hope you will. I want it to be your house."

"Some of the furniture is pretty old-fashioned, but I won't change anything till I've lived here a while. I'll get used to some of it that I may not like now. Oh, I'll spend money."

"Well, I anticipated that. By the way, did your father give you an allowance?"

"Yes. Fifty cents a week."

"Good. We'll continue that," he said, and looked away from her as though there would be no further discussion, but she saw that he was joking.

"That's very kind of you. When I join the ladies' sewing circle they'll all be so envious of me, getting fifty whole cents a week. Think of it. To spend any way I want to."

"Any way at all."

"I'll go to the candy store and buy all the licorish sticks I want. And will you buy me a doll at Christmas?"

"You're a sly one, you are."

"If you're ever stingy with me I'll just let my braids down and roll a hoop down Main Street."

"You're a born blackmailer."

"Think how mean I could be to you. I'd have Moses put a sandbox out in the middle of the lawn, and then when people go by I'll sit there with my little pail. I should have bought one in Atlantic City. I'll put a swing in one of the trees."

"Be sure and wear pantaloons. The ruffled kind."

"I will not. I won't wear anything. And all the little boys will come and watch me swing."

"The big boys will, too," said Robert. "Such as Bart Vance."

"Well, that's the only way he'll ever see anything, so don't worry."

"I'll always worry, Hedda. But I'll try not to let you know." He put his arms about her waist. "Will you give me your first kiss in your new house?"

She nodded and kissed him.

"We can be happy," he said. "I'll try my best."

"So will I," she said. "Now go away, because there are other things I have to do in the bathroom besides take a bath."

"I'll knock on your door at a quarter past eight."

No man of fifty-one, who was a member of the upper or middle class of Lyons, had ever married an eighteen-year-old girl. Such marriages had been known to occur among the poor and there were instances of fifty-year-old men who lived with girls of fifteen and younger. But such unions, legalized or not, were not entered into by members of the upper and middle classes, and those who were parties to the arrangements were looked upon as freaks. The community had its social and physical freaks. In the Valley there was a farmer's widow who every year or two had a new man on the farm, and a succession of illegitimate children. There were several bold homosexuals who would walk slowly past Kleckner's poolroom on Saturday night until two or three young men who had lost their money at pool would detach themselves from the group and follow the fairies down the alley. There were four or five men whom Constable Tommy Fenstermacher called his steady customers: town drunks, who had no steady jobs but occasionally found work as gravediggers, street cleaners, and porters, and would perform small tasks for Fenstermacher in exchange for a night's lodging in the lock-up during severe weather. There was a female dwarf and there were several bad cases of histrionic spasm and of cerebellar and *grand mal* epilepsy. There was a

278

white-bearded Union veteran who beat a snare drum and marched from Johnsville to Lyons every Saturday afternoon. There was a legless young man of twenty-five, who rode on a little platform and carried a switch under his arm, with which he would lash out at the legs of children. And there was the hermit, who was believed to live in an abandoned mine tunnel and who came to Lyons to warn citizens that the world was about to end and to beg some salt from Langendorf and MacMahon.

In the middle and upper classes there were men and women who had eccentricities, quirks, peculiarities, habits and odd accomplishments. Some of these wore unusual or out-of-date clothes, some would interrupt sermons in church; one man could touch either eyeball with the tip of his tongue, another man was said to have a well-developed female bust, several men and women were remarkably double-jointed; one man could drink a sechsel of beer without leaving the table; two sisters could recite the names of all sixty-seven counties and county seats, forward and backward, and do the same with all forty-five states and their capitals; there was a man who could play Mendelssohn's Spring Song on the violin while standing on his head; another man had not eaten meat, fish, butter or cheese in thirty-five years; and one woman had visited her mother's grave every day, regardless of weather, for twenty-two years. All these people were members of families, and the families took pride in the accomplishments of some, endured embarrassment for the eccentricities of others, suffered shame for the antics of a few. But the upper class and its close connection, the middle class, successfully maintained the appearance of respectable normality, and if genius was occasionally stifled, Lyons did not know it and was more comfortable in conventionality. Lyons was a proud town, and in the community of towns regarded itself as unique and distinctive and superior, but the source of its pride was in its approximation of compact, continuous conventionality, never in its eccentrics or their caprices. And in this atmosphere Robert Millhouser, fifty-one, had married an eighteen-year-old newcomer.

Now she was twice a newcomer in less than a year's time: completely new as a beautiful schoolgirl, and even newer as a very young wife; a member of the town's womanhood before she had been included among its girls. In all Lyons there was not a woman, and scarcely a girl, who did not understand all the implications of a wedding trip, and there was not a man who either could not remember or anticipate the pleasures that Robert Millhouser had been enjoying—although neither fondest memory nor wildest dream would permit the men to cast Hedda Millhouser as their partner.

"You know what it's going to be like at first," said Robert, on their second day home.

"Oh, my, yes," said Hedda Millhouser. "All I have to do is remember what I used to think. Only now, *I'm* the bride. But you. They're going to look at you, too."

"I know they are, and I know what they'll be thinking. I'd have thought the same things myself, ten, fifteen years ago."

"Don't let them worry you, Robert. If I look happy, they'll stop wondering." She put her hand on his arm. "Have I said something wrong?"

"God, no."

"But you're in pain."

"No, no, girl. It isn't pain. What you're seeing is love. The pain is the years without you, all my life till now. Do you know that you called me Robert?"

"Haven't I before?"

"Not that way. Never that way. I've never liked it when you called me Millhouser."

"I knew that, but I couldn't call you Robert."

"But now you did. Yes, if you look happy, they'll stop wondering."

"I am happy. What else could I be but happy? You are, aren't you?"

"Am I indeed."

"The mine whistles woke me up this morning, and I sat up in bed and didn't know where I was. I've never gotten used to those whistles. But then I remembered you were just across the hall and I went back to sleep and slept like a log. The second time I woke up I felt like a queen, with my own bathroom and a button to push for my breakfast. No disagreeable girls with their hair falling down over their faces, pushing each other out of the way to get to the sink, or the w. c. Did you see what I had for breakfast? Or didn't you notice? I had figs and cream, and eggs and bacon and four pieces of toast, with apple butter. And coffee. And *after* breakfast—a cigarette."

"Why is a cigarette so remarkable? You had one after breakfast every day in Atlantic City."

"That was in a hotel. This was at home, in my own bed, in my own room. I got a look from Margaret."

"Margaret had better watch her looks."

"Too late."

He laughed. "I didn't mean it that way."

"I know how you meant it. She can stay till she gets used to me. But if she doesn't *try*, I'll give her the sack. Not you. *I* will. If she doesn't try, then *fuff*."

"Would you like a personal maid?"

"No! At least, no thank you. If I didn't hate to clean, I wouldn't let Margaret in my room except to bring me my breakfast. I'm so used to making my own bed I almost did it from force of habit, today. But I hate cleaning. No, I don't want to be that much of a queen. I don't want any woman that close to me. I hate to have a woman touch me, even powdering my back. If we ever go out in the evening, you'll have to powder my back."

They had Ed and Ruth Steele in for dinner that night. From the moment of the Steeles' arrival Hedda Millhouser proclaimed her independence of her mother, while at the same time—sometimes in the same sentence—re-establishing a cordial relationship with her father. Ed Steele had lapsed into a puzzled, awkward formality toward Hedda when Ruth told him that Robert Millhouser was to marry the girl. The age objection—Hedda's youth and Robert's lack of it—was easily disposed of by Ruth's presentation of the many arguments in favor of the marriage, and Ed Steele, with some misgivings but considerable relief, turned the problem over to his wife. It was a matter for her to decide, in much the same way that he would attend to a short circuit in the household electrical system. Knowing as much as Ruth had told him about Hedda, he could not pretend to himself that his daughter was liable to be ruined by the shocks of intimacy with a very mature man. And indeed he had only to recall that Ruth had been far more advanced in the sexual mysteries than he had been. The Swedish virgin he married had had to overcome his American-English ignorance, and Ed Steele's belief was that any woman had a better understanding of any other woman than any man could possibly have. It had been a much better thing, for instance, for Ruth to have known so long about Hedda's erotic experience and to have told him about it after a delay of years. If he had made any of the discoveries, he might have killed the man involved. But Ruth had known all along, had kept the secret, and had shown her husband that if there was to be any salvation for the girl, any hope of a peaceful future for her, violence and melodrama were to be avoided. And what Ruth had done—with considerable assistance from Hedda's own inclinations—was now proving out to be successful: she had given the girl and the man the opportunities that could end in one of two ways; in an affair that would not do much more harm to Hedda than had already been done, or in a marriage that had its less than perfect aspects but that represented all the difference between a protected woman and an irresponsible, unprotected wanton. Hedda was now Millhouser's responsibility.

After the first few minutes the party of four was split into sub-parties of two each. Ruth devoted herself to Robert, while father and daughter went about the business of creating their new relationship. Ruth Steele had had two anxious weeks, and her curiosity was concentrated on the question of how much Hedda had told Robert about herself, and the possible consequences to the marriage.

"Suddenly Hedda seems very mature," she said to Robert. "She likes this new role."

"The role of hostess?"

"Yes," said Ruth. "Oh, the role of wife would come easily to her, with the right husband. And I can see you're that."

"Thank you."

"It all goes back to what we've talked about before. And I never told you this, because it would have given you a wrong impression of our home life. But the fact is, Robert, Hedda wasn't happy at home. She wanted this. A husband. Her own home. She really *wanted* it at the age when most girls aren't sure they want it. I was never as pretty as Hedda, so I can't be sure what pretty girls think. But it always struck me as strange that she had this great desire to be alone. I would think that a pretty girl would thrive on attention, having people around her. They flocked around Hedda, but the crowd didn't mean anything to her. She'd pick out the most interesting person and ignore the others. When I was a girl the beauties all wanted to have as many around them as they could, but Hedda never did. She must have told you that."

"No. I've guessed part of that, but she hasn't told me that. In fact, Ruth, we haven't had much time to dip into the past."

That seemed to answer the unasked question, but Ruth went on. "Well, both of you have so many memories, Hedda living in so many different places and always interested in people. And you."

"I spent about eight months in Europe almost thirty years ago. That's the extent of my travels."

"I thought you were there for several years."

"No. That legend persists, but that's all it was. And that long ago. If there's anything you want to know about Lyons, I can probably tell you. But I've never been to Boston, or Pittsburgh, or Washington, D. C. I've been to New York twice in my fifty-one years. Let me see. I've been to Philadelphia, Fort Penn, New York, London, Paris, Florence, Naples, and Rome. Oh, yes, and Switzerland, which I hardly remember because I drank so much wine the few days I was there."

"Well, then you got a lot out of your travels. You give that impression. I remember a man we knew in Quebec. He was English, and he'd never been anywhere but Quebec City, Montreal, and Ottawa.

He'd never even been to Toronto. And yet I'd have said he'd been all over the world."

"Did you like him very much?"

"Why? Why do you ask?"

"Well, did you?"

Ruth looked quickly at Hedda before replying. "I've never cared for anyone but Ed Steele, but like? Yes, I've liked a lot of Ed's friends. Engineers are wonderful people. They have to have brains, and they travel a lot, get to see the world. Just as long as they know when to settle down. This is our last job as gipsies."

"Where are you going to settle, or where would you like to?"

"China. I've never been there, but so many of our friends have been, and now that things have quieted down there—I don't think I could ever live here at home again. The company gives you a house and servants, and you meet the very nicest people. Embassy people, and the officers and their wives. And I'm told the dollar goes a long way in China. We haven't been able to save much, but if we lived in China for the next twenty years we'd be able to save half of Ed's salary, and all the people that have ever lived there want to go back. It's the one place they all want to go back to. And you and Hedda could come out and visit us. And I'm told the big companies are looking for men that will stay, and Ed's just the right age. We have two more years and a little over in Lyons, and by that time Lars will be halfway through college and Ed will have something good to go to. And he'll be almost sure to have his bonus from here. Maybe two. He can't count on a big one for money saved, because Outerbridge was figured very close so the company'd get the contract. But the bonus for finishing ahead of schedule, he'll get that, and it could be a big one. They pay such high wages to people in the States, but Ed is a worker, and he can get the work out of the men because he's on the job day and night. So he's really counting on that bonus, and then—China."

"Did I hear you say China?" said Ed Steele. "Ruth has her pipe dreams before she even gets there."

"They're not pipe dreams."

"Yes they are. She's tired of our wandering around like gipsies, but where does she want to go next? To as far away as you can get. She's been listening to descriptions of lotus-land by people that haven't been out there in years, and if it was so good they'd be there now. I want to live in California, that's close enough to China for me."

"What is there in California? Oranges, and they wouldn't have them if they didn't have irrigation," said Ruth.

"Have you been to California, Robert?" said Ed Steele.

"Never. I don't even know how far it is."

"It's about three thousand miles. But if I told you that there are millions of acres of land, millions of acres to be had for two cents an acre, and all they needed was water and anything would grow there, would you turn down that chance to be a millionaire?"

"Robert doesn't want to be a millionaire," said Hedda.

"Oh, yes, I do."

"No you don't. If you did you wouldn't be living in Lyons."

"Well, if you look at it that way," said Robert.

"Be that as it may, California has this land and I'm an engineer. I'm in favor of buying as much land as I can afford and using my engineering experience to learn all about irrigation, and I'd be willing to bet that in ten years' time I'd be a millionaire. And if I weren't, at least I'd be living in a healthy climate."

"Politics has something to do with irrigation," said Ruth.

"Of course it has. But they need engineers, too. I wouldn't just buy any cheap land. I'd study it carefully before I bought. How far the water has to go and so forth. And the transportation problems."

"Yes," said Ruth. "Who's going to buy all these oranges?"

"Chicago, New York. *Lyons!* The same people that buy them now."

"But meanwhile we'd be living in a tent again."

"Well, we've lived in tents before."

"And I had to carry a revolver all the time and wear high leather boots. No thank you, not at my age. I've shot all the snakes I care to."

"She's a good shot, too," said Ed.

"I forgot about that," said Hedda.

"You wouldn't be here if your mother hadn't been a good shot. When we were in Montana."

"But we weren't living in a tent," said Hedda.

"No, we weren't," said Ruth. "We were living in a cabin and the snakes didn't like our intrusion. We'd have been much better off in a tent. No more cabins *or* tents for me, thank you. I want to live in a house, with plenty of servants, and knowing that I'm not going to have to move in two years or six months. And I don't want to live in California. They have earthquakes."

"They have them in China, too. If we lived in California for ten years, I'd be so rich at the end of that time that we could live anywhere we wanted to."

"I'm sure Robert isn't interested in our family problems," said Ruth.

"Of course I am. But I must say this discussion makes me glad I stayed home all these years. Unless, of course, Hedda gets restless."

284

"I won't. If this is where you want me to live, it's where I want to live."

"Thank you, my dear," said Robert.

"And I know I wouldn't want to live in China," said Hedda. "I wouldn't want to be surrounded by Chinese people."

"Why not? When did you suddenly take a dislike to foreigners?" said Ruth.

Her question created not one but three silences, all angry: Robert's angry silence directed at Ruth without his knowing the factual reason behind her question; and Hedda and her father, silent and separately outraged by Ruth's treachery.

Hedda looked at her mother with loathing. "I don't *know* all about *you*, Mother," she said. "And maybe you don't know so much about me." She looked down at her ice cream and strawberries and lifted her spoon to her mouth. Neither Robert nor Ruth nor Ed Steele could think of anything to say and the meal was finished in confusion and silence.

"Ed, shall we go out on the porch and have a cigar?" said Robert.

"Mother, do you want to come upstairs?" said Hedda.

"No thank you. I don't think we'd better stay. Ed, will you take me home? I'm sorry, Robert. But there's no use pretending I'm not very cross, because I am. I think a mother is entitled to more respect, even from a married daughter."

"Then for heaven's sake don't stay," said Hedda. "I *am* married, and this is my house."

Ed Steele and Ruth left immediately.

"She felt she was being backed into a corner. Your father, and you."

"Do you know what she was hinting at?"

"Well, I don't *know*. But I *guess* it was something that happened in some foreign country."

"It was. I'll tell you anything you want to know."

He sat in one of the wicker chairs. "Do you remember the first time you came here, and sat over there?"

"Yes."

"Well, I tried to find out then and it was the wrong time to try to find out anything. Since then, of course, I learned there was somebody else before you married me. There was me, for one. And if you and I hadn't gotten married, I'd have been somebody that your husband would have had to know about. But then I don't know. *Would* he have had to know about me, and any others there might have been? If I think about it much I'm consumed with jealousy and curiosity.

But good God in heaven, I've done things I'm ashamed of. And—"

"I didn't say I was ashamed."

"Let me go on, please. I didn't say you were, either. But I am ashamed of some things I did, and of some things I didn't do. I'm almost as ashamed of some of the things I didn't do. I'd almost rather not have you tell me what you did do than tell you what I didn't do. But now that I've said that, I've aroused your curiosity, and I'll tell you what I didn't do. I never slept with a woman till I was past twenty-five years old. And then it was a whore."

"Were you one of those men that do things with another man?"

"No, I never did. But my best friend did. He had relations with men, and I was so ignorant that he could have had relations with me. I admired him so much that—I don't know, Hedda. When I learned the truth about him I was disgusted and broke off our friendship, and I've never seen him since. That was close to thirty years ago. But I've often thought since then that he was much more admirable than I was. He was stronger than I was, and the fact that we didn't have relations is probably more to his credit than mine."

"But you like women."

"I like you. I love you."

"And you like my mother, too."

"Now how do you know that? I don't like her, but in totally different circumstances I would have an affair with her."

"No you wouldn't. But she'd let you think you could."

"Well, that would be up to her."

"Shall I tell you about the Mexican boy?"

He smiled. "It was a Mexican? I was right about that, then?"

"Shall I tell you about him? You've told me one thing."

"No, I'd rather not hear about it."

"You're lying to yourself, Millhouser."

"Yes, I am. But don't tell me about him."

"I have to, now."

"All right, tell me about him."

"His name was Johnny and he was seventeen years old. His father and mother were friends of my father and mother, and they lived two houses away from us."

"How old were you?"

"I was fifteen, and I had never been alone with him. He was very quiet and didn't speak English very well. He knew how, but his accent was so thick he had to repeat everything. Then one time I was in my room and he whistled to me and I went to the window and he tossed me an envelope and it was full of pictures of men and women. Do you know the kind of pictures I mean?"

"I can imagine."

"And then that night he climbed over the wall and got into bed with me. And after that he came to my room whenever he could."

"With your permission, I take it."

"Yes. Then my mother found out and we left Mexico."

"What did your father do?"

"She didn't tell him."

"Your father still doesn't know?"

"Not unless she told him lately."

"Actually I told you two things about myself, Hedda. So I feel entitled to ask you to tell me one more thing about yourself. Was this Mexican your first?"

"No."

"Who was?"

She shook her head. "Don't ask me any more questions unless you want me to tell you everything in my whole life. But if I do that I won't like it. And I won't like you, either, Millhouser. Now I wish I hadn't told you about Johnny."

"Why?"

"It was better before I told you."

"Yes, it was. All right, Hedda. No more questions."

"Good. I hate her enough for everybody."

"But in a way it's a good thing you told me what you did. This way if she says anything like that again I'll know what she's talking about, and I may even tell her I do. But at least I know. I'm talking gibberish, and I'm trying to say something that shouldn't be hard to say."

"My mother will know that you know about Johnny, so it'll be useless to bring that up again."

"Right. Why couldn't *I* have said it that simply?"

"Because you think too much. You try to be too fair to both sides. You always think too much. If you want something, go after it."

"That's not always the best idea. I wanted you, and if I'd gone after you—"

"You'd have gotten me."

"So you say. But we also agreed that it was better to have waited."

"No. What we agreed on was this house. It was more respectable to be married before we did anything in this house. The other house didn't count."

"It didn't?"

"Nothing counted that happened before we were married."

"An interesting point of view."

"Well, why should it have? I wasn't your wife then."

"That's an interesting point of view, too. In other words, now that you are my wife, and I'm your husband, it does make a difference."

"Sure it does."

"You believe in being faithful, Hedda?"

"Sure I do, as long as you're nice to me. But if you did it with somebody else, I would, too. What would be the use of not?"

"Then neither one of us will ever have to worry about that."

"Maybe not."

"Well, I certainly intend to be strictly faithful to you."

"You intend to be, but say my mother went after you—"

"That's ridiculous."

"If she wanted to have you, she could. Men are so easy, they're so excitable."

"That statement gives rise to a lot of questions I'd better not ask."

"Well, then let's change the subject. I'm not going to answer any questions."

"All right, let's change the subject, after I point out that I didn't ask the first question. You did. You asked me if I knew what your mother was hinting at."

"You see? You do think too much. Thinking."

"Well, I can't help that, Hedda. I've only had my own company for most of my life, and thinking takes the place of conversation."

"Oh, I like conversation," said Hedda Millhouser.

Summer entertainment in Lyons was chiefly porch entertainment. A man and his wife would stop in for "just a minute or two" and sit on the porch, have lemonade and cookies, and be on their way. People with large porches would invite friends to view the Fourth of July parade from their house. And groups of women would meet and sew on a friend's porch in the afternoons. Only three sizable parties, all with the same personnel, were given for the newly married Millhousers: the Steeles' party, the Langendorfs' and the Williamses'. They were Saturday night suppers, with sixteen persons present at each. The Steeles' party, which was the first, was also the least successful. Ruth had made the mistake of offering corn on the cob to a group of men and women whose teeth were not as good as hers and Ed's. The Langendorfs offered chicken à la king, and the Williamses, on a very warm evening, provided chicken salad and watermelon. The right food was extremely important at these parties. They were big-eating people, and since most of those present had children older than Hedda Millhouser, food took the place of conversation. No alcoholic beverage of any kind was served at either party, and after the eating was over the men and women retired separately and did not again come together until someone would announce it was his bedtime, whereupon the men would come in from the porch and the women would come downstairs from the hostess's bedroom and for an hour the general conversation would be devoted to such topics as the trolley line, the issuance of municipal bonds for roadway improvements, a second shift at the mines, and other such matters that would allow the men to express opinions. The women would remain silent but with a fixed show of interest until some wife would ask her husband how late it was getting to be, and the party would then really come to an end, all departing within five minutes.

But if they were tedious affairs, they were also favorable in their effect on Hedda Millhouser's new standing in the community. "She's really a shy little thing," the women said. "If you can get her to open up, she's polite and intelligent. But did you notice how she practically clings to Robert? It may work out." The dissenting opinion maintained that Hedda Millhouser was merely bored, not shy, and it was only a question of time before she would be bored by her husband. "If Robert has good sense they won't take long having children."

In any event, the newly married couple were seen, scrutinized, criticized, and at least tentatively assimilated before the dog days set in.

Only the children, not the parents, in the Lyons upper class took advantage of the swimming dam in the Glen, where there was cool shade on the picnic ground. Nothing had come of the talk of building a private dam upstream, with a clubhouse in which people could change their clothes and cook supper. Lyons had a lawn tennis court, enclosed by a high fence of chicken-wire, and the key to the padlocked door was left in the office of the nearby lumber mill, where it could be picked up by any member of the Tennis Club, except when members forgot to leave the key and took it home with them; but the Tennis Club did not even have a shelter to protect the players from sudden downpours, and it was the only upper-class club in the town. Consequently the well-to-do had no place to swim or to sit together and complain of the heat.* The grounds of the Millhouser place were rich with trees: the walnuts, elms and spruce in the immediate vicinity of the house and on the sloping lawn; the apple orchard that lay between the flower garden and the north fence; random Seckel pear, cherry, horse-chestnut trees; and besides the trees, the grape arbor. The air stayed hot under the grapevines, but elsewhere on the property—in the well-culled orchard and the semi-grove—the temperature was always noticeably lower than in the town. The areas of shade gave relief to the eye, and even the stirring of the leaves in the high limbs of the walnuts and elms was a cool sound. But the heat of the dog days in Lyons was inescapable. The street dust was laid twice daily by the

* The Johnsville Country Club, which many Lyons citizens joined, was not organized until 1927. The clubhouse was erected in 1929.

289

borough water-sprinkler, and citizens who possessed garden hose would soak their roofs and yards and the brick sidewalks; the ice wagon, driven by Iceman-Constable Tommy Fenstermacher, was on the road from seven to seven; the two hotels and several saloons provided water troughs for the horses as well as beer and shade for the drivers, and other kindly citizens placed washtubs on the curbstones so that horses might drink. In every house in Lyons there was some cool liquid to offer the casual visitor, even if it was no more than a pail of water with a tin dipper; and there were saucepans of water for dogs, earthenware bowls for birds, saucers of rapidly souring milk for cats, tumblers of homemade root beer for children. At a time when no one was unaffected by the sun, nearly everyone had a thought for the comfort of other men and of the friendly beasts. The burning, parching heat made every effort twice as costly as usual, and yet every man's and woman's greeting to a friend or stranger was an offer to take shade or cooling drink or rest, or all three. Tempers were short and patience easily tried, and every man and woman was engaged in a private struggle with the glare, the heat, the thirst, the dust, and the debilitating effect on spirit and flesh; and in a few cases the struggle was that of a weakened will-to-live against actual suffocation. Nevertheless it was a time when men and women seemed to be eager to alleviate the distress of others, very nearly as eager in that concern as in their own interest.

It was the season for palm fans and eau de Cologne, short haircuts and fewer petticoats, linen suits and leghorns, fly nets and straw hats on horses, great umbrellas on delivery wagons, open cars on the trolley line, citronella and Hires mugs, Tanglefoot and cold cuts. Children had convulsions, the flag hung limp at borough hall, horses expired in harness, diarrhea was endemic, and a Lithuanian and a Pole settled it forever with daggers. The world ten miles away did not exist, and philosophy consisted of the wish to be able to remember this in January. And through all this walked Hedda Millhouser, crisp and cool in white dotted Swiss, something to see and to touch.

"I'd ask you to go with me," said Robert. "But the sleeping accommodations aren't the best, and the dust and the chaff get in your nose and your ears and your eyes and lungs. The farmers all wear bandannas over their mouths and noses, like highwaymen."

"Do you wear a bandanna?"

"Of course."

"Why do you go if it's so uncomfortable?"

"Why does your father watch his men at work? Just being there is a good idea. But I'll tell you another reason. You can estimate how many bushels of rye you're going to have after thrashing, and you won't be far wrong. But there are two farmers, if given the chance they'd steal. I know which ones they are. But if I only appeared when *they're* thrashing they'd know I was suspicious. I don't mind a few bushels of wheat, but I keep them honest in other things, just by being there."

"If they're dishonest why do you keep them?"

"Two dishonest farmers out of fifteen isn't so bad, and if the other farmers know that I'm keeping the dishonest ones from stealing, the others won't be tempted. And there's another consideration. Both these farmers have sons that so far haven't misbehaved. If the boys are honest they'll be given the chance to own the farms. I'm going to sell all the farms in the next few years, and put my money in common stocks. The farms are getting to be more trouble than they're worth, and if anything happens to me, you'll be better off with securities than with farm land."

"If anything happens to you? For instance?"

"For instance, if I die. Or if I become an invalid. At fifty-one I have to be prepared for anything."

"I wish you wouldn't say things like that."

"I wish I didn't have to, but those are the stern realities, Hedda."

"If you died I'd be all alone."

"Not for very long."

"I wouldn't know *what* to do."

"The natural thing would be for you to marry again."

"I wish you hadn't said anything about dying. You don't look as if you were going to die."

"Thank you. But in five years I'll look older and *be* older. And you'll be twenty-three, a beautiful young woman. In ten years you still won't be thirty."

"How old does a man have to be before he can't do anything with a woman?"

"Well, I've heard of some remarkable men that had children when they were seventy. On the other hand, I've known of men that lost interest in their forties."

"When does a woman stop?"

"Well, I suppose most of them stop having children at forty or thereabouts, but I'm told they still go on having pleasure."

"I know they do. My mother is over forty."

"Well, you'll stay young, too."

"You shouldn't have said anything about dying."

"Why not? Whatever time I have with you I treasure."

"You think I ought to be pleased because you say that, but I'm not."

"And why not?"

"Because I didn't marry you for a few years. I married you for life. But now how long is life going to be? You talking about five years and ten years. It's just as if you bought me or hired me, for five or ten years."

"As usual, you see things your own way, and as usual, you have a very good point. However, I seem to be in good physical condition, and from what I know of my family—my mother was seventy-five when she died, and my father was sixty-one. If I strike an average there—sixty-one and seventy-five. One thirty-six. Divided by two. Sixty-eight. I ought to be around for seventeen more years, Hedda. I'm not worried, so don't you be . . . What are you going to do while I'm away?"

"I don't know."

"You're very lucky not to mind the heat."

"I've lived in much hotter places than this. And I'm not fat."

"Neither am I, but I'm always glad when the dog days are over."

"If you'd been I wouldn't have married you. Some of those men we saw in Atlantic City. I'd never want a fat belly on top of me."

"You always come out with the frankest statements."

"Well, I wouldn't. A fat sweaty man pumping into me."

"I don't like the picture you paint, either. But I don't like you in that picture with a thin man, any more than I do a fat man. However, we're not settling what you're going to do while I'm away."

"What is there to settle?"

"Well, have you thought about meals? You could have your mother and father and your brother here."

"Not likely. I don't want to have her prying into my affairs."

"Then why not just ask your brother to stay here?"

"Maybe I will."

"You see, I go away about once a month. When I'm on a trip to Fort Penn, you can come along. Do you like vaudeville? We can always go to the Orpheum, the bill changes twice a week. And in the winter there are always things to see at the Fort Penn. Music, if you like opera. And concerts. I can plan my trips so that when there's going to be something worthwhile you and I can take in the opera, and concerts, and the New York plays. But they don't start till October, as a rule."

"I don't mind being alone. Nobody wants to do anything in this weather. You don't even see as many people on the street. Don't fuss over me, Robert."

"I don't mean to fuss. It's to my own selfish interest to have you un-bored."

292

"Well, if I get bored I'll go for a drive."

"That's a good idea. Moses can show you a lot of things about this country that I don't know."

"I didn't mean with Moses. I meant by myself."

"Oh. All right, if you promise me you'll stay on the main highways, and don't go into the woods alone. I mean out past the Glen. The road gets very rough and narrow, no place to turn around. The ruts are so deep you can break a carriage wheel, and not to alarm you, but it's no place for a woman by herself."

"Why? On account of those Indians?"

"I wasn't thinking of human beings. I was thinking of other creatures. Animals. I'm not exaggerating. If a wildcat attacked your horse —no, I'm going to put my foot down on that. No driving past the Glen. It's foolhardy. I wouldn't go into the woods by myself, even with a gun, and I've hunted in First and Second Valleys since I was a boy. Does that convince you?"

"I didn't say anything about going into the woods."

"Well, I did."

His tone caused her to look at him quickly and with quick anger, which he did not miss.

"Therefore," he said. "I must ask you to give me your word that you will not drive past the Glen."

She stared at him coldly and defiantly and said nothing.

"Now look here, Hedda. I could very easily tell Moses that the horses are not to go out while I'm gone. If you're going to behave like a child, that's the way I'll treat you."

"If you treat me like one, that's how I'll behave. I'm going up to bed, and you can stay in your own room."

She barely spoke to him the next day and the next, which was the day before his departure for the farms. In the evening after dinner he said: "I'm taking the early train, so I won't see you in the morning. Here is some money for household cash, and if you need any more, cash a cheque and I'll reimburse you. I'll be back Saturday afternoon. This is a list of the farms where I'll be spending the night, and the nearest telegraph stations. Is there anything you want to ask me?"

"Yes. What did you tell Moses?"

"I haven't said anything to Moses. Goodnight, Hedda. I'll see you next Saturday."

He went to bed, and at long last to sleep, with only the sheet to cover him. His first awareness was not so much of her as of himself and the lazy sensuality that she was creating in him, lying nude beside him in the blue light of the moon. "Are you awake now?" she said.

"Yes."

"You wouldn't come to me, so I came to you."

"Did you just come in?"

"No. I've been here."

"Long?"

"I don't know. I was making you dream about me."

"You did, too."

"I know."

"Maybe I'm still dreaming."

"You know better."

She left him after he went to sleep, and when Margaret knocked on his door he was rested and at peace with himself. He dressed and entered Hedda's room quietly. She was asleep, with her sheet twisted around her right leg. He straightened the sheet gently and placed it over her. "Thank you," she said, smiling, and turned her face back into the pillow and slept again.

Hedda Millhouser had planned the week. In the mornings she got a list from Theresa and Moses drove her to MacMahon's, Langendorf's and any other stores on Theresa's lists. In the afternoons she called on the women who had entertained for her, Mmes. Langendorf, Williams, MacMahon and Holland. Lars Steele came to dinner the first four nights of the week, and Ed Steele and Ruth on the fifth. She was proud of the report of her activities she would make to Robert, but it would not be complete. One incident would be kept out of the report.

On the Thursday evening her brother went home as soon as he finished dinner, and Hedda went to her room and put on a nightgown and dressing gown. "You're wanted on the telephone," Margaret called out from the hall.

"Which one?"

"The Keystone."

The Keystone instrument was in the little room on the first floor. "It's a man, but not Mr. Robert," said Margaret.

"My father, I guess . . . Hello?"

"Where's that husband of yours?" said the man.

"Who is this? Lars, is this you?"

"Oh, you have a friend named Lars? Well, that sounds promising."

"Who is this, please? If you don't tell me who you are I'm going to hang up the receiver."

Margaret was plodding along as slowly as possible toward the kitchen.

"This is an old friend of yours. In fact, we took a train ride together."

"I don't recognize your voice," said Hedda Millhouser, and she

294

heard the swinging door between the diningroom and kitchen going back and forth.

"Then you must take a lot of train rides."

"Oh, cut the comedy, will you please, or I'm going to hang up the receiver."

"It's Bart Vance."

"Oh. Well, Robert's away. He'll be home Saturday."

"I know. Wouldn't you like to go for a drive, cool off? I'm sure Robert won't object to your going for a drive with an old friend. Not that I'd give a damn whether he would or not."

"Mr. Vance, you sound slightly intoxicated."

"I am slightly intoxicated, with the wife of my old friend Robert Millhouser, my very old friend. Too old, if you ask me."

"I have nothing more to say to you, Mr. Vance. So I'm going to ring off."

"Wait, just a second, Hedda. If you can't tonight, how about tomorrow night?"

"Not tomorrow night or any other night, thank you."

"I've got something the girls seem to like, and I'll bet you would too. I've got my hand on it right now, Hedda. Can you guess what it is?"

She hung up the receiver, turned the crank, and went to her room. She was infuriated by his treachery and his arrogant confidence in her silence. He knew she would say nothing to Robert, but he knew it was not to spare Robert. She loathed him for knowing that what he had said to her was exactly what she expected from those lips. And some day he might say the same kind of thing at precisely the right moment. This time he had been wrong by less than a week.

She had three letters from Robert, which came on Thursday, Friday, and Saturday, after Monday, Tuesday, and Wednesday on which she could not hear from him. Thus on the days when he could express himself to her, she was hearing nothing; on the days when she could read his letters, he was unable to say anything to her. For him it was all silence; it had not occurred to her to write him a letter. She had never written a love letter to anyone.

She was at the depot when his train arrived on Saturday at noon. She sat in the trap, which had a square umbrella, and she was shocked at his appearance. He wore clothes well and it was not the wrinkled suit and soot-speckled Panama, but the weariness in his eyes and drawn-down set of his mouth that she saw with alarm. He nodded and greeted several acquaintances on the way to the trap, but she knew before he spoke that he was exhausted. He kissed her. "I missed you, did you miss me?" he said.

"I missed you a lot," she said. "Do you want to drive?"

"Much rather you did," he said. "Has it been this bad all week?"

"At this time of the day, yes," she said.

"You look good, you smell good, and it feels good to be this close to you."

"And I've been good. Wait till you hear all the things I've been doing." She told him about her party-calls and her marketing, and was still telling him when they reached the stable.

"Hello, Moses. Anything new?"

"Only news I got, we better pray the Lord we get some rain pretty soon."

"We had a shower down-country on Thursday, but it didn't last very long. We went right on with the thrashing."

"Some barn gonna get hit by lightning and *it* aint gonna catch fire. It gonna explode."

"Yes, just when the farmer's got all his grain in. Anything else new?"

"Yessir." Moses looked at Hedda Millhouser. "I want gonna tell this before you come home. Thursday night, night before last. A white man prowlin'. I chased him away."

"When? Were you here Thursday night?"

"I slept in the stable every night you was away."

"Good for you, Moses. You see, Hedda, you were protected all the time."

"Thank you, Moses. I'd have felt better if I'd known that. Not that I was scared," said Hedda Millhouser.

"I'd have felt better, too," said Robert.

"Dog days, no tellin' how people gonna act, so I told Cora I sleep in this stable till you come home."

"Did you know the man?"

Moses hesitated. "No, I didn't rightly know him. I know him did I see him again, but not f'm before."

"What did you do?" said Hedda Millhouser.

"I come up behind him and I said, 'Man, you get off this property or I hit you over the head with this here club.' And I gave him a little push to get him started and away he went."

"Good for you. Did he run?"

"He run as good as he could run. He run like he was intoxicated. He smell like it, too."

"Well, Hedda, an adventure, even if you didn't know it."

"I'm glad Moses was here," she said. "Come on, you get a bath and a nice cool glass of iced tea."

"And a nap, if you don't mind."

The heat was broken that night by a storm that lasted three hours, starting while Robert and Hedda Millhouser were at supper. "This storm's coming from the east," said Robert. "Usually after a hot spell we get our storms from the southwest."

"What's the difference?"

"Wind. A storm like this has more wind behind it. Listen to it."

"I love it."

"You do? So do I. But some people are going to church tomorrow and be surprised when there's no steeple."

"Here? In Lyons?"

"Here, maybe. Somewhere in the Valley. And it's going to raise the devil with the trees. Tomorrow there'll be branches all over the place. Only branches, I hope."

"Why only branches?"

"Well, when it's been so dry for so long a wind like this can pull a tree over. Not to mention the lightning. Do you realize that in all my life we've only had one tree struck by lightning? I'm glad you like storms. 'Lo, the poor Indian! whose untutored mind/ Sees God in clouds, or hears him in the wind.' Did your tutors teach you to rhyme wind with mind?"

"My tutors? How did you know I had tutors?"

"I didn't. I was just speaking elegantly. Tutors instead of teachers."

"I had tutors galore. I was always behind in something. Oh, now what was that?"

"Let's go see," said Robert. A heavy object had struck the house. She put on his canvas hunting jacket and a fedora hat; he put on a cap and a mackintosh. "What about boots?"

"I'll go barefoot."

"All right. Out we go." They stood on the porch in darkness that was brightened only by flashes of lightning. "We'll never know what it was. It could have been any of those branches. Didn't it seem to you to hit the side of the house?"

"There, or the roof of the porch. It was something heavy."

"A limb from one of the trees, more than likely. Shall we go down and talk to the horses?"

"Can you find the stable?"

"Blindfolded. But you hold on to me or you'll blow away. On second thought, you'd better put something on your feet. My arctics."

"All right."

"Otherwise you'll surely cut your feet."

She went back inside and came out wearing his arctics, and they ran to the stable, where he switched on the light. The mare whinnied, and Robert spoke reassuringly.

"Let's stay here all night?" said Hedda Millhouser, clinging to Robert's arm.

"I know exactly how you feel. It's much snugger here than in the house. I guess it's because you feel that something *could* happen here, more so than in the house. I used to love to come here when I was a boy. Moses had a stove, and as a matter of fact Ryan had the stove first. The coachman before Moses. I know the house was warmer, but it always seemed warmer here. Cozy. The icicles would be hanging down outside the window, but in here we were very comfortable. Ryan letting me do his work, sponging the harness with harness oil. Moses used to make soup, and nothing I ever ate at home tasted as good as Moses' soup. On Saturdays I'd often spend the whole day down here. If my father hadn't left me some money I'd have ended up as a coachman."

"And I'd be the rich girl that came to see you."

"Would you? How nice. And what would you do?"

"Make you want me."

"Even if I were only the coachman?"

"If I liked you. I . . ."

"What?"

"Nothing."

"But you *were* going to say something."

"No I wasn't."

"Well, shall we go back?"

"Let's stay here a while. Pretend you are the coachman."

"And you're the rich little girl?"

"Yes. You sit over there, on that box."

"That's a bin."

"Now lie down as if you were taking a nap."

"All right. Now what?"

"Close your eyes. Pretend you're asleep, and you don't hear me."

He obeyed her, and then she went to his side and put her hand on his belly, moving her hand downward in circles of decreasing size. He opened his eyes and looked at her and saw that she was smiling, but she was not looking at his face. Then the smile left her face and she reached inside and held him roughly. "You do it to me, too," she said.

"Lie down," he said. "Get on the bin."

"I don't want to," she said. "Your hand, damn you."

He did as she asked and then she let him go and held his head with both her hands and covered his face with kisses; his mouth, his eyes, his cheeks. "Oh, how lovely," she said.

He put his arms about her waist. He gently sat her beside him. "What is it, Hedda?"

"Oh, just how lovely."

"Is that what you'd rather do?"

"No, no, no, no. But I wanted that now."

"Because I was the coachman?"

"Yes. *Because you were the coachman?* What do you mean?"

"I'm not sure."

"Then don't say things if you're not sure what they mean. Aren't you my husband? Can't we do anything we want?"

"Yes."

"Well, you don't always want everything the same way. So I don't have to either."

"Will you have a cigarette?"

"No. Let's go back to the house."

He switched off the light and they went out, but she did not wait for him. Guided by the lights in the house she strode through the dark and rain, and although he called to her she kept on.

In the hall she took off his arctics and jacket and hat and hung them in the closet. "I'm going to bed," she said. "Goodnight."

"Aren't you going to kiss me goodnight?" he said.

She turned her cheek and *he* kissed *her,* and she left him.

In the autumn they went frequently to Fort Penn, more frequently than was strictly necessary for his business trips. Ben Rosebery and Esther Baumgarten Parkinson had parties for them that in turn led to more invitations than they could accept. "I never expected Fort Penn to be like this," said Hedda Millhouser.

"I told you. It's the capital, and the State is as big as some kingdoms. Would you like to live there?"

"No, not yet. Maybe some day."

"I'm glad to hear that, for one reason."

"What reason?"

"Well, if we ever have a child, I'd like it to be born in our house, in Lyons."

"Why?"

"Sentiment. I was born there, my mother and father died there, and I'd like it to be the home of three generations of Millhousers. My father built it for himself and my mother."

"But we're not going to have any children for a while."

"No, but some day. You decide, but we can't wait forever, remember," he said. "By that time I'll have got rid of the farms and—"

"And you can sell our house."

"No. I'll never sell our house. Not as long as I can pay the taxes. Even if I don't rent it, I want to keep it. I could never sell that house, Hedda, or anything in it. If we *should* move to Fort Penn, and I don't find the right people to rent it, I'll close it up tight. The taxes aren't much, and even if it's an extravagance it's worth it to me. It's like buying a lot in a cemetery." He frowned. "Now why did I say a thing like that? It isn't at all like buying a lot in a cemetery."

"It must have been, or you wouldn't have said it. You always think things out so carefully. You're so percise."

"Pre-cise," he said.

"It's like buying a lot in a cemetery, the place you'll finally go to. I know you think of the house that way, but I don't."

"Don't you? How do you think of it?"

"I think of it as our house, where we live now, but we don't have to live there forever, so we probably won't."

"I thought you'd gotten to like it."

"I do. I like it better than any other house I've ever lived in. But it isn't only the house. It's Lyons. I have so much time when I have nothing to do."

"But two minutes ago you didn't want to live in Fort Penn."

"I said I didn't want to move there now. But I said *some* day. Maybe next year."

He smiled. "Ah, you see. Some day, to me, means in the distant future. To you it means next year, because I keep forgetting that at your age next year is the distant future. Do you feel that you've known me a long time?"

"I have. Over a year."

He nodded. "And to me, we met the day before yesterday. As we grow older the time goes so fast, so unbelievably fast. You'll never know the happiness I've had with you. A young person couldn't know. I think the young are terribly unhappy. I was. And then I got older and had a sort of semi-happiness that you get in middle age, when life itself begins to be precious. And then you came into my life and I could love someone, and that made the semi-happiness a new, complete happiness."

"Robert."

"Yes, dear."

"When you go on like this, are you talking to me, or to yourself? You say these things to me. I'm here, and I'm listening. But your voice has a different sound than when you're really talking to me. And you don't look at me, either."

He thought a moment. "I guess I am talking to myself. But I'm speaking my thoughts, that I want you to hear."

"Well, I don't always follow you."

"There's a reason for that. The reason is, you are the only person

300

in my whole life that has ever heard my thoughts, as they come to me. In all these years I've never opened up to anyone."

"Well, that's all right as long as you don't expect me to understand everything."

"I don't, Hedda. In fact I have a lot of mysteries that I don't understand myself. Some day—not next year, but what *I* mean by some day—maybe we'll have been together for so long, so closely, that we'll understand each other without words, the way some husbands and wives do. The way I'm sure my father and mother understood each other."

"Well, that will be a lot easier than trying to fathom some of the things you say now. They're too deep for me."

"There's nothing too deep for you. But you're young."

"I know I am, and I don't want to be anything else. I like to be young. I just don't especially like other young people. But that's not saying I want to look old, or get tired so easily."

"All you want is everything."

"Well, yes, of course. So do you. If you could have been happy when you were young, you wouldn't have said, 'No, I don't want to be happy till I'm fifty-one years old.' If you told me that I wouldn't believe you."

"And I'd be a damn liar. All that being older teaches you is the value of compromise."

"That word. We had it in American history. The Missouri Compromise. And if a girl is compromised the man is supposed to marry her. I'd rather talk about what kind of a house we'd live in if we moved to Fort Penn."

"All right. Let's talk about it."

"Are you sure you'd rather? I'll talk about the other stuff, or at least I'll listen to you, but I won't understand half of it."

"The half you understand you understand much better than I understand any of it."

"Now that's what I mean, Robert. Remarks like that."

In January, 1907, Robert received a letter from Fred Langendorf, informing him that the annual meeting of the bank stockholders would take place at two o'clock on a certain Thursday afternoon. Robert made note of the time and the date; he already knew that the place would be, as always, the directors' room on the second floor of the bank building. When he appeared for the meeting all the other directors were seated. "I beg your pardon," said Robert. He looked at his watch and at the wall clock. "Fred, didn't you tell me two o'clock? It's ten minutes of."

"You're not late," said Langendorf. "We were early. Have a seat."

"Well, I will if you'll get up and give me my chair."

"I have," said Langendorf. "There's your chair." He pointed to the place where he had always sat. The others began to laugh.

"You're up to something, Fred. What is it? Come on, now."

"I'll let Jerry tell you," said Langendorf. "Jerry?"

"I don't know why I should be the one," said Jeremiah MacMahon. "It's your place to tell him."

"Hear, hear," said the others.

"All right, then," said Langendorf. "Robert, we here in this room, we all know that you've always refused to take any part in politics. Darn it, I'm starting out wrong. What I should have said first was that we've been saying for some time that it was high time we showed Robert Millhouser what we thought of him. But you'd never run for public office, so we couldn't vote for you there. And just about the only way we could show you our appreciation for what you've done in this town, we met here at one o'clock, and unanimously voted to elect you president of this bank. So here is this gavel, signifying your election. And if you'll read what it says on this silver band, here—well, here's the gavel, Robert, and there's your new seat. So I guess that's all I got to say." He handed the gavel to Robert, who looked at it and then at Fred Langendorf, and clasped Fred's hand as the others applauded and got to their feet.

Robert went to his new position at the table. He remained on his feet, but he could not speak.

"Like to borrow my handkerchief?" said Billy Williams.

Everyone, including Robert, laughed. "Yes, damn it, I would," said Robert. His voice quavered. He looked at each of the directors in turn and he saw that some of them, like him, had tears in their eyes. "Well, I'd better say something, quick, or I'll make a spectacle of myself. And I don't want to have to borrow Billy's handkerchief, because everybody knows that Billy uses those blue ones that the miners use, and the dye will come off." There was some laughter at this.

"Not true," said Billy Williams. "I buy my handkerchiefs at the company store. Good fast dye."

"Well—what *can* I say? I thought it a bit strange that the annual meeting this year was for two o'clock instead of one. Now I see why. And this gavel—obviously you must have had it marked before you voted for me. And it wasn't unanimous, Fred. I still have all my stock in this fine institution, and I didn't vote."

"George Holliday voted your stock," said Langendorf. "We had to stretch a point. George doesn't have power of attorney, but he is your attorney."

"Then I guess the record will show that I was immodest enough to vote for myself."

"The vote was unanimous by those present, constituting a quorum. And there were no nays, proxy or otherwise," said George Holliday.

"Well, frankly, I'm not going to protest, and I'm certainly delighted to accept this honor, as you good friends knew I would be. I don't want to say too much about my lack of qualifications. I'd like to have this honor for a year, anyway. As you know, my father was one of the founders of our bank, which makes this a great source of pride for me. We have the oldest charter in the Valley, and the bank has always stood for fair and decent dealings with the people of the Valley, whether or not they were customers of ours. And in that connection, I want to say what a particular honor it is to accept this gavel from Fred Langendorf. We all know that Fred has given nearly as much time and devotion to this bank as he has to his own business."

"If he hadn't given so much time to the bank I'd have never caught up with him," said Jeremiah MacMahon. "Three cheers for the bank."

"Well, now I'm glad you interrupted, Jerry," said Robert. "Because here we have you two, you and Fred, rivals in business, but setting an example that the whole business world could well copy. And it typifies what I said a moment ago about fair dealings with the people of the Valley, and ethical principles among ourselves. It's my hope and my intention to copy Fred's conduct of the affairs of our bank, and as long as I do that, and counting on Fred's help and advice, the bank will continue usefully and profitably. In fact, I am going to start right off by copying Fred. I'm not going to use this gavel. I'm going to take it home with me, and instead of using it to rap for order, I'll do what Fred always does. Knuckles on the table. That was all that Fred needed, and I'll always treasure this symbol."

"Read the engraving," said someone.

"Oh, excuse me. I overlooked that detail. 'To Robert Millhouser, president, Lyons Bank & Trust Company, 1907, in appreciation of his services to the bank and to the community.' " He looked up and said: "I don't know what I ever did for the community, but I'll at least try to earn those last three words. As to my services to the bank, one of the proudest moments of my life was when our beloved friend Dr. Willetts told me I'd been made a director, and I've never ceased to be proud of it. My good friends, thank you."

He sat down, and the others again applauded.

303

"Mr. President?"

"Chair recognizes Mr. Williams," said Robert. "We're not going to do that all the time, I hope. But today is all right."

"I move that a committee be appointed to arrange a dinner in honor of the new president, such dinner to be held in a place where liquid refreshments can be served and the proper toasts made. The only damn trouble with this meeting today, we can't let the people find out that we had booze here on the bank premises."

"The chair has a better idea. Let me give the dinner at my house, but in honor of the retiring president."

"Have you got enough dishes? We're going to have to have the wives," said Williams.

"Well, we may not all eat off the same set, but we can manage," said Robert.

"All right. This way, your way, it won't cost the bank any money," said Williams.

Hedda Millhouser's appreciation of the honor bestowed on her husband was limited by her knowledge of the functions of a bank: it was a place where people saved their money, cashed cheques, and stored jewelry. She understood the reason for the burglar-proof vault, but she did not understand why so many of the most important men in Lyons had to bother themselves with chores that could have been performed by honest clerks and honest watchmen. But Robert's pleasure and pride indicated that he considered the election a high honor, and she noticed that he had less enthusiasm for the prospect of living in Fort Penn. Her intelligence did not fail to relate the lessened enthusiasm to the recent honor, and after the first days of genuine effort to appreciate what she did not understand, she began to think of the bank as a threat to the move to Fort Penn, as an enormously heavy anchor that she had not dropped. Consequently as hostess to the Langendorf dinner party she was not at her best, and when the last guest had gone home she immediately retired to her room.

Robert knocked on the door and she told him to come in.

"Why did you knock?" she said. "You never knock."

"I wasn't sure you'd be awake. I expected you to be sound asleep."

She was sitting in a nightgown, a cigarette burning as she brushed her hair. She was quite awake, gazing at herself in the triple mirrors of her dressing-table. "Why did you expect me to be sound asleep?"

"Because you were so weary all evening, and you were so much in a hurry to go upstairs."

304

"Sometimes I'm in a hurry to go upstairs because I can hardly wait to get naked for you."

"I don't think that's the case tonight."

"No, it isn't."

"All right, Hedda, what the hell's the matter?"

"Everybody here tonight talked as if you were going to be president of the bank till 1920!"

"Everybody but me. I only wanted it for one year. Three, at the most. There are some things I'd like to do that will take more than one year, but when they're finished I'd like someone else to have the job."

"Three years!" she said. "I think I'll have a bath after all." She got up and started the water, and when she returned to the bedroom she had taken off her nightgown, but continued to brush her hair. She took another drag on her cigarette before putting it out, and she kept moving about the room, continually in motion, finding things to do and doing them slowly, picking up stockings, hanging up lingerie, inviting inspection of her body while pretending to be ignoring his presence. Once she stopped in front of the mirror and stood with her shoulders back, looking at herself and pressing a hand to each breast.

"What are you trying to do?" he said.

"Seeing if my bust isn't getting bigger."

"Very interesting. What else are you trying to do?"

"I'm not trying to do anything. Can't I walk around this way if I feel like it? I'm getting ready to take a bath."

"You never walk around this way unless we're going to make love, and you have no intention of that."

"No, I have no intention of that."

"Then why are you showing off your body—"

"If you don't like to look at it, go to your own room. I didn't ask you to stay. I didn't even ask you here."

"Let me finish. Why are you flaunting your body at me. There's some reason for this, and I think it's insulting."

She suddenly stopped walking and faced him, with her feet far apart and her hands at her sides. "You'd better do what I want or I won't let you play with me," she said.

He got up and walked out of the room, and as he closed the door something that sounded like a china dish was smashed against the inside, and she called out in anger but he could not understand the words. He left his own door slightly ajar, and he heard more noise of breaking china, and then silence. He went back to her room, and she was lying on the bed, weeping, but he continued through to her bathroom, where the tub was overflowing. He opened the stopper to drain the tub, and returned to his room. He undressed and got into bed and turned out the light. In a little while she came in and lay beside him. Neither of them spoke, but she made love to him in ways that he had never experienced or seen, but that had been described for him by Ben Rosebery in bygone years. In the midst of such intimacy and controlled passion he had a sense of participation in an impersonal act, and yet she seemed to be showing him how bad and how generous she could be, and he chose to believe momentarily that she was asking forgiveness. But if that was the case, and she was surrendering, he knew that the humility, the docility, would not last. Even while she was inspiring pleasure in him and enjoying the power of creating it in herself, he doubted that love was her incentive or very much a part of the event. She went back to her room, unseen by him and without speaking to him, and left him to ponder the degree and incidence of hatred, humility, erotic hunger, inverted revenge, and threatened possessiveness that had sent her to his bed. Plainly, the postponement of Fort Penn had been on her mind earlier, but he was less concerned over that as a problem than in the motive behind her calculated efficiency as a woman giving pleasure to a man. Long after she left him the answer came to him: intentionally or not, she had given him a warning. The night's display, until now withheld and only released in anger, never in moments of love, was never meant by her to be part of love, but was intended to frighten him with what she could offer another man, equally without love. He, Robert, was any man.

Curiously, when he had satisfied himself that he had discovered her motive, he accepted her warning as though it had been a message wrapped in a snakeskin. Curiously, too, he regarded her warning as a fair and honorable gesture. If she was capable of all that she had shown him tonight, she had her special rights as an accomplished woman, separate from her rights and duties as his wife. At least she had never pretended not to be what she had been tonight. Moreover, in arriving at the fair judgment of her, he was entirely honest toward himself: she was what he wanted, for however long she would belong to him. Beyond that, he would not speculate.

Hedda Millhouser now had a campaign, a personal cause, which she had not had in the first six months of their marriage. Wanting everything was wanting nothing, but now her ambition was to move to Fort Penn. What she had seen of it made it seem like a miniature Paris (where she had never been). The substantial capitol and the other Commonwealth buildings; the wide, tree-lined residen-

306

tial streets; the shops, where she was called madam; the hotels, busy and ornate, and with music always in the background; the bridle path along the river front; the quite numerous automobiles; the fashionable confectioner, Yaissle's, where the prettiest women stopped for an ice cream soda in the late morning, and for tea in the afternoon; the many men in silk hats (in 1907 the only silk hats in Lyons were worn by the undertakers and, during the Christmas holidays, by Robert and a very few other men at the Assembly); the colored butlers in knee breeches; and the sordid atmosphere of the railway stations—Fort Penn was a city. And it was a city that could be hers, as Quebec City and Mexico City, Denver and Milwaukee had not been hers. Those men in silk hats flirted with her, and those pretty women at Yaissle's treated her with none of the condescension that the dowdy women of Lyons displayed toward her youth. She was sure that when she was ready to move, Fort Penn would be ready to receive her. She had noticed that at Fort Penn parties Robert and the most attractive men commingled, and that they and Robert eventually stood apart from the others. She was, in fact, more impressed by her husband in Fort Penn society than in Lyons, where he was merely unique. Under the same conditions her own father would have been compatible with the most attractive men, but more comfortable with the others. It was funny, she thought, that her father, who wanted to get away from Lyons, really belonged there; while Robert, who loved Lyons, more suitably belonged in Fort Penn. And in considering her mother as an imaginary resident of Fort Penn, Hedda found that she was passing the same judgment on Ruth Steele that the pretty women at Yaissle's would pass: respectable, good-looking, but uncongenial. Hedda already saw herself as a member of the Yaissle set; there had been mutually understanding looks between her and one or two of its members. She had missed one phase of her growth, largely by choice, but she was determined to get all she could out of young wifehood, and the maximum opportunities were not available in Lyons.

She had an ally in Ben Rosebery, the licentious man who completely misjudged her. Ben's infirmities had curtailed most of his nighttime activities and had paradoxically brought on a mellowness to replace the working cynicism by which he had always lived. He was protective of Hedda, convinced of her innocence, careful of his language in front of her, and had actually suggested that she call him Uncle Ben. She, on the other hand, saw him for exactly what he was, or had been, and found him amusing company. She refused to call him Uncle Ben, and he was flattered by her refusal: "I don't want you for a relation, I want you for a friend," she told him. As a friend he fell in with her campaign to persuade Robert to move to Fort Penn, and as a lawyer with a good memory he reminded Esther Baumgarten Parkinson of her own, long past reluctance to live in Lyons. "We must get them out of that dump," he told Esther. "It's going to make Robert old before his time, and little Hedda is wasted there."

Esther, who was generally without guile, was not in complete agreement with her cousin's opinion of Hedda, but since she had no reason to be suspicious, she saw to it that Hedda Millhouser met the right people under the right conditions. Esther was grateful to Robert Millhouser for her own happiness, that would not have come into being if Robert had been a more effectual lover, and her gratitude took the form of a sisterly affection for him. Hedda Millhouser partook of the advantages of this relationship; and Harold Parkinson, who was a handsome, heavy man of forty-five, was so engrossed in his surgical practice that he was under the impression that Robert Millhouser had always lived in Fort Penn. (He was so uncurious about extraneous matters that he had never taken the trouble to inquire into his own possible connection with James Parkinson, 1755-1824.) Esther had a daughter only three years younger than Hedda Millhouser, two smaller daughters and a small son, but her children were at Miss Holbrook's and Esther easily managed to find time for her social life. This fell into two categories: hospital and charity work that was directly helpful to her husband's career, in the course of which she entertained and was entertained by many women whom she would not ordinarily have seen; and the parties she gave and attended at which she saw people she had known all her life. And her secure position in the second category inevitably made her presence a more valuable contribution to the first. She was a capable administrator and a skillful snob, able to outmaneuver the social climbers who were always (at first) deceived by her quiet friendliness, which they took for simplicity, that it was, and stupidity, that it was not. The Sunday at-homes of her girlhood had been good training. Esther Parkinson, as a matter of fact, was often called the nicest woman in Fort Penn.

As the 1906-1907 winter season passed, socially and meteorologically, Robert and Hedda Millhouser became a more familiar unit as a married couple. Either one alone was always asked about the other, and seen together they were no longer stared at on the streets of Lyons and the Fort Penn trains. Their more frequent appearances in Fort Penn society had likewise accustomed men and women of the capital to the bright young beauty and her attentive older husband. Fort Penn was ruled by conservative thought, but as the capital its social life was more active than that of cities of comparable size, and this produced a social manner that would have been more usually encountered in much larger cities. It was a worldly manner, and part of it was to show no middle-class, small-town surprise at such phenomena as May-December marriages. There was, after all, ample precedent for such marriages at home and abroad; and indeed it was recalled—as usual, inaccurately—that Robert Millhouser had spent a great deal of time as an expatriate in his youth. As the semifact was recalled and repeated, Robert took on some of the aura of a man who had lived to the full before settling down; and there were even those with long memories who now looked back on his brief romance with Esther Parkinson as a rather cold, if happily unsuccessful, attempt at seduction, nipped in the bud by the timely intervention of crafty Karl Baumgarten and his wife. But obviously Esther had forgiven him, and there was no doubting that he was devoted to the young creature whom he had finally married. Robert gained some good will among the husbands by making it possible, and respectable, to chat with and dance with a lovely young woman who was quick at give-and-take and who did not wax indignant over every little thing. Only a chronically jealous woman would risk saying what some of the others thought, and have her husband retort that Hedda Millhouser's youth and beauty were not a crime but that envy and suspicion were. The wives, jealous and not very jealous alike, were insatiably curious about Robert, and almost without exception they would begin by expressions of admiration for Hedda's beauty and continue to the questions relating to his meeting with her and their courtship and marriage. But when that was told, the other questions remained unasked and unaskable, except for the question that could have only one possible answer: "You're very much in love with her, aren't you?"—for which there was a variant statement: "Anyone can see you're very much in love with her." From such inquiries the wives could draw the conclusion that Robert and Hedda Millhouser had sexual intercourse, but the only satisfactory aspect of the inquiries was that the wives could base their inferences on conversation with Robert. This was somewhat better than making the same inference from a chair across the ballroom.

Robert enjoyed the parties and he did nothing to discourage Hedda from enjoyment of them. But the train rides to and from Fort Penn were a precisely mixed pleasure: Robert enjoyed the ride home, Hedda enjoyed the ride to Fort Penn.

The election of Robert to the bank presidency was more than a routine event in the life of the town. Fred Langendorf had been president of the bank for so many years that the citizens assumed he had life tenure, and Robert's election was widely discussed and his stature in the town had a sudden growth similar to the occasion of his election to the Fair board. But the bank presidency was the highest honor in Lyons. The office of chief burgess was lowly in comparison, since the chief burgesses were always active politicians; and Billy Williams's superintendency of the Big Company's holdings was not a position that the Lyons citizens controlled. Consequently Robert Millhouser, selected by the most important men for the most important honor in the Valley, was suddenly transformed from one of several rich men to the rich men's leader. The implications were not lost on the citizens.

For both men and women the election was the stamp of approval of Robert's marriage, as surely so as if the bank directors had come out and said so. The directors, of course, were fully aware of that implication; it had been discussed in the informal meetings that led to Robert's election. Fred Langendorf was now an old man and it had been known for some time that he wanted to resign the presidency in favor of Jerry MacMahon, who was in his early sixties, in good health, and expanding his business interests. But Jerry, in conversations with Langendorf, refused to be considered. There was strong anti-Catholic feeling in the Valley, and such posts as the bank presidency, superintendency of the various collieries, the higher divisional jobs on the railways, presidency of the Fair, judgeships, and state senatorships belonged to the Masons. Ed Steele, coming in from the outside to do the reconstruction work at the Outerbridge collieries, would have been unacceptable if he had not been a Mason. Lower in the business and social scale were organizations such as the "P. O.'s" and Junior Mechanics (Patriotic Order Sons of America and Junior Order United American Mechanics) in which anti-Catholicism was almost the sole *raison d'être;* and while there were not many men of such organizations who were admitted to the Masons, there were many P. O.'s and Junior Mechanics who held membership in the Blue Ribboners. "Electing me could be the ruination of the bank," said Jerry MacMahon. "But thanks anyway, Fred. Robert Millhouser's your man."

"He's not a Mason."

"No, but he's a Protestant, and it's getting to be an old Lyons name."

"I thought of him."

"I'm sure you did. And I can tell from the way you say it what's on your mind."

"Well, Jerry, if you know what's on my mind, what's *your* opinion?"

"That a man's better off married than not. St. Paul said it's better to marry than to burn. She's very young, and she'll take a bit of handling, but in the long run—they'll be having a family before long. Robert's your man. Always interested in the bank, and has enough time to spare."

"We'll see what the others think."

"Fred, they'll think what you and I want them to think. It's a long time since any of them stood up against you and I."

"Jerry, it's a long time since *I* stood up against *you*."

The election of Jeremiah MacMahon would have been the only possible action of the bank that would have been badly received by the citizens; the announcement of Robert Millhouser's election had the effect of a *fiat*. Discussion was permissible, but there was no protest. The Masons still had their majority on the board, and Robert Millhouser was safely Protestant; and as to the Millhouser marriage, it was no longer startling. In any case, the bank directorate was too formidable, collectively and individually, for the organization of resistance, and rather than engage in any futile criticism of the election, the citizens made the best of it.

Actually there were several beneficial effects. On the practical side, Fred Langendorf's resignation was overdue. Robert Millhouser was not expected to be less conservative than Langendorf, but there were innovations within the limits of conservative banking practice that Langendorf had opposed for no other reason than that they were innovations. Lyons was a payroll town, where of necessity nearly all business transactions were based on credit, from the purchase of a spool of thread to the freight bills of the coal companies. As a result the bank, under Fred Langendorf, carried small checking accounts of only a few privileged persons. But Lyons was also a thrifty town, and Robert Millhouser had argued that it would be good policy to relax the bank rules governing such accounts, on his theory that a man who kept $20 in the bank instead of in the family Bible was likely to become a time depositor as well as a demand depositor, and the establishment of this relationship was worth the nuisance of the checking account. The three leading authorities on the citizens' credit were on the bank board: Fred Langendorf and Jeremiah MacMahon, as merchants, and Billy Williams as an ex-officio director of the company store. The bank was thereby protected against the bad credit risks who would be abusers of the checking privilege. Robert's goal for years had been the fantastic ambition to have a bank depositor in every home in the Valley, and Fred Langendorf had once lost his temper on that subject. But Robert's argument was that as the Valley prospered, a second bank in Lyons was almost inevitable, and it was cheaper to fight such competition with the citizens' own money, now, in the form of small accounts, than later when the second bank was organized. Fred Langendorf, whose fortune had been built on small accounts, preferred to carry no small checking accounts at all, and he made it difficult for those who wished to open them. This, he knew, would change under Robert Millhouser's presidency, but at least he was prepared to be proven wrong so long as the innovations were not adopted under his administration. And when he stepped down, he did so graciously.

The beneficial effect on Robert was obvious, and for a time the vote of confidence gave him some hope that he could be as deliberately persuasive with Hedda as he had unconsciously been with the bank people. But she never appreciated the significance of the presidency, either in what it meant to Robert or to his standing in the town. She considered it a good mark on his report card, and said as much. "Why do you take on so about being president of a Lyons bank? My mother said you can buy and sell most everybody in town."

"Very flattering, but not true. I could never have bought this. Some of the bank stock has been held for three generations in one family. As far as selling them—they aren't people I'd want to sell."

"No? Well, I'd *give* them away, most of them."

He abandoned his attempts to show her that the election amounted to an approval of their marriage. "I didn't ask them for their approval, and I hope you didn't," she said. "Did you?"

"Certainly not," he said. "But it's a nice thing to have, and it couldn't be bought, either."

"It makes me mad to think you care so much what they think."

"I suppose it would," he said. "But it would have made you madder if they hadn't approved."

"Oh, would it? Well, they didn't approve, and they don't now, no matter what they elect you to. All they did was say they're not holding it against you."

He knew immediately that she was right, as she so often was. She, in turn, knew that she had uttered a telling truth, and she quickly followed it up. "You think you have to stay," she said. "I say that this is the best time to leave. You'll never be higher in their estimation, so let's move now."

"No," he said. "We're staying two more years."

"Will you promise me that on the first of January, 1909, we'll leave Lyons?"

"I can't promise you that."

"What *will* you promise me?"

"Under this kind of pressure, nothing."

"I knew it! You have no intention of moving."

"I have every intention of moving, but I have no intention of submitting to the command of a nineteen-year-old girl."

"Oh, is that so? There's one command you'll submit to. You can stay in your own damn room."

He laughed. "I may not even submit to that."

"Take my advice. Don't ever force yourself on me."

"I don't need your advice for that, Hedda."

He resumed his more frequent visits to the farms with the coming of spring. They had several quarrels and passionate reconciliations, but he noticed that the quarrels seemed to take place in Lyons and the reconciliations in Fort Penn, where he would meet her on his return from visits to the farms. There was one occasion when this sequence was varied: they had been to a party in Fort Penn, not on the best of terms, and had reconciled in the night, and on the next day he departed for the farms. She took the afternoon train alone back to Lyons and was seated in the coach, with the train under way, at peace with Robert and with the world.

"What luck!"

She looked up and saw Bart Vance.

"You're by yourself," he said.

"And I'd rather stay that way," she said.

"Will you let me apologize? At least you'll let me try to do that much."

"An apology isn't going to make up for the things you said."

"I agree with you. And even if I was slightly intoxicated, whatever I said I must have meant. *In vino veritas,* they say. Did you study Latin?"

"Yes, I know what that means. But please don't sit down."

"I want to sit down, and you're too much of a lady to call the conductor."

"I wouldn't be too sure of that."

"That you're not a lady? Of course I'm sure of that. I don't waste my time with the other kind."

"You're wasting it with me, and I have a book I'd like to read."

"He's got you reading books? Let's see what you're reading." He reached forth and took the book out of her lap. *"The Marriage of William Ashe,* by Mrs. Humphry Ward. Has it got any spicy parts to it?"

"I'm sure I don't know. I haven't started it yet."

"Well, I never heard of the book or the author, but it ought to be good. A woman writing about marriage. That is, if she doesn't leave out too much. Let me put it right back where it was. There."

"You're disgusting," she said.

"All I did was put it back where it was."

"If you don't go away I'll call the conductor. This minute."

"Oh, all right. But you're not fooling anybody, little Mrs. Millhouser. You've *never* fooled *me*."

"Yes, I did once. When you made a fool of yourself following me. You should have seen your face."

"You'll hear from me," he said, and left her.

Later the conductor stopped to speak quietly to Hedda: "Mrs. Millhouser—kind of an embarrassing question to ask a lady. But did a certain party on my train bother you? We had other complaints from ladies riding alone."

"No. Not really," said Hedda.

"Well, if you don't want to say anything, there's nothing I can do. But if you ever do want to complain, you won't be the first. Thank you, ma'am."

At Lyons depot Vance took Hedda's heavy valise out of her hand and followed her down the steps of the coach. "Just put it down," she said. Before he could do so it was snatched from his hand by Moses Hatfield.

"Nigger, you'd better mind your manners," said Vance.

"And you better watch you' trespassin'," said Moses. "Somebody accidentally shoot you some night." He led the way to the trap and Hedda Millhouser followed him without a word to Vance.

They rode in silence until Hedda maneuvered them out of the depot traffic. "Moses, was he the prowler that night?"

"Yes ma'am."

"Next time, shoot him," she said. "No, I don't mean that. But why did you pretend you hadn't seen him before?"

"I say that because if I tell Mr. Robert I see the man befo', he inquire who the man was."

"Yes, he would have. I didn't think of that. And you'd have had to tell him."

After a moment he said: "Ma'am?"

"What?"

"It be all right if I ask you sumpn?"

"Yes."

"He the man ring you up on the telephone that same night?"

"Yes. How did you know that? Margaret told you."

"Margaret didn't know it was him, but she told me somebody."

"I'm going to have to get rid of Margaret."

"You get rid of Margaret you only get somebody just as nosy. Maybe two-th'ee times as nosy. Margaret been with us a long time. She just an old maid, ma'am. Nosy old maid."

"Then why do you tell on her?"

"Why I tell on her?"

"Yes."

"You care to know why I tell on her? I tell you why I tell on Margaret. If she say things and they're the truth, I never tell on her in one thousand years. But she say things not the truth, I'm willin' to tell on her. She cut you in the back, I cut her in the back. She tell lies, I say to myself, 'All right, then I tell young Missus the truth about Margaret.' I got no right to tell on Margaret, but she got no right to tell lies."

"You're like Mr. Robert. You think all the time."

"No ma'am. I aint like him. He like me."

"Oh, you taught him to think."

"Sure did. I used to take him in the woods. 'Listen to them birds, screamin', chatterin'. Listen to them birds,' he'd say. And I say to him, 'Think, boy. Why all them birds screamin', chatterin'. Why they do that, boy? Think.' And I say to him, 'You better watch out where you walk, 'cause them birds see a snake even if you don't.' Yes, ma'am. I teach him thinkin'."

Away from Robert, hearing about his life before she met him, Hedda Millhouser was sometimes envious of those who had shared that life; but stories about his boyhood and young manhood and even the later years were more likely to have another result, that of raising him in her esteem because Robert had had a lasting effect on most of his acquaintances. They were fond of him, or they were mystified by him, or they disliked him. She was even a little jealous of Robert, to have known and affected so many people over so many years. There was a lot of memory for him to return to after the temporary, if complete, domination she held over him in their moments of physical intimacy. For that reason she had thoroughly hated him when he had shown for once that he could resist the usually exciting sight of her. On that night she had been wise enough, or well enough guided by instinct, to know that he must be made to feel excitement and yield to it, or she would lose her strongest hold on him. The intensity of the love-making cost her nothing in pride, for as against her loss of pride in going to his room there was the pleasure she had always taken in being the aggressor with other men besides Robert. It had always, since she could remember, been in her nature to originate the excitement, to choose the man and to take pleasure in

315

his bafflement at being superseded in the aggressive role. Bart Vance had correctly guessed her ready concupiscence, but he had not known enough to wait. The firmness with which he had placed that book deep in her lap had truly disgusted her, but for her own reasons and not for the reason he would infer. Consequently nothing he would say or do—no speech, no touch—would make him attractive or dangerous. Nothing, that is, except what he proceeded to do: he ignored her.

She fully expected another telephone call during the night of her return from Fort Penn, but the telephone did not ring. After she turned out the lights in her room she stood at the window and looked down among the shadows under the trees, but he was not there. In the morning she did her marketing and she saw him sitting on the porch of the hotel, smoking a cigar and obviously waiting for someone, but he made no sign of recognition. In the afternoon she made an unnecessary trip to town on foot, and she saw him twice, the one time alone, the second time walking with George Holliday. George Holliday spoke to Hedda, but Vance did not even raise his hat. Whether it was Moses's threat, or the indignity of being jostled by Moses, or her own haughtiness, that had made Vance so angry, he was determined to snub her. After dinner, and after the servants had gone to bed, she telephoned the hotel and asked to speak to Vance. "Sorry, lady, he checked out this afternoon for the evening train," said the clerk. "Back in two weeks."

In the morning Margaret brought her breakfast, but instead of leaving immediately, as was her habit, Margaret stood with her hands folded.

"Do you want something?" said Hedda Millhouser.

"I'm giving notice."

"You are? What for?"

"Because I don't relish working here any more."

"Well, you never have, since I've lived here."

"Truer words were never spoken."

"What caused you to make up your mind today?"

"I just as soon not put it into words."

"All right. Then don't put it into words. I can't force you to say anything you don't want to say. When do you think you'll leave?"

"The customary two weeks."

"Oh, well, then you have it out with my husband when he gets back. Is Theresa trotting on behind you, too?"

"Yes she is, but mind I'm not speaking for her. She can give her own notice."

"Why should she, when she has you to do it for her?"

316

"Now you look here, young lady, I've given my notice, so I'm not working for you no more and I don't have to listen to your disrespectful abuse."

"Maybe you'll have to listen to a lot worse before I get through."

"You won't say much. Just you keep a civil tongue in your head."

"Don't you talk that way to me, you old biddy. Get out of here and stay out of my sight till you leave."

"Stay out of your sight, is it? You stay out of my sight would be more like it. That's the thing you'd like best while your husband is miles away. How convenient that would be, just like when the two old women pack off to bed and her ladyship can't wait to see is Mr. Bart Vance in town. Did I eavesdrop? Sure I eavesdropped."

"Oh. Well, you tell that to my husband when you give him your notice. I hope I'm there, because I'd like to hear what he has to say to you."

"He'll believe me. All these years he knows I'm no liar."

"That isn't what I was thinking of, that he wouldn't believe you. All you can tell him, Margaret, is that you heard me ask to speak to Mr. Vance on the telephone. And after you've told him that, what do you tell him next?"

"I can tell him I'll not live in a house where there's such goings-on."

"What goings-on? That's what my husband is going to ask you, and what are you going to say? You can't say anything unless you lie, and it'll have to be a damn good lie. But anyway it'll be a lie, good or not. And you know, you old bitch, you know it'll be a lie. And do you know what I'll do? I'll go to your priest and tell him that you lied about me to my husband. I know Catholics. You're afraid to lie to your priest because you'll go to hell. And that's what I'll do, go right to your priest and make him force you to admit you told a lie. So you'll be out of a job and your priest will know you're a liar, and you'll have to support poor old Theresa, because nobody will give her a job. Here, take this tray, and get out of my sight."

Margaret picked up the tray and carried it downstairs. Within the hour Theresa knocked on Hedda's door and announced herself.

"Ma'am, I come to tell you, I can't do anything with poor Margaret, she's that miserable. Turble distressful, there's no consoling the poor woman."

"Is she doing penance? She ought to be. I went to a Catholic convent, Theresa. Tell her to go and confess to the priest and make the stations."

"She'll do that, surely, this Saturday. But she wants your forgiveness. She'll get down on her knees if you want her to."

"I don't want her down on her knees. Just out of my sight till my husband comes home. Then let her say the things to him she said to me."

"She'll come up the stairs on her knees. I'm licensed to tell you that. Ma'am, she's on the stairs. I hear her."

"I can hear her. She sounds like a sick cat."

"Ah, don't be so hard of heart, ma'am. To err is human, to forgive, divine. And she's *not* a young *woman,* her on the stairs like that. Justice with mercy, ma'am."

"I don't know why I should forgive her, or you. An hour ago she was giving notice for you, now you're pleading for her. Both of you make me sick."

"She'd no right to give notice for me. Me mind was not made up."

"Call her in."

Theresa went to the door and spoke to Margaret: "She'll see you."

"Standing up," said Hedda Millhouser. "Don't come in on your knees or I won't look at you."

Theresa put her arm about Margaret's shoulders, and Margaret hid her face in her apron, her square jaw pressed down on her chest, and her cap hanging out of place.

"Answer this in front of Theresa," said Hedda Millhouser. "Did you ever know of any goings-on in this house since I've been here?"

"No ma'am," said Margaret.

"Do you swear that on the Blessed Virgin Mary?"

"I do."

"You heard that, Theresa," said Hedda.

"Yes ma'am."

"Did *you* ever know of any goings-on in this house?"

"No ma'am."

"Do you swear it?"

"On the Blessed Virgin Mary and St. Theresa, me patron saint."

"Then I hope you learned your lesson," said Hedda Millhouser. "The next time I'll go to your priest."

"Will that be all, ma'am?" said Theresa.

"Yes."

"Come, Margaret dear," said Theresa. "It's all right now. Isn't it, ma'am?"

"Oh, fuff. Yes, it's all right."

The old women withdrew and Hedda Millhouser sat on the edge of her bed and laughed. She fully appreciated the irony of the fact

318

that she had become mistress of the household when it no longer mattered.

Toward the middle of May the spring flowers became so profuse that Robert commented that it seemed a shame there were not more people to see them. From that thought came his idea for a first wedding anniversary party.

"I don't want to have an anniversary party," said Hedda. "I don't want people staring at us all over again, just after they've stopped."

"We won't call it an anniversary party. Just a garden party, but a big one. We'll invite everybody."

"You mean sixteen people."

"No. Fort Penn, too. I'll charter a special train, just for our guests. They can leave Fort Penn around say ten o'clock in the morning and be here before noon. No stops, you see. And have a big lunch party under a tent. Maybe a band, or an orchestra. If we have it on a weekday we might have dancing. And send them all back at four o'clock. Don't you think it would be a nice way to repay the Fort Penn people? Otherwise we'll have to wait till the fall, and you must admit, the yard is something to be proud of."

"A special train," said Hedda.

"It doesn't cost as much as you think. And a special train is a party in itself. We could arrange to serve light refreshments coming and going."

"Are you so rich?"

"I am, and I'm not taking anything out of your present. I've bought that. I'll pay for the party out of some money I made in the stock market last week. Ben told me to go in with him on a stock I'd never heard of, and I did, and I made close to eight thousand dollars."

"What did you buy?"

"As a matter of fact I didn't buy. We sold. We sold it short. Tennessee Coal, Iron & Railroad Company was the name of it."

"Tennessee? Why not Pennsylvania? You've never even been to Tennessee."

"Neither has Ben, but he was so insistent that I went in with him."

"How could you sell it if you didn't buy it?"

"I'll explain that some other time. Now I'm more interested in whether you'd like to have the party."

"All right, let's have it."

"Then let's get to work on the invitation list," said Robert.

Hedda's uneasiness over the party was clever thinking, and would have been accurate if the party had been a small and simple one. But it grew in size and splendor until the host and hostess were mere human details. A dining car was added to the train; the Johnsville Silver Cornet Band was engaged; Robert and Hedda abandoned all thought of hiring local help to serve the food and drink, and hired a Fort Penn caterer. Esther Parkinson, who was helping Hedda with the invitations and some other Fort Penn details, was tactfully informed that the governor and his wife would be pleased to be invited, and reluctantly Robert and Hedda put their names on the list. Hedda did not like the governor's wife, but Esther advised Hedda against refusing to invite her. The Millhouser party had become an after-piece to the already finished Fort Penn season, and the dressmakers in the capital helped to spread the word that it was quite likely to be the real climax of it. No such party had ever been given in Lyons, and even in 1907 Robert and Hedda were the only couple who could have given it and escaped the wrath of the uninvited. Robert had no business or professional enterprise that could be boycotted (it would not have been practicable to boycott the town's only bank); and while no Lyons woman who had been nice to Hedda in the first year of her marriage was left off the list, the others were numerous. Hedda exercised her privilege in another instance: Robert had put Bart Vance's name on the list, and Hedda later secretly crossed it off.

The day came, the third Saturday in June, and long before the special train had actually left Fort Penn there were citizens of Lyons and the Valley who were establishing their positions along the outer side of the Millhouser fence. Most of them brought their lunch and wore their Sunday best. The special train arrived shortly before noon, but many citizens who waited at the depot were disappointed when the train continued up the track to the point nearest the Millhouser place. By this time the Johnsville band had already been seated under a marquee in the far, northwest corner of the Millhouser property, and the musicians were the center of attention until the arrival of the special and the fashionable, distinguished guests from out-of-town. The governor, having used his office to wangle an invitation, did not appear; instead his wife was there, escorted by the adjutant-general in dress blues. "She's not going to sit at our table, and that's all there is to it," Hedda whispered to Robert. Only one table had place-cards, and when Hedda saw that the governor had stayed away, she ordered the caterer to remove the gubernatorial cards and reduce the table by two chairs.

Robert and Hedda received their guests under a small marquee at the beginning of the rose garden, so that the guests would move past them and along the brick walk and at the end of the walk wander about as they saw fit. At one o'clock sharp a cornetist sounded mess call and waiters moved among the guests announcing that luncheon was served. The last few guests were approaching the host and hostess, and almost the very last of them was Bart Vance.

"I never did get your invitation, but I came anyway," he said to Robert.

"I *know* we *sent* one. It must have been forwarded to New York, but anyway, you're here," said Robert. "Nice of you to come."

Vance moved on and Hedda said: "He didn't get an invitation because I didn't send him one. I crossed his name off."

"Why did you do that? He belongs here."

"Then he's your guest, not mine."

"I didn't mean him so much as his family. I saw him on the street the other day and he accused me of snubbing him, so I told him we'd invited him. Don't pay any attention to him. He's not worth the trouble."

The eating and drinking continued until past two-thirty. Most of the tables seated ten and Robert and Hedda had asked some of their Lyons friends, who were greatly outnumbered, to take charge of various tables as assistant hosts. Consequently at each table there was at least one Lyons couple, and it worked out rather well. Fred Langendorf, as a member of the Fort Penn Club, was acquainted with some of the visiting gentlemen, and Ben Rosebery was acquainted with a few of the Lyons natives. The ratio of approximately 120 visitors to forty natives made for a large number of strange faces for both groups, and in the matter of style the visitors were readily distinguishable from the Lyons folk; but the bright, comfortable weather, the musical background, the abundance of good food and drink and the novelty of the occasion created a cheerful atmosphere. To the citizens leaning against the fence and gnawing on their sandwiches it was such a sight as they had never seen, such a bunch of pretty women, such a bunch of rich-looking men, such laughing and talking, such a thing to talk about all summer. Many of the Valley citizens had never seen Hedda Millhouser, but few had not heard of her, of her youth and beauty. They therefore knew who she was when at the end of the meal she went to the fence and invited the citizens' children to come through the gate and finish up the ice cream and *petits fours*. She watched them until they began to eat, diligently and silently, and then she left them.

Robert and Hedda had decided against dancing, although it was a Saturday, and the ladies retired to the house, the gentlemen to the stable and the rambler-covered privy, and later they formed groups

321

under the marquees. The planking-and-sawhorse table had been cleared of the luncheon things, and cigars and cigarettes were available. A murmur, low but audible, went up and down the fence when one of the visiting ladies lit a cigarette, and several mothers immediately gathered their children and departed, but most of the fence people stayed to enjoy the sight of the musicians at their meal. For the guests the post-luncheon lethargy had set in, and a few gentlemen dozed off, to be awakened at four o'clock by the signal from the locomotive whistle that the train would be leaving in fifteen minutes. It left in something less than an hour, what with leave-takings, forgotten parasols and other small accidents. But when the last Fort Penn guest was accounted for, and the locomotive bell began to ring, it was generally agreed that it had been a delightful party.

The Lyons guests lingered, rather awkwardly because there had been no whistle or bell to tell them when to go home. But toward five o'clock they rose, more or less in unison, and said their thank-you's and then suddenly Robert and Hedda were alone.

"The party is all," said Robert.

"All what?"

"Just all. Didn't you ever hear one of us Pennsylvania Dutchmen say, 'The ice cream is all'? By the way, that was very thoughtful of you, with the kids. The ice cream."

"I was watching one little boy. He was watching somebody at a table. The man was eating his ice cream and the boy's head would go up, then down, then up, every time the man took a spoonful."

"It was a remarkable party. It isn't often you can get that many people together and not have some accident. But young Dr. Willetts didn't have a thing to do. Did you have a good time at your party?"

"Yes, but I'm glad it's over."

"So am I, for that matter. It was too long. We've been going for eight hours, really. But most people enjoyed themselves, and we'll never have to do it again."

"Why do you say that?"

"Why not? Isn't it your idea that the next big party we give will be in Fort Penn?"

"I hadn't thought of it."

"I had. I wanted the Fort Penn people to see exactly how we lived here. The size of our house and so on."

"Why did you do that?"

"So that when we move to Fort Penn they'll know that you're giving up something rather nice. A bigger house and yard than most people can have in Fort Penn. Beautiful flowers and trees. And good substantial friends. Quite a few people said, 'I'd give anything to live in a place like this.' Thought you'd like to know that, Hedda."

"You didn't have to give this party to tell me that. I know a lot of people would like to live here, but I'm not one of them."

"Well, another couple of years . . . What ever happened to Bart Vance? I must say I thought it was very bad manners for him to trot off without saying a word."

"Don't pay any attention to him. He isn't worth the trouble."

"Touché, as they say in fencing. And now, why *did* you cross his name off the list?"

"Because every time I see him he annoys me."

"You don't see him that often."

"No, but he still annoys me."

"Why didn't you tell me that, and I never would have put his name on the list in the first place?"

"Because he *isn't worth the trouble!*"

"All right, all right," said Robert, rising. "Well, the old man's going to retire. A bath and a nap for me."

Hedda Millhouser went to the kitchen to thank Theresa and Margaret for the slight extra effort they had made. Margaret was alone. She stood up. "Theresa thought she'd lie down a bit."

"I just wanted to tell you that Mr. Robert and I both appreciated your help today."

"Thank you, ma'am. And I've something to say, between you and I. I'm mortified, the thoughts I had that time. Now I know all you were doing was inviting that gentleman to a party. The one I overheard you telephoning."

"I thought we were never going to speak of that again."

"We weren't, but when I'm wrong I want to do what's right."

"All right. But now let's drop it for good."

•

The chapel bell tolled five o'clock. The man in the linsey-woolsey cassock got to his feet and blessed the hour. He stood for a little while and gazed at his work. It had taken him the full week to white-wash the inner side of the wall, but Brother Rafferty had told him that it took two laymen two weeks to whitewash the outer side. Now it was Saturday, the work was done and well done. "Never a first-rate painter," he said to himself. "But truly an expert with white-wash." He spoke humorously, but underneath the humor he knew there was boastfulness, and pride was a deadly sin. He picked up his brush and buckets and carried them across the fields to the barn. He cleaned his face and hands in the horse trough and went to join his brethren in the chapel. Humility, it seemed, was the last thing one learned, and it was the hardest.

•

Now THEY WERE in their second summer together, the first full year accomplished, the repetitions of the seasonal changes beginning. The slip covers were on the furniture, the fly nets on the horses, the kitchen range was cold and the gas stove was used for the cooking, woolens and furs went into the cedar chests, and the man had gilded the ball on the top of the flagpole. Everyone said—as they always did—that it looked like another hot summer, and cited from nature to justify their predictions. The horses had shed early, certain birds had nested ahead of time, children died of mysterious diseases that they did not get in wintertime, and milk did not keep quite so long. For Hedda Millhouser it had been a busy, busy year; so many new faces, so many new houses, new dresses, new authority, new kinds of compliments, the newness of her place in the world of men and women. But the recognition of last year's plans for the summer—precisely the same blankets put in precisely the same closets—stirred her discontent. In the autumn things would be got out of chests and closets as they had been in the previous autumn, and the storm windows would be hung again and the screen doors stood in the cellar, and now that she was no longer a bride there would be fewer parties in Lyons and Robert would be evasive when she tried to pin him down to a date for their final departure. He was already older, noticeably older, than he had been a year ago. In the evenings he would sit in the little room, lost in a book and foolishly happy. It was that way now, it would be that way in the autumn, and in the winter, and in the spring, and the next time the winter things were being put away and the summer things got out. Late at night they would lie together, but his thin lips were not the lips she wanted on her.

"How would you like to go to Asbury for August? I had a letter from Harold Parkinson, and his brother would like to rent his place there."

"What is Asbury?"

"You never heard of Asbury Park? It's quite well known. I've never been there, but I know what it's like. It's in New Jersey, on the ocean. But cottages, not hotels like Atlantic."

"Would it be any better than Lyons?"

"Of course it would. You'd have the ocean to bathe in every day, and it's always cooler at the seashore."

324

"It isn't the heat I mind."

"Well, I'm sure they entertain, and the people are from all over. New York. Philadelphia. Fort Penn."

"I'd much rather have a boathouse near Fort Penn."

"You would? Well, I'll try to find one, but I'm afraid they're all taken by this time. If you'd spoken to me earlier I might have done something."

"If *you'd* spoken to *me* earlier. We never talked about it before."

"Yes we did, Hedda. In March I asked you what you wanted to do this summer, and you said you'd let me know, but you never did. Shall I tell Harold we're not interested in his brother's cottage? I have to let him know right away."

"If his brother is anything like Harold it must be a very dull place."

"Then the answer is no?"

"Robert, I *told* you what *I* wanted."

"On second thought, I have a feeling we ought to wait a year. Don't you think it would look—strange? odd?—for us to take a boathouse on the Nesquehela? We aren't Fort Penn people, and all the boathouses are occupied by Fort Penn people. Let's wait till we get a real house there before we do anything about the boathouse. Yes, I think that's better."

"Well, you've decided everything, haven't you?"

"Not quite. *You* decided you didn't want to go to Asbury, a perfectly nice place that you'd enjoy a great deal more than one of those boathouses. You'd be so bored after one week in a boathouse that you'd be begging me to take you back to Lyons. I know you, Hedda."

"Then why ask me anything? Why not just do all the deciding yourself?"

"Sometimes that almost seems like the best idea."

At such moments, when he invoked the difference in ages and particularly her youth as an argument in his favor, her anger was too intense to dissipate itself, but no matter how long it took to subside, it lasted until it had been expressed in love-making. Of that he had become aware, and yet he would not allow himself to provoke her into passion. One reason was that he meant to deal fairly with her, not to take advantage of the woman he married as he might conceivably do with a woman who meant less to him. Another reason was that he was afraid. If he could arouse her only through quarreling, the time would come when the quarrels would have to be so intense that she would respond to nothing but violence.

Robert Millhouser now realized that Hedda no longer loved him, even in the restricted, special way she had allowed herself, or been able, to love him. He did not give up the hope that a child born to them would unite them in a marriage that had more promise of success than the present arrangement. But it was all too clear that the next two years, half in Fort Penn and half in Lyons, and the first year or two in Fort Penn, meant at least three years before she would welcome a pregnancy. And she had quite as much right, he recognized, to enjoy her youth as he had to enjoy fatherhood and the last years of middle age. She had specifically told him that she wanted no children before she was twenty-five, and that was six years away, and he had married her with that understanding. The marriage as it now stood was a mistake, at least for her. It could never be the same mistake for him: for however long it endured, he had and would have had that much time with her, the young excitement and the possession of her, the aesthetic pleasure of the nearness of this exquisite creature where nothing, nothing at all, had been for so many years, and where nothing would be if the marriage were to end. He had nothing to offer in exchange for the presence of her at his table, the sight of her walking in his garden, the feel of her in his bed, or even the promise of her being there when he came home. It began with her beauty, which in itself was enough; but he had mated also with her mind, that made her see quickly the evil in people. Standing still, with her hand on the back of a chair, she would mislead a painter who saw only cold, bright perfection at rest. But then she would move or speak, and her speech, her movement, would begin giving the answers to the questions that a good painter would want to ask. Chester Calthorp would have appreciated her. It amused Robert Millhouser to concede that Hedda would have loved Chester Calthorp more than she did him. There would have been a great, passionate, unclimaxed love between those two, the height of the passion unattainable but inexhaustible and satisfactory. Robert wondered why he had not seen that before, that there was no love lasting after they had made love, that she did not then lie in his arms or on the next day smile in the secret exchange of recall. Yet now he knew, thinking of her in an imaginary friendship with Chester Calthorp, that for her orgasm was only immediate release, temporary and quick, but with no continuing satisfaction, no joy of sharing since the extreme of excitement was, for her, an ecstatic interruption but an interruption nonetheless. There had been nights when Hedda had said to him, "I don't feel like it," and he had wondered why on some such occasions he had not felt a rebuff but had actually felt she was transmitting a mystifying message of tenderness and trust. She was, of course, magnificently the only woman with whom he had ever been in love.

He contrasted her with Esther, with whom he had shared a love of love. In his mind he had married Esther, they had had four children, he was comfortable and protected, and he had reached the age of fifty-two without knowing himself or Esther or anyone else. And if that had been the case he would be, at fifty-two, wondering what *had* happened to him instead of, at fifty-two and with Hedda, what was to happen, to him, to Hedda, to anyone else who came into their life.

To keep what was left he was willing to make concessions within himself, to placate her unbeknownst to her. He would space out the concessions so that they would last until she was willing to have a child, hoping that there would still be remaining enough of the affection and respect she had for him to form, appropriately, an embryo of a new marriage. To concede everything at once would be to lose everything, and her; but he was confident of the rightness of his intuitions and his recognition of the moment to yield to a demand. She could have all, or nearly all, that she wanted, but not for the mere asking. He had not told her so, but he had already decided on two years, not three, as the time he would require for his program at the bank; he had asked Ben Rosebery to keep him informed on the residential prospects in Fort Penn; he had sounded out the most reliable of his farmers on their attitude in regard to ownership of their farms. On only one subject did he refuse to think clearly or at all: he would not give her up to another man. This represented a rejection of his earlier philosophical resignation to what he had once considered the inevitable, when he had told himself that love would come to her and that he would be gracious and graceful, and grateful for whatever years he could have with her. If the concessions he was making and would make were bribing and buying her, he was glad to be able to hold her in any fashion, and no one—if he was sufficiently adroit, possibly not even she—would know that she had been held by a system of bribes. But the reversal of his attitude toward her falling in love with another man was not an intellectual exercise. It had simply happened, as her presence in his life became more and more necessary. He destroyed at once every incipient thought of her with another man, and the most significant product of his analysis of her emotions was his tolerant view of the love she might share with Chester Calthorp, the homosexual and monk. They could have that kind of love, but it was not a kind of love that he would fear.

He was almost grateful to Bart Vance. Of all the men who had been courtly, flirtatious, friendly to her in their first year together Bart Vance had been the only one whom he was prepared to hate. There had been a mutual attraction, even if Hedda herself did not suspect it. But Vance had blundered himself out of her esteem, and Robert could recall with pleasure Hedda's surreptitious attempt to contemn Vance in the preparation of the party invitations. It was the more satisfactory because she had done it on her own.

Late in July, on an evening when Robert was at the farms, Hedda went to her mother's house for a family supper, and after supper a team came and took Ed Steele to the colliery for the night shift. The mother and daughter relationship was now devoid of affection, but was somewhat easier for that reason; they were separate women who had known each other a long time. They talked for a while about Lars and his romance with the Lloyd girl, and when that exhausted topic was re-exhausted Ruth said: "By the way, that's a pretty story going around about Bart Vance."

"I haven't heard it."

"Oh, you must have. The Stiegel girl?"

"Yes, I know her, but I don't know any story about her."

"Well, you know how old she is. She's a year or two younger than you are, but her mother's dead and her father has a hard time keeping a job. He drinks. Well, it seems he came home one night about two weeks ago and found her upstairs in bed with Bart Vance. Mr. Stiegel attacked Bart, and Bart fought back and Mr. Stiegel got the worst of it. So then he got out a warrant for Bart's arrest, or tried to, and that's how the story got out."

"What happened?"

"Nothing happened, that's the awful thing about it."

"Is that all there is to the story?"

"Yes. I understand that Bart paid Mr. Stiegel some money and he's been seen leaving the house late at night. The neighbors are up in arms, but there isn't much they can do."

"Vance has a wife and children in New York."

"I know, but he doesn't seem to be worried about that. He, uh, he got quite fresh with me one time. I met him on the street and he walked home with me, just as far as the gate, you may be sure. If your father ever knew some of the things he said in that short space of time—honestly."

"What did he say?"

"What didn't he say? I think the man must be a little off. Don't *you* ever have anything to do with him. I'll tell you one thing he said. He said he'd like to collect the rent for this house, and if I was on hand to pay him there might be a reduction."

"Do you consider him handsome?"

"Handsome? I couldn't consider a man handsome that was as forward as he was with me. And it's not the kind of looks I like. I

328

prefer your father's looks, and Robert's. There has to be something more than mere handsomeness. You could almost tell about Bart Vance just by looking at his mouth."

"What's the matter with his mouth?"

"Haven't you ever noticed it? Those lips? I should think even Dorothy Stiegel would shudder when he kissed her."

"Maybe she does."

"I don't see how she could help it," said Ruth. "If I ever had to kiss him it would give me nightmares."

"Well, you don't have to, so you're lucky."

"They were stark naked when Mr. Stiegel walked in. One report I heard said they were actually having intercourse. Think of it, walking in on a scene like that, and what a woman must feel, having someone see her. Especially her father. A woman must feel so ashamed that she never wants to look at a man again."

"But I guess Dorothy didn't feel that way."

"Not from all accounts, no." Ruth looked far away at nothing, and then involuntarily shook her head.

"What were you thinking?" said Hedda.

"Something I've never thought of before." She shook her head again. "No, I don't know how to say it. And what's more, I don't want to say it."

"Oh, come on. You can say anything to me. I'm a married woman, now."

"And goodness knows we've had to talk about such things," said Ruth. "Well, I'll tell you what I was thinking. I was wondering what we must look like, we women, when we're with our husbands. Suppose somebody walked in, I'd hate to have somebody see me."

Her mother had obviously been imagining herself in just such a situation, and less obviously the man in the situation had been Bart Vance, not Ed Steele. By degrees, in recent months, Ruth Steele had descended from the position of authority and superiority that belonged to her as Hedda's mother. Hedda had consistently spurned all advice and interference, even of friendly counsel, and Ruth no longer had any influence over her daughter. Concurrently a somewhat subtler change had occurred in their relationship: now that Hedda was married, and the marriage seemed to be going well, her misbehavior in the years before the marriage became, as it were, retroactively legitimized, condoned under the same sanction that covered the sexual acts in her married state. The result in the relationship between mother and daughter was that Ruth, who had known only one man, was often frankly curious to the point where she was consulting Hedda, the one who had had the greater experience. The new relationship would not have been possible if there had remained any illusion of affection or maternal domination, but Hedda had unequivocally declared herself free of Ruth and made it plain that if there was to be any relationship it was to be on her terms. If this was not entirely satisfactory to Ruth, who had always dominated her husband and her children, it had its compensations. The responsibility for Hedda was completely transferred to Robert, and Lars and Ed still needed Ruth.

Every time anyone—her husband, her mother, a Lyons woman, Moses Hatfield—spoke disparagingly of Bart Vance, and no matter on what grounds, Hedda Millhouser felt an advantage gained. She wanted him to have no friends—and he had few enough—so that when she was ready and the opportunity arose for her to possess him, he would be desperately and completely her own. He was always in her thoughts, and the mention of his name had so telling an effect on her that she was as much surprised as relieved that there was no revealing blush in her cheeks. MacMahon's store was a block away from the hotel, but conversely the hotel was only a block away from MacMahon's store, and when she was doing her marketing she was conscious of the nearness because it was where he kept a room. When she saw Bart Vance on the street she did not speak to him nor he to her, and in the process of avoiding him and of being avoided there were enough artificial movements to disguise her inner excitement, and she was in no danger of blushing. But she wanted him, and therefore loved him, more than she had ever wanted anyone. As the summer dragged on her only fear was that they would meet accidentally in circumstances which would give him the advantage of the first minute. She needed that first minute, that advantage, and thereafter she would be in command. The moment finally came, and it was not quite as she had planned, but the advantage was hers.

It was in August and she had gone to the depot to meet Robert. All the passengers, Bart Vance among them, got off the train but Robert was not among them. She waited until the locomotive was uncoupled and proceeded up the track to the turntable and there was no likelihood that Robert had gone inside the depot or was somewhere about. Then she heard Bart Vance's voice behind the trap. "If you'd been polite to me I'd have saved your waiting," he said. "Robert asked me to tell you, if he wasn't on this train, he'd be spending the night in Fort Penn."

"Thank you," she said. "Where did you see him?"

"He was on the train and just when it was ready to pull out he remembered something he'd forgotten. So he gave me the message for you and got off the train."

"Thank you," she said. "Consider yourself kissed."

"Do you mean that?"

"Just what I said. *Consider* yourself kissed." She saw with exultation the absurdly eager excitement she caused.

"I'd rather have the real thing," he said.

"Would you really, Mr. Vance? Would you really?" She slapped a rein on the gelding's rump and drove away.

At the house, a few minutes after she arrived, she had a long-distance telephone call from Robert. "What a foolish thing," he said. "I had a large envelope with a bond in it and I stopped to buy the new magazines. I paid for the magazines and got on the train and suddenly remembered the bond. Negotiable, it was. And the first person I saw was Bart Vance. Did he give you my message?"

"Yes."

"Well, I'll have to stay at the club tonight, but I'll be home on the morning train."

"Did you find the bond, all right?"

"It was right where I put it, fortunately. Someone could have picked it up and walked off with it, a thousand dollars richer. I must be getting old."

"Well, I'll meet the morning train, if you don't mind doing the marketing with me."

She made sure that Moses Hatfield had gone home and that Margaret and Theresa had gone to their rooms, and then sat in the little room until the telephone rang. The call came shortly after nine o'clock.

"Hello," she said.

Without any introductory words he said: "I tried to consider myself kissed, but it won't work."

"Well then why don't you go down to Fourth Street?"

"I'd never go to Fourth Street if I could go to North Main. Do I have to go to Fourth Street?"

"You don't *have* to do anything." She hung up and rung off.

From the darkened front room she could barely see him, half an hour later, slowly walking past the gate twice and, the third time he came to it, entering the grounds and standing in the early darkness among the chestnuts and elms. She watched him move closer to the house, from tree to tree. He stood for at least five minutes behind the last tree and then apparently decided to risk the porch. As he put his foot on the bottom step of the porch she opened the door and

331

let him in. "Take off your shoes," she said. She waited, and then she led him by the hand to her room. The entire house was in darkness. She helped him to take off his clothes and put them on a chair, but when he attempted to embrace her she whispered, "Quiet," and left him for a while. When she returned she allowed him to kiss her and to fondle her but she put him off again and again until she knew that his anger was getting out of control, whereupon she became the aggressor and directed the movements of his body and his lips until the last seconds. He was noisy at the end, but not enough so to be heard elsewhere in the house, and when it was over she kissed him on the mouth. "Now go to Fourth Street," she said.

"Why should I?"

"Why shouldn't you? This can't ever happen again."

"Maybe it can't, but it will."

"It won't if you ever see Dorothy Stiegel again. We can't talk. You must go."

"When will I see you again?"

"Probably never."

She led him downstairs and he put on his shoes. "When am I going to see you again?" he asked.

"I'm not a Dorothy Stiegel, to see when you want to. First you have to break off with her, and when I'm sure of that I'll tell you when you can see me."

A week later Lyons was discussing the departure of Dorothy Stiegel, who was said to have gone to Philadelphia to learn to be a hairdresser. Her father was going with her, and there seemed to be little doubt as to who was putting up the money. At all events that disgraceful situation was rectified, and it was generally believed to have been a letter from Fred Langendorf to Chauncey Vance that had done the trick. Fred stubbornly denied having written any such letter, but he was practically the only man in town who could have written it, and Chauncey Vance was known to be the only relative who had any influence over Bart. If Fred wanted to deny it, that was his business, but facts were facts, and Fred Langendorf could still be counted on as the most dependable man in the Valley.

"I don't believe Fred Langendorf wrote any such letter," said Robert Millhouser.

"Oh, but I do," said Ruth Steele. "You know all these people better, but I've seen Mrs. Langendorf shut up like a clam whenever the subject is mentioned, and I think she's sworn to secrecy."

"I agree with Robert," said Ed Steele. "My guess is that Vance got tired of the gossip and decided to move the girl away somewhere.

332

What I've seen of Fred Langendorf, he'd stay out of a thing like that."

"I think Mr. Vance just wanted to get rid of her," said Hedda Millhouser.

"But he's not rid of her, necessarily," said Robert. "He can see her as much as he wants to in Philadelphia. That's on the way to New York. In fact, he can see her oftener this way. Coming and going."

"Well, I'll be interested to see who Bart Vance goes after next," said Ruth Steele.

"Goes after, or gets? He goes after every woman, Ruth," said Robert. "I'm surprised he hasn't made overtures to you."

"His kind don't interest me," said Ruth.

"That isn't what Robert said," said Ed Steele, laughing. "I hardly know the fellow, but he certainly has a bad reputation."

"He isn't worth bothering about," said Hedda Millhouser. "Is he, Robert?"

"No, he isn't, but here we are, all talking about him just the same," said Robert.

•

IN MID-OCTOBER the first invitations for the Fort Penn social season arrived at the Millhousers' and Robert announced first to Hedda and then to Margaret and Theresa that he had decided he would rent a parlor, bedroom and bath at the Schoffstal House in Fort Penn. They would be spending a great deal of time in Fort Penn, and it was a great convenience to have a place they could always go to and leave things, and it was not prohibitively expensive. On a monthly rate it was $75, but that included maid service and laundry. Two days after he made his announcement Robert said to Hedda: "Have you been having any trouble with Margaret?"

"No, why?"

"She's given notice. So has Theresa. I asked her why they came to me instead of you—Margaret, that is—and she said she considered herself my mother's servant. She gave a good enough reason for wanting to quit. She said it was obvious that sooner or later you and I were going to leave Lyons for good, and we wouldn't be taking the two of them. And they're getting old and they can board in town. But I wondered if you'd had any trouble with her."

"No, not that I can think of."

"That's good, because I always planned to give them a pension when they finally retired, and I couldn't do that if you'd had trouble. I couldn't be disloyal to you, if you know what I mean. In other words, I could give them a lump sum, but I wouldn't keep paying them the rest of their lives if you'd had some difficulties with them."

"Dear knows I won't miss them, but there hasn't been anything that I know of."

On the day that was to be Margaret's last under the Millhouser roof Hedda made her only mention of the topic: "I'll be sorry to see you both go," she said.

"Save that for somebody that'll believe it," said Margaret.

"Oh, so that's the way it is?" said Hedda.

"You ought to know," said Margaret. "And don't bring in the holy priest of God this time. You deceived me and deluded me with that before, but not this time. I falsified the reasons I give your husband, but God will find you out and we'll be away from this house when the truth becomes known. That what I know should happen in this house that was decent and peaceful these fifty-two years. God forgive you, is all I can say. God forgive you, but sweet Jesus don't ask me to. You had me fooled the one time, and I come to you on me very knees beggin' your forgiveness. But I caution you, woman, don't ever let Moses Hatfield find out what I found out, or Mr. Bart Vance's throat will be an ugly sight to behold. And maybe your own as well. We loved and cherished this house and those in it, and Moses as much as Theresa did or I."

"All right. But I haven't admitted anything."

"No, nor denied. What'd be the use? From the day your husband missed the train last summer I have the dates, if you want my proof. All written down in black and white, what time he come, how long he stayed. I doubt that I missed any, because woman, there wasn't a night your husband was away, not since you let me come to you on bended knees, that Margaret Dillon went to sleep before the hour of midnight. Not a night did I miss when your husband wasn't here to watch you. I know every creak in every board in this house, and many's the night I shut my ears to your licentious conversations coming through the register."

"Then what's keeping you from telling my husband?"

"I'm no avenging angel. I'll never be the one to tell him."

"Margaret?"

"What?"

"Wouldn't it have been awful if I'd turned out to be a good little girl? You couldn't have stood it."

"I always wanted him to have a good wife. I used to put it in me

334

prayers. But from the moment I first laid eyes on you I knew me prayers went unanswered."

"You may go now."

"With pleasure, with pleasure." She stood still for a moment.

"Well?"

"One last look at you, so's I won't ever forget what evil can come in a pretty package."

"Would you like to see it all, Margaret?"

"I've seen it all, thank you, marching and parading down the stairs with Mr. Bart Vance."

Through Esther Parkinson the problem of successors to Margaret and Theresa was quickly solved. Sophie Green was the new cook, Henrietta Lee the new maid. They came from the large colored section of Fort Penn, had been in service all their lives, and began taking orders from Moses Hatfield on arrival. Both women were in their middle forties, widowed and with working children. Hedda Millhouser and Robert had had little to do with hiring them; Esther Parkinson had an excellent reputation among the Negroes of Fort Penn, and her recommendation of the Millhousers was as valuable as her recommendation of the Millhousers' new servants. But for Hedda their chief recommendation was their color: they would not overstep as Irish servants did. Irish servants were outwardly respectful, but they were always on the verge of a personal relationship, with their jokes and advice and sentimentality. Hedda had had enough of Irish servants, and she was pleased that Moses, who had never been a butler, had taken the office of major-domo, since it enabled her to deal with Sophie and Henrietta through him and to remain aloof. But Hedda had been getting careless, and with the coming of the new servants and the adoption of a policy of extreme remoteness from them, she grew more careless than ever. She put her trust in the anonymity of the dark new faces of Sophie and Henrietta, forgetting that her very remoteness as well as her young beauty stimulated their curiosity about her. The difference in Robert's and Hedda's ages was a new fact to Sophie and Henrietta; the separate bedrooms were related to the question of age. And Hedda was careless.

At that stage in the history of the Lyons & Johnsville Telephone Company the Lyons switchboard was located in a one-story, three-room building on Main Street. "Central" was one of three operators, two of them women, and the night operator a man. Few local calls were made by number; the caller would say to the operator: "Mary, see if Jane Doe is home, will you?" Sometimes the operator would reply that she knew Jane Doe was not home but over at a friend's house. Anyone could leave a message with the operator, such as to say: "Mary, if anybody wants me, I'll be back in about an hour." In spite of Bart Vance's suggestion that she make minimum use of the telephone, Hedda spoke to him over the wire nearly every time he was in town. This was a carelessness because their rendezvous were made through the U. S. Mail. Hedda would write a note, giving the time of Robert's departure and return, but she would telephone Vance to confirm the information and to find out when she could expect Vance's visit. Thus the closest friends of the three operators knew that there was "something going on," even though Vance and Hedda were never together in public.

She had him in her suite at the Schoffstal House in the first week of her occupancy and she went to his room in the same hotel but on a different floor, a carelessness that was observed by elevator operators who disliked Vance and who did not dislike Robert. There was an incident in the Fort Penn depot that should have frightened her but did not. She had gone to the station with Vance, who was on his way back to New York, and they were standing in a corner of the train-shed when a uniformed railway policeman suddenly appeared and said: "Lady, you gotta cut that out."

"Cut what out?"

"Don't make trouble. I been watching you for five minutes, and you got your hand some place it oughtn't to be. If you want to go to bed, rent a room."

"It's all right, Officer. My wife's just sorry I'm going away," said Vance.

"Your wife? Mister, don't insult my intelligence. I know this lady or I'd have pinched her right away."

"If you pinched me I'd have you arrested," said Hedda.

"All right, but maybe a city policeman won't know you, Mrs. Millhouser. You either, Mr. Vance. Next time it won't be me. It'll *be* a city cop."

On her way to the hack-stand she saw the policeman and smiled at him, and a second policeman nudged him and made a rude joke.

For months there was whispering, and then one day, overnight, for no particular reason but because whispers were not enough, the gossip of the day before became the situation of the present, and Hedda had a visitor. It was Esther Parkinson and the place was Hedda Millhouser's suite in the Schoffstal House.

"Hedda, I'm a lot older than you—"

"I know you are," said Hedda, irritably.

"Don't be rude. I'm here as a friend of Robert's, not of yours,

336

although I could have been a friend of yours and tried to be. But I'm afraid you're not made for friendship, or loyalty, or any of the things I believe in. I came to tell you that yesterday there was a meeting of the committee for the St. Valentine's Ball. You're not going to be invited this year, and you were, last. Robert is going to ask why, and he's going to be very angry because he'll think we've snubbed you. Well, we have. At least five ladies on the committee. They won't have you sent an invitation, and they're not going to have you in their houses, ever again. As far as Fort Penn is concerned, you are through."

"Well, what if I am?"

"Just this. If you ever cared anything at all for Robert, go away from Fort Penn before he has to find out the truth. He's very apt to come to your defense and make some foolish mistakes, and then he'll have to be told why the best people are not going to receive you. Go to Florida, make him take you to Europe. But go away from here—and Lyons. You're extremely young, and a year from now— Robert's a forgiving sort and he may forgive you. But I could cry for what you're doing to him now."

"You and Robert used to cry a lot together, didn't you?"

"No, we never cried together. What we felt about love you'd never understand. We would never have disgraced ourselves in a railroad station."

"Dear me, this is Lyons all over again. Why do you think Robert doesn't know anything?"

"Are you implying that he does, and condones this?" said Esther. "If you are, you don't know Robert Millhouser. And if you're deliberately trying to implant the idea that all this is with his consent, I say you're a liar. And a nasty little liar, too."

"Strange he hasn't found out when everybody else has, don't you think?"

"Not at all. People are fond of Robert. You'll find that out, possibly to your sorrow."

"You have to go now, Esther. I'm expecting another visitor."

"Well, at least thank you for sparing me that. I can hardly bear to look at him in the best of circumstances."

"That's not nice. He's looked at you and said some very funny things about you. Complimentary, but maybe you wouldn't think so. Does that pique your curiosity, Esther?"

"It most certainly does not."

"I don't believe you. I don't think you've ever had any real pleasure."

"Oh-ho-ho. You ignorant little slut."

In a few minutes Vance appeared. "I just missed bumping into Esther Baumgarten. I mean Parkinson."

"I tried to make her stay, but she wouldn't."

"She was here? What for?"

She reported the facts of Esther's visit. While she was speaking he pinched his lower lip with his thumb and forefinger, always with him an indication of deep thought.

"She left here mad as could be," said Hedda Millhouser.

"At something you said? Or you might say on general principles?"

"What difference does it make?"

"She's very highly thought of, you know. It might have been wiser if you'd handled her with kid gloves. Now it's only a question of days."

"What days?"

"Before it gets to Robert. Unless you decide to take Esther's advice. You could have a tantrum and make him take you to Florida. Or, as Esther said, to Europe. You'll have to give up all thought of ever living in Fort Penn."

"Well, I was thinking we could move to New York. Or Philadelphia."

"Philadelphia would be just as bad as Fort Penn. New York would be better. Then I could go on seeing you."

"You could go *on* seeing me? Are you running away?"

"Hedda, haven't you been paying any attention to what I've been telling you? Doesn't Robert ever talk about business to you? My wife has lost almost everything she ever had. If I didn't have the mineral rights in Lyons we'd be strapped. Don't you know what's been happening in the stock market?"

"Oh, I know that Robert was worried."

"Worried! Don't you know that Robert saved the Lyons bank? By himself?"

"Oh, that time before Christmas? Yes, I knew that, but I never understood what was going on. I understand you, though. You're afraid, and you're running away."

"Robert Millhouser is a hero in Lyons. Whatever they thought of him before, he's a hero now. And I'm the man that's been having an affair with the hero's wife."

"You're good and scared, aren't you? Well, so am I. I think I'm going to have a child, and it's yours. I don't want a child, not before I'm twenty-five. And if I do I'll bet it'll have your mouth and everybody'll know it's yours."

"What's the matter with my mouth?"

"Hasn't anybody ever told you that you have an ugly mouth?"

338

"No."

"Then I'm telling you now."

He put his fingers to his lips. "What's the matter with it? It's just like everybody else's."

"No it isn't. It isn't like *anybody* else's. Go look at it in the mirror."

"I've had the same mouth for forty-two years and you're the first one to tell me it was ugly. You never objected to it before. And I'll tell you this, it didn't stop me from having as many God damn women as I wanted."

"I've told you that I'm going to have a child, and all you can think of is your ugly damn mouth. Robert was right. You're just not worth bothering about."

"You went to a lot of bother to prove the opposite, it seems to me. I'm sorry you're having a child, but whose fault is that? You wanted to be the one to take precautions. How far along is it?"

"Two months, at least."

"Have you seen a doctor?"

"No."

"Then you may be worrying over nothing. And anyway, why are you so sure it's mine?"

"Because there were several times when I didn't take precautions with you, and no times when I didn't with Robert."

"Well, my advice to you is see a doctor, and save your worry till you hear from him. God damn it, everything happens at once." He looked at her, sitting erect in her white shirtwaist and gray skirt that made her seem like a very young girl dressed up in her mother's clothes; the blond beauty of her with her braids wound about her head in a personal defiance of the current pompadour style; the sapphire eyes embedded in the powder-white face that were together convincing proof of the innocence that had been left out of her at birth. "Do you hate my mouth?" he said.

"Yes," she said.

"Do you hate me?"

"If I hated you I'd tell you to come in the next room with me."

"Aren't we going in the next room?"

"No."

"Why?"

"Because I don't hate you or love you and I don't want you."

"I could make you want me."

"You could *never* make me want you. You never did. I can want a man, but no man can make me want him. And I'll never want you again."

"Hedda, you're the one that's afraid."

"Maybe. But you don't know what of. Afraid Robert will divorce me? Afraid of what people will say about me? Do you think I couldn't take Harold Parkinson away from Esther if I wanted to? That's how much I care what people say about me. As soon as she tells him about me, that's when I could take him away from her. But what's the use, if I don't want him? That's what I'm afraid of. I don't want anybody. And I've always wanted somebody."

"You're growing up, Hedda," he said. "You'll see somebody tomorrow and want him."

"I hope I do." She reached up and unpinned the cameo at her throat. "My mother gave me this. It belonged to her grandmother. You like my mother, don't you?"

"Yes."

"Well, you'll never have her, but you can have me just this one more time. I'll be my mother and you be you. My mother's going to surprise you, Bart. Oh, I know a lot about that woman. She sits on my father's lap, like this . . ."

•

THE HERO of Lyons became testy whenever anyone spoke words of gratitude. "I was only saving my own neck," he would say, an over-modest half-truth. Robert had no more inside information than any other citizen of Lyons, but late in October, when the Knickerbocker Trust Company failed, he reasoned that if the Knickerbocker and other New York banks were unable to raise money, the New York situation was already serious and the effect would be felt so soon elsewhere in the nation that he had no time to lose. Accordingly he acted quickly, before the word panic had begun to appear in print. He planned carefully, and on his personal note he borrowed $10,000 from Ben Rosebery. "You can have the money because I can afford to lose it," said Ben.

"Why do you expect to lose it?" said Robert.

"Because you do, too."

"What makes you think I expect to lose it?"

"Because you don't need $10,000, not on your personal note. Not from me, at least. If you needed $10,000 you could go to any bank in the State and borrow it, and you haven't, have you?"

"No, not yet. All right, Ben, I'll tell you what I'm doing. I'm protecting the Lyons bank."

"With your own credit."

"Yes. I'm going to borrow from you and Harold Parkinson. That's two in Fort Penn. Fred Langendorf and Jerry MacMahon, that's two

340

in Lyons. And I'm going to try to get the rest from banks in Lancaster, Lebanon, and Gettysburg. Banks I've done business with."

"You're going to put up the farms for that money?"

"Yes."

"Well, I knew there was something that didn't meet the eye. Put down Brock Caldwell."

"I hardly know him. I can't go to him."

"He's a friend of yours, whether you know it or not. He doesn't like many people, but I know he'd be pleased if you'd ask him."

"Well, if you say so."

Robert proceeded to borrow $5,000 apiece from Parkinson, Caldwell, Langendorf, and MacMahon. On an impulse, while Robert and Ben were dining at the rathskeller, Ben called the proprietor, Fritz Gottlieb, over to their table. "Fritz, Mr. Millhouser wants $5,000 cash. He'll give you his I.O.U."

"You want it bick bills or little bills?" said Fritz.

"He wants little bills," said Ben.

"I be back, chust hold your horses," said Fritz. Before they finished their dinner Fritz handed Robert a large envelope. "Here she is."

"I'm not going to give you an I.O.U., I'm going to give you a note," said Robert.

"No sir. A banker takes notes and a stenographer takes notes but I don't *take* notes. I aint a banker and I aint a stenographer yet. Only such a saloonkeeper."

"And a terrible jokester," said Ben.

"Ah, well, I like chokes. A man don't laugh, he better be deat yet."

"Well, I hope the laugh isn't on you, Fritz," said Robert.

"You chust keep it warm a while," said Fritz.

At the banks there were papers to sign and more formality, but the bankers knew the value of the farms and the money was forthcoming. Robert had a total of $55,000 cash, which was converted into 2,000 $5 bills, 1,000 $10 bills, 250 $100 bills, and 200 $50 bills. They made a bundle about a foot high, which he took home to Lyons and hid behind a row of books in the little room. On the first day of November, 1907, Robert was having his hair cut and he heard the word panic for the first time in Lyons. He looked in the barber's mirror to see who had said it, and the speaker was Albert Connor, owner of the wagon works and a good man.

"I hope you're not afraid, Albert," said Robert.

"Oh, Robert. I didn't reccanize you," said Connor. "Well, I don't know if I'm afraid or I'm not afraid, to tell you the truth."

"Well, I'll tell you what you do. When you finish your haircut you come down to the bank and I'll show you something that you ought to see. But meanwhile, don't frighten people that *aren't* afraid."

Robert went to his house on foot, obtained the bundle of cash, and had Moses drive him quickly to the bank. In a few minutes Albert Connor arrived and went to the directors' room on the second floor. On the table Robert had spread out the money in the four denominations. "That's $55,000, and it's all mine," said Robert. "I want you to count it."

"Oh, hell, Robert, I'll take your word for it."

"No, I want you to count it."

"That'll take me all day."

"No it won't. There are only 3,450 bills there," said Robert. "One a second is, uh, six into 34-50 is—"

"About fifty-seven minutes. Just under an hour," said Connor. "Robert, I got better things to do."

"You're damn right you have, Albert. One of them is to go around and tell people this bank is safe, and you know it's safe, because there's $55,000 of my own money, cash, backing it. This money is not on deposit, Albert. This is money I'm willing to put up to keep people from getting nervous."

"All right, Robert. I learned my lesson," said Connor. "But I'd like to do one thing. This pack here, this is 250 $100 bills? I just want to hold $25,000 in my hand. That's the most I ever felt at one time."

"Anybody that wants to can come in and do the same thing. And by the way, Albert. This is five thousand more than we're capitalized for."

"Robert, they oughta have your picture up there instead of Fred's."

"Well, I painted that one. Maybe Fred will paint one of me." Both men laughed and Albert Connor departed, to spread the good word.

Tommy Fenstermacher was hired at $2 a day to stand guard, complete with revolver in holster, and for four weeks the only near-run on the bank was caused by men and women who were eager to hold $25,000 in one hand. As conditions in the nation improved, Robert deposited the money and sent out cheques with interest to repay the loans. There was hardly a man or woman in the Valley who had not heard of what he had done, and at first he was touched by their words and by the shy smiles of those who were not accustomed to speaking to him. But he knew that this was the last as well as the biggest thing he would ever do for Lyons. Hedda was not even making much of a pretense of living in Lyons; at Christmas she protested against missing the Fort Penn Charity Ball and the Bachelors

Club cotillion, and they were away from Lyons throughout the holiday season. Late in January he heard the first gossip, not a word of which was spoken, for it came in the form of a sudden silence.

Robert seldom went to Fritz Gottlieb's Rathskeller alone, and never alone for lunch. At lunch the patronage was almost completely male and he preferred the all-male company at the Fort Penn Club to the all-male patronage at the rathskeller, where the laughter was too hearty and the voices too loud. But on this day he was nearer to the rathskeller, the sidewalks were slushy, the snow had turned to rain. He walked through the main diningroom to the smaller room where he usually sat with Ben Rosebery. In a booth seating six there were a party of men whose raucous laughs could be heard over the noise in the main room. But the moment he entered the smaller room he heard one man's voice uttering the warning sound, "Uh-oh," and all six men looked at Robert, stopped laughing, and stared at him. He knew one or two of them by sight and nodded to them, and was nodded to in return. But the men looked at each other and it was all too evident that they had been discussing him. He went to his usual table, but it was unmistakable that his presence made them uncomfortable and had silenced them. There were no friends of his among them; it was a group of men who had businesses in the vicinity; shopkeepers, minor lawyers, insurance men, who could set their own time for the return to their business. Since he was known to them only as a friend of Ben Rosebery's, he considered the possibility that they had been discussing Ben; but he rejected that momentary comfort. There had been a look of angry, startled guilt on their faces, and even a trace of fear, as though *he* might punish them for what he might have overheard. And then he knew that whatever they had been saying about him, Hedda had been mentioned. When they all left together Robert, with an effort at casualness, said to the waiter: "They're a noisy bunch, Karl."

Karl tapped his head: "Well, you know how it is. The bass drum makes the most noise, but hollow inside. Today it was some woman they was talkin' about. Near always it's some woman. Women, women, women. I don't have that to worry about no more. Like these fellows here today. Today some story how a railroad cop at the depot, they're always trying to shoo away the hookers. But this cop seen a woman playing with a fellow's privates and he was gunna take her in, but she was some rich lady. Women, women, women. Rich or poor. If I was to run them in for every time I seen that in this place. It's a good thing I aint a cop."

"It *is* a good thing, Karl," said Robert, with intentional lack of enthusiasm that he hoped would send Karl away. For the moment he was a captive; he could not leave immediately, as he wanted to do, since to do so would cause comment and questions by Karl and just possibly indicate that he had been disturbed by the six men's sudden silence. Moreover he did not even want anyone to see his face when he put his mind to work on the reason for their silence. Therefore he ate what he ordered and occupied his mind with a fancy that had lately occurred to him. He had read in a newspaper a brief article which reported that a man who lived somewhere on the South Shore of Long Island had put a dollar bill and a note in a bottle, dropped it into the ocean and seven months later had received an answer to his note from a fisherman in Portugal. It was an item that would have had no more than moderate and passing interest except that when he read it Robert had been doing some thinking about probability, chance, coincidence, and life expectancy. He had, in fact, been thinking of life insurance, with Hedda as the beneficiary, which led him into his semi-philosophical considerations. The newspaper article belonged in the realm of probability and chance, and then Robert created his own embellishment of the story. Suppose that the Long Island man had dropped a *second* bottle into the ocean and that once again it had been returned by a Portuguese native? It would be a remarkable coincidence, highly improbable, with the chances enormously against such a happening. But Robert was sure that the Long Island man, instead of marveling at the mathematics of the double improbability, would quite likely be slightly bored by the second occurrence. Coincidence, probability, chance? They ceased to be forbidding factors in a man's thinking when once the novelty was gone. He was suddenly returned to the table and the room and the six men who had lately left the room: what were the chances against his walking in at the moment they were discussing him, a stranger, and his wife, whom they had never seen? The fact remained that he *had* walked in, that they *were* discussing his wife, and that three lives would never again be the same.

He paid his bill and went to the reading-room of the Fort Penn Club, not noticing until he was actually inside the clubhouse that he had come through the slush and rain without his overshoes, which he had left at the rathskeller. He was seldom forgetful of such things; he was neat and orderly habitually; and as he seated himself in the reading-room, with his wet shoes off and pretending to write a letter so that he would not be disturbed, he himself was the disturber of his thoughts. It was unlike him to forget his overshoes in this kind of going, and he regarded the lapse as a measure of the disturbance that already existed in his soul, even before he had begun to ponder the problem of Hedwig Steele Millhouser. Between this moment and her ultimate confession there would be accusations and lies, and tears and violent anger, perhaps a reconciliation and passionate love-making before the repetition of the accusations and lies and anger. But even as he tried to anticipate the future in systematic fashion, Robert knew that the conclusion had been reached. He was going to have to kill Hedda, and reason, love, appreciation of beauty, tolerance of her frailty and indeed his own guilty inadequacy would not singly or together be enough to stop him.

He stayed at the club through the afternoon and then put on his damp shoes and summoned a cab and was driven back to the hotel in the slush.

She put up her cheek to be kissed. "Where were you all day?" she said.

"Business in the morning, lunch alone at the rathskeller, and in a brown study all afternoon. I've been at the club. Have you been out?"

"In this weather? No, I've been here all day."

"Let me change my socks and I'll be right with you. I forgot my rubbers. Left them at the rathskeller and sloshed my way to the club."

"That isn't like you. You must have something on your mind. Were you doing some of your deep thinking again?"

"Very deep indeed." He went to the bedroom and put on dry socks and bedroom slippers.

"Well, I've been doing some thinking, too. I want to go to Florida."

"Florida? You must mean Palm Beach. You overestimate my resources. Only millionaires go there."

"Aren't you a millionaire?"

"I am not. Why do you want to go to Palm Beach?"

"Well, then some place away from here. Why can't we go to Europe?"

"What you have in mind is some *distant* place. We're practically living in Fort Penn. Why do you want to go away?"

"I'm sick of Fort Penn, as sick of Fort Penn as I am of Lyons. Oh, you're going to hear about it, so I might as well tell you. We're not being invited to the St. Valentine's Ball."

"Of course we are. We were invited last year and they never take your name off that list."

"Well, they did ours."

"Who told you that?"

"Does it make any difference who told me? I know it for a fact, and *fuff* on this town. I want to get away from here and Lyons and Pennsylvania. And the United States. Now."

345

"Well, first I want to inquire about the Valentine's Ball. I've been invited to that all my life, and you and I were invited last year. I certainly want to know why we're suddenly dropped."

"Why do you care? If some of those women have it in for me the whole place can go to hell."

"They didn't have it in for you at Christmas. If anything we had too many invitations then. What's happened since? I can find out by asking Esther."

"Esther! She's on the committee. She won't tell you anything."

"She'll tell me."

"Don't you dare ask her!"

"But I'm going to." He started for the telephone.

"If you do I'll leave you."

He sat down. "Will you have a cigarette? I see you've had quite a few."

"I can't even smoke without somebody spying on me."

"Do you want one, or don't you?"

"No."

"Have *you* spoken to Esther?"

"No."

"Are you sure?"

"Oh, all right. I have. She was here the day before yesterday and told me."

"Without saying why? Esther wouldn't come and tell you that without telling you why. Are you sure Esther didn't give you a chance to explain something or other?"

"Explain what?"

"Whatever it was that caused them to drop us. You know, it isn't like Esther to—excuse me." He interrupted himself to sneeze. "I'm catching cold. But to go on, Esther took you under her wing, so to speak, the first year we were married. It isn't like her to drop a friend without an explanation."

"Who is she a friend of? You, not me."

"Of both. She did a great deal more for you than she'd have had to do as a friend of mine only." He sneezed again. "I want to get to the bottom of this."

"What for? So you can hear a pack of lies about me?"

"Yes, Hedda. I'd like to hear a pack of lies about you. I think I'd rather hear them than the truth."

She stood up and slapped his face. "Take that. I hope you get pneumonia and die."

"That might save a lot of trouble, but it's only a cold." He stood up and went to the telephone. "I'm not calling Esther. I'm going to get another room so that my dear one won't get the sniffles. But I am going to speak to Esther."

"I told you. If you do, I'll leave you."

"Yes, that might be one of the consequences, if I speak to Esther. You leave me, I leave you. Why don't you tell me the truth? Why were you dropped from the St. Valentine's Ball? You know why, so why don't you tell me? How long do you think it's going to be before I find out? . . . Let me speak to the front desk, please. This is Mr. Millhouser. Could I have a room near where we are now? I'm coming down with a cold? Thank you . . . They're giving me the room across the hall."

"They can give you the whole hotel, for all I care. I want to leave here and I want to leave this town."

"You've made that point clear. What I want to know is why you suddenly have to leave this place that only a short while ago was heaven on earth. I'm sure to find out, but I'd like *you* to tell me."

"You're going to talk to your friend Esther anyway."

"I'd much rather not talk to Esther, but I will if you leave me no alternative. I'm going to put some things in a satchel." He went to the bedroom and packed for his removal to the other room.

He heard the knock on the parlor door and opened it for the bell-boy. "Afternoon, Mr. Millhouser. I got the key for five-fourteen."

"Good afternoon, Jimmy."

Robert saw that Jimmy was not looking at him but at Hedda. "Hello, Mrs. Millhouser," said the bellboy.

"Good afternoon," said Hedda.

There was an absence of respect in the bellboy's greeting to Hedda that could be interpreted as active disrespect, as though the man had insisted on making her speak to him and thereby put her on terms of familiarity. Instinctively Robert put the bellboy among the party of men at the rathskeller.

"Take my satchel, will you please?" said Robert.

"Ugly weather out, ma'am," said Jimmy. She did not reply or look at him, and he picked up the satchel and went to the door and held it open for Robert. "Good day, ma'am," said Jimmy. She continued to ignore him. Robert followed him to Room 514.

He did not see Hedda again that night nor the next day until late afternoon, when she knocked on his door. "Have you had anything to eat?" she said.

"I don't want anything, thanks," he said. "You may be getting your wish."

"I'm going to send for the doctor. What doctor do you go to here?"

"The only one I can think of is Harold Parkinson."

"Well, didn't you tell Esther you were sick?"

"Very clever, Hedda. But I haven't spoken to Esther. If you want to help, you can call the hotel doctor. I suppose there is one."

There was not a resident physician, but a plodding practitioner who smelled of laudanum and was oversolicitous came and took Robert's temperature. "Don't you have a regular doctor in town, Mr. Millhouser?"

"No."

"Mrs. Millhouser, your husband by rights oughta be in the hospital."

"Then let's take him there. Will you make the arrangements?"

"I don't happen to be connected with a hospital, but—"

"Do you know Dr. Parkinson?" said Robert.

"Yes, sure. At least I'm acquainted with him. Do you know him? He's more a surgeon, but if you know him, that's different."

Robert was taken in an ambulance to the hospital and a private room, and for the next few days, which were one long day and many short days of brief consciousness, he saw the faces of Hedda and of Ruth Steele, two nurses, Harold Parkinson, a younger doctor, and other nurses, over and over again. Sometimes he would hear a name and he would think he saw the face that belonged with the name, but when he tried to speak to the face it became the face of one of the nurses. The strange younger doctor became Gianni, the friend of Alfredo di Cattaneo, and the face of Leonard Vance became the face of Bart Vance, and Harold Parkinson was Dr. Willetts and Hedda was a girl named Zaza. Then one day, in the morning it was, he opened his eyes and saw clearly, breathed without struggling, and spoke to the woman in the blue dress and white apron whose back was turned to him. "Good morning," he said. "What's your name?"

"Miss Fogarty," she said. "I'm your day nurse. How do you feel?"

"I feel very well, thank you."

"You've been a very sick man. Will I get you the bedpan?"

"Is my wife anywhere near?"

"She's generally in about ha' past nine, ten o'clock."

"What time is it now?"

Miss Fogarty looked at the watch on its fleur-de-lis pin. "Just after ten. Four minutes."

"Then she's a little late."

"She generally comes with her mother, Mrs. Steele. You go on the bedpan and I'll fetch Dr. Schertlinger."

"Who's Dr. Schertlinger?"

"The intern on duty."

"Gianni."

"No, not Johnny. Heber. Heber W. Schertlinger."

"Was I supposed to die last night?"

"Such talk. You're very weak, now, and don't waste your strength asking those kind of questions."

"I have a feeling that—it's ten o'clock now—I was supposed to die around four o'clock this morning."

"I wasn't here, if that's when the crisis was, but do what you have to do and then I want you to go back to sleep."

"Saddle my horse and have him at the door in half an hour."

"Oh, Lord," she said, and took his pulse.

"I was joking. I'm not delirious, Miss Fogarty. You can stop squeezing my wrist, and I'll make water for you."

"Will I run the water in the sink for you?"

"I have a surprise for you, Miss Fogarty. You can take the pan away. Now I'd like to sit up."

"You'll do no such thing, but if you're quiet I'll get you some orange juice. If you're quiet, that is."

Hedda and Ruth Steele arrived while the intern was in the room. "Good morning, Hedda. Ruth," said Robert.

"Good morning," they said.

"Dr. Parkinson will be down in about an hour or so," said the intern. "If you want anything, tell Miss Fogarty." He left and the nurse followed him out.

"Well, I'm still here," said Robert. "I have a feeling I kept you up very late last night."

"Oh, that's all right, Robert," said Ruth Steele. "I'll leave you two for a few minutes."

"How is Ed?"

"Ed's fine. He telephoned every day to see how you were."

"That was nice of him."

"I'll go now, Robert, but I'll be right outside," said Ruth.

"Well, how are you, Hedda?" he said, when they were alone.

"I'm all right, I guess. How do you feel?"

"Weak. But beginning to make sense, I guess. But you look rather tired."

"We were here till five o'clock this morning, Mother and I. They wanted to give us a room down the hall but I hate hospitals. I wouldn't have been able to sleep."

"You didn't get much sleep at the hotel, either."

"I will this afternoon. You're going to be all right again, the doctor said."

"Yes. Have you been coming every day?"

"Yes."

"That was nice of you. Thank you."

"Well, you're my husband, and if I'd have been sick you'd have come. You spoke to me, didn't you know it was me?"

"Not always."

"You had trouble saying my name. Zaza instead of Hedda, but that's the way you were talking. Mumbling. It was hard to understand you."

"I've always been a hard man to understand, haven't I, Hedda?"

"Sometimes."

"You don't have to stand. Why don't you sit down? You must be very tired."

"All right," she said. "When do you think you'll get out of here? Did they say anything?"

"No, but I'd guess in another week or so. You can go home, if you want to."

She was silent.

"Or go stay with your mother and father, if you'd rather not be in the house alone. Or have your mother stay with you. But I should be up and around in a week or so."

"I don't know what I want to do. I don't want to go back to Lyons, and I don't feel much like staying at the hotel, by myself, but Mother's going to have to go back to Lyons. The only person I've seen outside of my mother was Ben Rosebery. There's nothing for me to do in this town."

Suddenly he was aware of the appalling loneliness she faced when her mother returned to Lyons. Whether or not she had brought it on herself through a quarrel with Esther and the rest of Fort Penn, she was a lost child and he pitied her.

"I'm sorry about everything, Hedda. No, not everything. That isn't true for a minute. But I wanted to make you happy."

"Oh, let's not talk about it while you're sick in bed. What's the difference anyway?"

"Don't stay in Fort Penn. Go back to Lyons with your mother."

"I guess that's what I'll do if you don't mind."

"Yes, do that and I'll be home as soon as I can be. You *are* lovely to look at, Hedda."

"You're not going to be saying that much longer," she said.

"I'll *always* say *that*," he said.

Ben Rosebery insisted on accompanying Robert to Lyons. "Maybe it's a case of the blind leading the halt," said Ben. "But I'd feel better if you'd let me go along."

"I'm not going to put up much resistance," said Robert. "I'm still a little weak in the knees. Not accustomed to hospital food." Ben, the clever lawyer, should have known that his impassivity in recent weeks had been more revealing than a frank discussion of the problem of Hedda. All sorts of gossip reached Ben; political, social, business, personal. He was the confidant of many men and women in all classes and grades of the life of the city, and Robert reasoned that Ben must have been one of the very first to hear stories about Hedda. It was curious that with so far nothing to go on, Robert believed that there was gossip aplenty, but again not so curious. The silent awkwardness of the men at the rathskeller was enough for a man who was not completely obtuse; the conversation with Hedda had been circumscribed without getting specific in detail of accusation or denial, and it was a case of two people who understood each other so well that everything was said while the committing words remained unspoken. Robert was sure that Ben was hoping he still had heard none of the gossip; he was equally sure that Ben had some hope that he could "iron things out," an expression he often used to cover some of the most intricate legal maneuverings. But Robert saw no point in maintaining his own silence, and by chance an opportunity occurred on the train to Lyons to bring up the subject of Hedda. He had the afternoon newspaper on his lap. "Ah, let's have a look at this," said Robert. "The names of the Valentine's Ball committee." He read the list quickly to himself. "No clues," he said, when he had finished. "Just about the same people as every year." He waited, but Ben did not ask what clues. "I suppose there's not much use asking you."

"Asking me what?"

"Who blackballed us this year."

"Well, *are* you asking me? And *do* you want to know?"

"I suppose not."

"I could tell you who I think might have blackballed you, but I'd refuse to be drawn out on the next question. You have to work that out yourself."

"I guess I haven't been fair to you, Ben. You're trying to remain a friend of both parties, and that's difficult."

"Not when you really are fond of both parties, and not as long as neither one of them tries to get anything out of me," said Ben. "There's a situation, and all three of us know it, and I want to keep my services available if they become necessary. That's a little obscure, but it's as far as I'll go."

"Nothing obscure about it. I understand it, and so would Hedda."

"Hedda does understand it."

Of that there was no doubt, for Hedda evinced neither surprise nor curiosity about Ben's making the trip with Robert. The three dined together and Robert retired early, weary but not so exhausted as he might have been after dinner alone with Hedda. He did not expect Hedda to come to his room, and she did not come, and Robert was thankful that Ben stayed over another day and another night. He was deliberately keeping Hedda and Robert apart, postponing the confrontation that all three knew was inevitable, but giving Robert an extra day or two of rest and Hedda an extra day or two in which to consider the advantages of a quiet life in Lyons, now that Fort Penn was a failure.

But Ben Rosebery was not in possession of all the facts. He was actually not in possession of any facts, but even if Hedda had confirmed the gossip in regard to Bart Vance, there still remained the fact that meant more to Hedda than any other. She needed no doctor to tell her she was pregnant, and consequently there was no peace for her in the quiet life of Lyons.

In the time she spent in Lyons before Robert's return she had observed the subtle difference in the way people spoke to her: they would look first and then speak, instead of speaking and looking at the same time. Also it had happened too often that some women were not speaking at all—too often, that is, to be accidental. While she was at her mother's house she stayed at home in the morning, but when she went home she did not resume her custom of doing the daily marketing.

She got through the first day after Ben's departure only by pretending to a nurse-like solicitude, impersonal attention to small comforts and keeping a distance. But on the second day Robert said at lunch: "We have things to talk about, Hedda. Will after lunch suit you?"

"All right," she said.

They went to the little room and he closed the door. "What do you want to do?"

"I want to go away."

"Yes, I know that. But how do you want to go away? You don't want to go away with me."

"No, I don't."

"Speak up, Hedda. Don't force me to ask you a question every time. What do you want to *do?*"

"If you'll give me the money, I'll go away and never come back here."

"How do you know that that's what I want?"

"You told me to tell you what I want, but isn't that what you want too?"

352

"You want a divorce, I suppose. But is there any reason why I should give you the money to go away with another man?"

"No, unless you want to get rid of me. Then it would be worth it."

"There is another man, of course."

"This reminds me of when I first knew you. You're trying to find things out without asking the questions. Well, ask your damn questions, but I'm not going to tell you anything unless you do. You're not going to get anything for nothing. If you want to know anything, you'll have to take a chance and ask your questions. You're a coward."

"All right. Have you had an affair with another man?"

"Yes, I have."

"Who?"

"Bart Vance."

"How long has it been going on?"

"Oh, I don't know. Long enough. How many times have I had relations with him? Ask me that."

"How many times?"

"So many times that I've lost count. More than I've ever been with anybody except you."

"Where?"

"Where? Here. Fort Penn."

"When I was away?"

"Of course when you were away. No, once in Fort Penn when you were in town."

"In this house?"

"Of course in this house, once in this room. But usually in my room. If you'll ask the questions, I'll tell you everything you want to know."

"Why?"

"Why not? If I admit it once, isn't that enough? The rest is you torturing yourself, so go ahead. I don't mind you torturing yourself."

"What happened in the Fort Penn depot?"

"Oh, you even knew about that. Nothing happened. I was feeling him and a policeman came and told us to stop. He knew us. He knew Bart and he knew me."

"You were feeling him?"

"Yes. I was trying to make him miss the train. He was going back to New York and I didn't want him to. What else would you like to know? I'll tell you every single thing. Ask me what I did to him and he did to me . . . You ought to see your face. You're not sure whether you want to throw me on the floor or kill me."

"Yes I am."

"Well, you don't have to throw me on the floor. We have a comfortable bed upstairs, and I'll go if you ask me. But you have to ask me, Robert."

"You'd really go upstairs with me?"

"Yes, I said I would. We're just like any two people now. We're not a husband and wife any more." She stood up. "I'm ready any time you are."

"I'm not like you, Hedda. This doesn't excite me the way it does you."

"There you're wrong. It isn't talking about it that excites me. It's your face. You might as well be a different person. You're another man, but I know your name. Come on, Millhouser."

"I am another man. You've completely destroyed the one you knew."

"All right. So much the better."

"You don't mind destroying the one that loved you?"

"Loved me? You never loved anyone but yourself. You can't. You never will. You might just as well be another woman. You're built like a man, a man's physique, but you're not a man inside. There's something wrong with you, Robert. Me, too. But I'd rather have what's wrong with me than what you have. I never saw your face like this before, and you say I destroyed the one that loved me? Maybe I did. Who knows? Maybe that's why I really wanted to go upstairs, a minute ago. And maybe you will love somebody, if you've changed. But maybe I'm wrong about that. Maybe you haven't changed."

"Is this the young woman who complains that *I* think too much?"

"Yes," said Hedda Millhouser. "But I do too, sometimes."

He rose. "Shall we go upstairs?"

"No," she said. "I changed my mind."

"But let's."

"All right," she said.

They went to her room and she lowered the shades. They took off their clothes and he lay beside her, touching her everywhere gently, kissing her. But whenever he looked at her face she was watching him warily. "You must help," he said. "Why are you so calm?"

"What do you want me to do?" she said. "I think you must be too tired."

"I've never had to tell you what to do."

She touched him and kissed him, but there was no response. "You're tired," she said. "It's too soon after the hospital."

"Do you think that's what it is, Hedda?"

354

"I don't know."

"Would you mind if I went to sleep here?"

"No, I don't mind."

"Maybe if I slept for a little while."

"Do you want me to stay?"

"Of course I want you to stay."

He went to sleep. When he awoke she was sitting at her dressing-table, smoking a cigarette, brushing her hair. "Have I been asleep long?"

"I guess about an hour."

"Come here," he said.

She took off her dressing-gown and got into bed again, but it was no use. "I've lost you," he said. "Haven't I?"

"I don't know," she said.

"Meaning I have. Well, I'm almost fifty-three."

"Maybe you ought to try with another woman."

"I won't, and I don't want you with another man."

"You won't be able to stop me. You always knew this would happen, and now it has." She spoke matter-of-factly, without much anger. "Why don't you ask your friend Esther, she might help you. She's always helping people. I honestly wouldn't mind if you had her here."

"With you and Mr. Vance in the next room, I suppose."

"Not Mr. Vance. I don't want him any more, but what difference does it make who it is? It'll be somebody. I'm not dead yet."

"Hedda, it won't be Mr. Vance, and it won't be anybody."

"But it will. I'm going to leave here tomorrow and I'm not coming back."

"Where are you going?"

"I don't know. Maybe to my grandmother's out west. I guess you won't give me any money, but I can pawn the jewelry you gave me."

"If I were going to let you leave I wouldn't be stingy. But I'm not letting you go, Hedda. Why do you refuse to understand that?"

"Because you can't stop me. I'll get dressed and leave this minute."

"Don't do that. At least give yourself one night to think it over."

"One night won't change my mind."

"Do me that courtesy."

She laughed. "I'll stay, because my father has three engineers staying at their house, not out of courtesy."

"You're an exquisite creature, Hedda."

She got up and put on her dressing-gown. "Thanks," she said. It was the last word she ever spoke to him.

He left her room with no plan but to be alone and by being alone to hide from her anything that might show of his humiliation. She had provided him, out of her kindness, with an explanation for his impotence: he was too soon out of the hospital, he was physically weaker than he had ever known himself to be. But something of what he now felt was very much the same vertigo that he had fought against in the side room of Fritz Gottlieb's Rathskeller. Then he had been able to overcome it by concentrating on the bottles that floated to the coast of Portugal, but now he could look back to that time and from it fix the moment that was the beginning of the end of his desire of Hedda. A puncture had been made, and almost literally the desire began to leak away. So it had continued during his illness, when strength and desire both were being drained from him by pneumococci and by a realized fear. In the hospital he could pretend, but not well, that disease was taking away his strength and with it desire; but he had never kissed Hedda in the hospital, and after the first few days she had ceased to kiss his forehead. The realized fear, denied but recognized at the rathskeller, was much less a matter of simple jealousy of a known or unknown man than a loathing of the inevitable, predictable, predicted atrophy of a function, the function called making love but that symbolized life and power even when it was loveless. He could not believe Hedda; he *had* loved her. Why else had he been so terrified by the realization of the loss of his power to give her pleasure? Why was he now so searchingly looking at his reflection in the mirror? What did she see in his face?

He could see nothing that had not been there a day ago. The skin drawn a little more tightly over the cheekbones, a little more looseness in the skin below his jaw, a paler shade to the eyes, the look of a man who had been through a critical illness. It was not in Hedda's powers to see more than that. And yet she had been afraid of him. Her fear of him had not dispelled his impotence, but it had created in her an absence of lubricity that was itself impotence. It would not last longer than it would take her to discover a man to lust after. But he was forgetting: there would be no such man. This was the night she was to die.

Odd that he had known—how long? three weeks?—that she was to die, that he would kill her, but that he had never given any thought to the method by which he would end her life. It was as though he would will her to death, that his wish was so intense that she would die of it. It was totally uncharacteristic of him, both as a man of precise habits and as a man who had never made a claim to extraordinary powers, that he would not have chosen a weapon or that he could have accomplished her death without one. The thought of a weapon immediately suggested the method.

He put on some clothes, stopped in the hall for an overcoat, and went to the stable. Moses was drowsing beside the stove.

"Moses, I want you to go to the drug store and ask them to give you a bottle of my cough medicine."

"Now?"

"Right away. And I'll wait here till you get back."

"You don't have to wait here. I bring it up the house."

"Will you do as I say?"

"You cranky since you been sick."

"I'll be a damned sight crankier if you don't hitch up and get on your way."

As soon as Moses had driven through the gate Robert opened the drawer where he knew the pistol was kept. The pistol was there, loaded and well oiled. He put it in his pocket and went back to the house and hid it in a bureau drawer. In due course Moses returned, and Robert was lying on his bed.

"I look all over for you down the stable way."

"I got tired waiting."

"Here's your ee-lixer. Doctor Brown, he say you wasn't to take too much of this stuff. No more'n four teaspoons a day. Say you got a bottle two days ago and you oughta have some left."

"I have, but I didn't want to run short."

"Mr. Robert. What's the matter? What's the trouble?"

"No trouble."

"Ever since you was a boy wud I always tell you? You feel sumpn's wrong—sumpn's wrong. I got that same feelin' when I look around for you down the stable way. Sumpn wrong here, I say. *You* din get tired waitin'. If you was waitin' there you never woulda let my stove go out. You din wait no time at all. What's—wrong?"

"Nothing. Will you tell Sophie that I'd like some clear soup in my room, about seven o'clock. I won't be down for dinner. And tell Mrs. Millhouser."

"Me tell Mrs. Millhouser? Why don't you tell her you'self? Is that what's wrong?"

"Now don't be nosy, don't ask about things that are none of your business."

As soon as Moses left Robert drank half of the six ounces of cough medicine. It always made him sleep, even a teaspoonful of the stuff, and a good dose of it now would surely take him through the evening.

At seven o'clock Henrietta knocked on his door repeatedly, but when she got no answer she reported to Hedda. Hedda opened the door of his bedroom. He was lying on his back, snoring. "We won't wake him," she said. She went in again at ten o'clock, on her way to bed, and he was still asleep but the snoring had stopped. "I guess he's going to sleep all night," she said to Henrietta.

It was eleven or twelve o'clock when he awoke; he was not sure of the count of the bell in the borough hall. His head ached and he was thirsty, but he was so groggy that the thought of the effort of getting up for a glass of water made him sleepy again and he slept. The next tolling of the bell he heard was for two o'clock. The household and the town were sleeping and he was alone in the world until returning consciousness brought with it the reality of his headache, now sharp and fierce, and his thirst, so strong that in spite of the pain that any slight movement caused in his head, he dismissed the fancy that he was alone in the world. Thirst and headache were real, and there were too many people in the world, as real as his dry mouth and the pounding on his brain. He went to the bathroom in the dark, fearful of the added pain that would come with a light in his eyes. He found the tumbler easily and drank glass after glass of water, which ran cold, cold enough so that he soaked a washrag and put it to his forehead, but the ache was not lessened.

He returned to his room and sat in the Morris chair. She should not have said those awful things. He had decided to kill her, that she must be killed, but it could have been put off until she ran away. She could have run away. He had not really decided *when* to kill her, no more than he had decided how. If she had not said all those terrible things she might have acted on her fear and run away from him. But she had been coldly and deliberately cruel; having destroyed the man that he had been, and that he had come to like, she expressed no regret. She had desecrated what was left of that man by her vicious taunting, by taking pleasure in her wildly free admissions and her nastily childish eagerness to turn confession into boasting. She had declared her intention of having another man, and finally she had forced him to humiliate himself in the most contemptuous way she could devise, challenging him by pretending to offer temptation, defying him to respond to the beauty of her body, and mocking him with the passionless rituals of her love-making. She had made it impossible for him to do anything but what he was about to do.

He heard no more striking of the borough-hall clock; it had become part of the outside silence, like the distant shifting of coal cars in the night sounds that he never noticed. He stood at the window, and the darkness was no less complete for the street lamps than the

358

silence for the familiar sounds. But then above the mountain ridge he saw first light, light before light, and the time had come. Time, sound and light had meant nothing until now, but first light was an excitement. What he had to do must be done while darkness remained. His hand found the pistol and he went to Hedda's room.

He stood at the foot of her bed until he could make out the outlines of her body; then there was more light, and he could see her slowly changing her sleeping position, so that she now lay with her right cheek on the pillow, her left arm extended so that the hand hung over the edge of the bed. He moved closer, put out his hand until the pistol was scarcely a yard away from her. He cocked the pistol, and fired into her heart.

She did not move. It was as though she were pinned to the bed. For a minute fraction of a second he believed he had not shot her, but only so long as it took for the shock of the pistol sound to take effect on him. The roar seemed a long time coming and he stepped back with the pistol still in his hand, his arm lying loosely at his side. He did not take his eyes off her until he saw some blood beginning to soak the sheet under her left armpit.

"I'm sorry, Hedda," he said, aloud.

Soon the blood stopped coming and Robert Millhouser wondered what to do next. He did not want to leave Hedda, but daylight had arrived and he had a crime to confess. He put the pistol in his pocket and covered Hedda's face and body with the silk counterpane that was folded and resting on a stool. He went downstairs and rang young Dr. Willetts's number.

The doctor's telephone was answered by one of his young children: "Dr. Willetts's residence."

"May I speak to your father, please? This is Mr. Millhouser."

"Yes sir," said the child.

Dr. Willetts came to the telephone. "Good morning, Mr. Millhouser. Anything wrong?"

"Very. Doctor, I've got to prepare you for a shock."

"I'm used to shocks. Go ahead."

"I've just murdered my wife."

"Just a minute till I close the door," said Dr. Willetts. Then: "Now say that again, please."

"I have just killed my wife."

"How?"

"I shot her in the heart, with a pistol."

"I see. I'll be right out. Meanwhile, leave everything exactly the way it was, and maybe you'd better telephone George Holliday, if you haven't already."

"Thank you, Doctor."

"Why did you call me? Dr. Dixon is the deputy coroner."

"Your father wanted me to get married."

"My father wanted you to get married? I think we'd better not talk any more till I get there."

Robert Millhouser next called the number of the borough hall, but the operator said: "There's nobody there now, Mr. Millhouser. Tommy Fenstermacher don't come to work till around eight, but you can leave a message with me if you wanta."

"No thanks. What time does Mr. Holliday's office open?"

"His girl's generally there a little after eight. She stops at the post office on her way, and that takes her about ten-fifteen minutes, and by that time Mr. Holliday's generally there too."

"Thank you. I'll try him later," said Robert Millhouser.

He had not yet come to any sense of the enormity of what he had done. He sat in the little room, conscious of the act of murder, but not yet saddened, not yet fearful, whichever would come first. He conceded the major importance of the act and the likely effects on his emotions and his safety, but his practical thinking was concerned with matters that were secretarial. There were people to notify. He found himself pondering the advisability of telephoning Ed and Ruth Steele, and went into that matter in some detail. Was it the honest and honorable thing to speak to Ed Steele, or to let him find out from someone else? Was it the brave thing to speak to Steele? The kinder thing to speak to him? It was only after some thought that he realized that his bravery, his kindness, his honesty, his honorableness were forever, forever, of no concern to the father and mother of the dead girl upstairs. And his slowness in coming to that conclusion was a measure of how little he had so far been affected by what he had done.

His first genuinely civilized reaction to his crime was impatience. When he began to be impatient with the doctor's slowness in arriving, he began to feel. Impatience with the doctor evolved into impatience with the avengers: let them come and hang him and get it over with. Then from impatience he proceeded to nervousness and from nervousness to self-protective fear, and fear had set in by the time young Dr. Willetts arrived.

Robert Millhouser heard the doorbell and got up to answer it, and was surprised, almost humorously surprised, that Henrietta also was going to answer the door. Henrietta and Sophie still had no knowledge of what had occurred. "Morning, Mr. Millhouser. I din know you was down," said Henrietta.

"Henrietta, I'll go to the door." He hesitated. He did not know how to tell this woman. "Something very bad has happened."

"Sumpn bad? Mrs. Millhouser, she poorly?"

He nearly thanked her for that much help. "She's dead, and you and Sophie may want to leave this house. I killed her."

She looked at him blankly, fully believing him, but incredulous of the fact that he was so near her. Suddenly she screamed and ran to the kitchen.

Robert Millhouser opened the door. "That scream was the maid. I just told her what I've done."

"I'll have a look at Mrs. Millhouser," said the doctor.

"She's in the room at the top of the stairs and on your right facing out toward town. Do you want me to come with you?"

"No," said the doctor. Plainly he did not want to be in the house, and was repelled by Robert Millhouser. He remained upstairs less than five minutes.

"Do you think she felt any pain?"

"No," said the doctor.

"I hoped she wouldn't feel any pain."

"She didn't. That's not saying she didn't want to live."

"You don't like me, do you?"

"Like you? This was the most cold-blooded murder I've ever seen. Don't you know how I earn my living? I'm a doctor. As far as I'm concerned, you're at the opposite end of the human race. Where is the revolver?"

"Here." Robert Millhouser held the pistol, butt end foremost, for the doctor to take. The doctor unfolded a handkerchief and lay it in the palm of his hand before accepting the pistol.

"I've left word for Dr. Dixon. Fenstermacher should be here soon."

"Then there's no need for you to stay."

"Yes there is. I want to keep an eye on you."

"I'm not going to try to escape. And don't forget, I could have shot you."

"I doubt it. I'd have shot you first." The doctor showed Robert Millhouser a .32 Hopkins & Allen revolver. He put it back in his pocket. "For the time being, Mr. Millhouser, you're my prisoner."

"Prisoner? I'm your prisoner? I'm nobody's prisoner. I'm my own prisoner, but not anybody else's."

"Have it your own way, but if you try to leave the house I'll shoot you. After what I saw upstairs I could let you have all five shots."

"He won't run away."

The doctor turned and saw Moses Hatfield. "Oh, it's you, Moses."

"He aint gonna run away," said Moses. "Mr. Robert, you aint gonna run away, are you?"

"No," said Robert Millhouser.

"Can I get you a cup of tea, Mr. Robert?" said Moses. "Them women, Sophie and Henrietta, they ran."

"Maybe the doctor would like a cup of tea," said Robert Millhouser.

"I've had my breakfast," said the doctor.

"I guess I'll have a cup of tea, Moses," said Robert Millhouser. Moses departed for the kitchen.

"What did you mean when you said my father wanted you to get married? Why do you mention my father?"

"Nothing more than I said. Your father used to tell me I ought to get married, and I did."

"Are you in any way trying to blame my father for any of this?"

"I have no desire to blame anyone but myself for anything."

"I never understood what my father saw in you. Neither did my mother."

"Your father had compassion. Yes, even for murderers. I remember a long time ago, a woman hacked her husband to death. It's so long ago, and my brain isn't working very well, but the woman had a phantom pregnancy. That was what your father called it. A phantom pregnancy. She was out of her mind, unbalanced. Your father understood that. He had compassion. Your father knew things twenty-five years ago that other doctors are just beginning to find out. I wish he were here now. At least I could try to tell him."

"Tell him what?"

"I don't know. Everything. That's the worst thing about living longer than your friends. That's the worst thing about living. Your friends die, and so do you. When a friend dies, that part of you dies too, the part that was friendship with your friend. The part of me that was Hedda, that's dead now. But she killed it before I killed her. She destroyed me, and I was nice. She should never have done that. If I hadn't been nice, that would have been a different story. But I was, and she deliberately humiliated me."

"Listen, I'm going to be asked to testify against you. You'd better shut up."

"That was deliberate. When she destroyed me, maybe she couldn't have helped that. But to deliberately humiliate me, that was a different story."

Moses came in with a tray. He set it on the desk. "If them eggs is too hard I fix you some more. They's a little over two minutes."

"As long as they're not boiled too hard," said Robert Millhouser.

"Moses, where were you when this happened?" said the doctor.

Moses turned and frowned, and he did not answer the question. Moreover, his manner showed that he would answer no other questions.

"I had another friend, before your father and I got to be such good friends. His advice was quite the opposite. He told me not to get married. But he became a monk. A Catholic monk. Moses, will you get me a teaspoon, please?"

"Forgot a teaspoon," said Moses, and went to fetch it.

"Both of them knew me very well, and yet when it came to giving me advice, one said do one thing, and the other said do something entirely different. But your father's advice was what I wanted to do, and Chester Calthorp's—that was my other friend's name—his advice went against the grain. I had always wanted to get married and be like my father, so naturally your father's advice was more acceptable. It probably doesn't pay to do what you want to do. I'll never believe that Chester wanted to become a monk. I'll never swallow that. He was a real sybarite, but now I'm told he has to dig ditches and get up at four o'clock in the morning. Pray every few hours. Who does a man like Chester pray to? Bacchus and Venus, when I knew him."

Dr. Daniel Dixon, the deputy coroner, arrived. He was a small young man with pointed chin whiskers that did not make him look older. He was obviously taken aback to find Robert Millhouser having breakfast.

The doctors were punctiliously courteous to each other, thus confirming Robert Millhouser's quick impression of professional hostility. "I haven't touched anything, Doctor, except to pull down the counterpane for a superficial examination of the wound," said Dr. Willetts. "The body is in the same position it was in when I first saw it."

Dr. Dixon, who was a newcomer to Lyons, said: "This man is calmly eating his breakfast."

"But talking gibberish," said Dr. Willetts.

"It isn't gibberish just because you don't understand it," said Robert Millhouser.

"I took a pistol away from him—"

"I *gave* it to you," said Robert Millhouser.

"—and here it is. I'm armed, myself, and I've made him my prisoner pending your arrival."

"I don't know that he's *my* prisoner," said Dr. Dixon. "To tell you the truth, this is the first murder I've been called in on."

"Homicide, I believe they call it, Doctor."

"Oh. Were you ever deputy coroner?"

"Yes I was, years ago. You can place him under arrest, if you wish to, Doctor. You're a sworn officer of the county. But if I were you, Doctor, I'd wait for Fenstermacher."

"I'm not going to run away."

"He keeps repeating that, but that's not to be depended on. I'll keep an eye on him while you make your examination."

"Thank you, Doctor."

"While it's on my mind, would you let me be present when you perform the autopsy?"

"The autopsy. By all means, Doctor. I wish you would. When shall we do that?"

"Well, some time this afternoon, I suggest. If you like, I'll call the undertaker and get the body out of here and we can start some time around two o'clock. We should be finished by about half past five, six o'clock."

"Stop saying those things!" Robert Millhouser shouted.

The outburst startled Dr. Dixon and he excused himself and went to the bedroom.

"How can you be so cold? 'Get the body out of here.' She was my wife, and this was our home."

"Yes. Your home."

"I murdered her, but I have respect for her. I don't *want* you to say things like 'Get the body out of here.' She isn't a bundle of something to get rid of."

"She is now."

Robert Millhouser rushed at Dr. Willetts and slapped his face. Willetts, who was built like his father, stood up and easily shoved Robert Millhouser into a chair.

"You're so cruel," said Robert Millhouser. He put his hands to his face but he did not weep. He and the doctor did not speak again until Dr. Dixon reappeared and whispered something to Dr. Willetts, who nodded and whispered a reply.

"Mr. Millhouser, will you tell me what happened?" said Dr. Dixon.

"What is there to tell you? I held out the pistol and took aim, and then I fired."

"Your wife was sleeping?"

"Yes."

"What time was this?"

"I don't know."

"But some time after daylight. Say six-thirty?"

"I don't know. It wasn't daylight. I could hardly see her at first."

"But you took aim."

364

"Yes."

"Then either it was daylight or you lit the electric light."

"It was just before daylight."

"You said you could hardly see her at first. Does that imply that you were in the room for some time before you fired the pistol?"

"Yes. Long enough to be able to see her."

"Describe her position in the bed."

"When I fired the pistol?"

"Yes."

"She was lying on her back, her face was turned to the right and I think her right hand was under the pillow. Her left hand was hanging over the edge of the bed."

"And you took aim and fired. Where were you standing?"

"At the foot of the bed. I leaned forward a little to take aim."

"And you took very careful aim?"

"Yes."

"A moment ago when I asked you to describe her position in the bed, you wanted to know whether I meant at the time you fired the pistol."

"Yes. She had changed her position."

"I see. That's what I was coming to. In other words, you had been standing there for quite some time. Long enough so that when you first went into the room it was dark, and then when you finally decided to pull the trigger it was light."

"I don't know how long I was there. It must have been a long time, but it doesn't seem long when I think of it."

"But your common sense tells you it was a long time."

"I guess it was a fairly long time."

"You know it was a long time, don't you, Mr. Millhouser?"

"Oh, now I begin to see what you're driving at. You want me to say that it was deliberate murder, that I'd had time to think it over. Oh, I'll admit that, Doctor Dixon. I made up my mind to kill my wife three or four weeks ago. It was deliberate murder."

"That *is* what I wanted to know."

"Just as deliberate as the way she destroyed me. But I didn't do it for revenge. I honestly didn't. At least I honestly think I didn't."

Dixon and Willetts exchanged glances.

"I didn't have anything to go on till yesterday. She admitted it all yesterday, but it was three or four weeks ago I knew I was going to kill her. And that was before she and I talked about it."

"Dr. Dixon isn't interested in your suspicions," said Dr. Willetts.

"I didn't say anything about suspicions, but you did. So you must have heard the gossip, too. I'm not going to cause any trouble. I'm going to plead guilty and they can hang me."

"If they let you plead guilty," said Dr. Willetts.

"How can they stop me? I'm guilty. I murdered my wife. Have I tried to deny that?"

"You're an educated man. You know that if you're allowed to plead guilty you won't hang."

"I didn't know that."

"If you didn't, you do now. And that's what your lawyer is going to try for. A plea of guilty, and life imprisonment."

"I'd rather hang."

"Nobody would rather hang, Mr. Millhouser," said Dr. Willetts.

"I tell you you're wrong. *I'd* rather hang. Don't judge the human race by what you've seen of it. You haven't seen it all, and you haven't seen it except with your own cold eyes. I would rather hang."

"Then why didn't you shoot yourself after you killed your wife?"

"I never thought of it. My life was over three weeks ago, and I very nearly did die of pneumonia. But I didn't. If you want to, you can say that I had such a strong desire to kill my wife that it kept me alive. And maybe that's true. I got over pneumonia, and men of my age usually die of it, don't they? Who is that?" He stood up when he heard voices in the hall.

"It's the undertaker, most likely," said Dr. Dixon. He went out to give orders and Dr. Willetts remained with Robert Millhouser.

"If I tried to run away, you'd shoot me, wouldn't you?"

"I wouldn't have to shoot you, but if I did I'd aim for your leg."

"I see. You don't want to kill me. You want someone else to do it. Yesterday in this room I was called a coward. Now I call you a coward, and the worst kind. You want to see me dead, but at no cost to yourself. At least I did my own killing, Doctor. Don't ever forget that."

"I'll never forget any of this. The most cold-blooded murder I ever knew about."

"Your father would despise you for what you're doing to me. I know what you're doing. You won't be satisfied till you see me groveling."

"That won't satisfy me."

"What will? You want to see me afraid. *I am afraid*. But I'm not going to go into hysterics for you."

"Mr. Millhouser, I have a daughter not much younger than your wife, about two years younger. She's in high school. That's why I want to see you hang."

"There's the doorbell. That should be Tommy Fenstermacher." He got up and, followed by the doctor, went to the front door. It was Fenstermacher. "Tommy, I'd have gone down and given myself up but I didn't want anyone to think I was trying to run away."

"That's all right, Robert," said Fenstermacher. "I didn't come to arrest you."

Robert Millhouser looked at him gratefully. "I did it, though," he said.

"You get a lawyer. Don't say nothing to me," said Fenstermacher. "Or if you want me to, I'll tell George Holliday to come out myself. You go have some rest."

"Why aren't you putting this man under arrest?" said Dr. Willetts.

"Do I take orders from you, Doc?" said Fenstermacher.

"I charge him with the murder of his wife," said the doctor. "You can't ignore that."

"You say I can't, but I can."

"Dr. Dixon is here, and the undertaker. Go on upstairs and see the body. What's more, Dr. Dixon has the pistol Mrs. Millhouser was shot with. Now what are you waiting for?"

"Maybe somebody has to arrest him, but it won't be me."

"You'd better arrest me, Tommy. I'm guilty," said Robert Millhouser.

"No, it goes against my principles, Robert. If Leon Bensinger wants to arrest you, he can. But I won't."* Tommy Fenstermacher left the house.

"It's too bad Tommy Fenstermacher's father wasn't a doctor," said Robert Millhouser. "Tommy would have made a good doctor."

"Whatever his father was, Fenstermacher has no respect for the law."

"I have a favor to ask you," said Robert Millhouser.

"It'll give me some pleasure to refuse it."

"It's a duty. It's only a favor to me—well, you'll see. Will you go see Mr. and Mrs. Steele? Will you tell them before someone else does?"

Dr. Willetts considered for a moment. "Yes, I'll do that. I'll take my wife with me."

George Holliday was the next to arrive. "Where's Tommy Fenstermacher?"

---

* In several particulars this version of the scene differs from the account given me by Robert Millhouser and reported by me in an earlier chapter. I have set down both versions to demonstrate the confusion existing in the mind of Robert Millhouser in the period following the telephone conversation with Dr. Willetts. The confusion was so real that his recollection of it twenty years later was faulty, one of the few instances in which Robert Millhouser's memory failed him.—G. H.

"He left. He refused to arrest him," said Dr. Willetts.

"I told him to, but he wouldn't," said Robert Millhouser.

"That was a mistake," said Holliday.

"You're damn right it was," said the doctor.

They all heard footsteps on the stairway and men's voices. "Swing it around a little more to your right . . . Easy, now. Easy . . . Don't start going down till you get a better hold on it . . . Hold it, now, hold it. I got the front end, I gotta turn around . . . For Christ's sakes don't drop her . . ."

The three men in the little room—Holliday, Willetts, and Robert Millhouser—stopped talking. They stood still, fixed in the positions they had been in when they heard the voices and first realized what was going on in the hallway. Holliday slightly bowed his head but gazed upward at Robert Millhouser. Now the sound of the footsteps came heavily and with a slow regularity until a man's voice uttered the word "There." Then someone said, "Who'll open the door?" and another voice said, "I'll open the door. It looks like I better open both doors." And there was a blast of cold air as the double door was opened. Then the doors were closed again.

"My God, Hedda," said Robert Millhouser, and slumped into a chair.

•

IT WAS ALWAYS DARK in the Fort Penn jail, the Nesquehela County Prison. The prison yard was so small in relation to the three cell blocks and fourth block of administrative offices and warden's quarters that surrounded it that there was never, except at noon, any real relief from the darkness. And at noon the prisoners were eating their dinner. There was the darkness and the overwhelming prison smell that gets into a new prison a month after it has been commissioned and never leaves while any of the prison is left standing. It is the smell of crude disinfectant, unwashed men, body gases, unhealthy breath, steamed soup, exposed plumbing, and sickness, and no other smell is like it except the smell of human blood in its assault on the sense and its lingering presence. There was, then, the darkness and the smell, and Robert Millhouser soon found that the silence he had expected did not exist. There was quiet, but it was not a silence, and at night especially the place was lively with sounds. The men never stopped talking and whispering, laughing joylessly, roaring in their sleep, groaning with pain. The guards would come only when the outcry was unmistakably that of the loser in a fight. The loud laughter and yelling of the pederasts and the other degenerates went unnoticed by the guards. Two of the guards had sweethearts of their own among the prisoners, who were protected from other prisoners by being placed in separate cells. As soon as Robert Millhouser was denied bail and put into prison uniform he was considered fair game until he would be claimed by a prisoner who would be able to drive off other claimants. On his first afternoon in the exercise period he was stared at in a way he did not immediately understand but soon—a matter of minutes—he learned. A man came up to him from behind and threw his arms about Robert Millhouser's waist and said: "You and me, huh, sweetheart?" Whereupon the man was punched in the chin by a second man who said, "I get this little old boy," and stood behind Robert Millhouser and squeezed his waist. The first man got to his feet and attacked the second, the guards blew their whistles and the yardful of prisoners slowly formed ranks, their exercise period ended. The men who had quarreled over Robert Millhouser were singled out as they re-entered the cell blocks and taken to the guards' room for their beatings. Robert Millhouser, in custody of two guards, was returned to his cell.

He had no cellmate, being charged with a capital crime. The cell door was made of riveted sheet iron, with a screened opening one foot square through which he could be observed by the guards. High in the wall of the cell was a single narrow window, six inches wide, with an iron bar on the outer side. A heavy screen made it impossible to touch the glass from the inside of the cell, a precaution against breaking the glass and using it for suicide. He was given carpet slippers instead of shoes containing laces as another anti-suicide precaution, and at mealtime he was provided with a large wooden spoon which was taken away when he had finished eating. The water level in the toilet was kept too low for him to drown himself in the bowl, and there was no point in the cell so high that he could dive head-first from it and fracture his skull.

His only visitor on his first day in prison was George Holliday. "I have been in touch with Ben Rosebery. He's in Wilkes-Barre but he'll be here tomorrow," said Holliday. "I hope that's all right with you."

"Of course."

"I've never defended a homicide case, and Ben's the best there is."

"I understand, George."

"Naturally I'll help as much as I can."

"I know you will."

"Is there anything I can do for you?"

"No, I guess not, thanks." Robert Millhouser almost pitied George Holliday, who was forcing himself to do his duty but was so relieved that Ben Rosebery was about to assume the responsibility. "It isn't your kind of case, George. Thank you for what you've done, but I wish you'd let Ben handle it. He doesn't live in Lyons."

"I'm not afraid of Lyons."

"Of course you're not, you've proved that, but it's better for all concerned if I have a Fort Penn lawyer."

Ben was admitted to the cell on the following morning, chatting familiarly with the guard as he was let in, and perfectly at home in the cell. "I came as soon as I could," he said. He shook his friend's hand and let his left hand rest on Robert's right shoulder.

"Thank you, Ben. Have a seat."

"I'll take the stool, if you don't mind. If I sit on your cot I'll be sure to pick up some bedbugs. I've learned from experience. Have they bothered you?"

"Yes. Last night."

"I'll speak to the warden. We get a blowtorch and kill those that are there now and the eggs, and I'll arrange to have some sheets and your own blanket. They'll be back in a week, the bugs, but we can keep you as comfortable as possible. Kerosene is good for them, but if you kerosene them the warden won't allow you to smoke. Now tell me the whole story."

Robert Millhouser told the story factually and as straightforwardly as his mental confusions would permit, uninterrupted by his friend. "Dr. Willetts said nobody wants to hang, and he's right. But I'm prepared to," he concluded.

"You're not going to. You don't want me to fight it, I know. But I'm going to anyway. As your friend I can't let you die, no matter how you feel now. But as your lawyer, friendship to one side, I have a responsibility that has no sentiment in it at all. If ever a man had provocation, you had. I was very fond of Hedda, but that's a sentiment that has no place in my thoughts until I get you off. She was flagrantly, continually unfaithful. Did you know she was pregnant?"

"No!"

"They discovered that in the autopsy. Obviously she was pregnant by Vance. That might be hard to prove in a court of law, but if this case ever comes before a jury, there won't be any doubt in any juror's mind when I get through."

"Don't do that to her."

"Why not? It isn't a matter of chivalry. The State is going to introduce that element, not you or I. The State will charge that you killed her in a jealous rage, a jealous rage, however, that lasted long enough for you to make elaborate plans over a long period. But never mind that aspect for the present. The point is, the State, not we, will have to introduce the element of infidelity. It's the only thing they can do. I got back from Wilkes-Barre late yesterday afternoon, and I've been busy ever since. I already have a tentative list of about thirty witnesses that will testify that Hedda was flagrantly unfaithful to you. Bellboys, chambermaids, people like that. One day she was almost arrested in the depot—"

"I know about that."

"Oh, you do. Then there's a whole slew of people in Lyons. Telephone operators. Hotel clerks. Your household help."

"No, Ben. I don't want that."

"Robert, I'm afraid there's no alternative. However, it may not be necessary to have them all testify in court. It depends on the district attorney. If he will let you plead guilty to a lesser charge than murder in the second degree, I'll talk turkey with him. On the other hand, I would be willing to go into court and defend a first-degree charge and get you off scot-free, and I'm prepared to do that if the district attorney is stubborn. But he won't be.

"Here is how he has to look at it. He knows damn well I can get the jury to acquit on a first-degree charge. That way he loses the ball game. But if you're allowed to plead guilty to one of the lesser charges, it'll go down as a conviction on his record, and the public will be better satisfied, too. Do you see what I mean? He is better off winning a little something than losing everything. Robert, all I have to do is put Bart Vance on the stand in front of a jury, and I'll bet you a thousand dollars they'd be back in the courtroom within two hours at the most. And the district attorney knows that, although he won't admit it now.

"I'm going to plead you guilty in spite of knowing I could win on the first-degree count. I'm going to do that because I'm a friend of yours and I know you so well. If I got you off you'd never feel right about it. I think, knowing you, that you actually want it on the record that you were guilty of taking Hedda's life. That's the way I analyze your conscience. On the other hand, *my* conscience would never permit me to see you die or serve a long term in prison for taking Hedda's life in these particular circumstances. The punishment never does fit the crime, according to my way of thinking. Punishment is a square peg, crime is a round hole. It's like what we were taught in school. You can't multiply a dozen eggs by a dozen oranges. Punishment is eggs, and crime is oranges. Oil and water. Two separate things. So they don't fit, they don't mix. However, the law prescribes certain punishments for certain acts, and I am going to make every effort to see to it that you receive the minimum punishment that the law will permit. The law says nothing at all about your unhappiness or the punishment that that will inflict on you, and yet it's often a very good point in court. Everybody knows that you're a decent man, who has lived a decent life. A respected citizen, as witness the fact that the night before last the best people in your home town came to your rescue. Incidentally, if we went to trial I'd have men like Langendorf and MacMahon on the stand to tell what the town thinks of you, and the difference between them testifying in your behalf and Bart Vance—oh, a question I wanted to ask you. Did you ever threaten Hedda?"

"No."

"Did you ever threaten Vance?"

"No."

"Did you ever discuss Hedda with Vance?"

"No. *Yes*. Before we were married, one time on the train." Robert Millhouser recalled the conversation for Ben.

"He's not likely to remember that unless someone prods his memory, and it isn't important if he does," said Ben. "It would be important if you'd ever had any such discussion after you were married, and in the course of which you threatened him. But as long as you didn't, we're in good shape. In fact, I admit that I'm getting a little bloodthirsty. Mind you, I'm not going to change my tactics. I'm going to have a talk with the district attorney and make him see reason. But the more I think of it, the more I want to put the screws on Vance, and that's the way I'm going to act with Stahlmyer, the district attorney. Henry is a thorough, uninspired man, a chess player, but not a brilliant chess player. And I'm going to hint at enough of my moves to let him figure some things out for himself. For instance, I want him to worry a little bit about that autopsy. I'm going to make him imagine Vance on the stand and me asking Vance if he knew that Hedda was pregnant. I'm sure Vance did know it. She'd tell him that. But either way I gain. If he tries to lie, the jury will see him squirming and probably losing his temper. On the other hand, if he admits that he knew she was pregnant he practically tells the jury that it was justifiable homicide. He practically directs a verdict of not guilty, as good as a judge's charge. There's even a third possibility, that he honestly didn't know she was pregnant, but I also know how to deal with that. I simply show that Hedda was careless, irresponsible. Hold your horses, I'm not going to do any of these things in court. I'm merely going to perform an operation on Stahlmyer's mind. Before I'm through with him he may be in a mood to hand the case over to an assistant so that he won't risk complete loss of prestige. But all I'm after is a lesser homicide conviction and a minimum sentence. And I may be able to get a suspended on that. Have a cigar, Robert."

"No thanks, Ben. I couldn't taste it, the air in here."

"That's why I'm smoking. I'm going to send over a box of club cigars for you, to get this formaldehyde or whatever the hell it is out of the air. Do you like peppermints?"

"Yes."

"I'll send you some. They'll help, too."

"Thank you. But Ben, what if I oppose you in court? What if I get up and tell the judge I'm guilty?"

"I'd ask to have them consider a plea of not guilty on grounds of temporary insanity. I thought of that right away, as soon as George telephoned me. But I don't want that. I don't want it on your record, for one thing. And I don't want to get into the kind of legal tangle that temporary insanity can get you into. Both sides hire alienists and that could be a very miserable experience for you. Then there's the question of sentence. You could be sentenced to do your time in an asylum and I think I'd rather shoot you myself than put you through that. Also, you could be put in an asylum for a while and then when they decide you've regained your sanity, you could be tried, convicted, and sentenced to death. No, we're going to rule out an insanity defense."

"And it wouldn't be true. I wasn't insane. Do you think I was?"

Ben was silent. "If you won't object to my using the word insane, yes. I think you were. The trouble is with that word. You don't want to think of yourself as insane because right away you think of the village idiots and people like that. But if you only consider the word in its literal meaning, and that you acted as a result of certain information that made you temporarily lose your reason—yes, you were insane. You could plead temporary insanity and it would be the truth. But if I can avoid it I don't want that taint put on you. Mind you, in a jury trial, I'd implant that idea in the minds of the jurors, but I'd keep the word insane or insanity out of it. Once you get that word in there, that starts any number of legal complications. For instance, you wouldn't be able to control your money, or vote, or do any number of things if you were declared insane. And it would have a bad effect on your descendants, in case you should ever marry again, or on the descendants of any of your relatives. By the way, what about relatives?"

"No close ones. I don't expect to be hearing from any of them."

"Just as well. They can be as much of a nuisance as a help in a time like this. I hope none of them do show up."

"They're not likely to."

"Good. Now I suppose you're wondering what happens to you in the immediate future, so I'll tell you. The Grand Jury is in recess, so you will be held without bail until they meet again in a week or so. Stahlmyer will then go before them and get a true bill, and your case will be put on the calendar for the next term of criminal court, a month away. You'll have to be here during that time, a prisoner. At the same time I'll be preparing our defense, but what I'll really be doing is working on Stahlmyer, making him see the light. Then I will ask for a postponement, because in all so-called crimes of passion, any and every delay acts in favor of the defense. I can get a postponement that will keep you here till the end of May. That would mean you'd be staying here a prisoner for about three months. If I thought you could stand it, I could probably get your trial put off till the September term, but this is a dreadful place to be in summer. It isn't hot. I'll say that for it. It's one of the coolest places in town. But it's hell. Insects, the smell, the guards are short-tempered, and summer's when the prisoners are at their worst. Stabbings and fights, and all the various sex troubles. I want to talk to you about that, Robert, straight from the shoulder. I understand there was a fight over you.

"You're going to see things here you never knew existed outside. Here they're common practice. This is a strict warden, Batson. By that I mean first of all, it isn't like some prisons where whores can be sneaked in. The whores here are men, other prisoners, and a prisoner can fall in love with his sweetheart as much as he ever did with a woman. And be just as jealous. It's something Otto Batson can't stop, and I understand a couple of the guards are queer. Now this is something I have to say to you, and I don't like to say it any more than you'll like hearing it. But don't you ever have anything to do with any prisoner or any guard. Face reality. You've been having regular sex relations with a woman and you're going to miss it, but don't yield to temptation to do anything with another man. There won't be any more incidents like the one you've had. I told Batson you were supposed to have your exercise separate from the other prisoners, because you're in on a murder charge. He agreed, and hereafter you'll be taken out once a day for a half an hour, with a guard. But it won't always be the same guard. You'll have all your meals in your cell until after your trial, and then I hope you'll be out of here. If you were convicted you'd eat in the mess-hall and exercise with the others, and you'd have a cellmate. But even now, if you're willing, you could have sex relations with other men. You could bribe a guard to bring a man to your cell, or a guard might want to go after you himself. You may think I'm insulting you by talking this way, but life in a

374

prison, with nothing to do, rots a man, even a good man. And most of the men here are anything but that. Don't feel defeated if you have temptations. Just don't let them defeat you."

"Am I going to be allowed to have reading matter?"

"Yes. As much as you like. Books. Batson will have to approve of the books, but that won't create any difficulty."

"What about writing materials?"

"Unfortunately, no. Not before you're acquitted or convicted. A man stabbed himself with a pencil some years ago while he was awaiting trial on a homicide charge, so they made that rule. On the other hand, you can have a barber in to shave you and cut your hair. I don't think that's consistent. A man could grab the razor away from the barber and cut his throat if he wanted to, but I didn't make the rules. You're not a religious man, but if I were you I'd get acquainted with the chaplain. They have two. Protestant and Catholic, both pretty good fellows. Jennings is the Protestant, a Presbyterian, and he won't try to make you pray if you don't want to, but maybe you will. He comes in twice a week and even if you don't talk about religious topics, he's a good man to relay messages to the warden, and he's easy to talk to. Man about my age. Been doing this work for as long as I can remember. Knows Esther Parkinson, although he isn't the big Presbyterian minister. He has a little parish over on the other side of the river."

"What other visitors may I have? Moses Hatfield?"

"You're allowed to see me any time, but you can only have one family or friend visitor a week, and that will usually be in a visitors' room with a guard present and listening. Who else would you like to see?"

"Nobody."

"I talked to Esther. She wants to visit you."

"Thank her, and tell her I understand her kindness, but I want to keep her out of this."

"Langendorf and MacMahon told George they wanted to visit you."

"No. I'm ashamed to see them. There is one man I'd like to see."

"Who?"

"Bart Vance."

"Not likely. He's going to stay out of the State as much as he can. But between you and me, if he goes to see Dorothy Stiegel in Philadelphia, he'll be subpoenaed."

"How did you know about Dorothy Stiegel?"

"My friend, I spent four hours talking to George, and I know how to ask questions. Next week I'm going to spend a couple of days in

375

Lyons. Those people are anxious to help, people like Langendorf and MacMahon."

"I would like you to do something for me. When is Hedda being buried?"

"Tomorrow, in Lyons."

"I would like you to order a blanket of spring flowers for the grave, but don't have it put on the grave until after the burial, and don't say where they came from."

"I understand."

"And will you try to find out—George will know—what Ed Steele plans to do. If he's going to finish his work in Lyons, or move away, or what. They haven't much money, and this was to be his last job before settling down somewhere. He likes California, and if he resigns his job maybe I could, through you, have his company pay him a year's salary. Without his knowing I did it, of course. I never thought that what I was doing would disrupt so many other lives."

"I haven't much of an answer to that. You might like to talk to Reverend Jennings about it."

"I wasn't looking for an answer, Ben."

"I could point out to you that you never knew the widespread effect of some of the good things you've done. There are people in Lyons that consider you a valuable citizen. They want you home and free."

"I'll never be free, and you know that."

"I'm afraid I do. But when I get you out of here you *will* be free, Robert. In one sense. You will be free to do what you want to do with the rest of your life, and I know what that's going to be."

"Then you know more than I do."

"I do. I can look at this whole thing from a distance, I can see you from a perspective that you haven't got. All my life I've been listening to men and women in trouble, sometimes getting them out of trouble, sometimes not. Whenever I take a case—I've turned down quite a few—but whenever I take a case, I fight to win it. Oftentimes I've regretted my part in getting a man off, but whenever I've had a client that didn't try to stay out of trouble the second time, I've refused to take his case. What I am saying, Robert, is that in spite of my reputation for taking questionable cases and for the kind of personal life I've led, I haven't had much trouble with my conscience. I have a talent, or a gift, whatever you want to call it, and a lot of people will tell you that I've misused it. But I haven't. I've gotten guilty people off to a new start and some of them are all right now. The ones that are all right compensate for the real no-good bastards.

There's a partner in one of the biggest stores in town, a rich man to-day and probably as well known for his charities and philanthropies as for his business. But thirty years ago I was the only lawyer in town that would take his case when he got into trouble. He stole some money, I won't say how. And he was through before he got started. But I pleaded him guilty, he did a year and a day, made restitution over a period of years, and since then I guess he's done as much good for this town as any one man I could name. I take some credit for that because when his mother asked me to take the case, all she thought of and he thought of was getting off. He was hysterical. If he didn't get off he was going to commit suicide. Well, I was God damn mad and I gave it to him straight from the shoulder. 'You've stolen this money, and now you want to avoid punishment. If that's the kind of man you are, get another lawyer. But if you take your punishment, own up to your crime, this is your one and only chance to get a new start.' He did what I said, partly because he had very little choice, but at least to some extent because what I said made sense to him and his mother. In later years there hasn't been a year that he didn't interest himself in at least one first offender, pay my fee, get me to plead the man guilty and make him take his punishment, and then when the man got out my friend would help him get a new start, either here or elsewhere."

"And has it worked out?"

"A little better than fifty percent of the cases. And I'll tell you something, Robert. We've had the most success with men that stayed right here in Fort Penn. Those that moved away tried to hide their records, take new names, but unfortunately made more of an effort to hide their past than to start over again. About twenty percent of the men were no-good bastards and a couple of them are right here in this building. Do you see what I'm aiming at?"

"Yes, I think so. Especially the part about those who stayed in Fort Penn. You want me to return to Lyons."

"I want you to *promise* me that you'll return to Lyons."

"All right. I promise."

"If you were one of the no-good bastards I'd still want to get you off, because of the provocation, the circumstances. But I wouldn't care whether you went back to Lyons, because there's no hope for a no-good bastard anywhere. But after you get out of here you must go home, Robert. Face the unpleasantness, not so much because you want to redeem yourself in the eyes of your Lyons neighbors. But because, Robert, all the rest of your life you'll be expiating your crime, and the place to do it is where everybody knows you and you know everybody."

"We have a long way to go before that begins to happen."

"Yes, and I know that better than you do now. Your first month here is going to seem like an eternity."

A short while later Ben departed, leaving Robert Millhouser with the rest of the unending day that somehow ended. Until his books arrived he spent unending minutes waiting, waiting for the next striking of the Nesquehela County courthouse clock, waiting for the next serving of a meal, the tramping of the prisoners' feet as they marched to the exercise area, waiting for the exercise period and the heavy murmur of their voices to end. In the nights he would doze off for undefinable periods of shallow sleep—his watch had been taken from him for no reason that he could imagine—and sometimes he would be awakened by the guard's bull's-eye lantern flashing through the opening in the door, sometimes his sleep was interrupted by the bite of the bedbugs. And all through the first half of the night and particularly of the latter part of the first half he would hear the ugly sounds of the prisoners' nightmares and the horrid laughter of the perverts. Then for the latter half of the night there was some silence, but though the silence was more general late at night, it was always broken by a scream, a moan, a shout. There was never a period between the striking of the hour and the half-hour that was not at least once broken by some outcry. Beginning at ten o'clock and sometimes until two in the morning at every striking of the hour some men would join in the chant: "Ten o'clock and all's well/ Otto Batson go to hell."

With the arrival of some books Robert Millhouser had something to occupy his mind while the narrow shaft of light from the window lasted. It was at night that he needed the books but there was no artificial light in the cell. After the fifth day in the cell Robert Millhouser began to lose track of time, an experience that he was undergoing for the second time in a year: in the hospital, in and out of delirium and in and out of consciousness, he had been unable to count the days or nights, but now his only check on the days was to recall each of Ben's visits and try to remember a particular topic that had been discussed during each visit. But the method was a failure; he could not be sure when Ben had brought a message from Jerry MacMahon or when he had brought the tiny flask of perfume that he sprinkled on the blanket. (The empty flask itself had to be handed over to the guard; it was made of glass.) Otto Batson forbade newspapers, candy, and about fifty other items, as though to make contraband any article that would allow a prisoner momentarily to forget he was in prison. But Ben was permitted to bring in sandwiches so long as they were eaten while he was visiting his client, and sometimes instead of a sandwich he would provide half of an apple pie. The prison budget

378

allowed a maximum expenditure of thirty cents per day per prisoner, and it was tacitly understood that the warden was entitled to pocket the difference between the thirty-cent figure and the actual twenty-six-cent cost of feeding the inmates. Nothing was bought outside that could be prepared in the prison. The prison had its own bakery and the big meal every day was bread and stew. Breakfast was coffee, black or with watered milk and one teaspoonful of sugar, and bread. The evening meal was coffee, bread, and a teaspoonful of jam. On Sunday the prisoners were given small bricks of Neapolitan ice cream, which, however, were paid for out of the proceeds of their basketwork, burlap sack-stitching, and shoe-repairing. Prisoners serving sentences—unlike Robert Millhouser, who was awaiting trial —were supposed to have some gainful employment, depending upon individual skills, but under a complicated system of bookkeeping their earnings never exceeded the cost of tobacco purchased at the canteen run by the guards. In most cases the tobacco was paid for by relatives on the outside and frequently was used to purchase casual sexual favors among the prisoners. Because of Batson's strictness only about a dozen prisoners were able to obtain cocaine from the guards, who were paid on the outside or waived payment in exchange for information. In spite of Batson's strictness the incidence of advanced syphilis was high, gonorrhea was nearly endemic, and tuberculosis was prevalent.

It was a long way from the house on the hill in Lyons.

Horace Jennings on his first visit to Robert Millhouser stayed only long enough, as he said, to get acquainted and to find out if there was anything he could do to make Robert more comfortable. He was a stout man of slightly less than average height, somewhere near sixty in age, who wore a dark gray broadcloth suit. A large size, old-style Phi Beta Kappa key dangled from a lapel chain, and he had starched cuffs and a gates-ajar collar. He was clean-shaven and nearly bald. If he had not known that Jennings was a clergyman Robert Millhouser would have guessed him to be an extremely religious businessman, but since he was prepared for a clergyman Robert's first impression of Jennings was of a man who was so imitative of the laity that he could not possibly be an effective minister. He obviously hated his genteel poverty, and got away from parish duties whenever he could. So Robert Millhouser surmised from the absence of spirituality and the briskness of the man and the effort to look and behave like a layman. "I'm not going to ask you if you'd care to pray with me," said Jennings. "Let our first meeting be a get-acquainted one. I'm afraid I don't hold with so many men of my calling, that whip out their Bibles and prayerbooks the very first thing. Prayer to me is such an intimate thing that before I ask a man to pray with me, I want to know does he have confidence in me. Is he ready to pray with me? Can we compose ourselves jointly and severally for the visit with the Lord Jesus Christ? I could cite you instances where I've called on a prisoner for as long as six months or a year before he would say to me, 'Reverend, I am ready to join with you in an humble supplication before the throne of the Almighty.' And whether it takes a week or a month or a year, whether it be the hardened criminal or the first offender, I never give up. You'll find it in Psalms. 'And call upon me in the day of trouble: I will deliver thee, and thou shalt glorify me.' And remember in Matthew? 'For where two or three are gathered together in my name, there am I in the midst of them.' How is Brother Langendorf?"

"Fred Langendorf? Do you know him?"

"Oh, indeed I do. My dear one who passed on two years ago was distantly related to the Langendorfs of your town, and Fred responded very generously to our appeal for a memorial fund. I have never actually met Fred, but our correspondence has brought us together. I wrote over a hundred letters to those I thought might wish to honor my dear one and her work among the needy of our parish. It's very difficult for me to struggle alone without her at my side, but how much more difficult for those that came to depend on her, whose needs were urgent. We're a small parish, and most of the help we get comes from elsewhere, and when my Elizabeth passed on I could not abandon her work, although in His infinite wisdom the good Lord saw fit to bless us with a devoted daughter who has been carrying on the good work her mother and I started over twenty years ago. But she's nowhere near the money-raiser her mother was. There's a lot more to it than just asking."

"I imagine so."

"Elizabeth had to learn, and so will our daughter, in God's good season. Well, Brother Millhouser, I've enjoyed our little chat, but you haven't said a word about what I could do for you. Is there anything you need? Warden Batson will usually grant any small request I make if it doesn't conflict with the rules."

"I can't think of anything, thank you."

"Well, you may think of something and you can let me know the next time I make my rounds. I'm usually here Monday, Wednesday and Friday except during August. Good day, sir."

Jennings rapped on the cell door, which the guard opened and closed, and Robert Millhouser heard Jennings say to the guard: "Let's go and have a look at the a. and b. they brought in last night.

I have his name here somewhere. Wasn't he in for one-to-ten for burglary a while ago?"

"That's him," said the guard. "Bad actor."

When Ben Rosebery visited him late that afternoon Robert Millhouser said: "I don't want to hurt that Jennings man's feelings, I'm sure he does good work. But is there any way I can keep him from coming here?"

"There is, but I don't advise it. Don't you like him? He's not a bad fellow."

"He's a bore."

"He is now, maybe, but he's from the outside, and after you've been here a while anybody from the outside is going to be mighty welcome. I don't want to give you any horseshit, Robert. Prison is no fun, and there isn't anything about it that you're going to learn to like. But Horace is going to be a break in the tedium, and he won't seem like as much of a bore as he does now. I'm going to try to arrange it so you'll be able to see at least one person from outside every day. Me. Horace Jennings, and maybe a doctor and the young fellow I have in my office. Young lawyer I'm breaking in."

"What does a. and b. mean?"

"Assault and battery. Why?"

"Just wondered."

"I could lend you some law books if you like."

"No thanks."

Ben nodded. "That's a relief. If you started reading law books you'd only confuse yourself and get in my way. The best things to read in prison are novels and travel books, for the very same reason that it's a good idea to see people from the outside. You have to keep your mind on outside things and outside people."

"Do I?"

"Yes. You're going to get out of here, keep remembering that. Don't get what they call a prison psychology."

"What's that?"

"Well, a prison psychology is what happens to men that are in for long sentences. They let go of everything, as if the outside didn't exist at all. That's why men have other men to satisfy them. None of the outside rules or manners or customs mean anything to a man that has the prison psychology. Most people on the outside don't know anything about prison psychology. For instance, escaping. People have the idea that every prisoner spends all his time planning to escape, but that's just not so. After a man gets the prison psychology he hardly ever thinks about escaping."

"Then I must have it already. I haven't thought of escaping."

Ben frowned. "You haven't? Not at all?"

"I don't believe so."

"When you look up at that little window with the iron bar in it, doesn't that make you wish you had a saw?"

"No."

"If I smuggled in a pistol, wouldn't you use it to escape?"

"No. Ben, I can't seem to make anyone believe that I came here expecting to die. I appreciate what you're doing, I'm grateful because I know why you're trying to help me. But I'm afraid that my appreciation doesn't go much deeper than politeness. The only word I can think of for the way I feel now is *numb*. Is that prison psychology?"

"Well—yes."

"I'm not going to let myself go. That is, I want to keep clean, I don't want to have relations with another man. But I don't care if I die. In fact, Ben, I don't even care if I live."

"The prison psychology got you sooner than most because you're more intelligent than most. I think that's it."

"Maybe so."

"I want to ask you something, partly as your lawyer, partly as your friend."

"Anything you want to know."

"Have you had feelings of remorse?"

"No, and that's the worst thing you could have asked me, because that's the worst thing that's happened to me. I have no feeling of remorse. *I have no feeling.* I think all feeling went out of me that morning. When was it? I don't even know how many days ago it was."

"You wanted to send flowers to her grave. You wanted to help her father with money. Those are feelings."

"They're nothing more than the way I was brought up. I know up here, in my brain, that there are certain things I ought to do. Polite things. But instead of feelings I have this numbness. I've been waiting ever since I was brought here for the regrets or the remorse, the contrition, the penitence. It won't come, Ben. I'm like a barren woman, I guess. I wait for it to happen, and it doesn't."

"You mean a frigid woman."

"No, I mean a barren woman. A frigid woman, there's hope for, with a different man. I mean a barren woman, that can't have a child by any man. Forget about women. I'm like land where nothing will grow. Rock that's been dead for a million years. I'm simply numb, Ben, and I know why."

"Why?"

"Forgive me, but I don't want to tell you."

"All right."

"Maybe I'll tell you some day, when I have it all worked out in my mind. But I just want you to realize that I'm without feeling or hope. I'll tell you this much. Do you remember the other day, when we were talking about insanity?"

"Yes."

"Well, I don't want you to try to use this in court or in my defense. It couldn't be used in my defense, because it was something that has happened to me since I killed Hedda. But literally I am insane. There is something missing, and it's what I've been saying. Feeling, that's what's missing. A normal, sane man would feel remorse for killing a beautiful creature. But I don't feel either remorse or pleasure, the pleasure of revenge. And I give you my word, Ben, I don't feel fear. When those men in the yard started those sexual advances, all I felt was disgust. But what is disgust? Isn't it just something we feel because we see something or experience something we aren't accustomed to? I've wondered about that. Those men don't feel disgust. Far from it. They fought over me because what they wanted is something they've become accustomed to."

"Ah, but they're not normal men, living in normal conditions. Prison has done that to them, as I told you before."

"Quite true. But I'm not a normal man either. Prison hasn't done anything to me. It never could. What has happened to me was my own doing, caused by an act of mine. I have done the worst thing a human being can do. I have taken another human being's life. And the worst thing that could happen to me has happened. I am devoid of feeling, and always will be. There, I've practically told you what I wasn't going to tell you. When I put the bullet in Hedda's heart I killed whatever it is that made me feel, too. And I've been wondering whether I didn't have that in the back of my mind. Why did I kill Hedda? Oh, the obvious reasons, to be sure. But you have no idea how many times since I've been here that I've asked myself, 'Was I killing myself as much as I was killing her?' Did I kill Hedda because I was secretly afraid that I wasn't only losing her, I was losing the beautiful and passionate side of my life that she represented? I'm not so sure of the answer to that. Those are things that are beyond my comprehension. If Dr. Willetts, Senior, were still alive he might have an explanation. He was always looking for motives behind motives . . . My friend, your expression is sad. You're a good man, Ben. You and Dr. Willetts would have made a wonderful team."

"I've often wished I'd known him better."

"It's been my great privilege to have known you both. I've had very good luck in my men friends, and I was married for a little while to the most beautiful creature I ever saw. My father, that I idolized, but when we were together I often thought of him as a friend. Leonard Vance—"

"Bart Vance."

"No, Leonard. His older brother, my boyhood chum. He was quiet, and a good runner and swimmer. That's almost all I can say about him now, after nearly forty years, but we got along well. Then Chester Calthorp. Stimulating and clever, in his own ways. Dr. Willetts. You. And never intimate or close, but Jerry MacMahon. And for that matter, Moses Hatfield. The women in my life? Only two, really. My mother, who tried to love me but couldn't. I guess I didn't measure up to my father or her first husband. I've often thought that my mother tried to love me because I was her son by my father, but that somehow or other she became motherly toward her first husband so that she could forget that she'd been in bed with him. And that complicated her feelings toward me."

"What about Esther?"

"Esther? Lovely, kind Esther. A friend with the body of a woman. How lucky she was to be protected from me! I'd have ruined Esther, destroyed her not the way I did Hedda, but through neglect. Love and domesticity were the things she was born to. No, we weren't suited to each other, and Hedda and I were. I killed Hedda, but she could as easily have killed me. In a way, in *her* way, she did. But that's something I *can't* tell you about, Ben. When I took the cough medicine I imagine Dr. Willetts would say I was hoping I'd never wake up, but that wouldn't be true."

"What cough medicine was that, Robert?"

"Oh, that's part of what I can't tell you either."

"Where did you get it?"

"Brown's drug store, where I have all my prescriptions filled."

"One of those soothing syrups, I suppose."

"I suppose you'd call it that."

"But you could buy the same thing at any drug store? In other words, if you caught cold here it's probably what the prison doctor would prescribe?"

"Oh. I was wondering why you were asking about it. Yes, it's one of those elixirs, they call them."

"I hope you don't catch cold here. Prison colds have a way of hanging on, and there's a lot of T.B. here. Well, I must be going, Robert. I'll be in again day after tomorrow. Anything you want?"

"They won't let me have *Leslie's,* will they?"

"No magazines or newspapers. That's one of the things Batson is strictest about. I could cut anything out that you wanted to read."

"I only wanted to look at the pictures. And I suppose if they won't allow me to have a pencil, they won't let me do any painting. But crayons? Charcoal? Will you ask him about them? I couldn't stab myself with a crayon, could I, very easily?"

"No, but I doubt if he'll let you have them. However, I'll try."

"Never mind. But you might bring me a book with a lot of pictures. I get tired reading, reading, reading. Then at night I don't sleep. Pictures might keep me awake in the daytime."

"I'll do that. So long, Robert."

"Thank you, Ben."

Robert Millhouser did not again confide in Ben Rosebery. Once having stated the fact of his emotional lethargy, he returned to it. He had owed that much, the statement, to the man who was trying to help him, but he owed no further explanation to anyone else. Moreover, by the act of stating the fact he had established a mode of existence. The explanation to Ben had clarified matters for himself. He saw that his apathy was limitless, which he had not recognized until his conversation with Ben Rosebery; but now that the numbness was defined as infinite he would no longer trouble himself or be troubled with his failure, his inability, to feel or to induce a feeling of remorse. Soon he noticed that he *no longer* noticed the cries in the night; they were voices, but they were separated from him by an iron door. He no longer was repelled by the prison food; if he did not feel like eating it, he left it untouched. When he had visitors he conversed with them, and when they had gone the conversation vanished. And in a month's time he had become so settled in his own torpid routine that almost nothing could rouse him. The original small irritations and discomforts ceased to bother him, just as the small luxuries allowed him now gave him little pleasure. His reading was a case in point. He read dutifully, with his mind. The printed words were there, and his mind knew what to do with them; he responded to the intent of the words, whether they were meant to create images, to reproduce speech, to ask him to reflect, to advance the story, to simulate experience. But when the experience that was to be simulated was an emotional one, Robert Millhouser read on untouched. He was entirely conscious of what was happening to him; he could observe it all as if from outside himself. But the observer observed was not affected. The small spectacle of the atrophy of a soul left him unmoved. It was during these days that he came upon Milton's lines:

All hope is lost
Of my reception into grace; what worse?
For where no hope is left, is left no fear.

Then he knew that someone—Milton himself, surely—had once wondered why fear was gone. It had gone when hope had gone, and now, much too late, Robert Millhouser began to believe that of all the Graces, Hope was the most precious. Hope was protective, but could not be protected.

And so went the hourless days and dayless weeks and weekless months that could not even be measured from so dramatic a moment as the discovery of despair. In the Nesquehela County Prison sat a man who was a phenomenon: he had been deserted by God, lived with that knowledge, and did not even suffer from the fear of it. The barber cut him with the razor, and blood came forth, and besides this there were all the other proofs that this man lived. He yawned when he was sleepy, and he shielded his eyes from the sun. He carried on conversations, he asked for water when he was thirsty, at night sometimes he snored. And at other times at night the guard would stand outside his cell door and listen to what the man was saying, but none of it made any sense. Little of what prisoners said in their sleep made any sense, but sometimes they were funny to listen to. This man was not even funny to listen to . . .

A date was set for the trial, Ben Rosebery asked for a delay, and it was granted. Robert Millhouser heard these details and many more as Ben reported them from time to time, but he made no effort to commit them to memory. When the time came, he would be taken to court, he would sit there until the trial was finished, and he would be led out of the courtroom to wherever a judge directed. There was nothing he could do, and nothing he wanted to do to accelerate or impede the machinery, and Ben had come to understand that this was so. Nevertheless he continued to report whenever there was a new development. "Well, my hunch was right," he said one day. "My man that I had watching Dorothy Stiegel's place, he served Bart Vance day before yesterday, and now I can talk turkey with Stahlmyer."

"Well?"

"Well, what?"

"You seemed to be waiting for me to ask you a question."

"I was. Don't you want to know about Bart Vance? Aren't you curious to know how he took it?"

"No."

"You ought to be, Robert. You say you're not letting yourself go, but you are. You must *try* to keep up your interest in things. Surely you must have some curiosity about Vance when he was served."

"I'm sorry, Ben, but I have no curiosity about Bart Vance. I should hate him, and I did hate him, but I don't now. The only way

I can convince you of that is to tell you something that I know will shock you, but doesn't shock me."

"Go ahead and shock me. Anything that will make me understand you better."

"All right. It's this: most of the time I don't even remember Hedda. I could draw you a picture of her that would be a good likeness. Recognizable. But Charles Dana Gibson could draw a better one from a photograph, one that would be more like her. I don't really remember Hedda, and I think that in a little while I won't remember her at all."

"Do you remember shooting her?"

"I can if I force myself to. Yes. But where she was on the bed, that's blank. The thing I remember most vividly now is the noise. It's like being inside a clap of thunder. That noise keeps out everything else. It may be what keeps me from feeling remorse."

Ben stroked his lower lip with his thumb. "I don't know what to do. Robert, do you want to go to prison?"

"I'm in prison."

"I mean for the rest of your life. Is this the way you want to stay for the rest of your life?"

"It *is* the way I'm going to stay the rest of my life."

"No, what I would like to know is, are you afraid to live on the outside?"

"What is there for me to be afraid of?"

"Well, you could be afraid of having people look at you."

"No, I'm not afraid of that. But I'm not afraid of anything else, either. Now maybe I can make you understand, Ben. I have no fear of anything. I could go to Ed Steele and hand him a pistol and tell him to shoot me."

"They've left Lyons. They've moved to California."

"Did you try to give them some money?"

"The Company refused to discuss it. I wasn't going to tell you that."

"It doesn't make any difference. I'm not insulted."

"I believe they're going to take care of Steele for three years, maybe it was two, and give him his job back if he wants it. But anyway, would you be afraid of things like that? Snubs. Rebuffs."

"I've only ever felt snubbed twice in my life. Once by a woman in Philadelphia, a cousin of Chester Calthorp's. And the other time by an old man, an Italian duke."

"Well, I've been asking you these questions because it has occurred to me that what I think is the right thing may not be the right thing. If you're going to be worse off outside, if you never want to live with people again, I could get you certified and then get the court to commit you to a private sanitarium."

"Wouldn't that be a lot of trouble?"

"It'd be worth it to me if I thought it was the right thing. But God help me, I don't know what *is* the right thing."

"And I'm not helping you at all."

"You're familiar with the old saying that the lawyer that tries his own case has a fool for a client. Maybe a man who hires a friend to defend him has a fool for a lawyer. Is there anyone you would like to talk to, not necessarily a lawyer, but a friend who could be of any help? Anybody in Lyons, for instance? Do you still refuse to see Langendorf and the rest of them?"

"There have only ever been three men I could really talk to. You. Dr. Willetts, who's dead these many years. And Chester Calthorp, a monk in a monastery."

"Would you like to talk to Chester?"

"We wouldn't speak the same language any more."

"Well, I'll just go on, then, the way I intended to. I'll plead you guilty on a manslaughter charge and try to get you a suspended."

"Anything you do will be acceptable to me, Ben. I'm sorry to put you through this."

Three days passed, and on the morning of the fourth day shortly after nine o'clock, having submitted to regular cell inspection, Robert was lying on his cot, reading the poems of Sir Walter Raleigh, when the guard rapped on the cell door with his key-ring and said, through the aperture: "You got a visitor." The door was swung open and Robert put down his book and looked at the visitor.

"Chester! Chester Calthorp!"

"Your servant, sir," said Chester Calthorp, smiling.

"Chester Calthorp," said Robert Millhouser.

"A half an hour," said the guard, and locked the door.

"Let me look at you," said Robert Millhouser. "I thought you were a, uh, monk."

"This worldly raiment? Not the latest cut, is it? It's the suit I was wearing when I entered the monastery, and I haven't worn it since."

"I thought you had to wear a brown cassock, and sandals."

"We do, and wearing shoes again is a minor penance. My feet have spread, but my shoes have not."

"How did you get here? I thought you were never allowed to leave."

"Your lawyer, my old friend and fraternity brother Ben Rosebery, and I'm sure God will forgive me for the touch of sarcasm. Ben came down and was very persuasive with Brother Hilary, our Superior. It was decided that no good purpose would be served by my appearing in public wearing my habit, and so they got these clothes out of a trunk."

"You've lost weight, but you're brown from the sun."

"I've lost fat, as you can see by my waistcoat, how loose it is. But I've developed muscles. One of our community, a Boston man, has compared me favorably with John L. Sullivan in his prime. Sullivan, the prize fighter. It used to be Nero that people were reminded of. If, that's progress, I leave it up to you."

"And you're happy. Anyone could see that."

"Yes, I'm happy. Your quarters aren't very different from mine. Slightly larger."

"I guess we haven't much time, Chester. What do you want to talk about?"

"Well, I didn't come to scold you," said Chester.

The childhood word *scold* was so out of place in the present situation and approaching context that Robert Millhouser laughed. But his first laughter in many months did not last long. "No, you came out of friendship, and I suppose a sense of duty."

"A lot of both," said Chester. "Duty runs through everything I do, although we don't exactly refer to it as duty. As far as friendship is concerned, we learn to think of that as brotherhood. And of course we *were* friends, Robert, until you very wisely went your own way."

"Wisely? Where did my wisdom get me? It turns out that the last advice you gave me was the best advice I ever got from anyone, but I was too busy showing my superiority to listen to your advice."

"What advice was that?"

"Don't you remember? You told me never to marry."

"Yes, I did, didn't I? But who was I then to give such advice? From what great knowledge and wisdom was I giving you that or any advice? Think back on the man that gave you that advice. Would you listen to a blind man's disquisition on color? Would you ask a legless man to teach you to waltz? You wouldn't knowingly pray to Satan, but it comes down to that, Robert. If you take the advice of a cynic, and especially the kind of cynic I was in those days, it amounts to the same thing as asking help of the devil."

"Nevertheless, it was good advice."

"No. It was mortal advice. Advice from a prejudiced mortal. It denied the doctrine of free will. A cynical young man, corrupt and conceited, presumed to foretell the future of an innocent, unworldly, but intelligent friend. You were right to reject my advice."

"How can you sit here and say that, in a prison cell to a murderer?"

389

"Because I'm not dealing with your decision to marry, or the reasons that caused you to marry, or the consequences of the marriage. I'm only trying to make you see that I was unfit to influence you in such a thing as matrimony. Matrimony is a sacrament, you know. It isn't only a convenience."

"You said you weren't going to scold me, but you're talking like a priest. Next you'll want to hear my confession."

"I can't. I'm not a priest. Never will be. I'll never be ordained, and therefore I couldn't hear your confession. No, I'm *not* here to scold you, Robert. Furthermore, I'm not here to convert you."

"Well, that's good, because it would be a great waste of time, and we haven't got much."

"So you're probably asking yourself why I came at all? I came because of some things that Ben must have told my Superior, Brother Hilary. I wasn't there during the conversation, but I gather that Ben is very much concerned for your soul."

"Ben Rosebery?"

"Yes, Ben Rosebery. He may not have spoken of your soul as your soul, but what he told Brother Hilary must have convinced Brother Hilary that that's where the trouble lay, and that the community rules should be relaxed to permit me to pay you a visit."

"I've never thought much about my soul, but your Brother Hilary is quite right. If we want to go on using that word, my soul no longer exists. I had a soul, or I'll concede that I had something that I'll call by that name, but I destroyed it when I killed my wife."

"No. You see we don't believe that. The soul is immortal. It may be saved, it may be damned, but it goes on through eternity. Why do you say you destroyed it?"

"Chester, it's my soul, isn't it? And I know when it's destroyed. I'm a human, animal body here, going on living just the same as you are, or that eavesdropping guard, or your Brother Hilary. But I no longer feel anything that has to do with the soul, and I've begun to lose some of the physical things, too. I'm no longer afraid of death, for instance."

"Neither am I, but I know I have a soul, a living, immortal soul."

"Very well. I don't care whether I live or die. You do, don't you?"

"I want to live so that I can devote my life to the greater honor and glory of God, and then die when my time comes."

"Well, you're a priest, or whatever you are. A man of God. I'm not."

"And you've arrived at, or nearly arrived at mortal despair. But if you were one of us, a Catholic, you'd know that that's a sin. I don't expect you to see why that would be a sin, but to a Catholic it's one of the worst sins. It amounts to the same thing as denying the existence of God Himself."

"Ah, now I think I can talk to you. Do you know these lines: 'All hope is lost/Of my reception into grace; what worse?/For where no hope is left, is left no fear . . .'?"

"It sounds like Milton, although I see you've been reading Sir Walter Raleigh."

"It's Milton, and it explains to me why I have no fear. I lost fear, when I lost hope. And other things besides. I have no remorse for the thing I did. I have no deep feelings of any kind whatsoever."

Chester smiled. "Why, my friend, you haven't lost hope at all. The fact that you acknowledge the absence of hope is enough to convince me that it's still there and alive."

"Chester, I never thought I would call you a stupid man, but that's what you are."

"It saddens you to say that, doesn't it?"

"Yes, it does."

"Well, it doesn't sadden me to hear it. The only thing that does sadden me is that you're saying it thirty years too late. It was when I was at my cleverest that I was at my stupidest, and you're apologizing to the stupid man you knew thirty years ago. The man you see today has the beginning of wisdom, which is fear of the Lord, and using Milton's thought, I accept fear because I know that it implies the existence of hope. As a matter of fact I've never thought of that until now, but I know that it's going to help me when I'm distressed."

"I thought you said you were happy. Why would you be distressed?"

"Robert, you mustn't think of us as living in a sort of limbo-on-earth, or a suburb of heaven."

"I'm afraid that that's exactly what I do think, although I wouldn't want to live there."

"Most people in the world do think that. But our life is quite different from that. We do manual labor, which we dedicate to God, but that leaves us an awful lot of time for doubt and temptation. We are living so close to faith, our minds are so continually occupied with an abstract thing that *isn't* an abstract thing but a vital force—that we're constantly tried by doubt and temptation. The layman, out in the world, may have his doubts a few times a year, and his blind faith is strong enough to resist those doubts. But when a doubt assails one of us it stays with us."

"Then how can you say you're happy?"

"Because we take refuge in prayer, and when our prayers are answered and doubt dispelled, happiness returns. But you're right, Robert. Hope is the thing, at least for you. Hope will keep faith alive."

"Hope can't keep faith alive if hope has been destroyed. And as to faith, it's never been a factor in my life."

"No, I suppose not, and that's what's missing now. It's what you miss most."

"That's nonsense. I'm thankful that along with all my other troubles at least I don't have to worry about faith, or the lack of it."

"And whom are you thankful to?"

"That's only an expression, and you know it."

"But it isn't *only* an expression. It's an instinctive act of faith, and if you examine it, consider it, you'll admit that you're not being thankful to any mortal that ever lived, but to God."

"The Indians and the Great White Father, Chester?"

"But of course. The Indians didn't come up from the primeval ooze of Wyoming, separately from the Egyptians or the ancient Slavs. Wherever they came from, Outer Mongolia or the Galápagos Islands, remember that the one thing in common they all had was some form of the Great Father. Through the centuries they may have forgotten how to make iron or roll a wheel, but the Great Father in one form or another is always, always there."

"Well, I must say I'd rather hear you on the subject than the Reverend Horace Jennings."

"But whoever he is, don't send him away."

"How much time have we left?"

"I don't know. I have no watch," said Chester Calthorp.

Robert Millhouser laughed. "You and I have come to that."

"Yes," said Chester Calthorp.

"Well, I guess neither of us really needs a watch."

"You will, shortly, so I'm told."

"So I'm told. Speaking of watches, I resigned from Delta Psi. They refused to accept my resignation, and I was quite touched."

"I resigned, and they accepted it," said Chester Calthorp.

"Well, after all, Chester, you turned Catholic. I only committed a murder. I'm sorry I said that. It was cheap. But you were always the witty one of us two, and I always wanted to shine."

"It was a rather funny remark."

"Is it true that you never talk to each other, you and your—what did you call it?—community?"

"Not literally true. But we haven't much time for frivolity, and it isn't encouraged. However, laughter isn't punished, and we enjoy our small jokes."

"What will they say when you go back?"

"Nothing, and neither will I."

"Not even to Brother Hilary?"

"Not even to Brother Hilary."

"He's not going to ask you what you did, and what you said to me and I said to you?"

"No."

"Amazing. What did he say when you left?"

"He called me in and told me the circumstances—"

"The circumstances being that I was in prison for murder?"

"Yes. And that I was to help you if I could. Then he told me I wasn't to wear my habit, and gave me carfare and said he'd expect me back this evening. And he gave me a dollar, which I'll return, what's left of it."

"Have you any money of your own?"

"Yes. If you mean in trust. There's a lot of it, you know, and the income goes to the Church, but I don't actually become a pauper till I've been in the Order for ten years. I can always leave, and stop the income."

"But meanwhile you get a dollar and carfare. They must trust you. Very sure of you."

"I'm sure of myself."

"Do they need money?"

"Did you ever hear of a religious organization that didn't need money?"

"No."

"Why? Are you thinking of giving them some? If you are, I'd rather you didn't tell me about it."

"Why not?"

"Because if you do give them money, *they'll* never tell me about it. I'll never even know what happens to you, Robert."

"Good God!"

"I can pray for you, and will, but we don't hear much of what's going on in the world."

"It's true I can't write to you?"

"Never, or me to you. When I die you'll get a small black-bordered card, and that's all. That will be the next thing you hear from me."

"If I die will you be notified?"

"No. You're not a relative."

"When you leave this cell, it will be the last time I ever see you, the last you'll ever hear of me?"

"In this world, yes."

"That's inhuman."

"I don't think so. It's been thirty years, Robert. I doubt if it'll be another thirty years."

"Don't talk that way. You believe that you'll shake hands with me and the next time we meet—"

"Will be in eternity. Yes."

"Suddenly I don't know you."

"But you should, Robert. I went through what you're going through now."

"But believe me, the outcome won't be the same."

"I hope it will be, in the only way that matters. I hope you'll find peace. And you can." Chester Calthorp stood up. *"Pax vobiscum.* You must remember that much from Mercersburg." He rapped on the cell door. "I'll pray for you, and sometime I hope you'll remember to pray for me."

Robert Millhouser rose as the door was swung open and then was swung tight again. And now, for the first time, he wept.

•

THERE WERE OTHER FACTORS than the persuasiveness of Ben Rosebery that dictated Henry Stahlmyer's decision to allow a plea of guilty of manslaughter in the Millhouser case. At the bottom, and at the top, of Stahlmyer's decision was the sure knowledge that if he tried for a verdict of first-degree murder, he would lose a sensational contest. But in between the first and the last considerations Stahlmyer, who was no fool when it came to sensing and reflecting public opinion, saw that he not only would be in danger of losing the case; as prosecutor of an unpopular action, and in a trial that Ben Rosebery would be sure to draw out at great length, he would continually appear as the personification of harsh, vindictive justice, so that even in the remote event that he won the case, he would be gaining nothing. Almost no one wanted Robert Millhouser to undergo any punishment at the hands of the law. For a man who was scarcely known by sight to more than a hundred men and women in Fort Penn, Robert Millhouser had become an amazingly sympathetic figure. The Fort Penn newspapers had played down the case, but Stahlmyer was told rather bluntly that if he persisted in his early intention to ask for a first-degree verdict, the newspapers would open up, give him all the publicity he had ever dreamed of, and turn it all against him. In Nesquehela County, Pennsylvania, no less than in a thousand other counties in the Union, a district attorney would listen to the words of a newspaper editor. The words were the editor's, but the wishes they expressed were the owner's and the owner's friends and associates. In the Millhouser case Stahlmyer was up against Ben Rosebery, whom he hated and feared, and who had closer blood and social ties to the men who owned the newspapers. In effect, Rosebery was representing the men whose support was the *sine qua non* of Stahlmyer's political advancement. Stahlmyer was at that stage of his political career where a few years out of office could be disastrous; if he failed to get the nomination for Congress or a county judgeship that was his next step onward, nothing would be left but private practice— and private practice after a sensational defeat was an unpleasant prospect. Stahlmyer naturally suspected that when Brock Caldwell ordered his editor to speak so bluntly about unfavorable newspaper publicity and implied the threat of political abandonment, he was doing so after a conversation with Ben Rosebery. Rosebery, Caldwell, and Millhouser were friends and second-generation members of the Fort Penn Club. Stahlmyer's moment of righteous indignation, such as it was, was years too late, since he was a politician and in no sense a crusader or reformer. He had always done as he was told and had got this far by so doing, and if he had expressed indignation at Caldwell's attempts to influence him, Caldwell, who was cognizant of Stahlmyer's record of obedience, would have regarded the protest as preposterous. And would have said as much.

But even aside from the effect on his political fortunes, Stahlmyer was influenced by the fact that he did not wish to call attention to himself as an irreproachable citizen. There would be times during the trial when he would be compelled to utter highly moral platitudes, especially if Bart Vance were on the stand. It would be necessary to contemn Vance's adulterous conduct while at the same time extracting from his testimony the motive for first-degree murder, and Stahlmyer was afraid that he would not be equal to the task. For it was unreasonable to expect that out of a panel of twelve Nesquehela County men not one had ever heard of Stahlmyer's weakness for women. And most of all he feared the faint smile and raised eyebrows of Ben Rosebery during such questioning. Rosebery would stay well within the bounds of proper court conduct, but he would make sure that the jury did not miss the by-play. The more Stahlmyer considered the hazards of the case, the easier it became to heed the demands of public opinion. In his own words, expressed to his closest assistant: "The poor son of a bitch shouldn't have shot her, but I'd a damned sight rather be defending this case."

Robert Millhouser was given his own clothes on the morning of his day in court. He had been shaved by the barber on the preceding afternoon and there was a faint white stubble on his chin. He was handcuffed to a prison guard, and Robert Millhouser and the guard, followed by another guard bearing a shotgun, went down to the exercise yard and got in the prison van, which was drawn by a single black horse. It was the last week in May and it had been raining since early morning. The van proceeded to the courthouse, a block away, and stopped at a side door, which had a barred window and was opened for the party of three by a uniformed court attendant who wore a belt with a holster from which protruded the staghorn butt of a revolver. The court attendant locked and bolted the door behind the party of three and another armed attendant led them up a winding staircase. The staircase was narrow and progress was slow because of the awkwardness created by the handcuffs. At the second landing the court attendant knocked on a heavy oaken door. "Me with the prisoner, Harry," he called, and the door was opened.

Now they were in a small room which contained an oaken table and six matching chairs and several brass spittoons on rubber mats. Ben Rosebery, wearing his reading glasses, was busy over some papers with his young assistant. "Good morning, Robert," said Ben.

"Good morning, Ben," said Robert Millhouser, and added a good-morning for the assistant.

"Be with you in just a minute," said Ben. "Guard, you can take off the handcuffs."

"I'm not supposed to," said the guard.

"Oh, for Christ's sake, don't tell me what you're supposed to do or not to do. I know this by heart. Unlock those handcuffs. You're supposed to stay within arm's reach of the prisoner, but he is *not* to be wearing handcuffs when he enters the courtroom. Now be quick about it, or do you want to be told by the warden? You with the shotgun, Bill Whatever-Your-Name-Is. Tell this horse's ass the rules."

"He's new," said Bill. "Yeah, you unlock the cuffs."

"Have a cigar, Robert? I'll be right with you. Just a few things to go over."

"No thank you. I might have a cigarette, though," said Robert Millhouser.

"Bud, do you have a cigarette for Mr. Millhouser?" Ben asked his assistant.

"Yes, sure," said Bud.

"Is there anything wrong?" said Robert Millhouser.

"Oh, this? These papers belong to another case," said Ben. "No, we ought to be out of there in less than an hour. It largely depends on how windy Stahlmyer feels this morning. Excuse me. Now where was I? Oh, yes. Now look, Bud, from here to here, down to here, let's change all that to what we were saying last night. If we have to get a new affidavit, the man is still in town and you can catch him at his store any time before the eleven o'clock express."

Ben and his assistant conversed in vague terms that told nothing to the others in the room. Robert smoked the cigarette and had a strange feeling that he did not belong in the room: the guards were staring at him blankly, while Ben Rosebery and Bud ignored his presence. In a matter of minutes Ben Rosebery would be using his mind, his talents, to effect the freedom of Robert Millhouser, but for the moment Robert Millhouser was forgotten. The guards were there to shoot Robert Millhouser if he attempted to escape, and they would do so without hesitation, but for the moment he was only a dull figure in a room with them on a rainy morning in May. The single plate-glass window was streaked with rain but not sheeted with it: the iron bars outside the window broke the gusts that would have evened the liquid patine.

"All right, Bud. I guess that's all for now. You know where his store is. Just so you catch him in before the eleven o'clock express."

Ben stood before his client and inspected him silently but critically, then nodded in silent approval. Robert Millhouser was now for the first time seeing his friend at his professional best. "Are your shoe-laces tied tight?"

"Yes, why?" said Robert.

"I don't want you to trip and fall. I don't want you to do anything or say anything or have anything about you that will attract attention to yourself. The closer to anonymous you are, the better. This is going to be between Stahlmyer and me. If the judge looks in your direction, be expressionless. Neuter is the word I'm trying to think of. Don't stare back if he stares at you, but try not to be shifty-eyed. Try not to listen to anything we say, and above all, don't show any sign of irritation at anything you hear Stahlmyer say. Or that I might either, for that matter. At the same time, don't give the judge the impression that you're not paying attention, or that you don't give a damn. The judge will take that as a sign of disrespect for the dignity of his court.

"Frankly, this is going to be pretty much of a cut-and-dried affair. The judge knows what's coming, and so does Stahlmyer and so do I. With the exception of one thing. We don't know till the last minute for sure whether the sentence will be passed today or at a later date. That we can't be sure of, Stahlmyer or I. Our guess is that it will be passed today. It's the end of the month and the judge will most likely want to go away on his vacation beginning the first of June, to be gone till September. Naturally if he does that I'll ask for bail, and he'll let you out on, say, $5,000. So you've probably got only one or two more nights left in prison, at the most. My guess is that you'll be sentenced today and that sentence will be a year and a day in prison, which he will then suspend, giving you credit for the time you've already been in prison so that the suspended sentence will amount to about nine months. You may be able to leave prison this afternoon."

"Is that true?" said Robert Millhouser.

"Yes. I haven't told you that before because I had to make certain that Stahlmyer wasn't going to oppose me when I ask for a suspended sentence. That is a very delicate matter. You can't ask a judge to suspend sentence in a homicide case. You have to let the judge think it's his idea, and if the district attorney shows that he's going to be unhappy about it—and he can show that, all right—the judge will reason that six months or a year in prison isn't too harsh a punishment for a homicide. However, I got Stahlmyer to go along with manslaughter, and I'll say this for him. He isn't out to punish you. He'd hang you if he thought he could, but once I got him agreeing to a plea of guilty he said he wouldn't fight it if I pursued the line that you had been punished enough and that additional time in prison for a man of your standing was not in the public interest. These are some of the things I'm going to be saying in court, and you probably won't hear most of them. The judge is Timothy Blankenship, one of the few older men on the bench that has no trouble with his hearing, so Stahlmyer and I will be speaking in ordinary conversational tones. Tim is a fair man, knows the law better than most, and won't stand for any monkeyshines, but I happen to know that he doesn't believe in capital punishment and has a long record of leniency toward first offenders and men involved in so-called crimes of passion. He's a bachelor, like yours truly, and I've never known why. He has a farm about ten miles outside of town and raises blooded cattle, but I've never been invited there and don't know anybody that has. Maybe he doesn't invite anybody there, but I somehow doubt that. I think Tim's had visitors when he was younger."

There was a knock on the door and an elderly tipstaff poked his head in. "Five minutes to ten," said the old man.

"That means in we go," said Ben Rosebery. "Tim always enters the courtroom while the clock is still striking."

"Do I follow you?" said Robert Millhouser.

"We go in separately. I'll go in alone, then you come in with the attendant and go to the table where I'll be sitting." Ben looked at his friend, and put a hand on his shoulder. "I won't say don't worry. You never have. But just remember what I told you, and God willing you'll be spending tonight at my house and maybe things will look differently."

"Thank you for everything, Ben."

"You're more than welcome, Robert. More than."

398

Judge Blankenship was a tall, broad-shouldered man with a great mass of gray hair brushed back on his large head. He was smooth-shaven and had a small mouth and thin lips. The clerk read unintelligibly from a large black book and the judge accepted a document which he examined quickly without putting on glasses. "Well, if we're all ready, gentlemen, let's proceed," said Blankenship, and for the first time he looked at Robert Millhouser, but his glance lingered no longer on him than on the other men who had business before the bench: Stahlmyer and his assistant, the court attendants, the tipstaff-crier, the shorthand reporter, the clerk, Ben Rosebery and three men at a table whom Robert Millhouser took to be newspapermen. Stahlmyer spoke first, and Blankenship looked at him all the time he was speaking. Ben Rosebery then spoke, followed by Stahlmyer again, and the two lawyers and the judge engaged in a three-sided colloquy, during which several legal papers were handed up to Blankenship, read by him, and handed to the clerk. Robert Millhouser could hear almost none of the conversation, which was serious but amiable. At one point the three men were silent and during the silence Blankenship, on his revolving chair, turned and faced the wall to his right. "What does Mr. Stahlmyer wish to say about that?" said Blankenship, after half a minute, and again facing Stahlmyer. The three-way conversation was resumed and then Robert heard Blankenship say, "All right, call the defendant."

"Robert Millhouser," said the crier.

"It isn't necessary to be quite so stentorian," said the judge. "We can all hear without raising our voices."

"You don't want him to take the stand, do you, Judge?" said Ben Rosebery.

"No. Just swear him and I have only one or two questions," said Blankenship.

Robert Millhouser was sworn, gave his name and occupation—farmer and banker—and Blankenship then said: "You are aware, Mr. Millhouser, that your counsel has entered a plea of guilty of the charge of manslaughter. Is that how you wish to plead?"

"Yes sir," said Robert Millhouser.

"Whenever there is a plea of guilty to a capital charge I like to hear from the defendant's own lips that he has been fully informed of the implications of such a plea, as well as the alternatives that are open to him. You do understand these implications and the alternatives that are open to you?"

"Yes sir, I do."

"That's all. You may sit down."

"Prisoner take his seat." said the crier.

"That was better, Tipstaff," said Blankenship. "The cause of justice is never furthered by shouting. Quite the contrary, I've always maintained."

There was another resumption of the colloquy, inaudible to Robert Millhouser, so much so that when the tipstaff-crier called out, "Prisoner will rise," Robert was not listening to him but to the murmur of the three voices of the judge and the attorneys.

"Prisoner will rise," repeated the tipstaff.

"Stand here, Robert," said Ben Rosebery, indicating a place between him and Stahlmyer.

"It is the sentence of this court that the defendant, Robert Millhouser, shall serve a term of one year and one day in the county prison. Taking into consideration the fact that the defendant has already been incarcerated for a period of more than three months in county prison, and the mitigating circumstances of the crime to which defendant has pleaded guilty, this court suspends sentence and defendant is released in custody of counsel for a period of five years. Court will recess for fifteen minutes before taking up the next case."

"Thank you, Your Honor," said Robert Millhouser.

Blankenship nodded but did not speak. He rose and left the courtroom and Robert Millhouser shook the hand of his friend. "Now what?" said Robert.

"You're free."

"I could walk out that door?"

"If you wanted to. It's still raining, I see. Come with me to the lawyers' room and we can go out the side door. I have a hired automobile with a driver."

Stahlmyer laughed. "Pretty sure of yourself, Ben," he said, picking up his papers.

"Is it all right for me to thank Mr. Stahlmyer?" said Robert Millhouser.

"Yes, but don't let anybody see you shake hands with me," said Stahlmyer.

"Very well, but thank you."

"You don't need anything from your cell, do you? I can send for your possessions," said Ben Rosebery.

"The warden has my watch and chain. That's all I want. They can keep the books and anything else."

"Good day, gentlemen," said Stahlmyer, and turned to go.

"So long, Henry. Or should I start calling you Congressman?"

"When the time comes, when the time comes," said Stahlmyer, and left them.

The automobile was standing in the rain at the curb. "I slipped up on one thing," said Ben. "This machine attracts attention. But I guess people won't be looking at us, not in this weather."

"Not so many people know me in Fort Penn," said Robert Millhouser.

"True," said Ben Rosebery. "Now what would you like to do first? A good soak in the tub? Then what? Don't worry about lunch. I've seen to that. But I know if I were you I'd want a good big drink of French cognac."

"Yes, I'd like that very much."

"And a woman. Most men that have been behind bars want a woman before they want a drink."

"Thanks, Ben, but I don't want a woman."

"Entirely up to you. Don't think of me as an unfeeling lout. I'm not. At the same time, I do face facts, Robert, and you will be wanting a woman, sooner or later."

"I wonder. I doubt it."

"Well, maybe not. But don't give up women just because you're afraid of what they may be thinking. There are some women that will shy away from you. You know that. But there'll be others that won't feel that way. And of course there are millions of women that don't know anything about you and don't want to inquire, that'll take you on without asking you any questions except have you got the price. That sounds callous now, but it's a good thing to remember."

"I think that as far as women are concerned, I'm crippled for life."

"Well, there are other things. As many times as I've dipped my wick, as many different women, there aren't more than one or two that I look back on with any sentiment. One or two. One was a whore, and she could always make me laugh because she never took anything seriously. And the other, she *wasn't* a whore. I never came near her, that way, but I was in love with her from the time she was a girl of sixteen. You know, I'm surprised you never guessed who it was."

"Surprised I never guessed? Then maybe I can guess. Was it Esther?"

"From the time she was about sixteen."

"And you never said anything to her?"

"What was there to say? I was in my thirties, and I certainly wasn't deceiving any of the older people in Fort Penn about my morals."

"I was in my thirties when I asked her to marry me."

"Yes, but you were different."

"Not very."

"Yes you were. We went to the same whorehouse, but nobody ever thought of you as a ne'er-do-well. By the time I was thirty I'd begun to look like a pig, besides acting like one. And by the time she was ready to be engaged to you, I was in my forties."

"She was in her twenties."

"I know."

The automobile stopped at Ben's house and they went in and sat in his den, a room that was furnished for masculine comfort but had an unused look about it. "This room has everything I want in it, but if I sit in it for five minutes I wonder what I'm missing at the club or Fritz Gottlieb's." He poured cognac into highball glasses and he and Robert saluted each other without a spoken toast.

"Tell me some more about you and Esther."

"Why?"

"Well, I've often wondered about you. Didn't you ever fall in love with anybody before Esther?"

"No, I never did. The only thing I wanted from women I could never get from girls like Esther."

"Did you think I was good enough for her? I wasn't."

"I thought you'd be better for her than anybody else that was around. However, if I have to be honest, I confess that down deep I may have been relieved when she broke your engagement. And I guess that was why I was hoping you and Hedda would turn out well. Conscience. I hadn't pulled for you when you were engaged to Esther, so I pulled extra hard when you married Hedda."

"Yes, you did. And now I know why you worked so hard to get me out of prison."

"Yes, so do I, although at the time I thought it was just friendship, plus professional pride. Yes, I'd have fought your case with every trick I knew."

"And did you? Is that what you meant by calling Stahlmyer Congressman?"

"That was part of it. But I wasn't the only one that put pressure on Stahlmyer. All the better element did, Robert. And if you don't mind my preaching, you owe something to those people. The first thing you owe them is to try to lead a normal life, as much as possible."

"A normal life won't be possible, and you know it."

"I do. But you can try. Start by getting rid of that prison psychology. I don't say try to mix with people. But let them see you trying to lead a normal life. Would you consider having a talk with Tim Blankenship?"

"No."

"That's too bad, but I didn't think you would."

"I know what I'm going to do, Ben."

"You do? What?"

"I'm going back to Lyons and live in that house for the rest of my life. Once a day I'll go for a walk so that the people will be able to see me, and won't suspect me of—oh, lying drunk in my room. Maybe I'll go to the post office every day. I'll speak to those who speak to me, and I suppose in time they'll all get used to me. But I'll never linger for conversation, I'll never ask anybody to come to my house, and if anyone should ever invite me to his house, I'll decline."

"Is that a normal life?"

"It'll become the normal life for me, Ben."

"When did you plan all this?"

"When I began to feel that you were going to get me out of prison. The past two or three weeks. If I go home and face them every day, they won't create legends about me, the way they would if I went some place else."

"And what will you do with your time, the rest of your time?"

Robert Millhouser smiled. "Well, you know in prison I often wished there was better light to read by, especially at night. I like to read. I'll help Moses with his chores. I may paint. I found out in prison that small things can fill the day. Meals. Shaving. The ritual of the bath. Reading the newspapers."

"Do you know what it sounds like to me? It sounds like an elegant prison."

"Do you mind if I correct you slightly?"

"Go ahead."

"Not an elegant prison. A comfortable monastery."

•

TWENTY YEARS and a little more have passed since I ended the story of Robert Millhouser, ended it in the only way that was satisfactory to me then and as I now finish rereading it. Will not the reader agree with me that Robert Millhouser's own words—"a comfortable monastery"—provide the beginning and the end of as much of his story as I could know? I think back to those days when I was a boy and Robert Millhouser was only a slightly strange but pleasant old gentleman who would pass my grandfather's house four times a day on his way to and from the post office. Then I think of the citizens of Lyons and their attitude toward him, most sympathetically reflected by the conspiracy of silence that my grandfather and others like him observed. Then I recall the awakening of my curiosity and my eventual, almost inevitable, involvement in the life of Robert Millhouser, up to the time that he used the phrase "a comfortable monastery."

403

I ought not to use an apologetic tone when I say that that was the only ending that was satisfactory to me. Robert Millhouser himself ended the story there, if not precisely at the utterance of that phrase. He never told me any more about himself, about the years in his comfortable monastery. He stubbornly—and cleverly—resisted my best efforts to draw him out. I spent considerable time in his company while I was writing the story, and I tried to make him tell me about those years after he came back to Lyons. Once I went prepared with a question that I thought would lead him into reminiscence: "Mr. Millhouser," I said, "I notice in your notes that you have your wife speaking of some jewelry you gave her. What ever happened to it?"

"I still have it. It's all here in this house," he said. "I thought of giving it to her mother, but after Ed Steele's company refused my offer of money, I realized that the Steeles wanted nothing from me, nothing."

"I see. Do you ever take it out and look at it?"

"I do not."

"Just for my own information, because I'm literal-minded, I guess —will you tell me how you happened to get hold of the jewelry? I mean literally that. Did you go to her room after you came home from prison and take it out of a drawer?"

"No. The day after I was taken to prison Margaret Dillon came back to work for me, to take care of the house. She packed all my wife's clothes and such-like and got word to the Steeles that they could come and collect it all, or Moses Hatfield would deliver it to them. That included the jewelry. They sent back word that they wanted nothing, nothing, that I had bought for Hedda."

"I see. And then Margaret Dillon—"

"Turned the jewelry over to George Holliday, and I don't remember what she did with the clothes."

"And when did you move to your wife's room, to sleep?"

"Some time later. After I got home from prison."

"When? How much later?"

"That belongs in the part of my life that I'll never discuss."

"Not even with me?"

"Especially not with you, Gerald. There is nothing to be gained by telling you about those years."

"But there might be."

"No. Some good might come of my experience, my life up to the time I came back to Lyons. I'm not entirely sure of that, but if you look at it the way a doctor does a medical case history, some good might come of it. But all that is composed of facts, isn't it? At least

404

facts and emotions that can be understood. After that, after I came home, all that belongs to me."

"You mean your suffering?"

"I don't mean my suffering. I have not used that word and I haven't implied it. What went on inside me will never be put into words. Words like suffering, particularly."

"And yet at some time you must have begun to live again, to get rid of what Mr. Rosebery called the prison psychology."

"Damn it to hell! There you are, trying to get me to admit or deny two things! Have I ever said I began to live again, or that I didn't begin to live again? Or that I got rid of the prison psychology or didn't get rid of it? I consider these questions, and this method of questioning, impertinent. Insulting. You are insulting my intelligence if you think I can't see through these tricks."

"I'm sorry, and I apologize," I said.

"And you should. You have no right to upset me so. You mustn't do that again."

"But there are some facts I want to clear up, and—"

"I've kept nothing from you."

"Some of the facts carry over beyond your coming back to Lyons."

"What do you mean by that?"

"Well, for instance, in Lantenengo County we had a rich saloon-keeper who kicked a man to death. Took him down in the cellar and kicked him to death. Bob Corrigan was the saloonkeeper's name. Corrigan was arrested, but there weren't any witnesses that would testify against him and Corrigan left town, lack of evidence I think was what got him off."

"How does this apply to me? I can see a connection, but I would like you to state it."

"The connection isn't so much a connection as some similarity to what happened to you. People simply forgot. But that isn't why I told you about Corrigan. I told you about him because I wanted you to know that I'm not naïve."

"I never thought that."

"Well, then, were there ever any repercussions over the fact that you were found guilty of manslaughter and given a suspended sentence?"

"Yes. One. Somewhere I have a clipping from a newspaper, a newspaper published by the miners' Union. It didn't mention me by name, but the meaning was obvious. It speaks of a miscarriage of justice, and one law for the rich and another for the poor."

"What ever happened to Henry Stahlmyer?"

"What would your guess be?"

"That he went to Congress."

"You're right. He went to Congress for two terms and now he's getting $25,000 a year as one of our Nesquehela County judges. But he wasn't bribed, at least not with money. He was threatened, but only threatened with political reprisal. Another man might have done exactly what he did without being threatened. On the other hand, another man might have gotten me hanged. I've never concerned myself over Stahlmyer's decision, either way. If he'd gotten me hanged, I wouldn't be here, and that's all I've ever felt about it for nineteen years."

"I see."

"Do you? And do you believe what you see?"

"Yes, I suppose I do."

"I wonder if you do. I wonder if a young man can really believe that."

"I believe that *you* believe that your life ended in 1908."

"Well, I suppose that's as much as I can expect you to believe."

"And yet, when Chester Calthorp left you that day in prison, you told me you wept."

"Yes, I wept."

"Ever since you told me that I've been wondering if that wasn't when you began to feel again."

"You saw me weep at your grandfather's funeral."

"Yes, I did," I said. "And that bears out my contention."

He was silent, not, I could see, from displeasure at what I had said, but because he was trying to remember something. Slowly he got to his feet and went to the bookcase. "A year or so ago I came across a poem that I'd never read before. I might not have read it then if the title hadn't seemed so relevant to a conversation you and I'd had. Do you remember a conversation we had, Gerald, about you and your girls?"

"Yes, I do. With some embarrassment."

"The poem is more applicable to me, my life, than to yours. Here, let me read part of it: 'Then each applied to each that fatal knife,/ Deep questioning, which probes to endless dole.' "

I interrupted him. " 'Ah, what a dusty answer gets the soul/ When hot for certainties in this our life!' "

He stared at me. "You know this poem? Obviously you do. Is it a well-known poem?"

"I know it because I'm reading a very good novel called *Dusty Answer,* by an Englishwoman named Rosamond Lehmann."

406

"A new novel?"

"Brand-new."

"Would I like the novel?"

"I think you would."

"I must order it." He turned his attention back to the poem. " 'No villain need be! Passions spin the plot:/We are betrayed by what is false within.' To think of discovering all this in a poem called 'Modern Love.' And to think of George Meredith calling a poem 'Modern Love.' " He put the book back on the shelf, and sat down again. "I wanted to give you an answer, you're so hot for certainties, Gerald."

"A dusty answer, of course."

He ignored my remark.

"I suppose I could just as easily have quoted Shakespeare. 'There are more things in heaven and earth,' and so forth. I'm not even sure that Meredith meant certainties the way I read it. I'm afraid I often misread the poet's intention. Do you remember my telling you that I went to prison thinking that Milton had been considering how his *life* was spent?"

"Yes."

"We *mustn't* expect the absolute answers!" He spoke with more passion than I had ever seen him display. "Chester Calthorp, with his vain, deluding joys. I wept, yes, I wept. *I* had no answer! I was dead, as I'm dead now, as I've been dead all these years. As dead as you're alive. But this man that I loved, deceiving himself with his penance and his prayers. Fighting, stifling his soul with prayers to the God that gave him a soul! Asking his God to benumb that soul. Does he believe in his God, or doesn't he? He doesn't, my young friend, or he wouldn't ask Him to crush his spirit."

"Why did you weep for my grandfather?"

"That's easier to answer," he said, after a moment. "He was one of the good people of the world. You must know that there are some people who are lucky. In the same way, some people are good. And some are unlucky, and some are bad. And some are like Ben Rosebery. Neither lucky nor good nor bad, but dead the day they die."

"And where would you put old Dr. Willetts?"

"I put each of them in a separate place. Dr. Willetts was good but not lucky. His only luck—I can say this—was that at least one man knew how good he was, even if that one man was me. That was the extent of his luck, Gerald. Perhaps someone else like him has come along and been luckier, and more people appreciate his goodness."

"Do you believe in luck?"

"I believe that you can toss a bottle in the ocean and it will be washed up on the shores of Portugal, and that you can do the same thing again and the bottle will be picked up by the same fisherman. It happened in 1907."

"So it did. But is that what you call luck?"

He smiled. "No, but luck is what I call tossing a bottle in the ocean, et cetera."

"And what else do you believe?"

He ceased to smile. "Nothing."

"But that's not true, Mr. Millhouser."

"It's true now. I make it true by saying it. You have had your last peek at my life, and even that was only what I let you see."

"But I can study what I've seen, and I will."

He made a cold chuckling sound. "Look out, Gerald. You may find what you're looking for. Yourself."

I left him then and I never saw him again. He would not see me, although he sent us handsome presents when Frances and I were married and when our children were born. I was in the Navy when he died, aged eighty-nine. Later I figured out that at the moment of his death I was at my battle station, and it was entirely possible that as I stared into the darkness above the Leyte Gulf I was thinking of him and the Portuguese shores on the other side of the world. I often tried to think of things like that to take my mind off Frances and the stories that had got back to me.